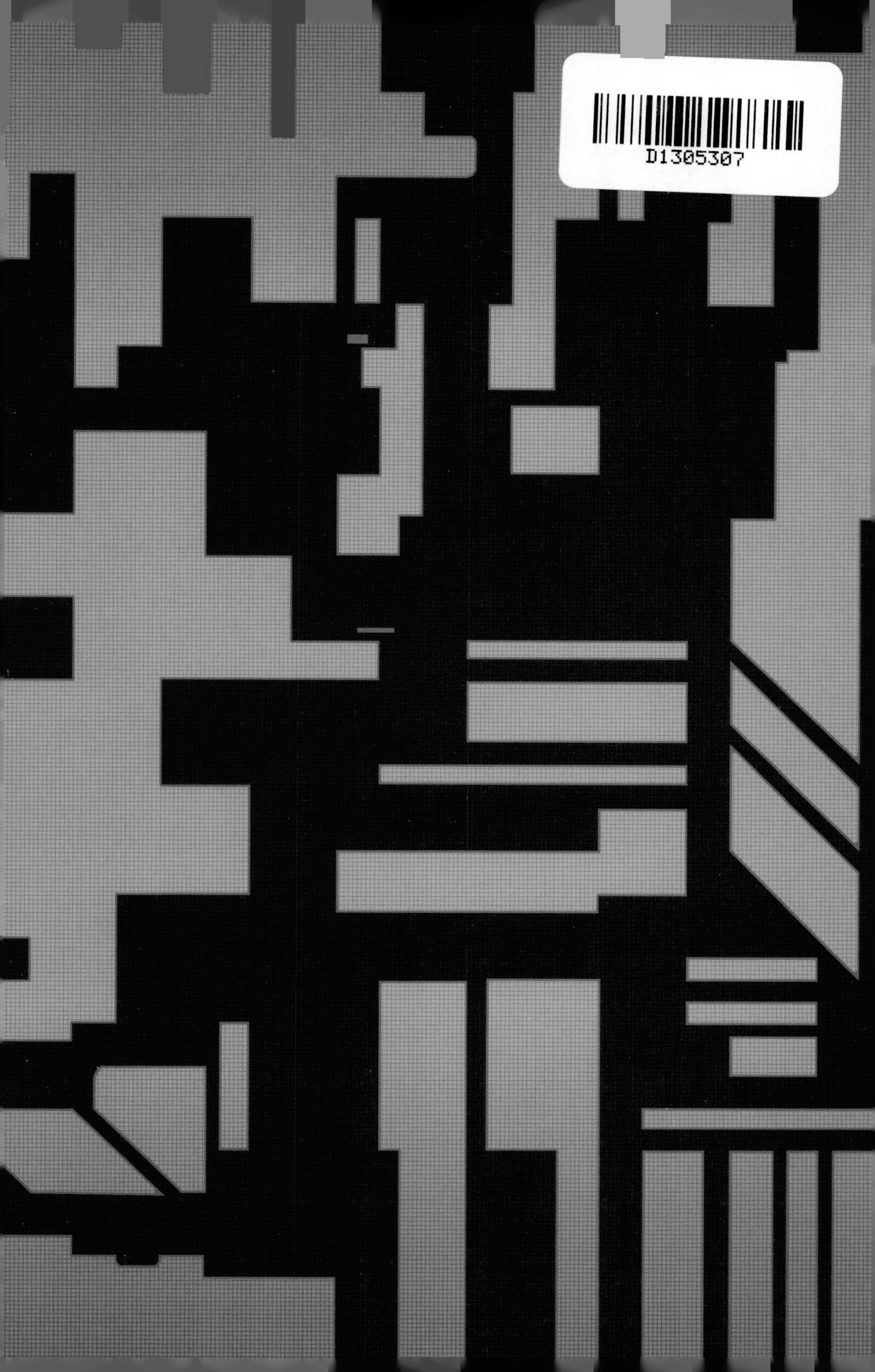

IMAGECOMICS.COM

AXCEND TP VOLUME 1. First printing. September 2016. Published by Image Comics, Inc. Office of publication: 2001 Center Street, Sixth Floor, Berkeley, CA 94704. Copyright © 2016 Shane Davis. All rights reserved. Contains material originally published in single magazine form as AXCEND #1-5. "AXCEND," its logos, and the likenesses of all characters herein are trademarks of Shane Davis, unless otherwise noted. "Image" and the Image Comics logos are registered trademarks of Image Comics, Inc. No part of this publication may be reproduced or transmitted, in any form or by any means (except for short excerpts for journalistic or review purposes), without the express written permission of Shane Davis or Image Comics, Inc. All names, characters, events, and locales in this publication are entirely fictional. Any resemblance to actual persons (living or dead), events, or places, without satiric intent, is coincidental. Printed in the USA. For information regarding the CPSIA on this printed material call 203-595-3636 and provide reference #RICH-704863. For international rights, contact: foreignlicensing@imagecomics.com. ISBN 978-1-63215-756-0.

cover art
SHANE DAVIS
MICHELLE DELECKI,
& MORRY HOLLOWELL

special thanks to
JOHN TYSZKIEWICZ

logo & publication design
GABE BRIDWELL

editor
MICHELLE DELECKI

creator
SHANE DAVIS

VOLUME ONE

THE WORLD REVOLVES AROUND YOU.

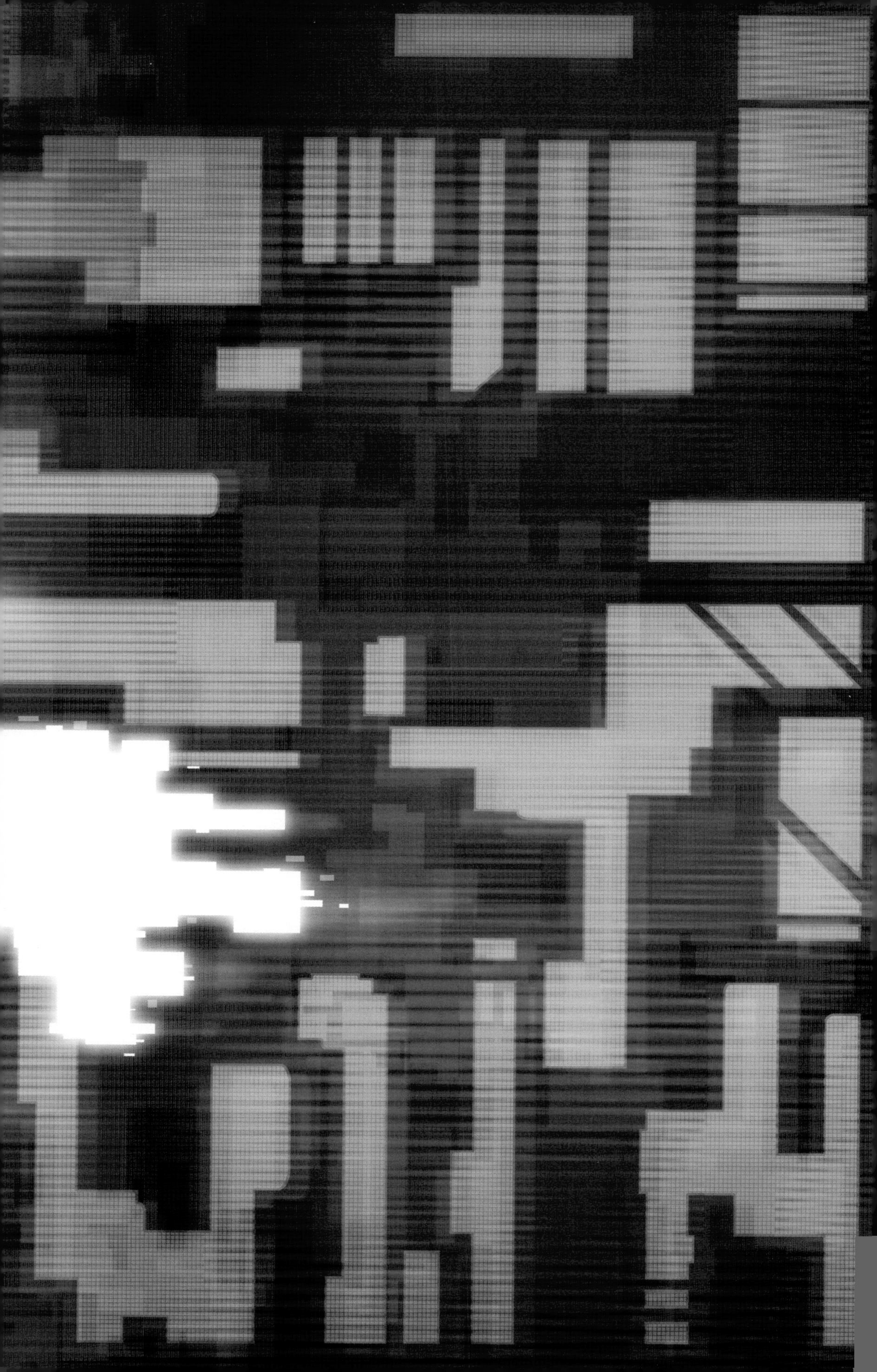

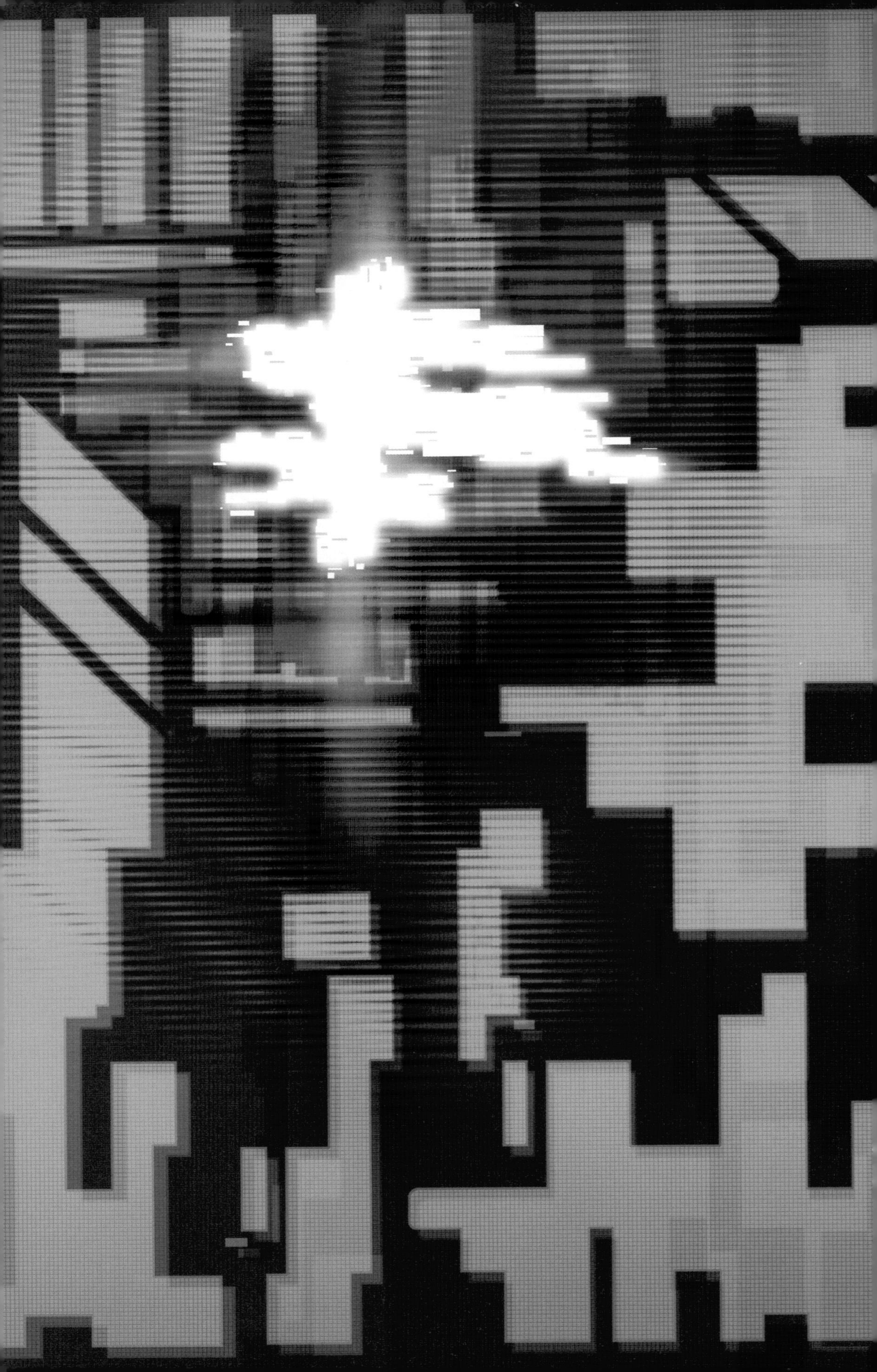

SHANE DAVIS
writer

SHANE DAVIS
penciler

MICHELLE DELECKI
inker

MORRY HOLLOWELL
colorist

PATRICK BROSSEAU
letterer

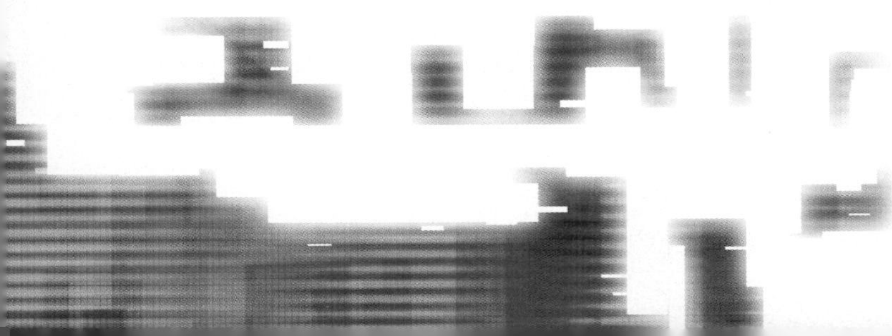

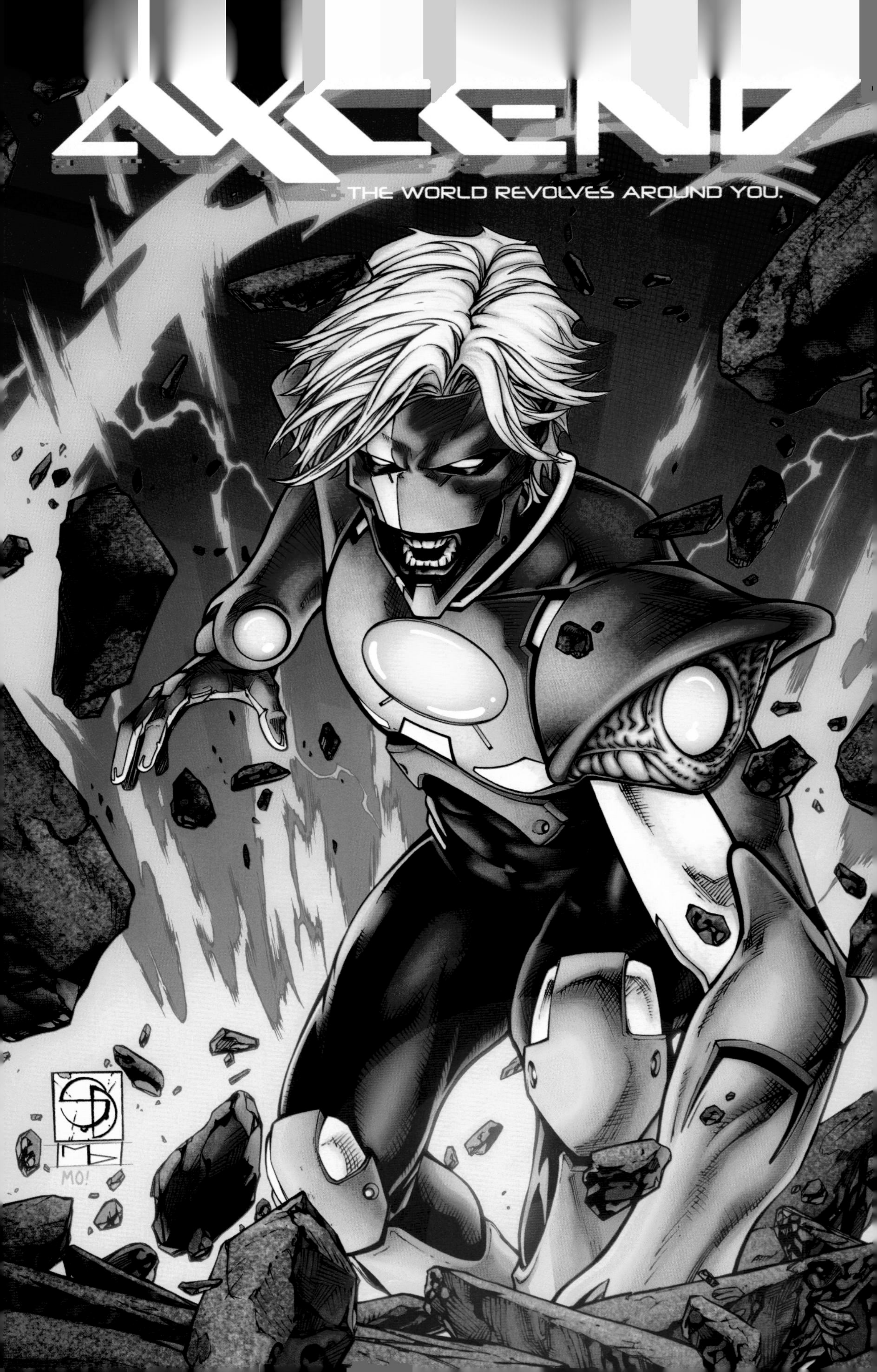
AXCEND
THE WORLD REVOLVES AROUND YOU.
MO!

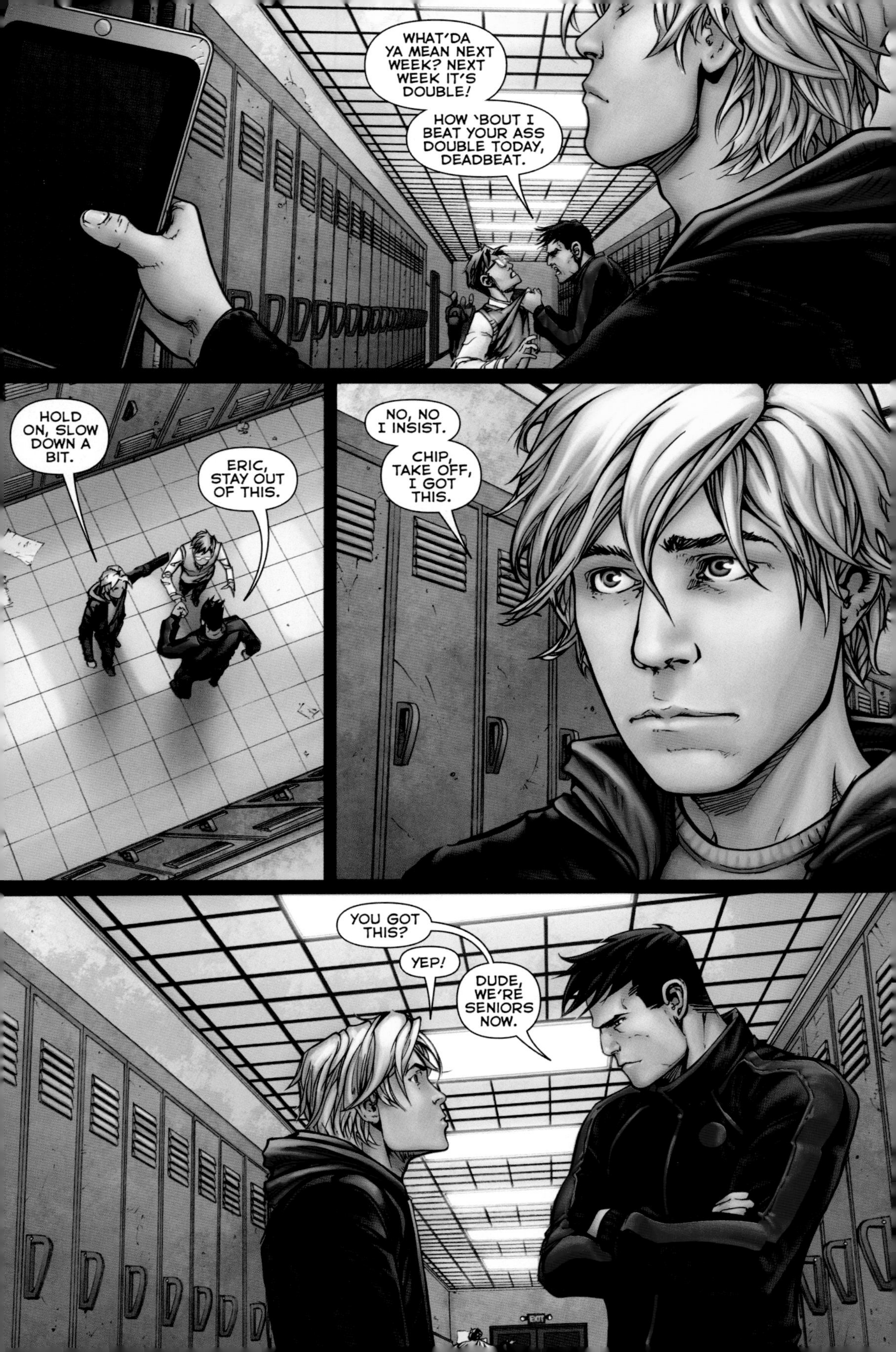
WHAT'DA YA MEAN NEXT WEEK? NEXT WEEK IT'S DOUBLE!
HOW 'BOUT I BEAT YOUR ASS DOUBLE TODAY, DEADBEAT.
HOLD ON, SLOW DOWN A BIT.
ERIC, STAY OUT OF THIS.
NO, NO I INSIST.
CHIP, TAKE OFF, I GOT THIS.
YOU GOT THIS?
YEP!
DUDE, WE'RE SENIORS NOW.

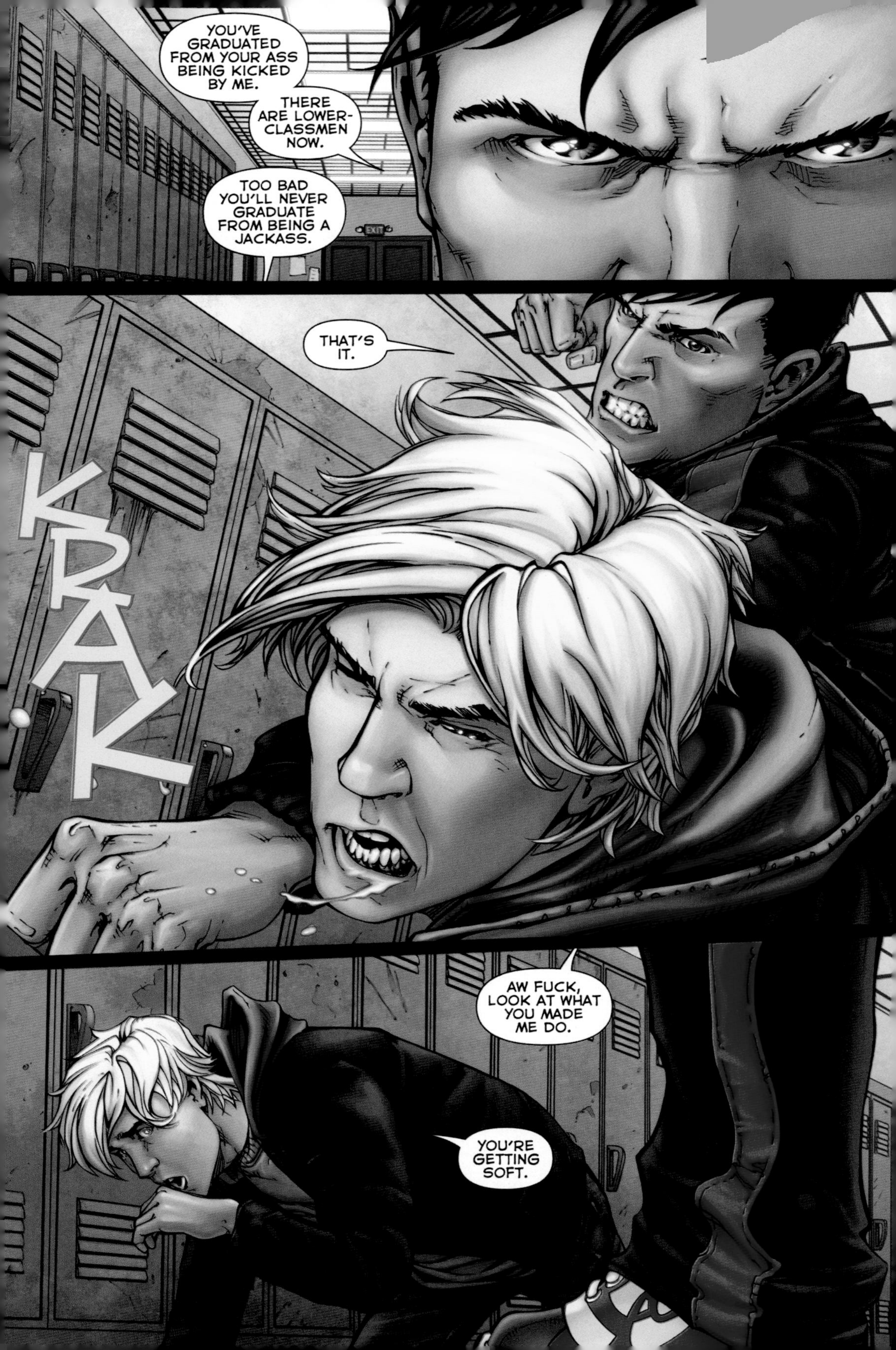
YOU'VE GRADUATED FROM YOUR ASS BEING KICKED BY ME.
THERE ARE LOWER-CLASSMEN NOW.
TOO BAD YOU'LL NEVER GRADUATE FROM BEING A JACKASS.
EXIT
THAT'S IT.
KRAK
AW FUCK, LOOK AT WHAT YOU MADE ME DO.
YOU'RE GETTING SOFT.

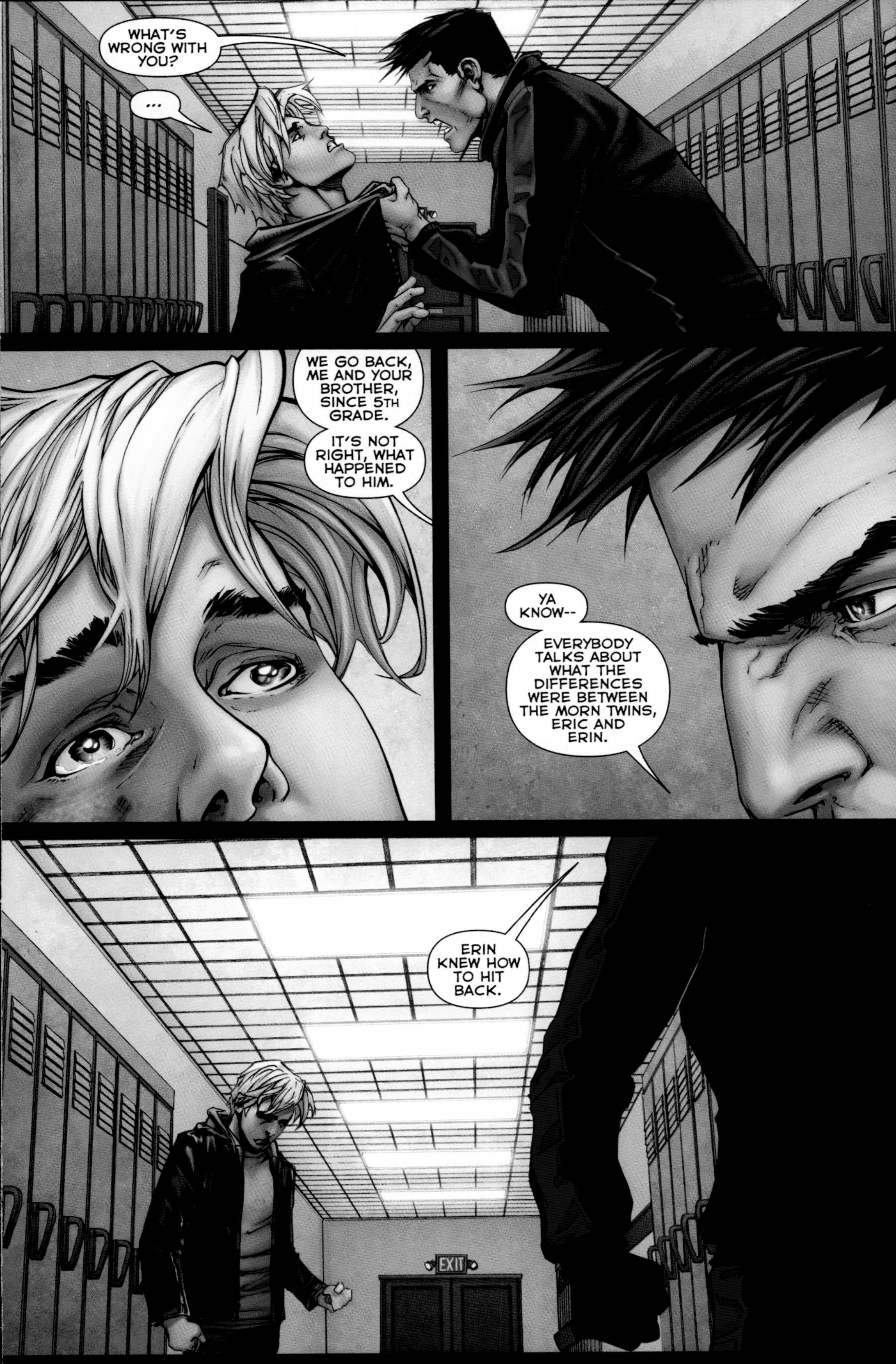
WHAT'S WRONG WITH YOU?
...
WE GO BACK, ME AND YOUR BROTHER, SINCE 5TH GRADE.
IT'S NOT RIGHT, WHAT HAPPENED TO HIM.
YA KNOW--
EVERYBODY TALKS ABOUT WHAT THE DIFFERENCES WERE BETWEEN THE MORN TWINS, ERIC AND ERIN.
ERIN KNEW HOW TO HIT BACK.
EXIT

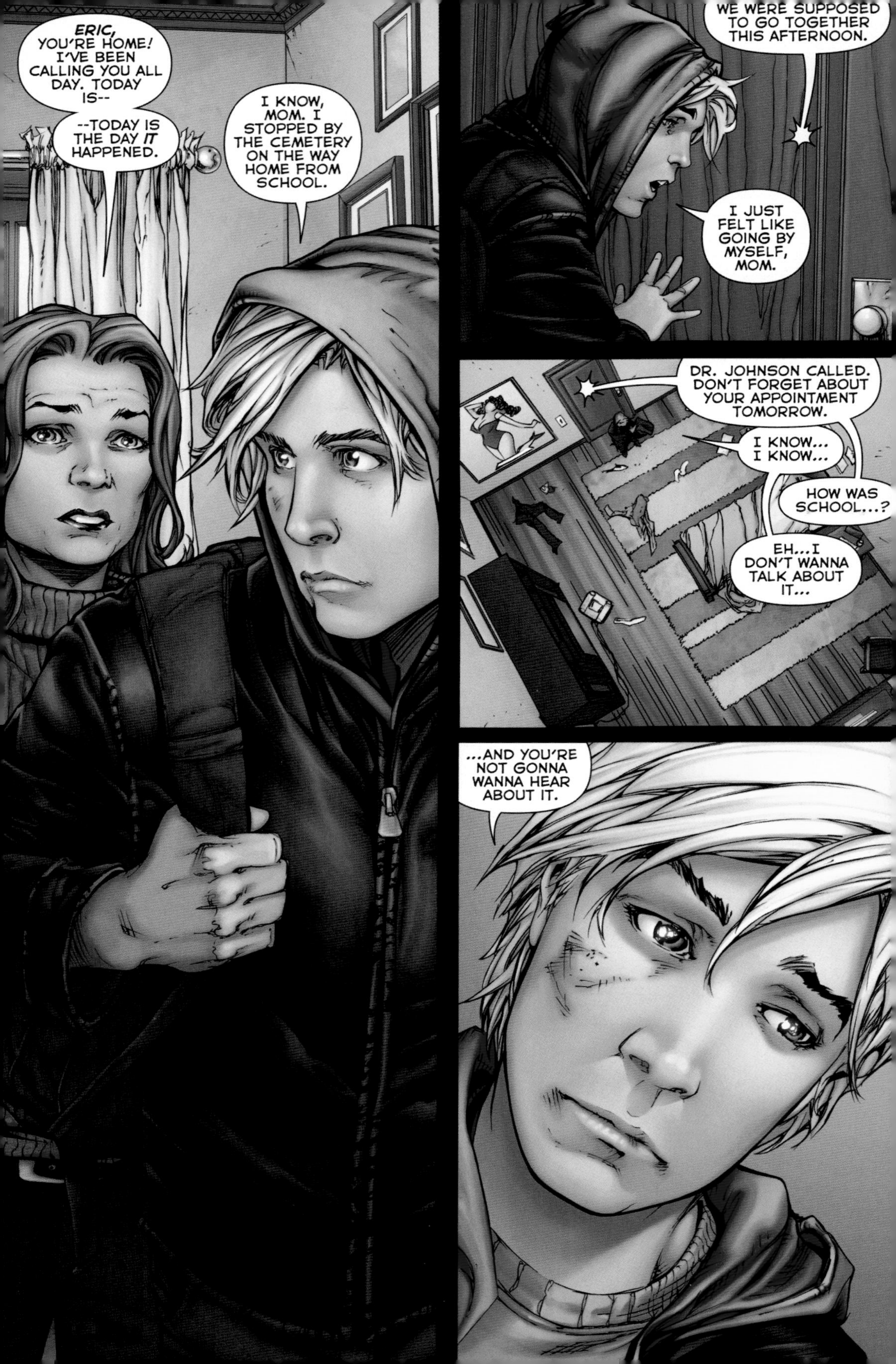
ERIC, YOU'RE HOME! I'VE BEEN CALLING YOU ALL DAY. TODAY IS--
--TODAY IS THE DAY IT HAPPENED.
I KNOW, MOM. I STOPPED BY THE CEMETERY ON THE WAY HOME FROM SCHOOL.
WE WERE SUPPOSED TO GO TOGETHER THIS AFTERNOON.
I JUST FELT LIKE GOING BY MYSELF, MOM.
DR. JOHNSON CALLED. DON'T FORGET ABOUT YOUR APPOINTMENT TOMORROW.
I KNOW... I KNOW...
HOW WAS SCHOOL...?
EH...I DON'T WANNA TALK ABOUT IT...
...AND YOU'RE NOT GONNA WANNA HEAR ABOUT IT.

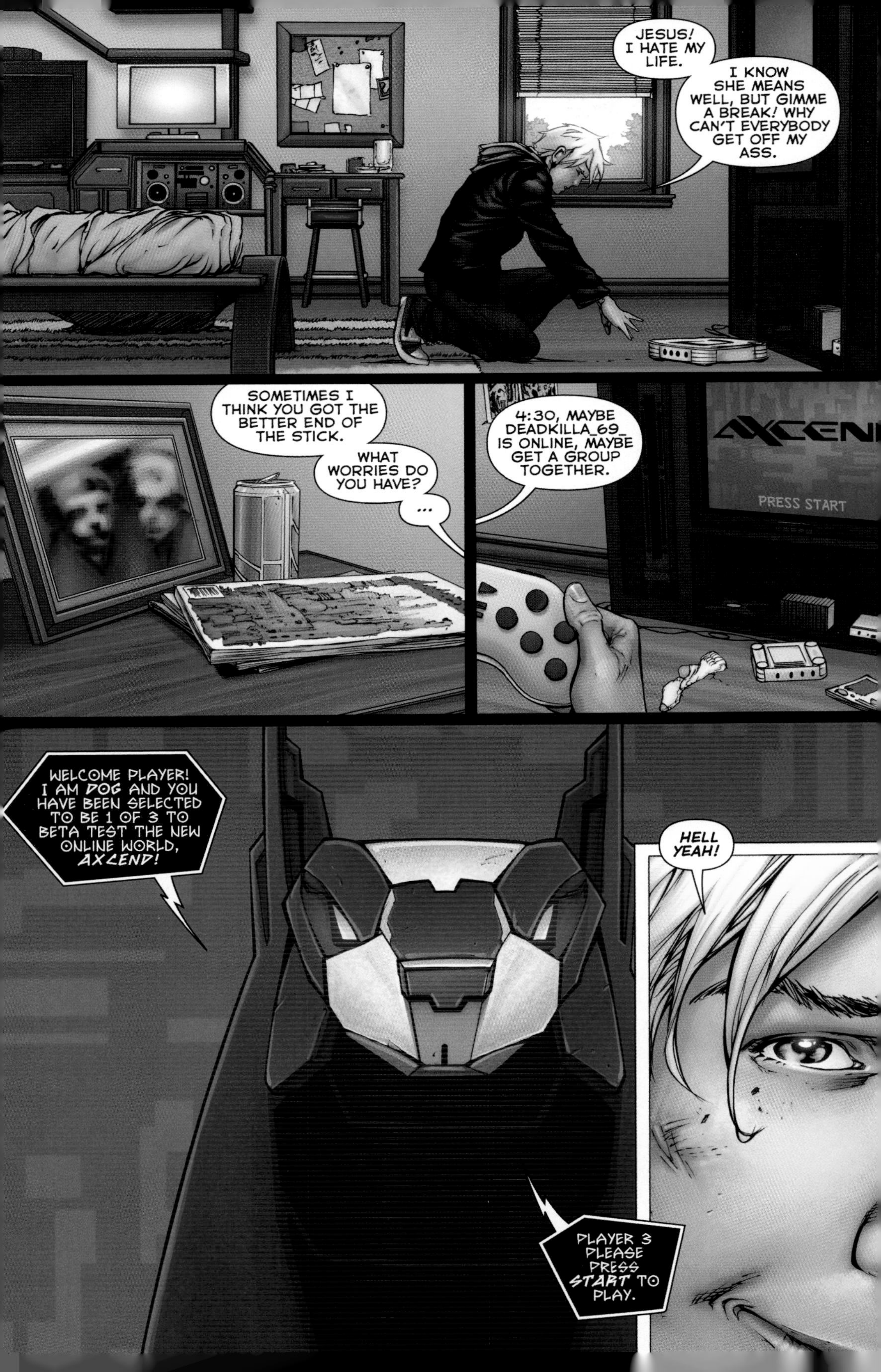

JESUS! I HATE MY LIFE.
I KNOW SHE MEANS WELL, BUT GIMME A BREAK! WHY CAN'T EVERYBODY GET OFF MY ASS.
SOMETIMES I THINK YOU GOT THE BETTER END OF THE STICK.
WHAT WORRIES DO YOU HAVE?
...
4:30, MAYBE DEADKILLA_69_ IS ONLINE, MAYBE GET A GROUP TOGETHER.
PRESS START
WELCOME PLAYER! I AM DOG AND YOU HAVE BEEN SELECTED TO BE 1 OF 3 TO BETA TEST THE NEW ONLINE WORLD, AXCEND!
HELL YEAH!
PLAYER 3 PLEASE PRESS START TO PLAY.

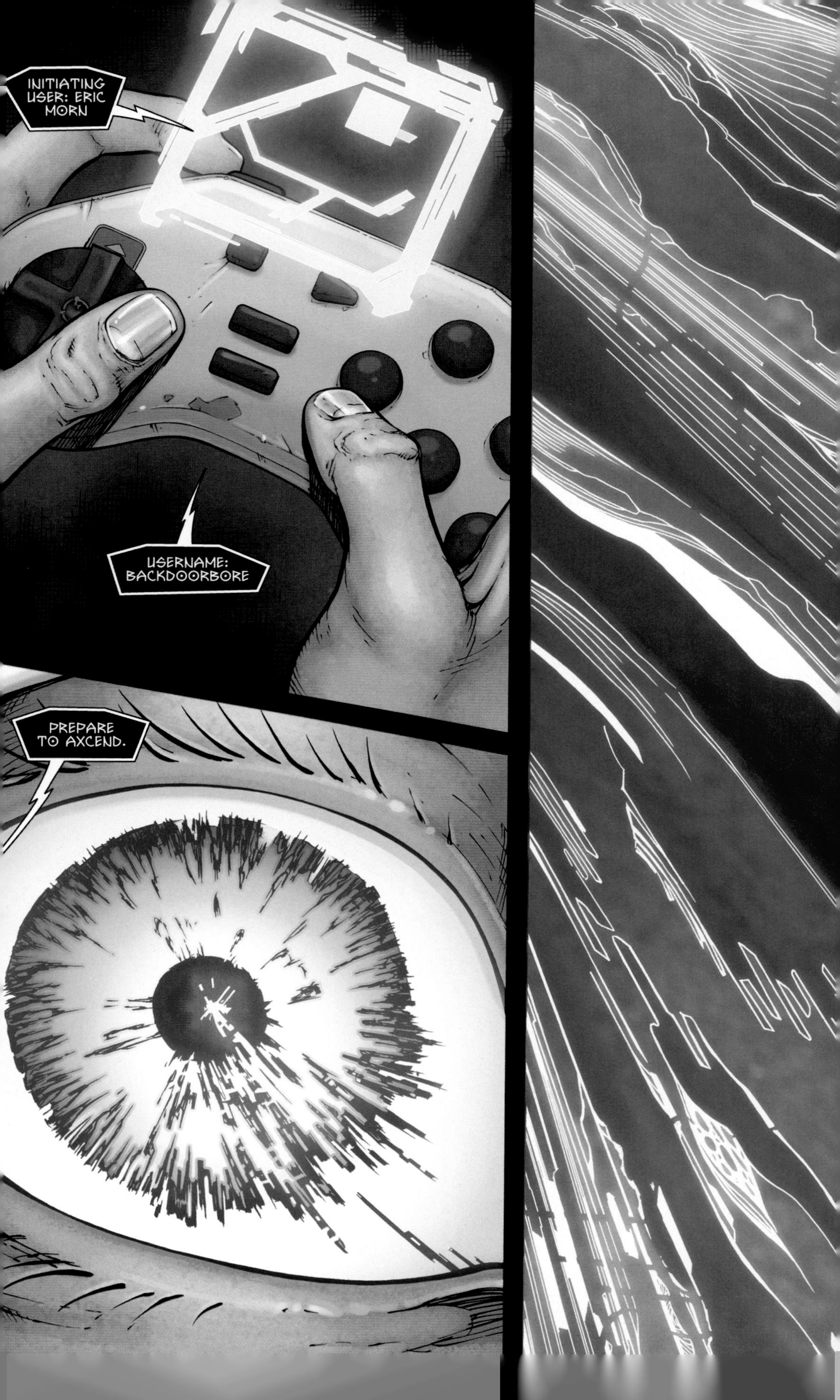
INITIATING USER: ERIC MORN
USERNAME: BACKDOORBORE
PREPARE TO AXCEND.

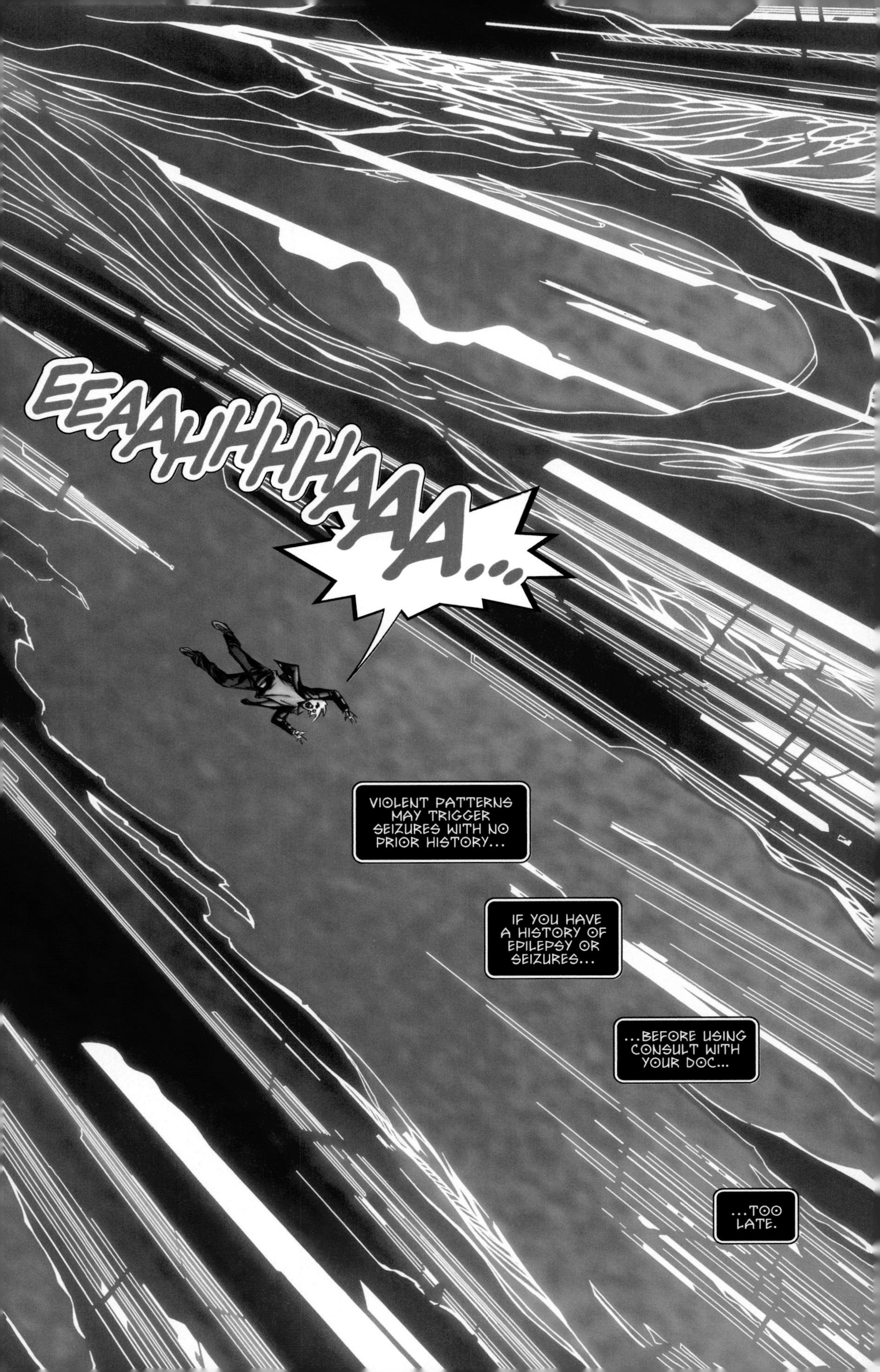
EEAAHHHHAAAA...
VIOLENT PATTERNS MAY TRIGGER SEIZURES WITH NO PRIOR HISTORY...
IF YOU HAVE A HISTORY OF EPILEPSY OR SEIZURES...
...BEFORE USING CONSULT WITH YOUR DOC...
...TOO LATE.

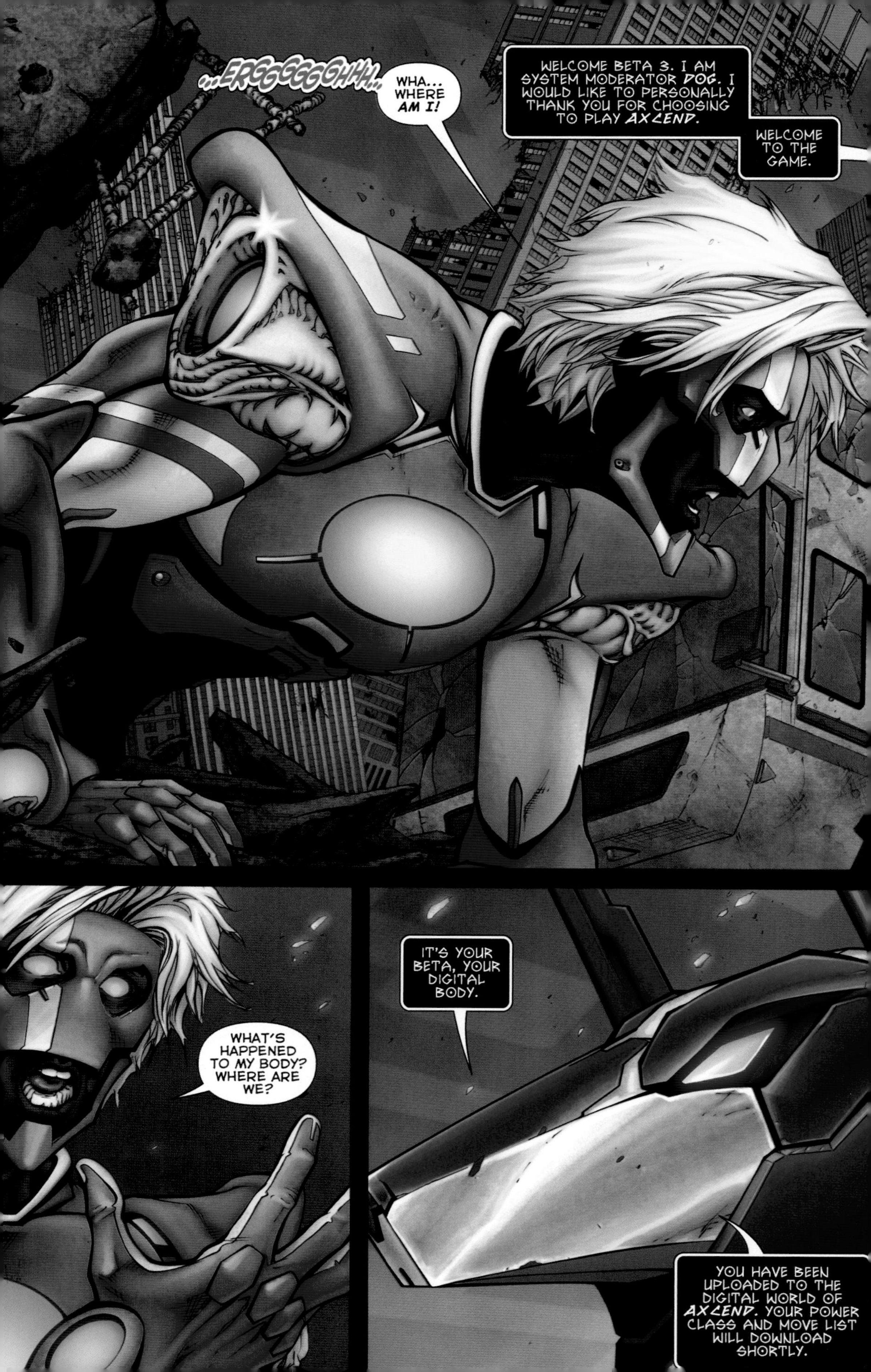

..ERGGGGGGHHH..
WHA... WHERE AM I!
WELCOME BETA 3. I AM SYSTEM MODERATOR DOG. I WOULD LIKE TO PERSONALLY THANK YOU FOR CHOOSING TO PLAY AXCEND.
WELCOME TO THE GAME.
WHAT'S HAPPENED TO MY BODY? WHERE ARE WE?
IT'S YOUR BETA, YOUR DIGITAL BODY.
YOU HAVE BEEN UPLOADED TO THE DIGITAL WORLD OF AXCEND. YOUR POWER CLASS AND MOVE LIST WILL DOWNLOAD SHORTLY.

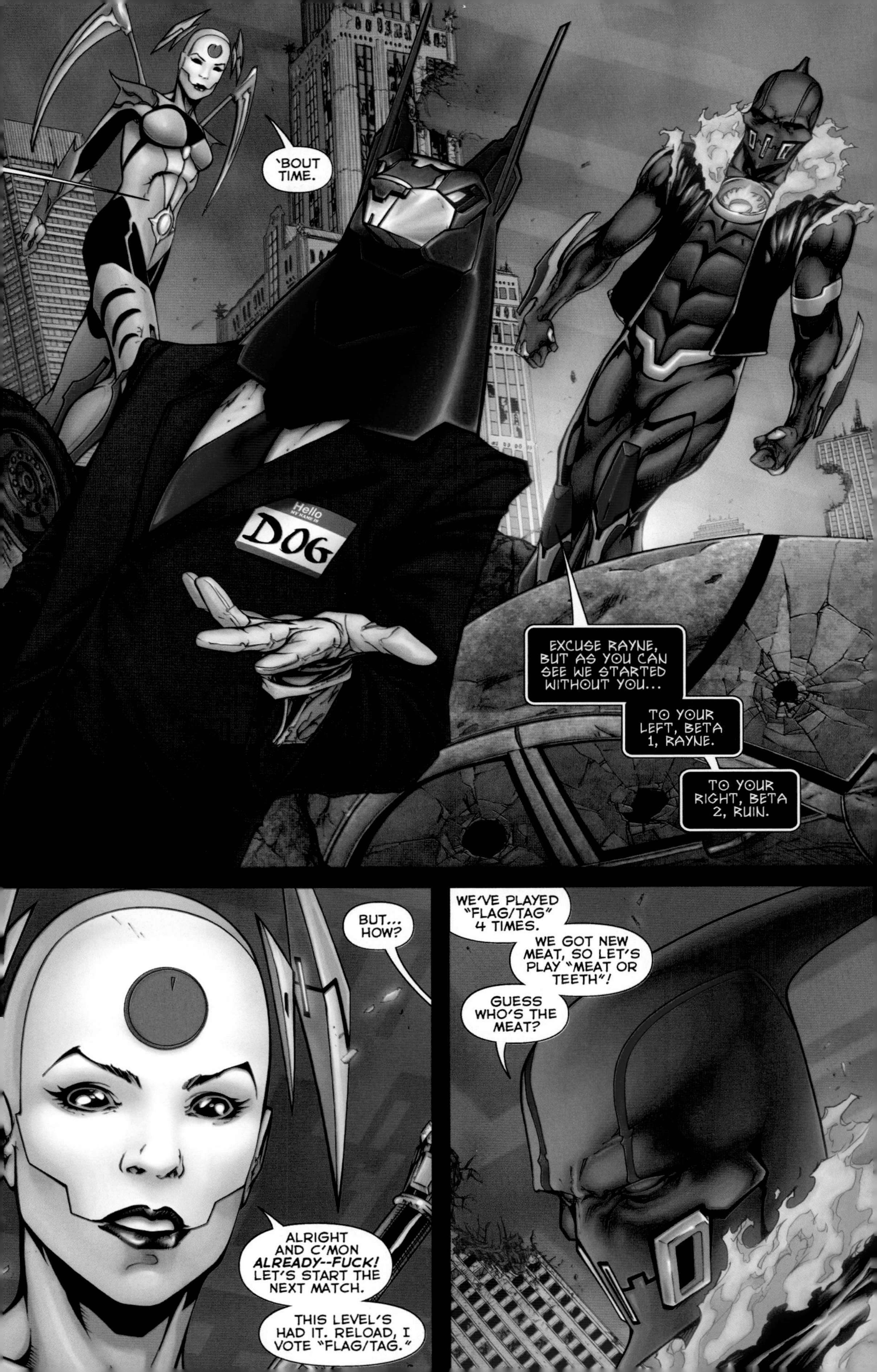
'BOUT TIME.
Hello MY NAME IS
DOG
EXCUSE RAYNE, BUT AS YOU CAN SEE WE STARTED WITHOUT YOU...
TO YOUR LEFT, BETA 1, RAYNE.
TO YOUR RIGHT, BETA 2, RUIN.
BUT... HOW?
ALRIGHT AND C'MON *ALREADY--FUCK!* LET'S START THE NEXT MATCH.
THIS LEVEL'S HAD IT. RELOAD, I VOTE "FLAG/TAG."
WE'VE PLAYED "FLAG/TAG" 4 TIMES.
WE GOT NEW MEAT, SO LET'S PLAY "MEAT OR TEETH"!
GUESS WHO'S THE MEAT?

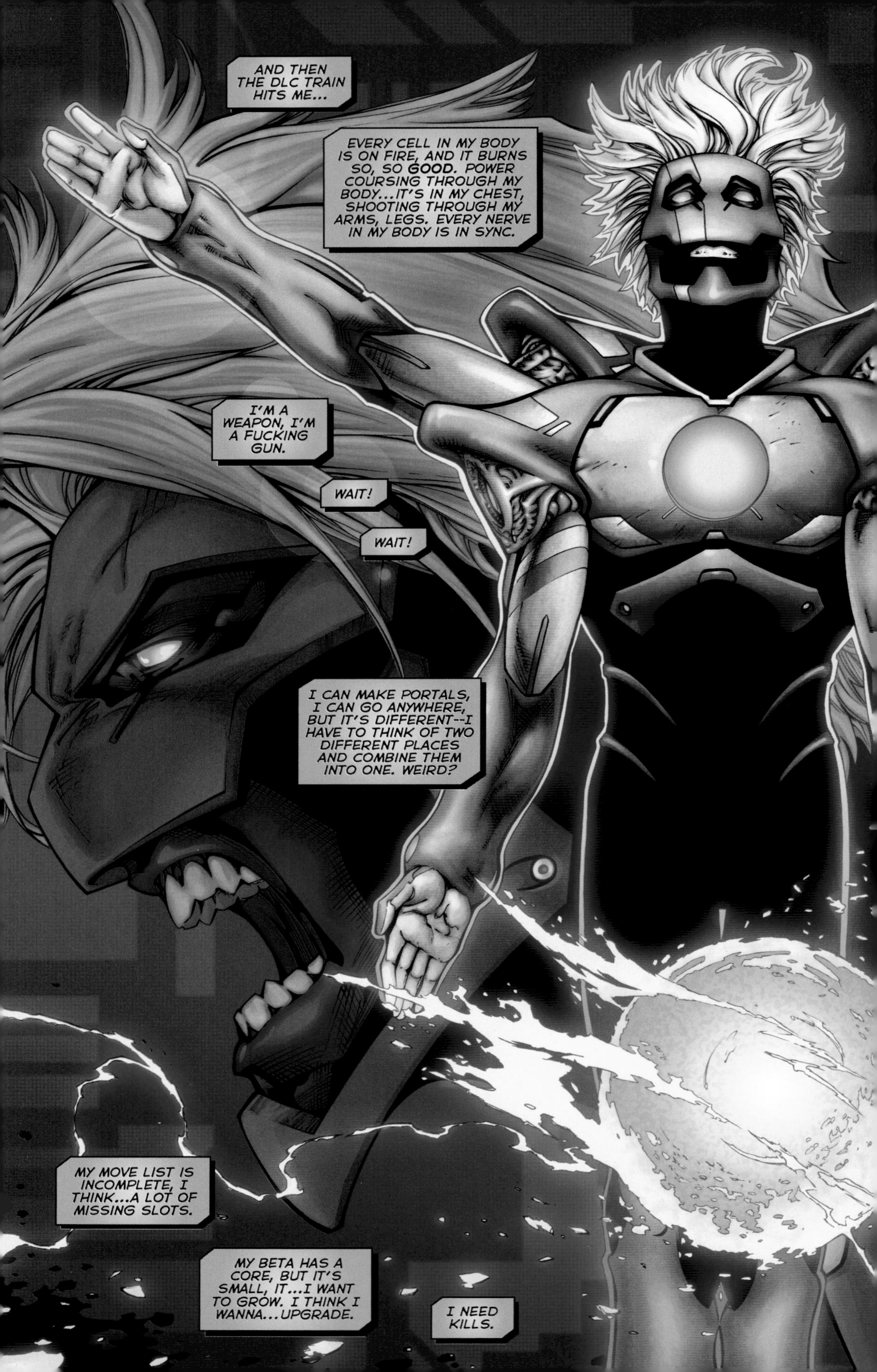
AND THEN THE DLC TRAIN HITS ME...
EVERY CELL IN MY BODY IS ON FIRE, AND IT BURNS SO, SO **GOOD**. POWER COURSING THROUGH MY BODY...IT'S IN MY CHEST, SHOOTING THROUGH MY ARMS, LEGS. EVERY NERVE IN MY BODY IS IN SYNC.
I'M A WEAPON, I'M A FUCKING GUN.
WAIT!
WAIT!
I CAN MAKE PORTALS, I CAN GO ANYWHERE, BUT IT'S DIFFERENT--I HAVE TO THINK OF TWO DIFFERENT PLACES AND COMBINE THEM INTO ONE. WEIRD?
MY MOVE LIST IS INCOMPLETE, I THINK...A LOT OF MISSING SLOTS.
MY BETA HAS A CORE, BUT IT'S SMALL, IT...I WANT TO GROW. I THINK I WANNA...UPGRADE.
I NEED KILLS.

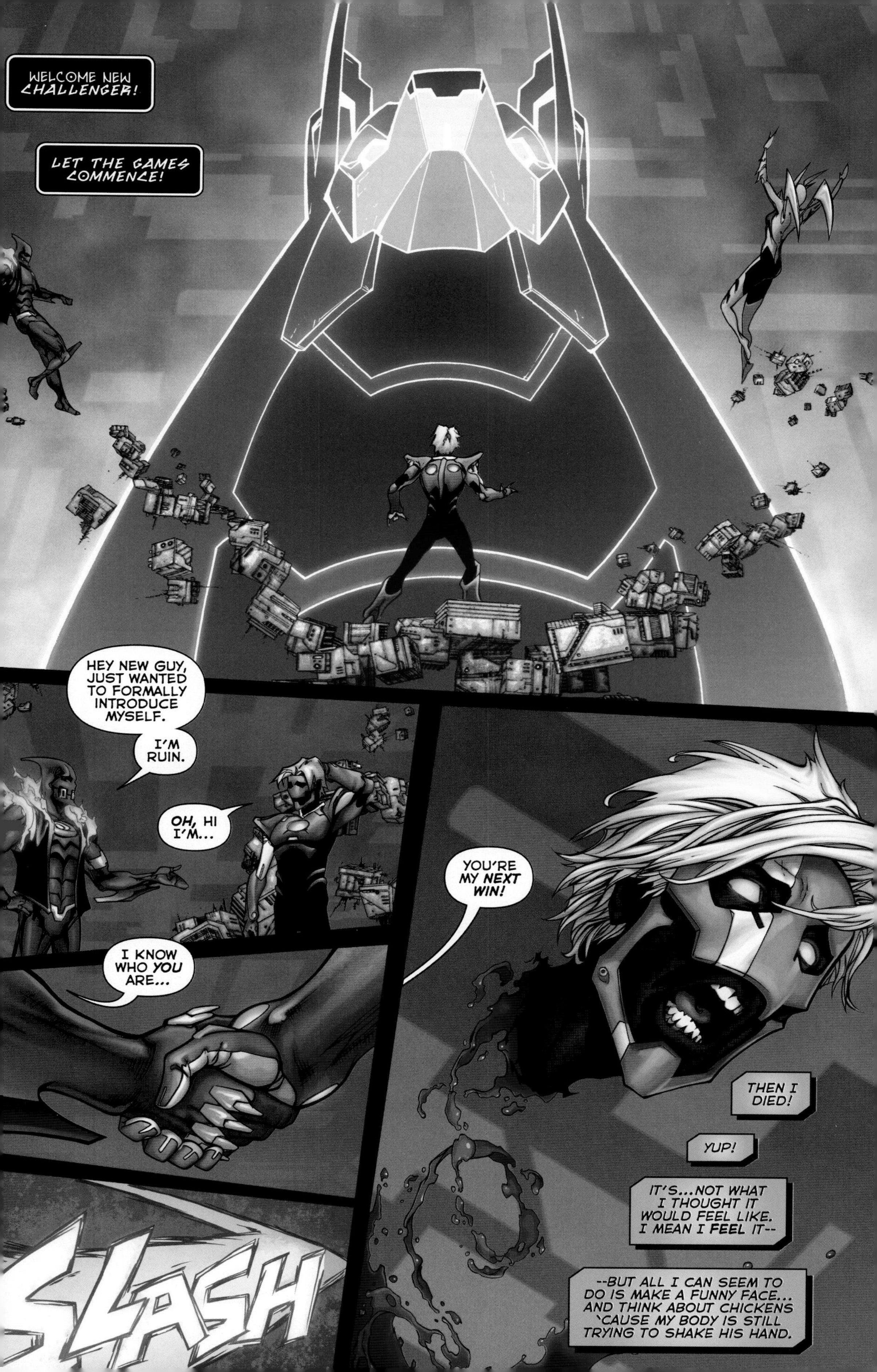
WELCOME NEW CHALLENGER!
LET THE GAMES COMMENCE!
HEY NEW GUY, JUST WANTED TO FORMALLY INTRODUCE MYSELF.
I'M RUIN.
OH, HI I'M...
I KNOW WHO YOU ARE...
YOU'RE MY NEXT WIN!
SLASH
THEN I DIED!
YUP!
IT'S...NOT WHAT I THOUGHT IT WOULD FEEL LIKE. I MEAN I FEEL IT--
--BUT ALL I CAN SEEM TO DO IS MAKE A FUNNY FACE... AND THINK ABOUT CHICKENS `CAUSE MY BODY IS STILL TRYING TO SHAKE HIS HAND.

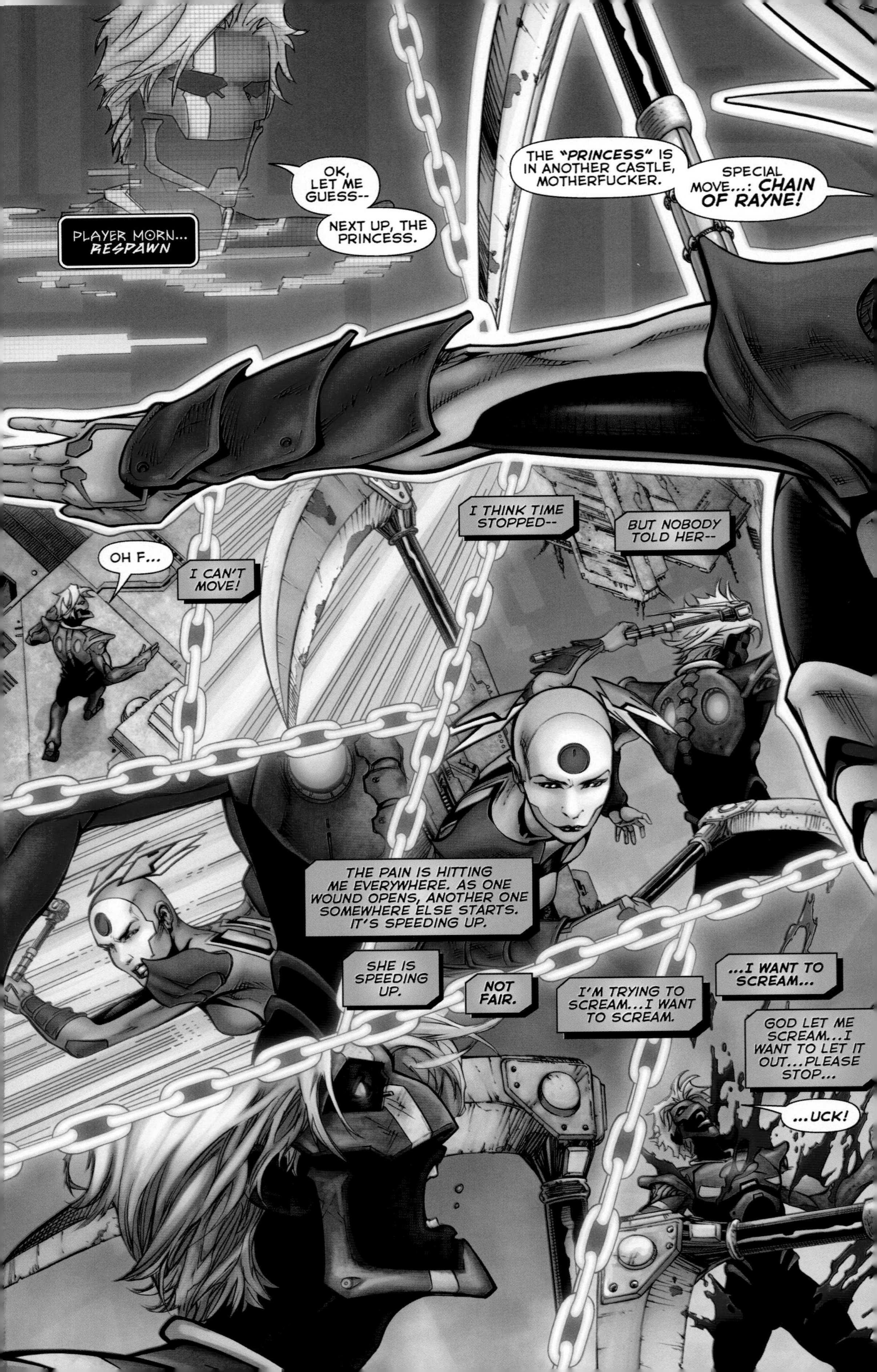
PLAYER MORN... RESPAWN
OK, LET ME GUESS--
NEXT UP, THE PRINCESS.
THE "PRINCESS" IS IN ANOTHER CASTLE, MOTHERFUCKER.
SPECIAL MOVE...: CHAIN OF RAYNE!
OH F...
I CAN'T MOVE!
I THINK TIME STOPPED--
BUT NOBODY TOLD HER--
THE PAIN IS HITTING ME EVERYWHERE. AS ONE WOUND OPENS, ANOTHER ONE SOMEWHERE ELSE STARTS. IT'S SPEEDING UP.
SHE IS SPEEDING UP.
NOT FAIR.
I'M TRYING TO SCREAM...I WANT TO SCREAM.
...I WANT TO SCREAM...
GOD LET ME SCREAM...I WANT TO LET IT OUT...PLEASE STOP...
...UCK!

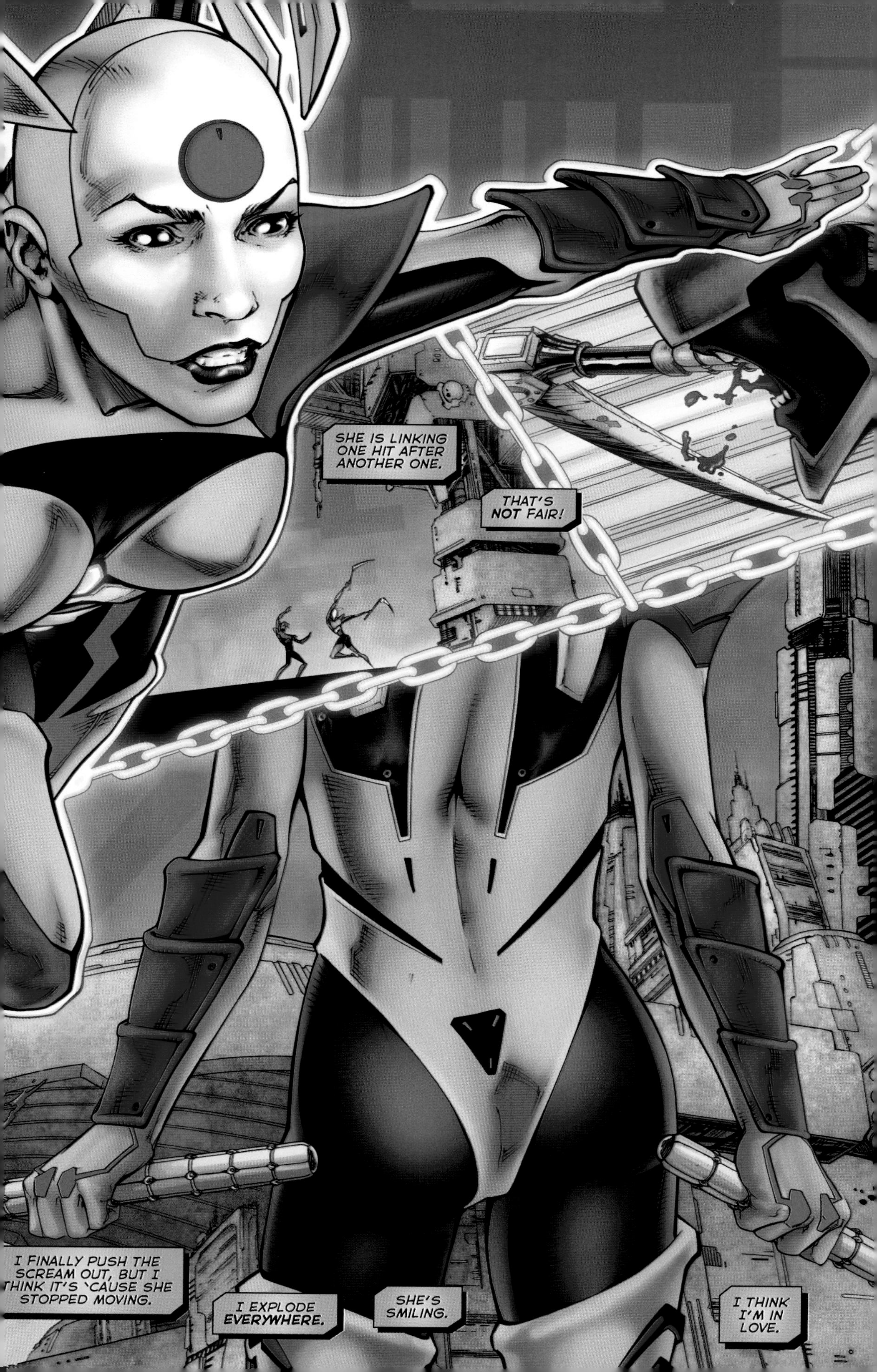
SHE IS LINKING ONE HIT AFTER ANOTHER ONE.
THAT'S NOT FAIR!
I FINALLY PUSH THE SCREAM OUT, BUT I THINK IT'S 'CAUSE SHE STOPPED MOVING.
I EXPLODE **EVERYWHERE.**
SHE'S SMILING.
I THINK I'M IN LOVE.

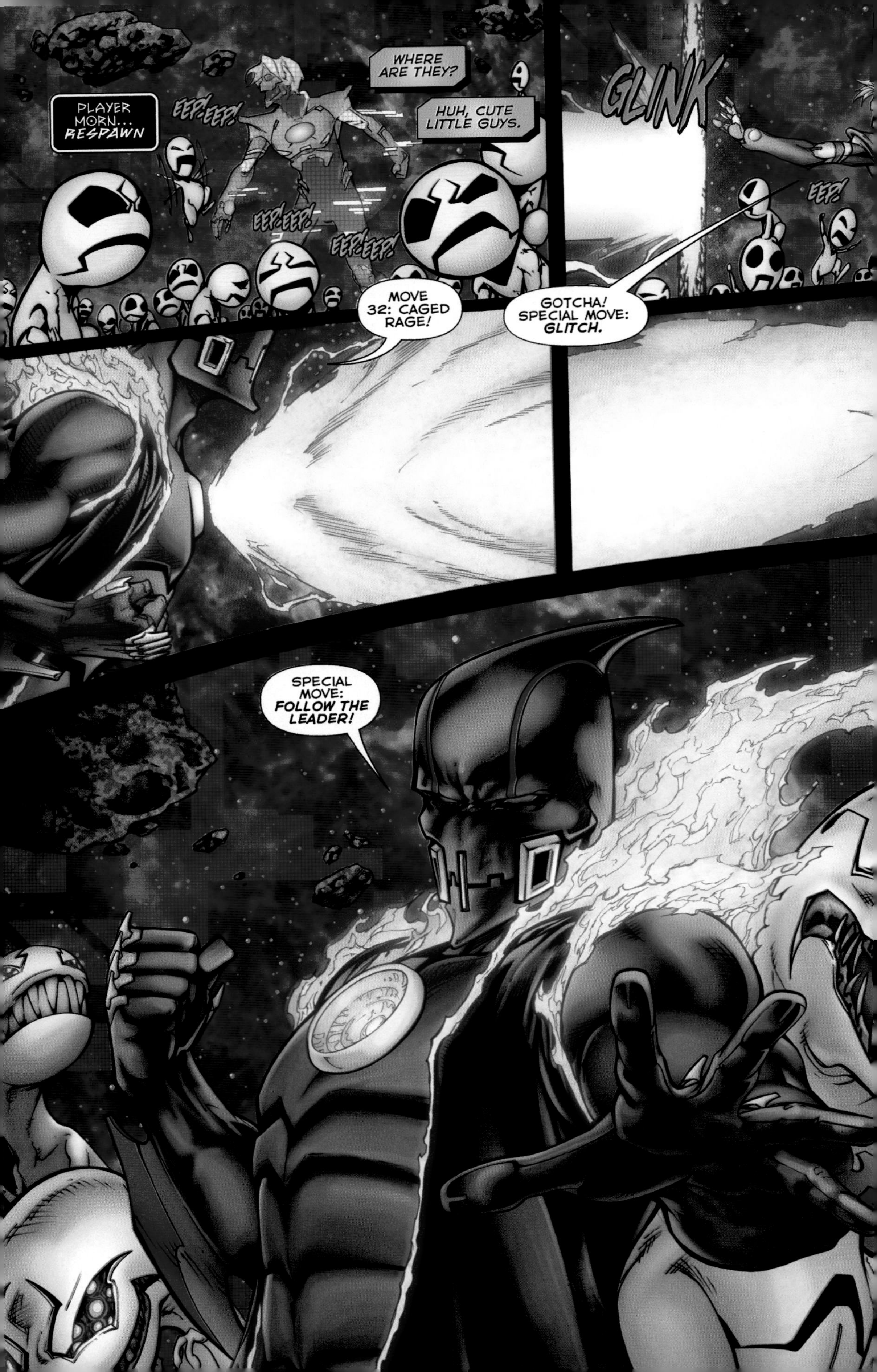
PLAYER MORN... RESPAWN
EEP! EEP!
WHERE ARE THEY?
HUH, CUTE LITTLE GUYS.
EEP! EEP!
EEP! EEP!
GLINK
EEP!
MOVE 32: CAGED RAGE!
GOTCHA! SPECIAL MOVE: GLITCH.
SPECIAL MOVE: FOLLOW THE LEADER!

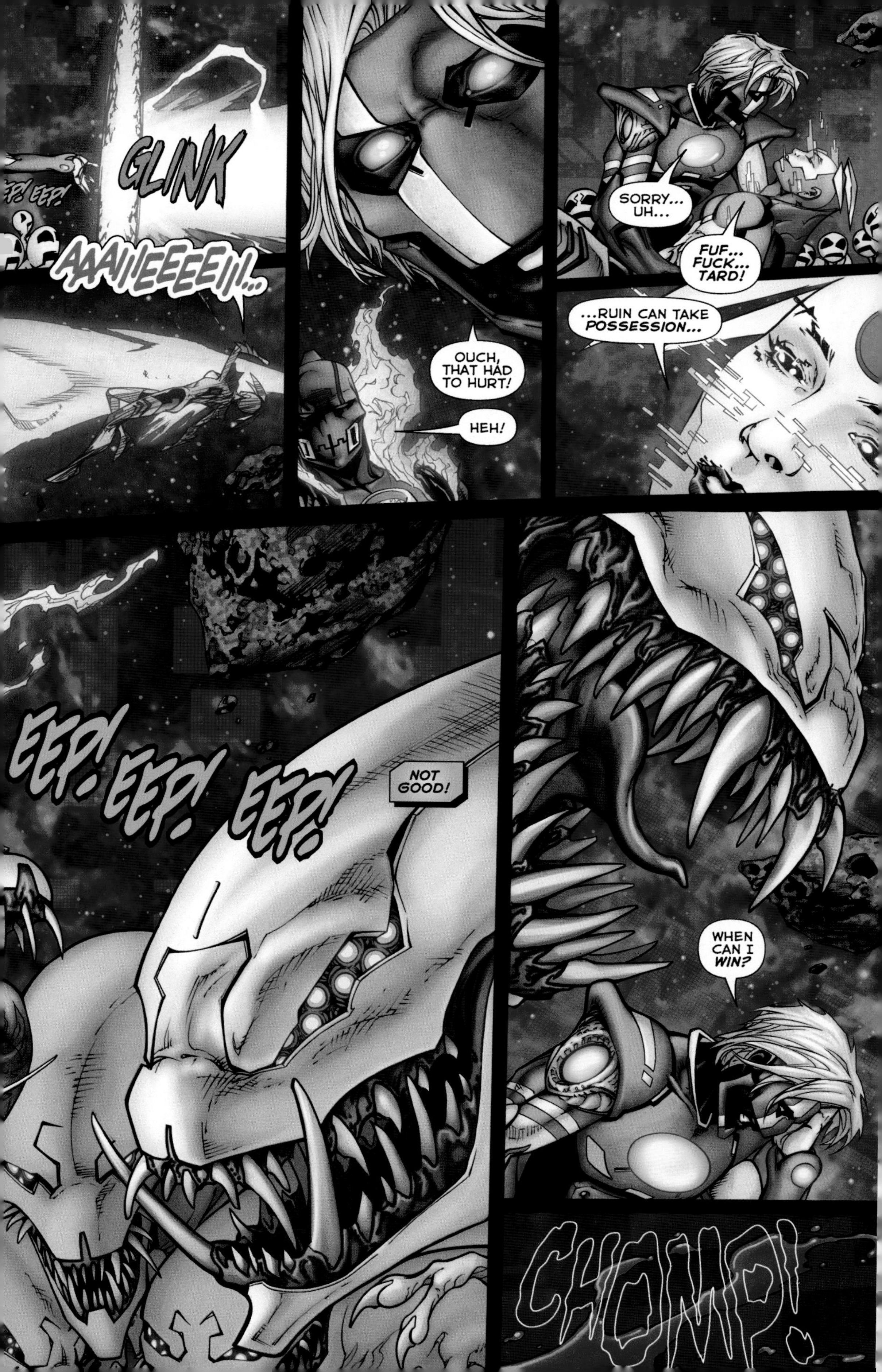
GLINK
EEP! EEP!
AAAIIIEEEE!!!...
SORRY... UH...
FUF... FUCK... TARD!
OUCH, THAT HAD TO HURT!
HEH!
...RUIN CAN TAKE POSSESSION...
EEP! EEP! EEP!
NOT GOOD!
WHEN CAN I WIN?
CHOMP!

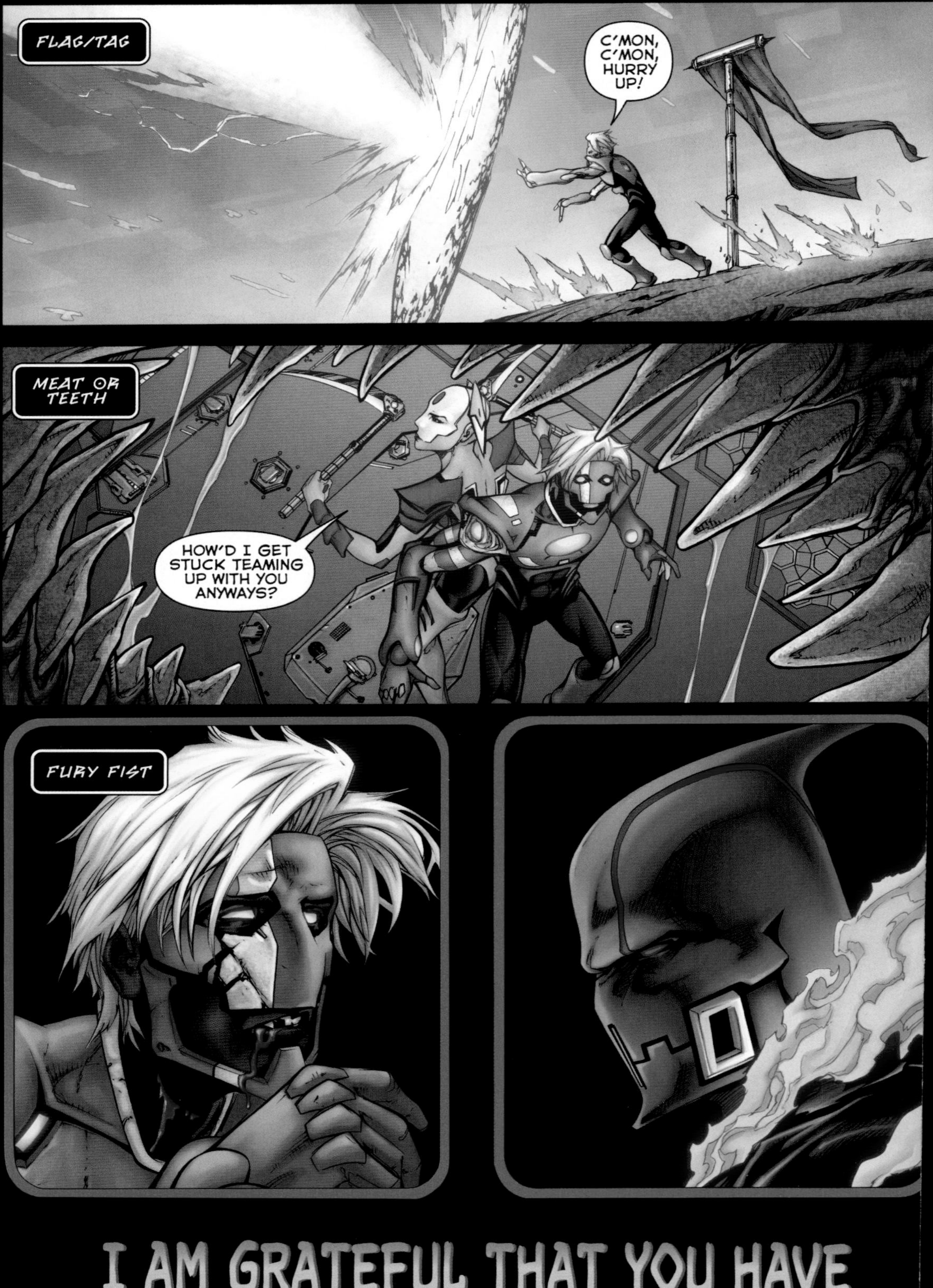
FLAG/TAG
C'MON, C'MON, HURRY UP!
MEAT OR TEETH
HOW'D I GET STUCK TEAMING UP WITH YOU ANYWAYS?
FURY FIST

I AM GRATEFUL THAT YOU HAVE SHOWN ME THE GREAT AND ANCIENT MYSTICAL ART OF SUCKING ASS!

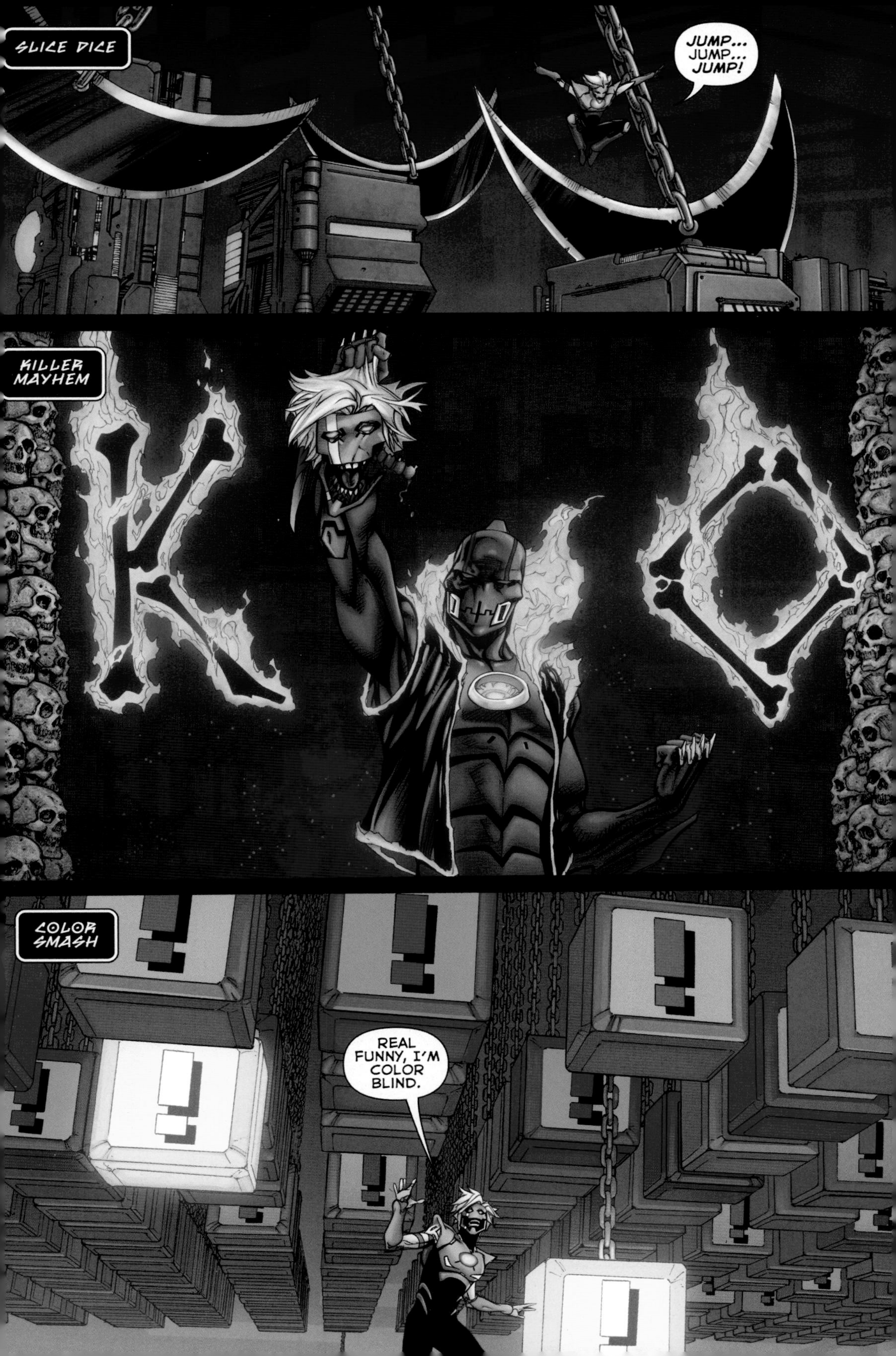
SLICE DICE
JUMP... JUMP... JUMP!
KILLER MAYHEM
COLOR SMASH
REAL FUNNY, I'M COLOR BLIND.

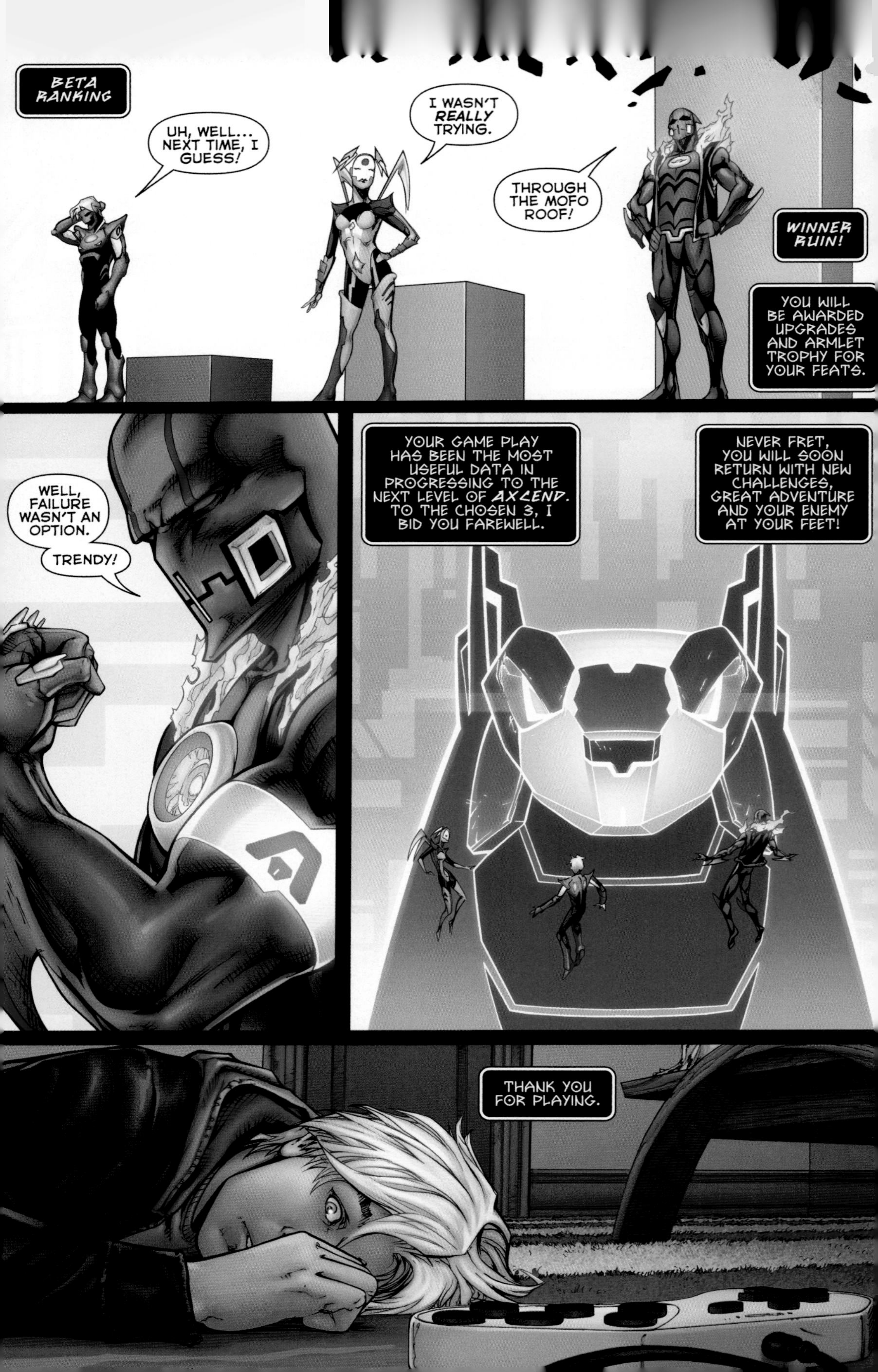
BETA RANKING
UH, WELL... NEXT TIME, I GUESS!
I WASN'T REALLY TRYING.
THROUGH THE MOFO ROOF!
WINNER RUIN!
YOU WILL BE AWARDED UPGRADES AND ARMLET TROPHY FOR YOUR FEATS.
WELL, FAILURE WASN'T AN OPTION.
TRENDY!
YOUR GAME PLAY HAS BEEN THE MOST USEFUL DATA IN PROGRESSING TO THE NEXT LEVEL OF AXCEND. TO THE CHOSEN 3, I BID YOU FAREWELL.
NEVER FRET, YOU WILL SOON RETURN WITH NEW CHALLENGES, GREAT ADVENTURE AND YOUR ENEMY AT YOUR FEET!
THANK YOU FOR PLAYING.

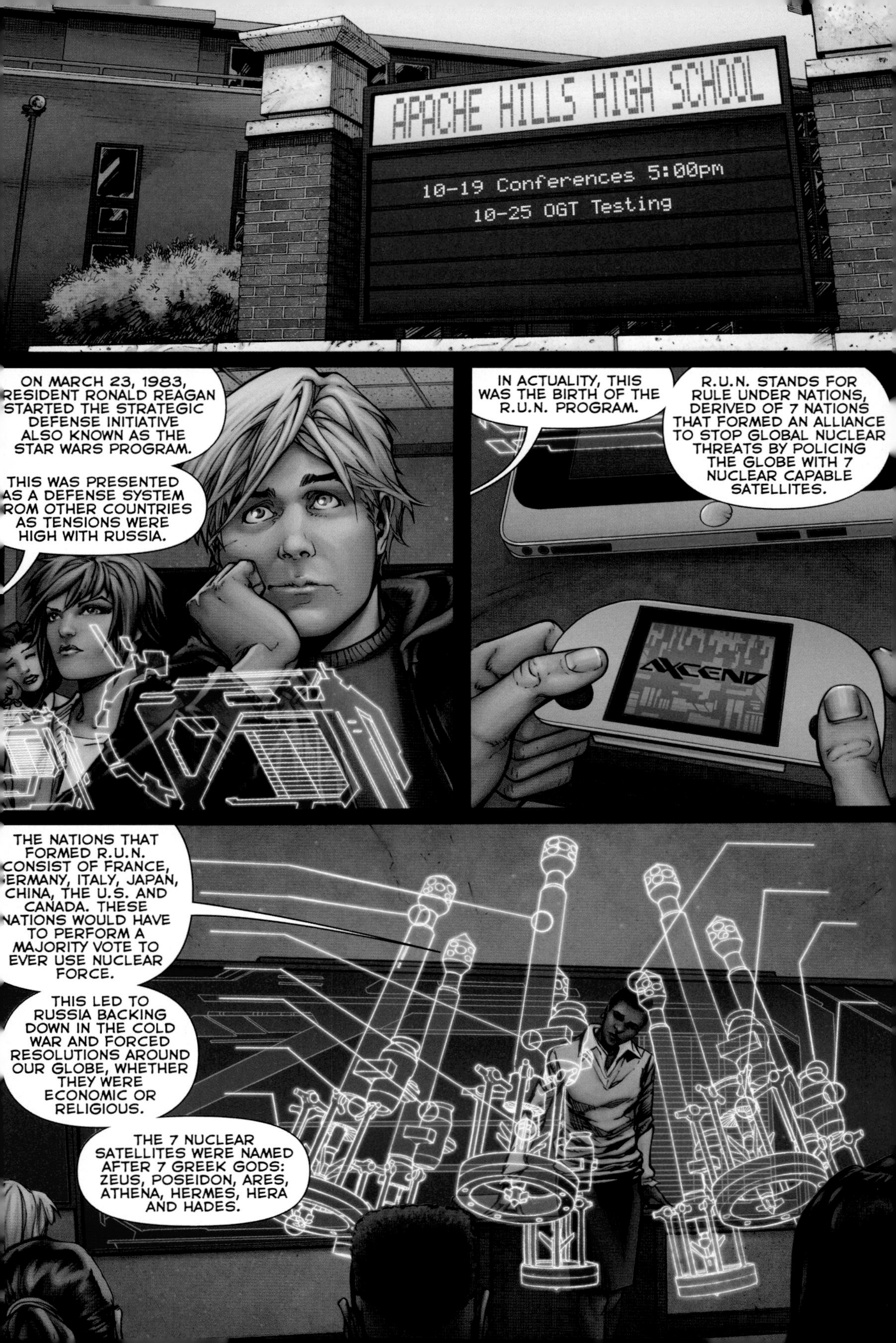
APACHE HILLS HIGH SCHOOL
10-19 Conferences 5:00pm
10-25 OGT Testing
ON MARCH 23, 1983, RESIDENT RONALD REAGAN STARTED THE STRATEGIC DEFENSE INITIATIVE ALSO KNOWN AS THE STAR WARS PROGRAM.
THIS WAS PRESENTED AS A DEFENSE SYSTEM ROM OTHER COUNTRIES AS TENSIONS WERE HIGH WITH RUSSIA.
IN ACTUALITY, THIS WAS THE BIRTH OF THE R.U.N. PROGRAM.
R.U.N. STANDS FOR RULE UNDER NATIONS, DERIVED OF 7 NATIONS THAT FORMED AN ALLIANCE TO STOP GLOBAL NUCLEAR THREATS BY POLICING THE GLOBE WITH 7 NUCLEAR CAPABLE SATELLITES.
AXCEND
THE NATIONS THAT FORMED R.U.N. CONSIST OF FRANCE, ERMANY, ITALY, JAPAN, CHINA, THE U.S. AND CANADA. THESE ATIONS WOULD HAVE TO PERFORM A MAJORITY VOTE TO EVER USE NUCLEAR FORCE.
THIS LED TO RUSSIA BACKING DOWN IN THE COLD WAR AND FORCED RESOLUTIONS AROUND OUR GLOBE, WHETHER THEY WERE ECONOMIC OR RELIGIOUS.
THE 7 NUCLEAR SATELLITES WERE NAMED AFTER 7 GREEK GODS: ZEUS, POSEIDON, ARES, ATHENA, HERMES, HERA AND HADES.

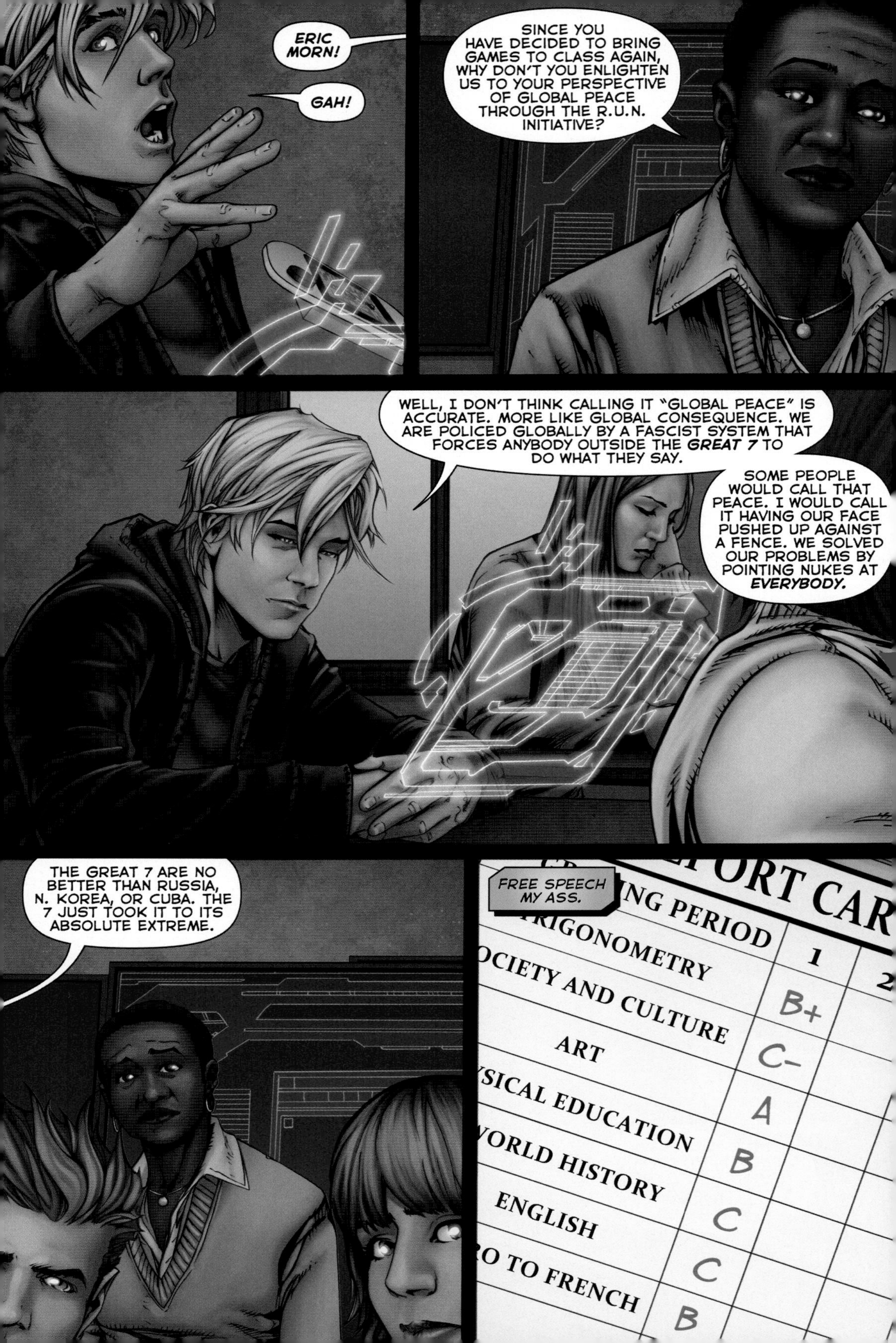
ERIC MORN!
GAH!
SINCE YOU HAVE DECIDED TO BRING GAMES TO CLASS AGAIN, WHY DON'T YOU ENLIGHTEN US TO YOUR PERSPECTIVE OF GLOBAL PEACE THROUGH THE R.U.N. INITIATIVE?
WELL, I DON'T THINK CALLING IT "GLOBAL PEACE" IS ACCURATE. MORE LIKE GLOBAL CONSEQUENCE. WE ARE POLICED GLOBALLY BY A FASCIST SYSTEM THAT FORCES ANYBODY OUTSIDE THE *GREAT 7* TO DO WHAT THEY SAY.
SOME PEOPLE WOULD CALL THAT PEACE. I WOULD CALL IT HAVING OUR FACE PUSHED UP AGAINST A FENCE. WE SOLVED OUR PROBLEMS BY POINTING NUKES AT ***EVERYBODY.***
THE GREAT 7 ARE NO BETTER THAN RUSSIA, N. KOREA, OR CUBA. THE 7 JUST TOOK IT TO ITS ABSOLUTE EXTREME.
FREE SPEECH MY ASS.
ART C-
ENGLISH C
B+
A
B
C
B

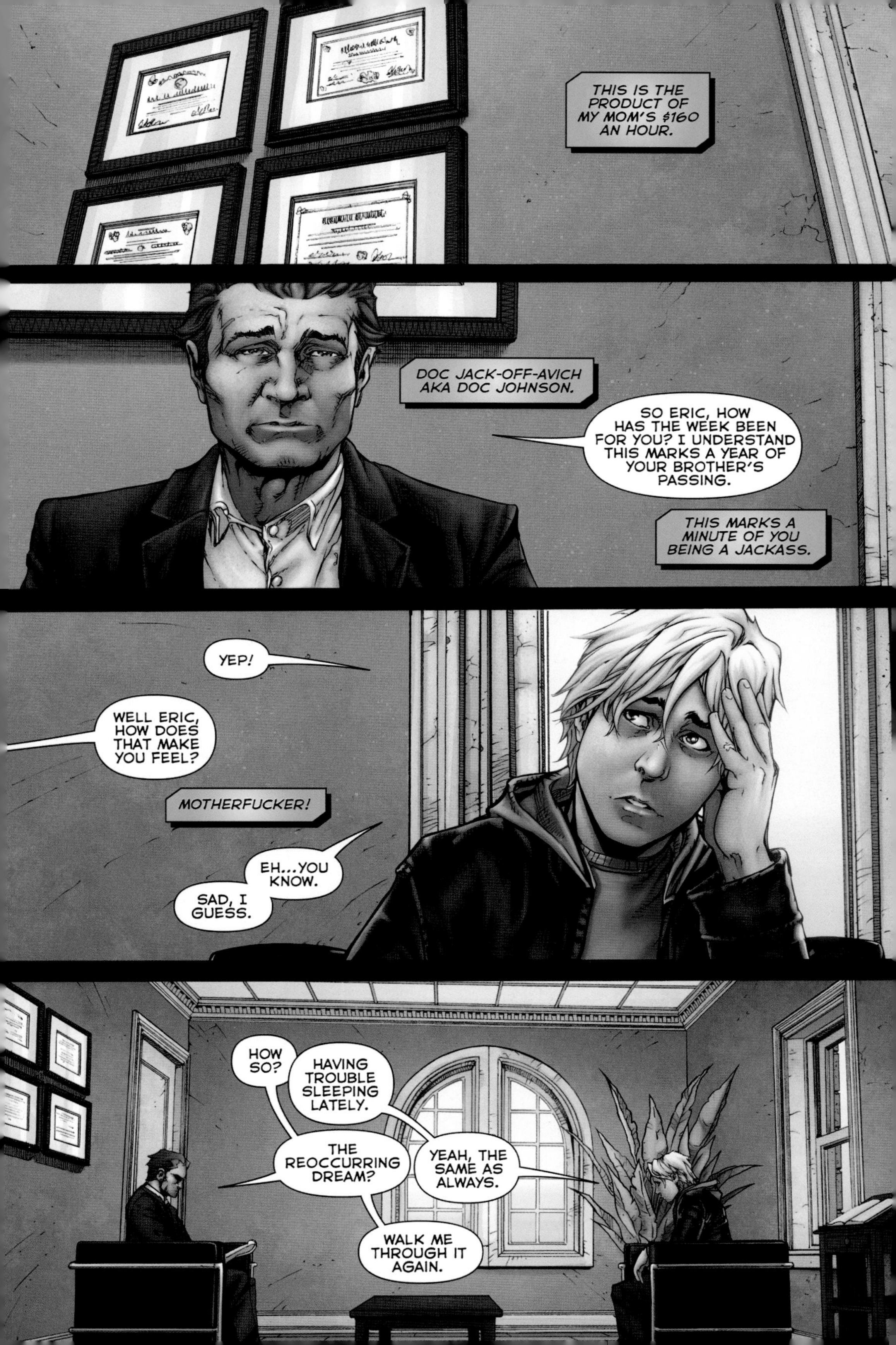
THIS IS THE PRODUCT OF MY MOM'S $160 AN HOUR.
DOC JACK-OFF-AVICH AKA DOC JOHNSON.
SO ERIC, HOW HAS THE WEEK BEEN FOR YOU? I UNDERSTAND THIS MARKS A YEAR OF YOUR BROTHER'S PASSING.
THIS MARKS A MINUTE OF YOU BEING A JACKASS.
YEP!
WELL ERIC, HOW DOES THAT MAKE YOU FEEL?
MOTHERFUCKER!
EH...YOU KNOW.
SAD, I GUESS.
HOW SO?
HAVING TROUBLE SLEEPING LATELY.
THE REOCCURRING DREAM?
YEAH, THE SAME AS ALWAYS.
WALK ME THROUGH IT AGAIN.

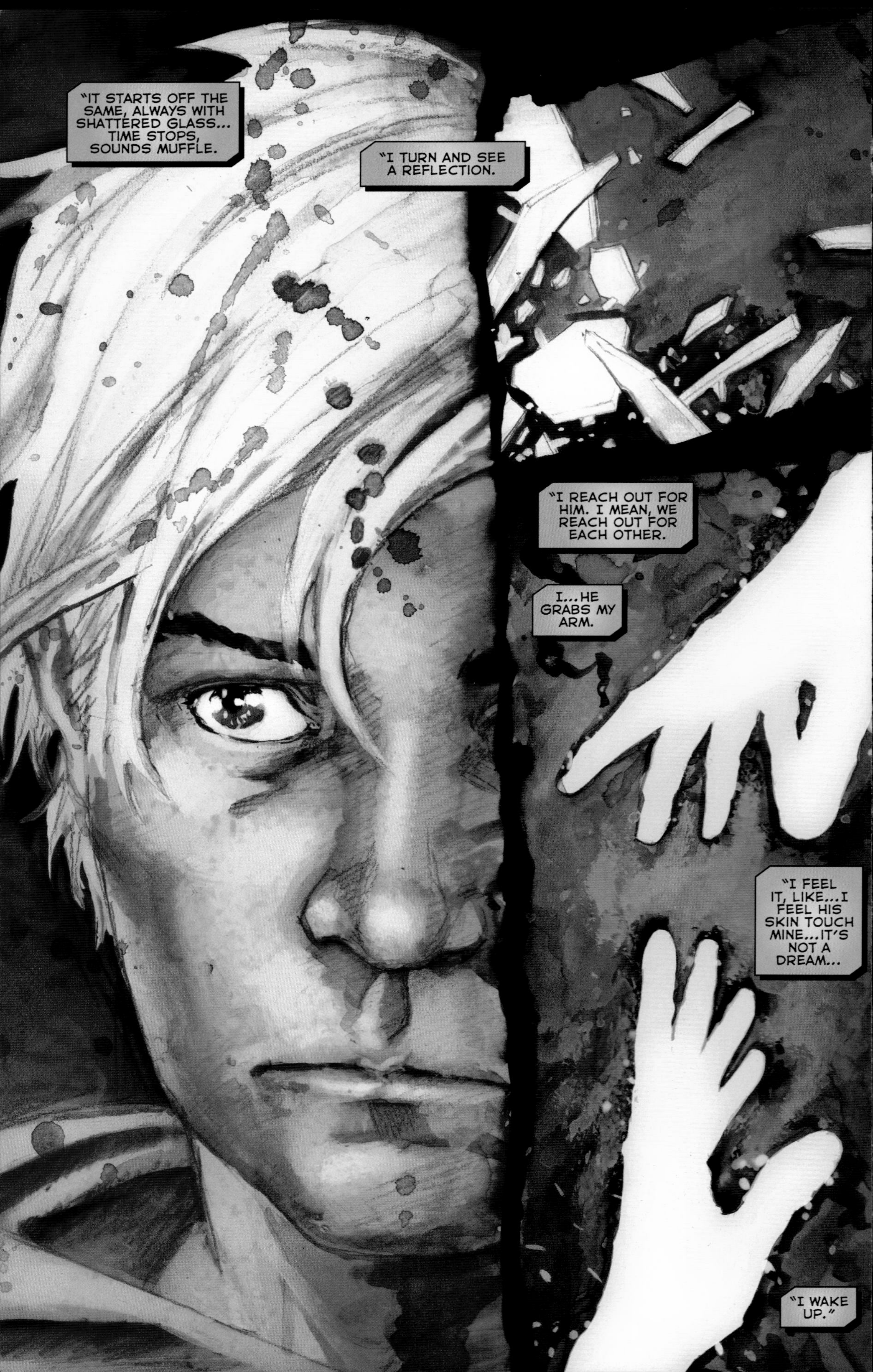
"IT STARTS OFF THE SAME, ALWAYS WITH SHATTERED GLASS... TIME STOPS, SOUNDS MUFFLE.
"I TURN AND SEE A REFLECTION.
"I REACH OUT FOR HIM. I MEAN, WE REACH OUT FOR EACH OTHER.
I...HE GRABS MY ARM.
"I FEEL IT, LIKE...I FEEL HIS SKIN TOUCH MINE...IT'S NOT A DREAM...
"I WAKE UP."

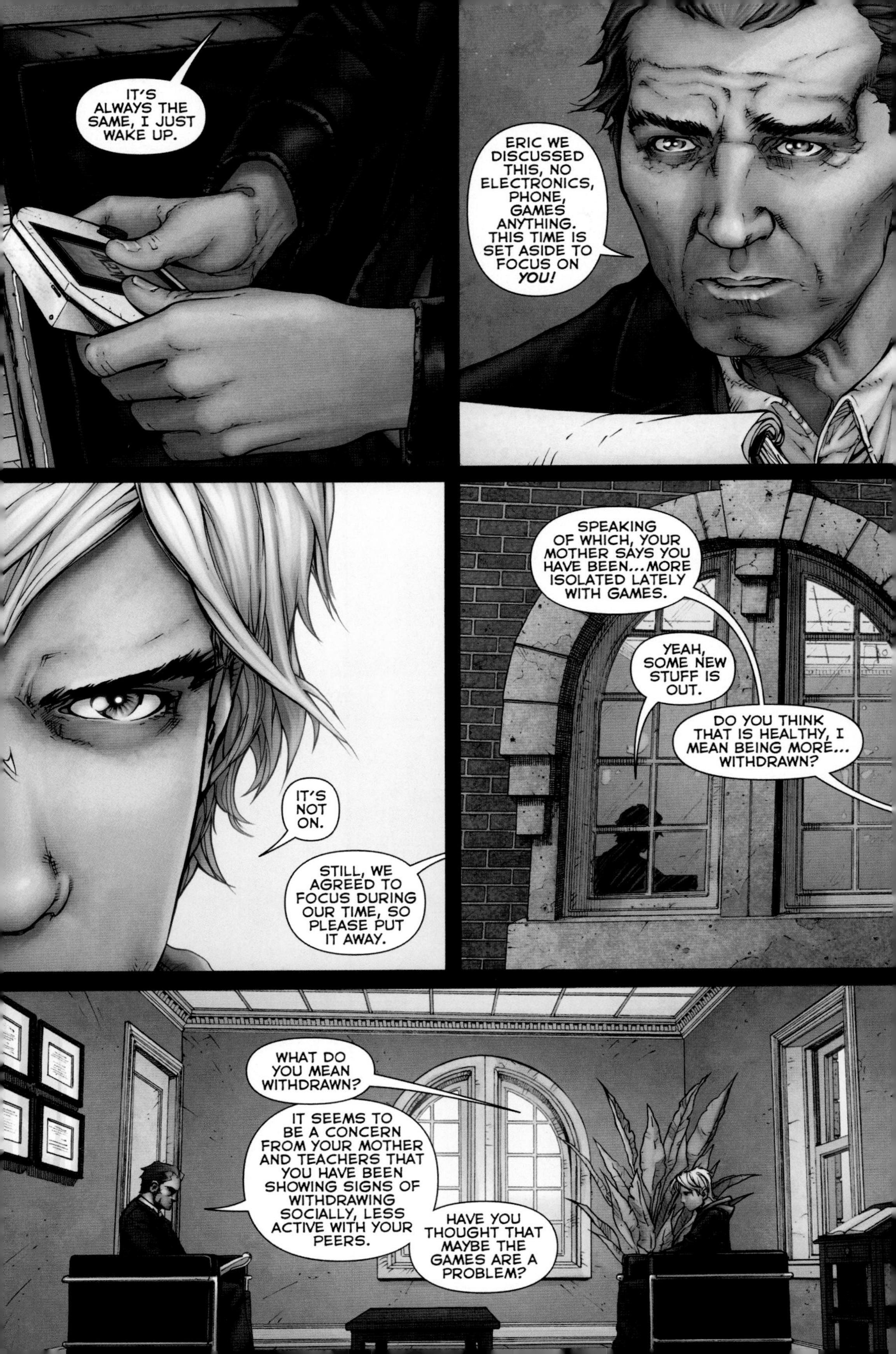
IT'S ALWAYS THE SAME, I JUST WAKE UP.
ERIC WE DISCUSSED THIS, NO ELECTRONICS, PHONE, GAMES ANYTHING. THIS TIME IS SET ASIDE TO FOCUS ON *YOU!*
IT'S NOT ON.
STILL, WE AGREED TO FOCUS DURING OUR TIME, SO PLEASE PUT IT AWAY.
SPEAKING OF WHICH, YOUR MOTHER SAYS YOU HAVE BEEN...MORE ISOLATED LATELY WITH GAMES.
YEAH, SOME NEW STUFF IS OUT.
DO YOU THINK THAT IS HEALTHY, I MEAN BEING MORE... WITHDRAWN?
WHAT DO YOU MEAN WITHDRAWN?
IT SEEMS TO BE A CONCERN FROM YOUR MOTHER AND TEACHERS THAT YOU HAVE BEEN SHOWING SIGNS OF WITHDRAWING SOCIALLY, LESS ACTIVE WITH YOUR PEERS.
HAVE YOU THOUGHT THAT MAYBE THE GAMES ARE A PROBLEM?

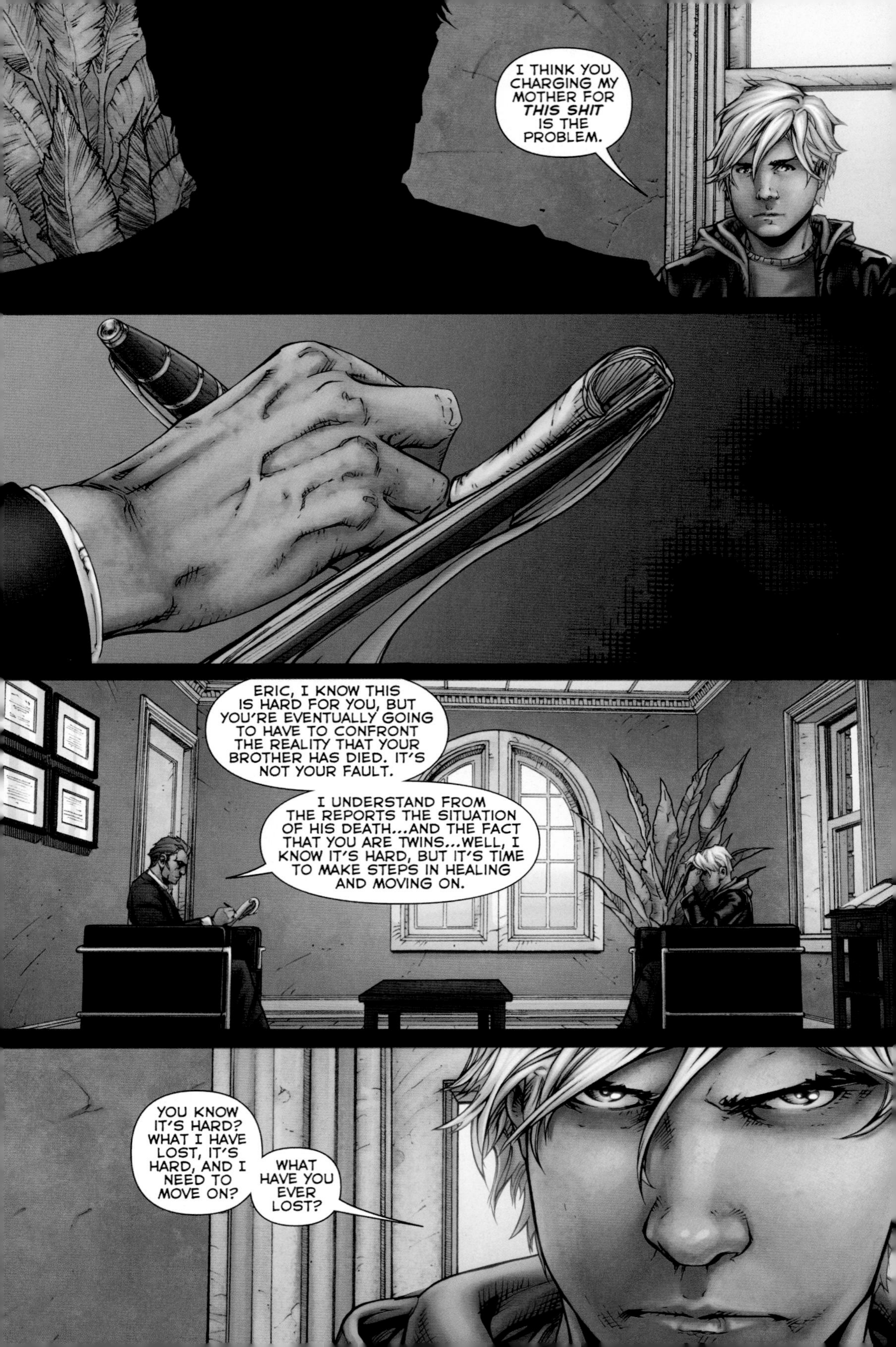
I THINK YOU CHARGING MY MOTHER FOR *THIS SHIT* IS THE PROBLEM.
ERIC, I KNOW THIS IS HARD FOR YOU, BUT YOU'RE EVENTUALLY GOING TO HAVE TO CONFRONT THE REALITY THAT YOUR BROTHER HAS DIED. IT'S NOT YOUR FAULT.
I UNDERSTAND FROM THE REPORTS THE SITUATION OF HIS DEATH...AND THE FACT THAT YOU ARE TWINS...WELL, I KNOW IT'S HARD, BUT IT'S TIME TO MAKE STEPS IN HEALING AND MOVING ON.
YOU KNOW IT'S HARD? WHAT I HAVE LOST, IT'S HARD, AND I NEED TO MOVE ON?
WHAT HAVE YOU EVER LOST?

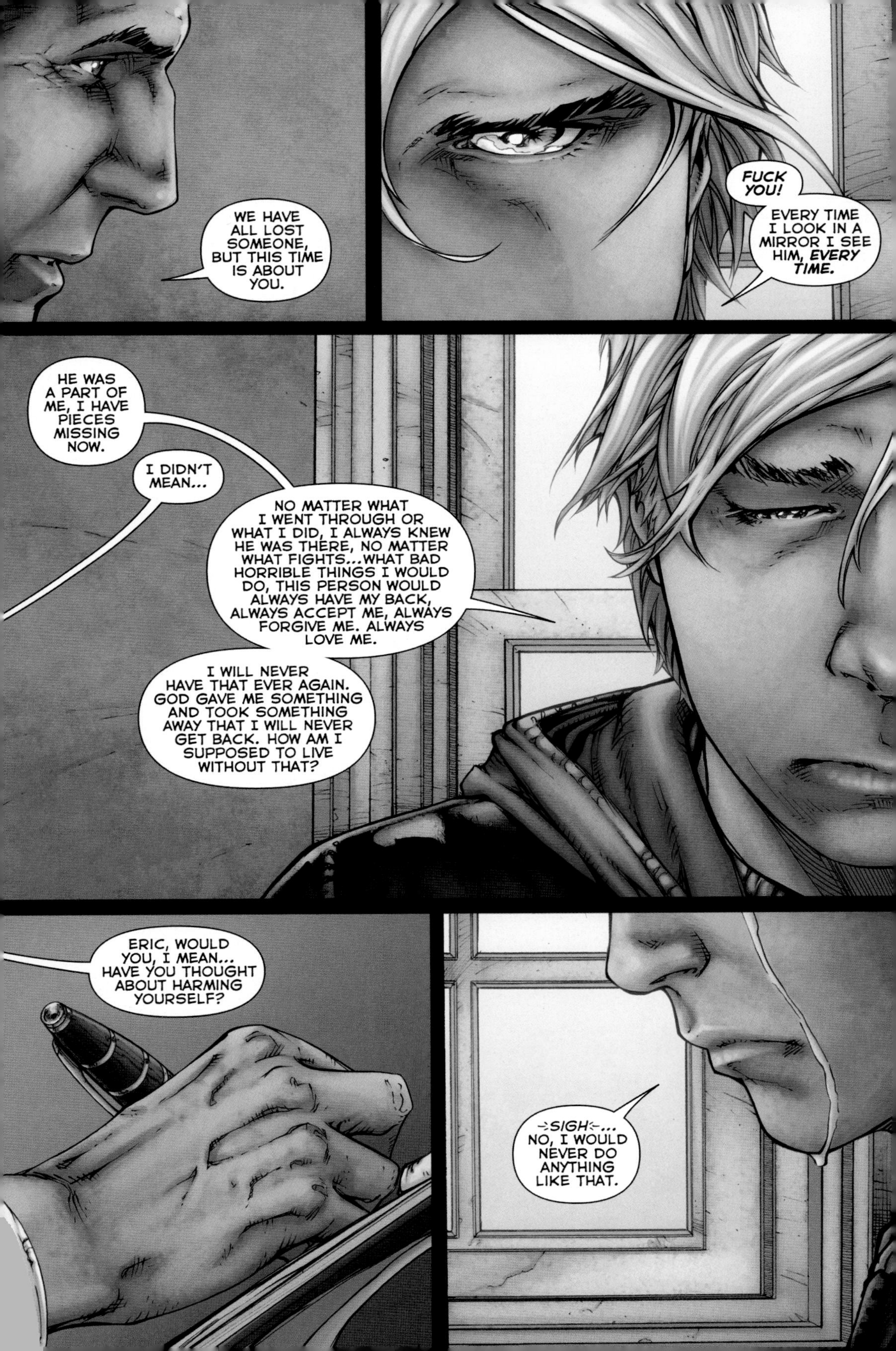
WE HAVE ALL LOST SOMEONE, BUT THIS TIME IS ABOUT YOU.
FUCK YOU!
EVERY TIME I LOOK IN A MIRROR I SEE HIM, EVERY TIME.
HE WAS A PART OF ME, I HAVE PIECES MISSING NOW.
I DIDN'T MEAN...
NO MATTER WHAT I WENT THROUGH OR WHAT I DID, I ALWAYS KNEW HE WAS THERE, NO MATTER WHAT FIGHTS...WHAT BAD HORRIBLE THINGS I WOULD DO, THIS PERSON WOULD ALWAYS HAVE MY BACK, ALWAYS ACCEPT ME, ALWAYS FORGIVE ME. ALWAYS LOVE ME.
I WILL NEVER HAVE THAT EVER AGAIN. GOD GAVE ME SOMETHING AND TOOK SOMETHING AWAY THAT I WILL NEVER GET BACK. HOW AM I SUPPOSED TO LIVE WITHOUT THAT?
ERIC, WOULD YOU, I MEAN... HAVE YOU THOUGHT ABOUT HARMING YOURSELF?
SIGH... NO, I WOULD NEVER DO ANYTHING LIKE THAT.

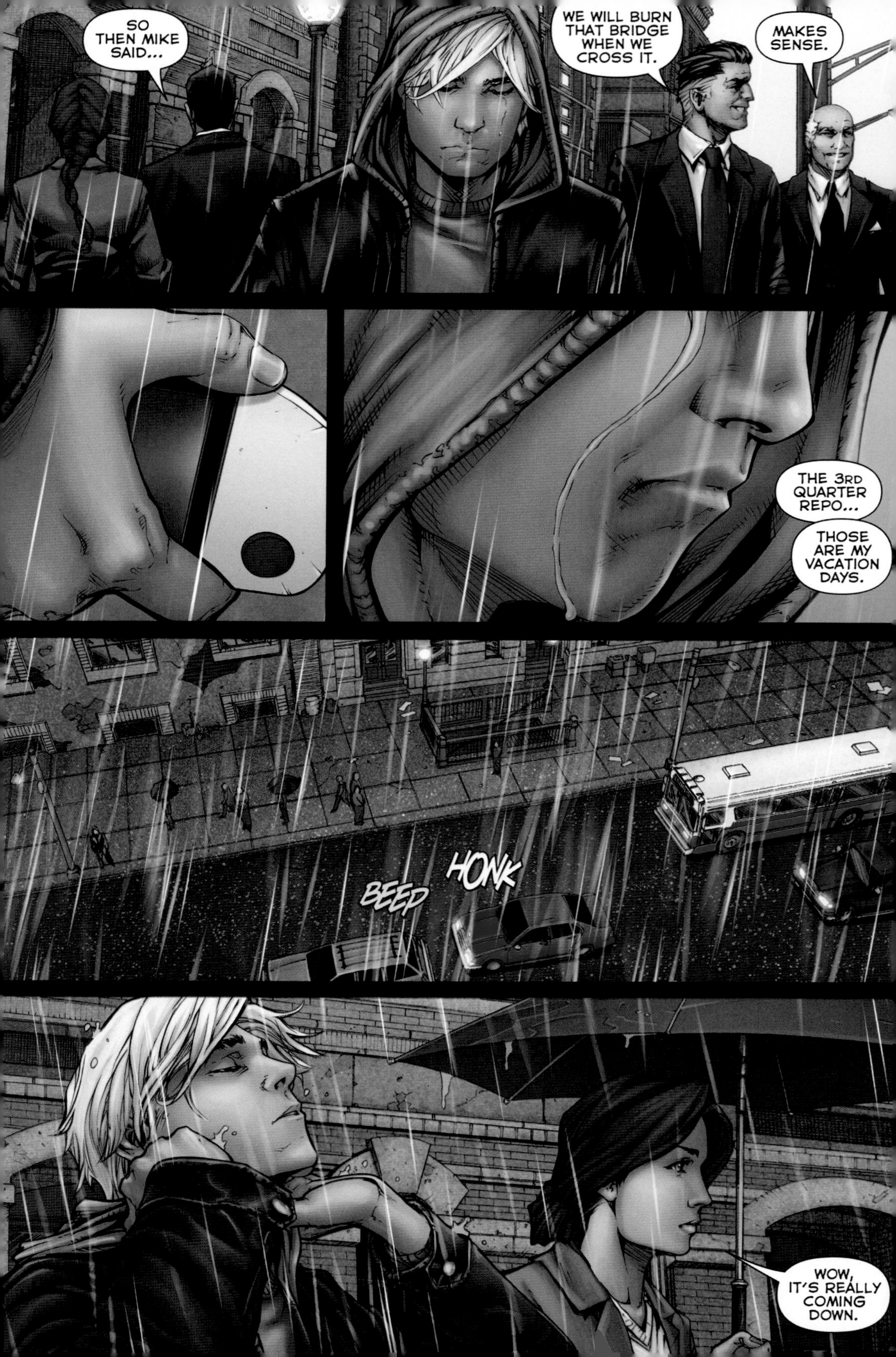
SO THEN MIKE SAID...
WE WILL BURN THAT BRIDGE WHEN WE CROSS IT.
MAKES SENSE.
THE 3RD QUARTER REPO...
THOSE ARE MY VACATION DAYS.
HONK
BEEP
WOW, IT'S REALLY COMING DOWN.

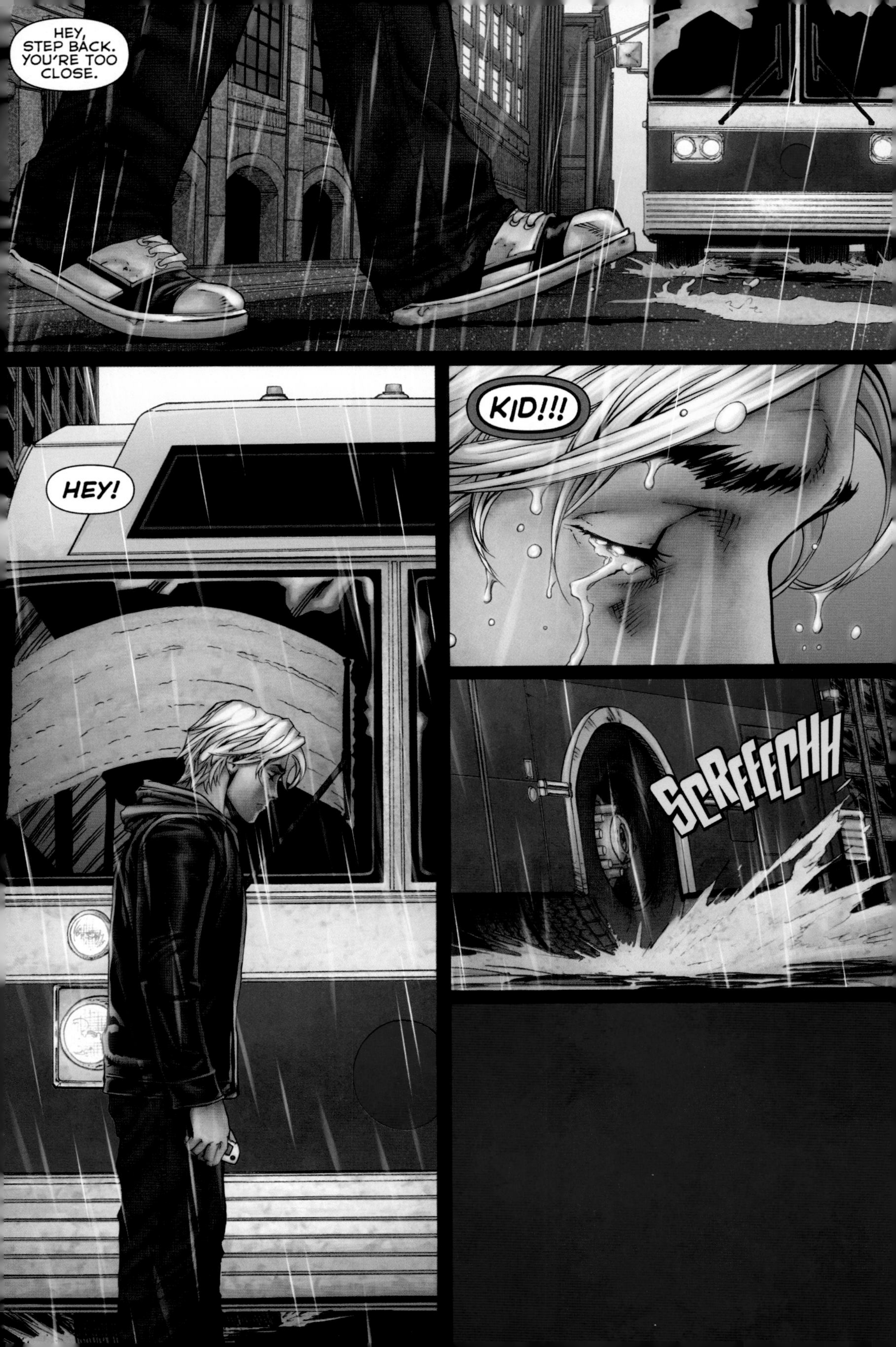
HEY, STEP BACK. YOU'RE TOO CLOSE.
HEY!
KID!!!
SCREEECHH

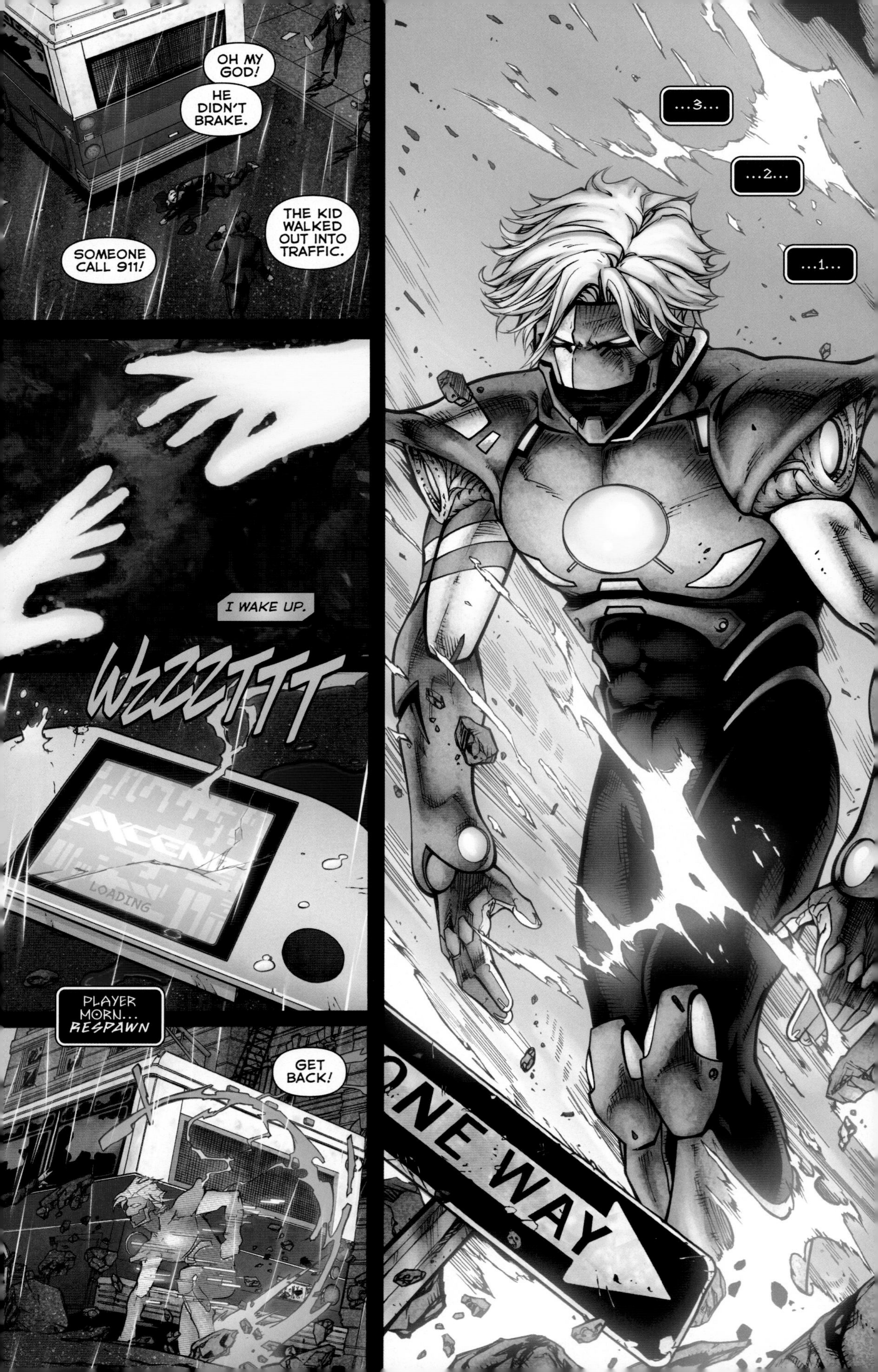
OH MY GOD!
HE DIDN'T BRAKE.
THE KID WALKED OUT INTO TRAFFIC.
SOMEONE CALL 911!
I WAKE UP.
WZZZTTTT
LOADING
PLAYER MORN... RESPAWN
GET BACK!
...3...
...2...
...1...
ONE WAY

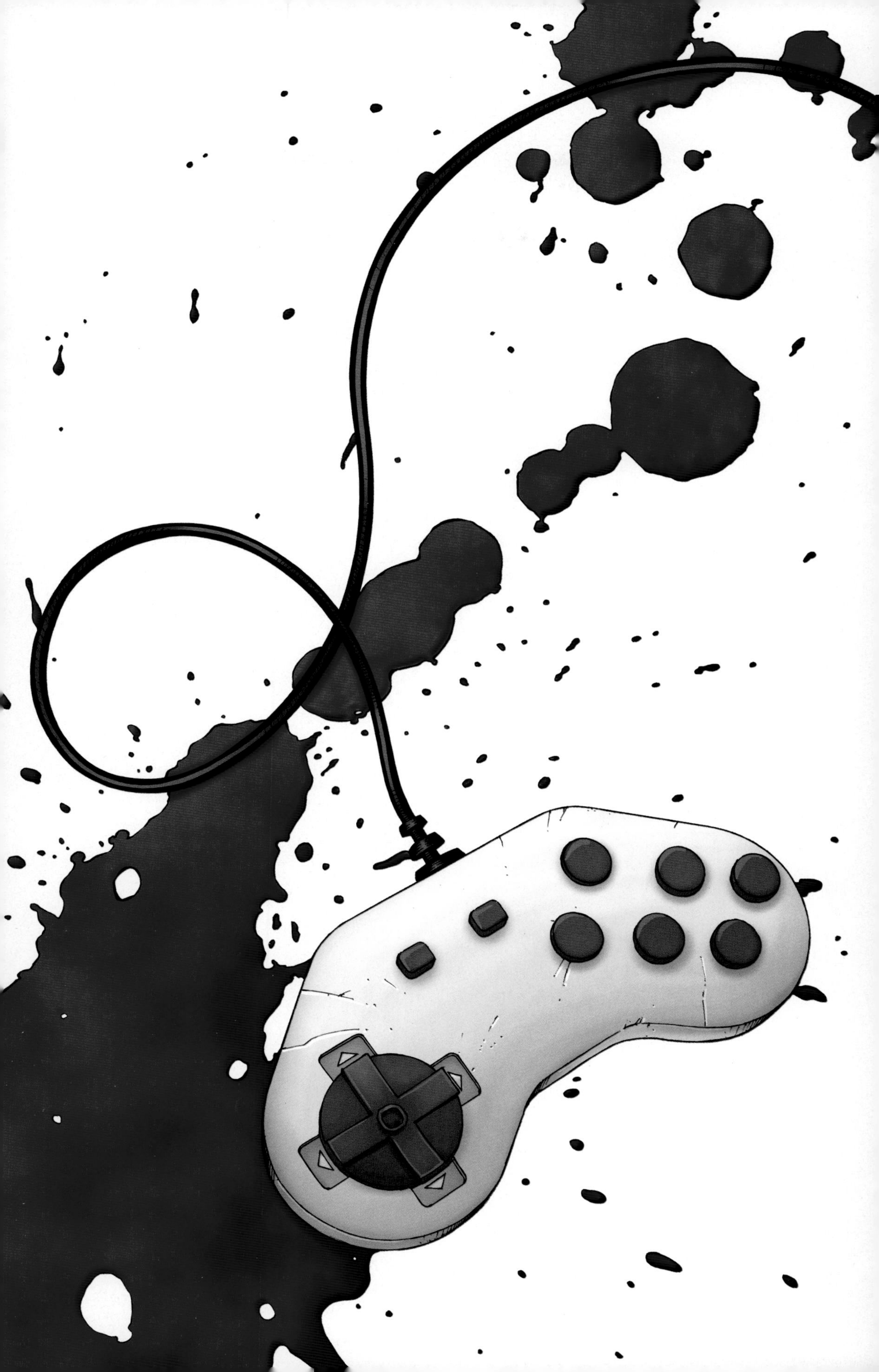

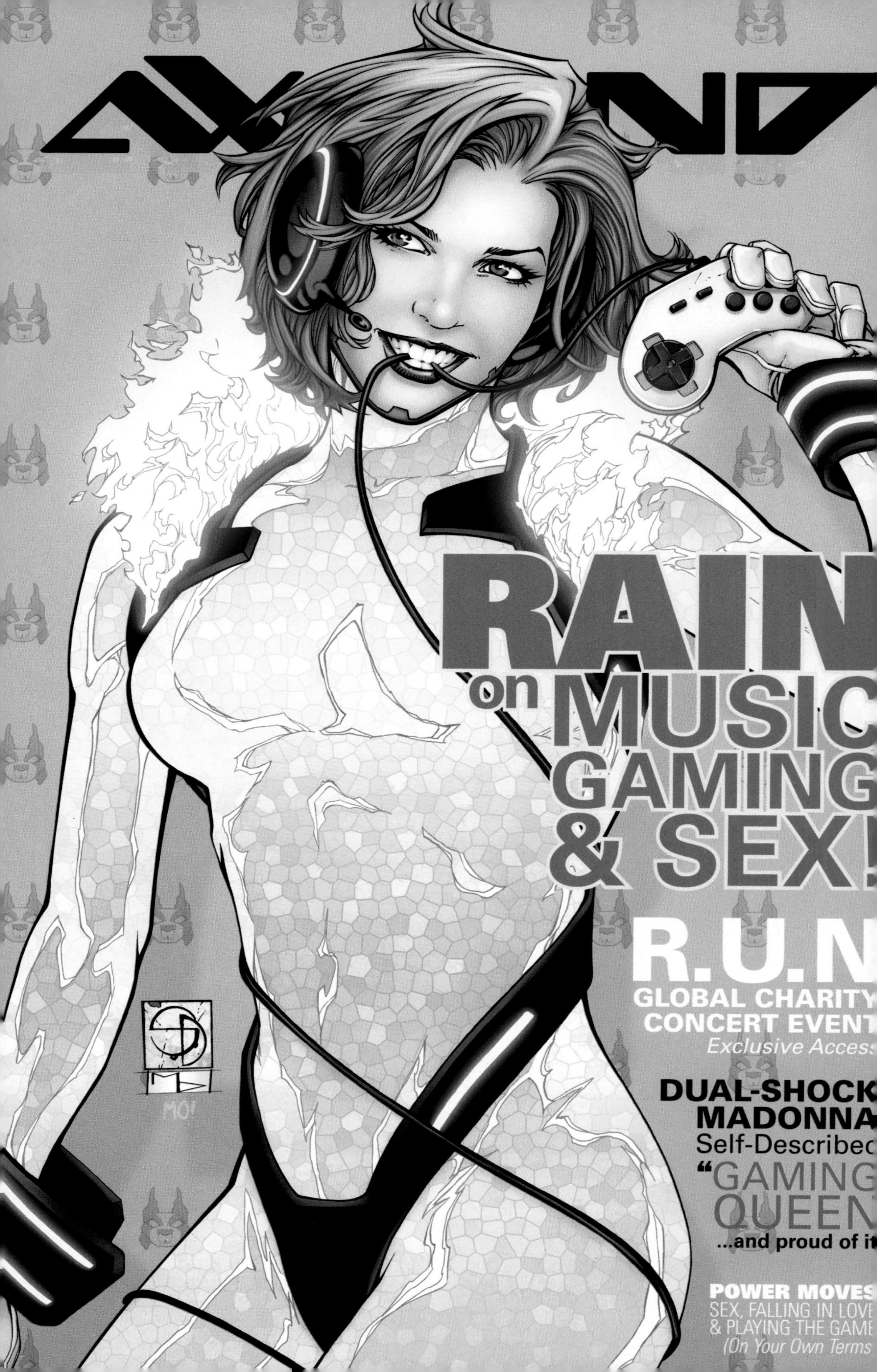
RAIN
on MUSIC
GAMING
& SEX!
R.U.N
GLOBAL CHARITY
CONCERT EVENT
Exclusive Access
DUAL-SHOCK
MADONNA
Self-Described
"GAMING
QUEEN
...and proud of it
POWER MOVES
SEX, FALLING IN LOVE
& PLAYING THE GAME
(On Your Own Terms
MO!

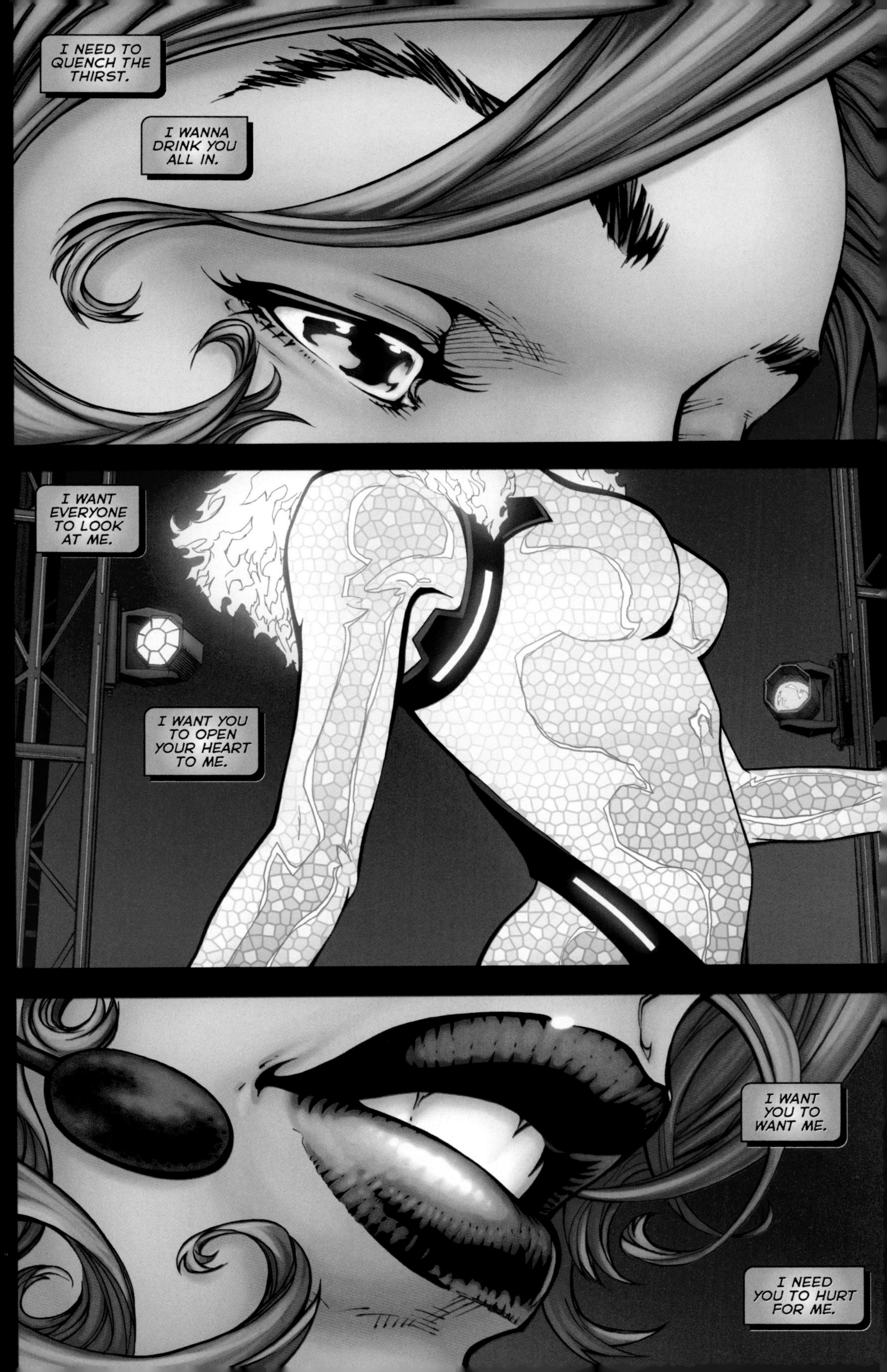

I NEED TO QUENCH THE THIRST.
I WANNA DRINK YOU ALL IN.
I WANT EVERYONE TO LOOK AT ME.
I WANT YOU TO OPEN YOUR HEART TO ME.
I WANT YOU TO WANT ME.
I NEED YOU TO HURT FOR ME.

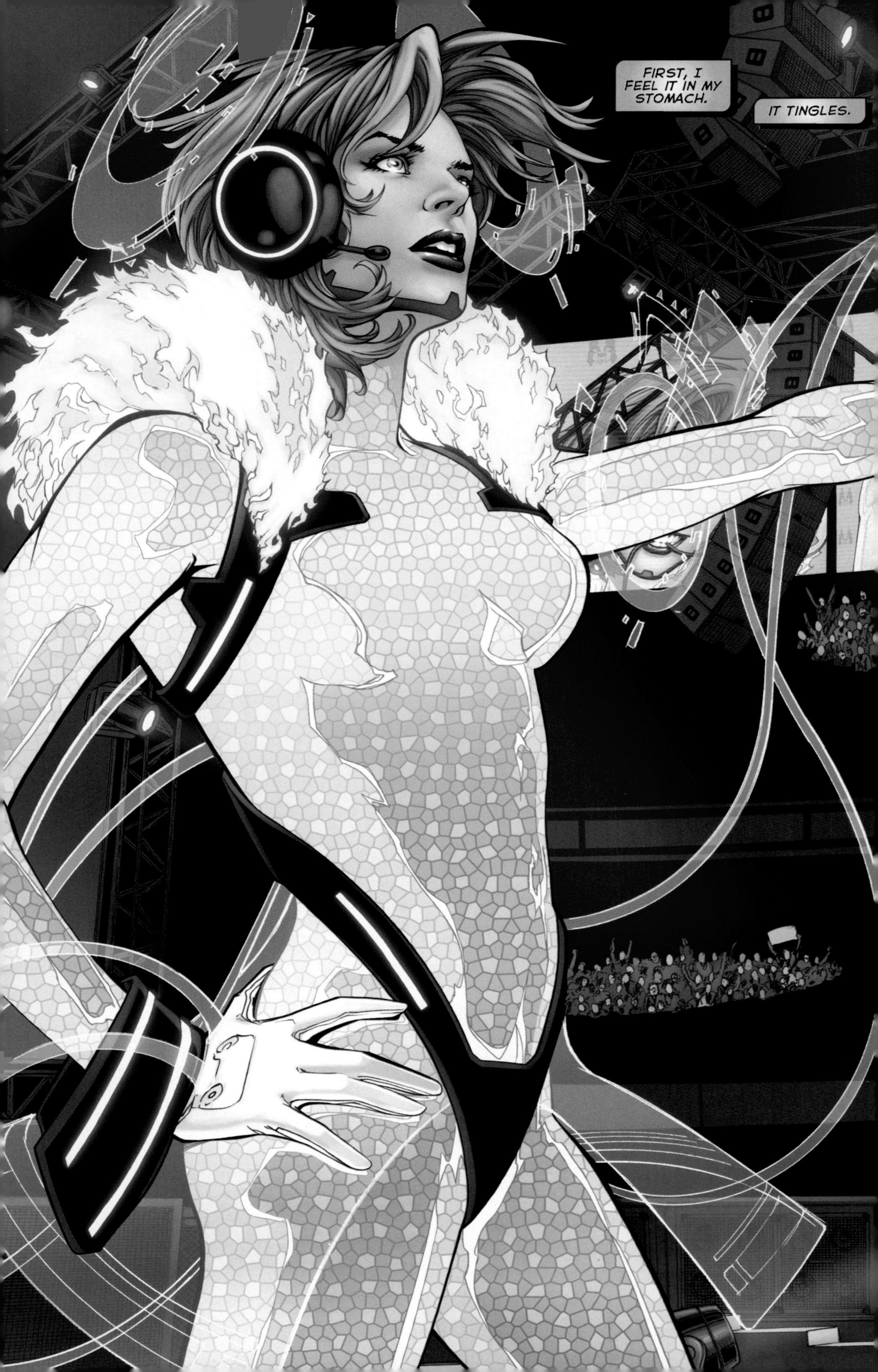
FIRST, I FEEL IT IN MY STOMACH.
IT TINGLES.

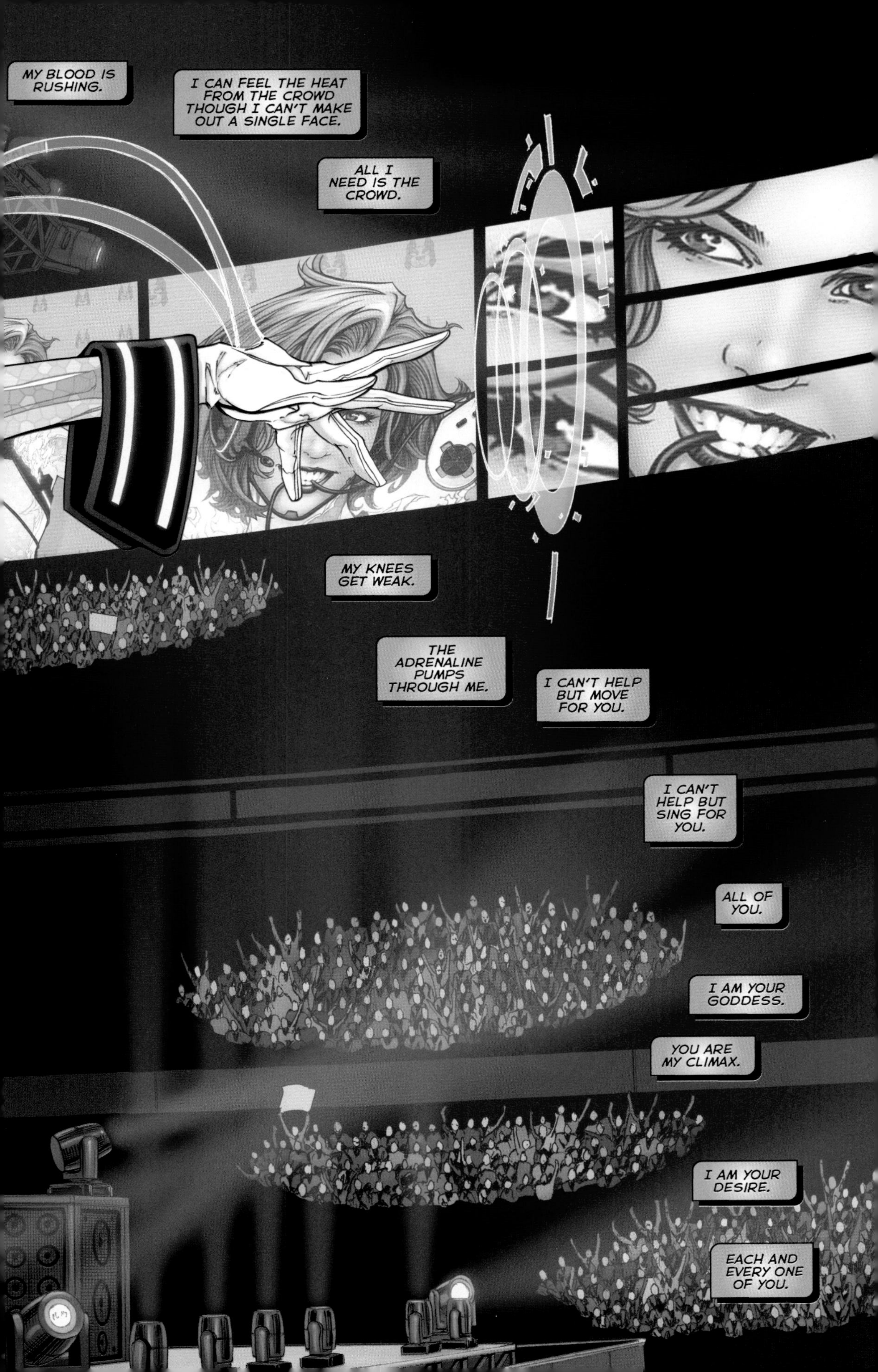
MY BLOOD IS RUSHING.
I CAN FEEL THE HEAT FROM THE CROWD THOUGH I CAN'T MAKE OUT A SINGLE FACE.
ALL I NEED IS THE CROWD.
MY KNEES GET WEAK.
THE ADRENALINE PUMPS THROUGH ME.
I CAN'T HELP BUT MOVE FOR YOU.
I CAN'T HELP BUT SING FOR YOU.
ALL OF YOU.
I AM YOUR GODDESS.
YOU ARE MY CLIMAX.
I AM YOUR DESIRE.
EACH AND EVERY ONE OF YOU.

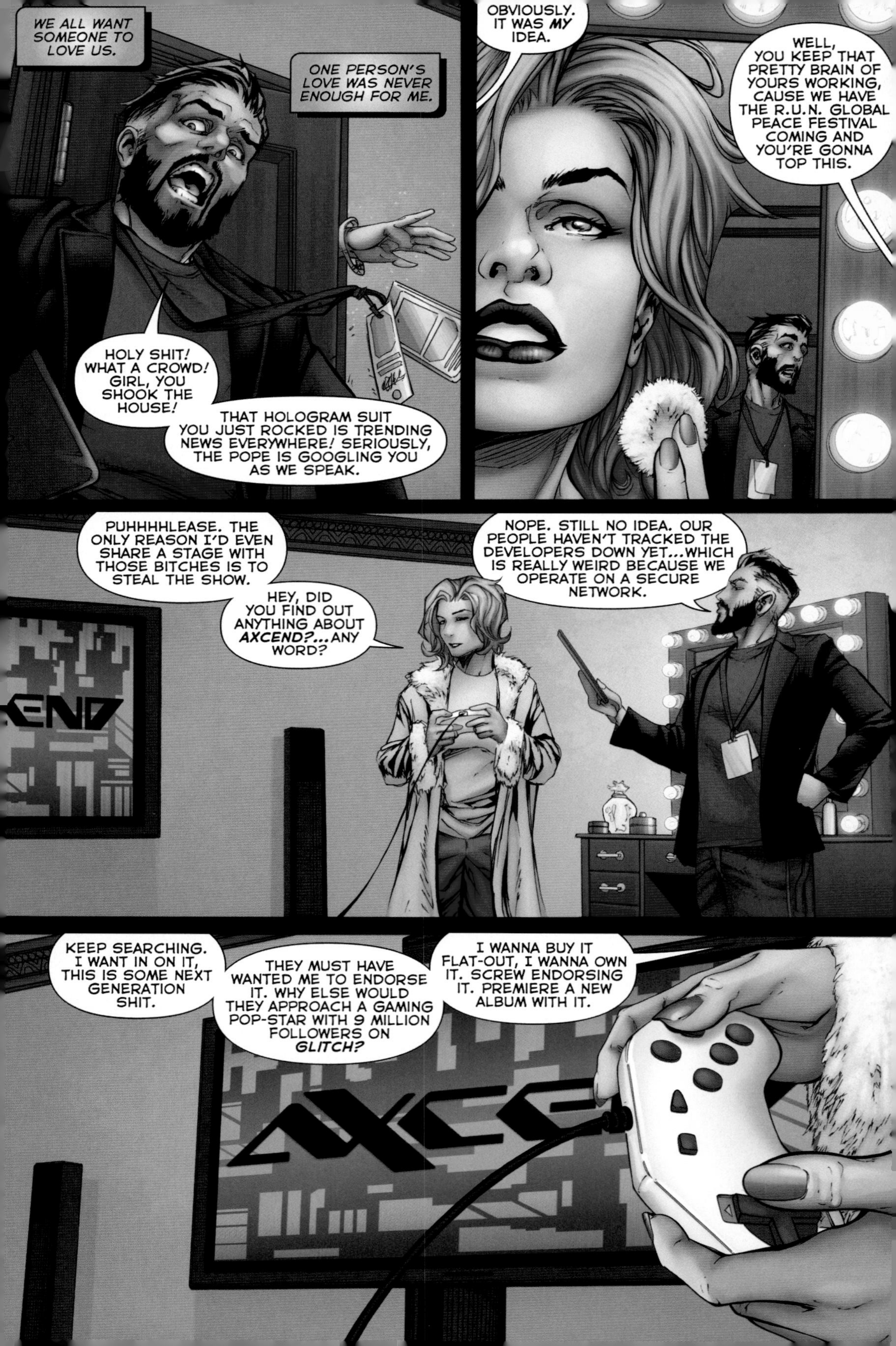
WE ALL WANT SOMEONE TO LOVE US.
ONE PERSON'S LOVE WAS NEVER ENOUGH FOR ME.
HOLY SHIT! WHAT A CROWD! GIRL, YOU SHOOK THE HOUSE!
THAT HOLOGRAM SUIT YOU JUST ROCKED IS TRENDING NEWS EVERYWHERE! SERIOUSLY, THE POPE IS GOOGLING YOU AS WE SPEAK.
OBVIOUSLY. IT WAS *MY* IDEA.
WELL, YOU KEEP THAT PRETTY BRAIN OF YOURS WORKING, CAUSE WE HAVE THE R.U.N. GLOBAL PEACE FESTIVAL COMING AND YOU'RE GONNA TOP THIS.
PUHHHHLEASE. THE ONLY REASON I'D EVEN SHARE A STAGE WITH THOSE BITCHES IS TO STEAL THE SHOW.
HEY, DID YOU FIND OUT ANYTHING ABOUT ***AXCEND?...*** ANY WORD?
NOPE. STILL NO IDEA. OUR PEOPLE HAVEN'T TRACKED THE DEVELOPERS DOWN YET...WHICH IS REALLY WEIRD BECAUSE WE OPERATE ON A SECURE NETWORK.
KEEP SEARCHING. I WANT IN ON IT, THIS IS SOME NEXT GENERATION SHIT.
THEY MUST HAVE WANTED ME TO ENDORSE IT. WHY ELSE WOULD THEY APPROACH A GAMING POP-STAR WITH 9 MILLION FOLLOWERS ON ***GLITCH?***
I WANNA BUY IT FLAT-OUT, I WANNA OWN IT. SCREW ENDORSING IT. PREMIERE A NEW ALBUM WITH IT.

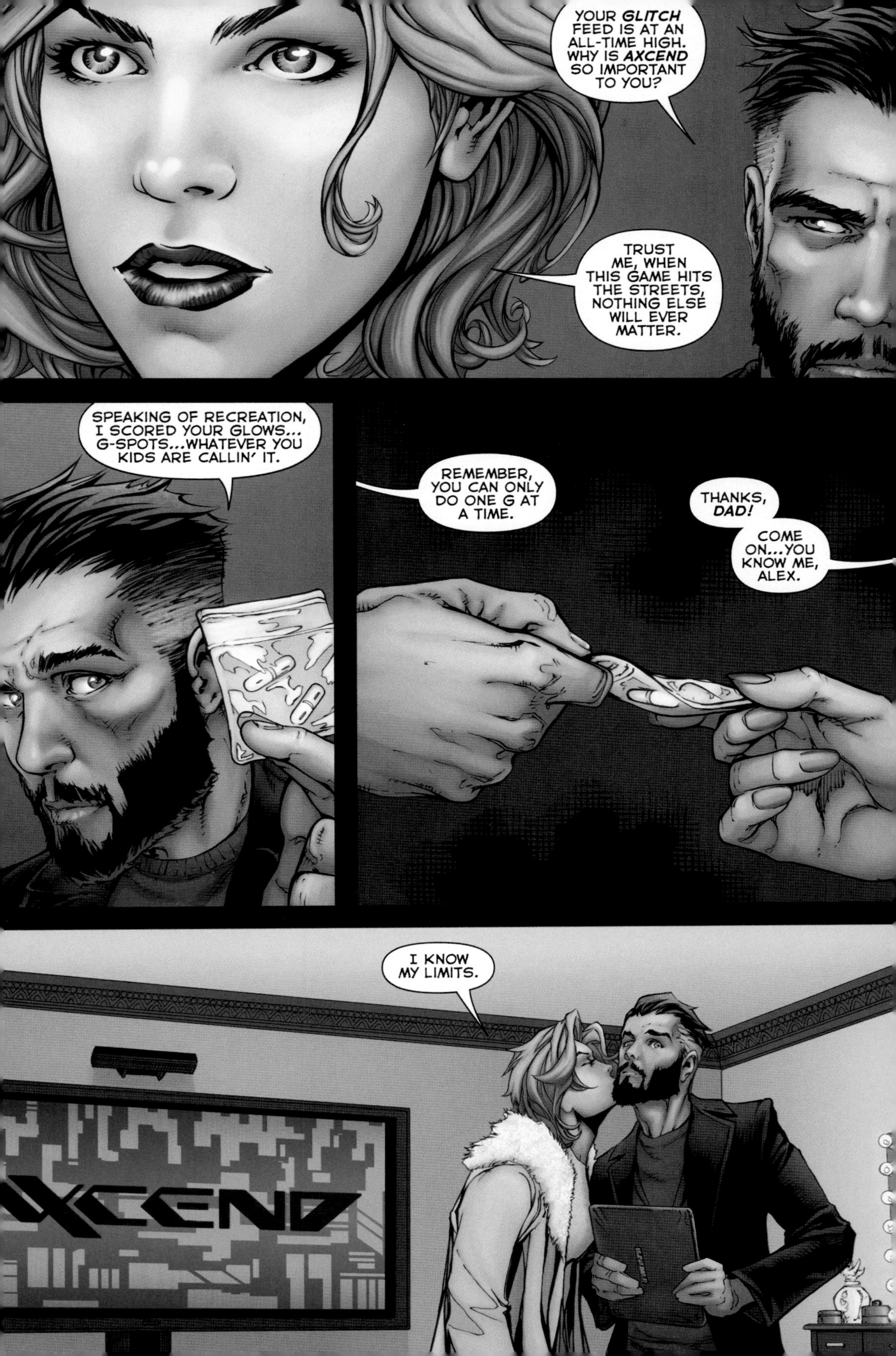
YOUR GLITCH FEED IS AT AN ALL-TIME HIGH. WHY IS AXCEND SO IMPORTANT TO YOU?
TRUST ME, WHEN THIS GAME HITS THE STREETS, NOTHING ELSE WILL EVER MATTER.
SPEAKING OF RECREATION, I SCORED YOUR GLOWS... G-SPOTS...WHATEVER YOU KIDS ARE CALLIN' IT.
REMEMBER, YOU CAN ONLY DO ONE G AT A TIME.
THANKS, DAD!
COME ON...YOU KNOW ME, ALEX.
I KNOW MY LIMITS.
XCEND

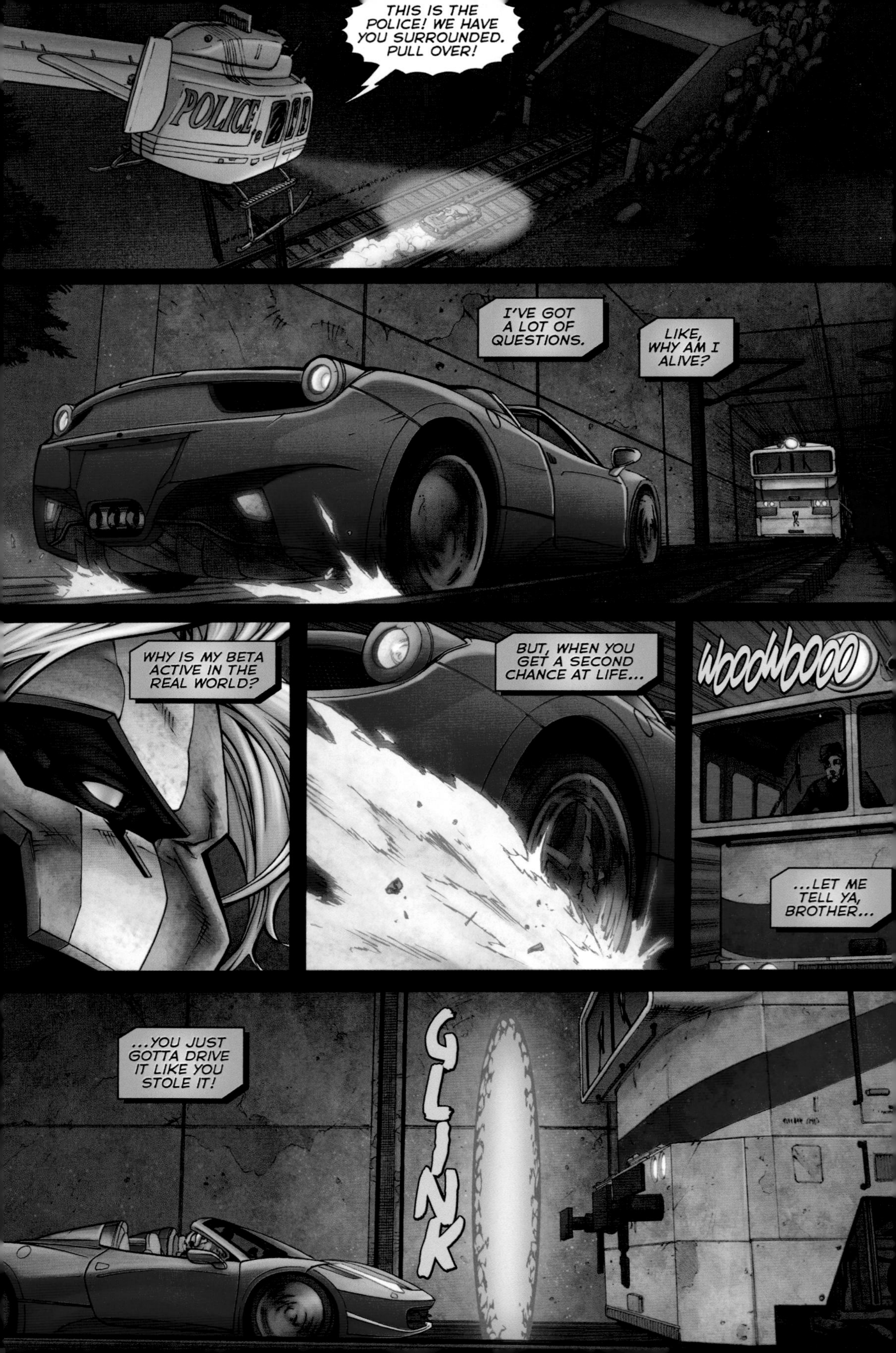
THIS IS THE POLICE! WE HAVE YOU SURROUNDED. PULL OVER!
POLICE
I'VE GOT A LOT OF QUESTIONS.
LIKE, WHY AM I ALIVE?
WHY IS MY BETA ACTIVE IN THE REAL WORLD?
BUT, WHEN YOU GET A SECOND CHANCE AT LIFE...
WOOOWOOOO
...LET ME TELL YA, BROTHER...
...YOU JUST GOTTA DRIVE IT LIKE YOU STOLE IT!
GLINK

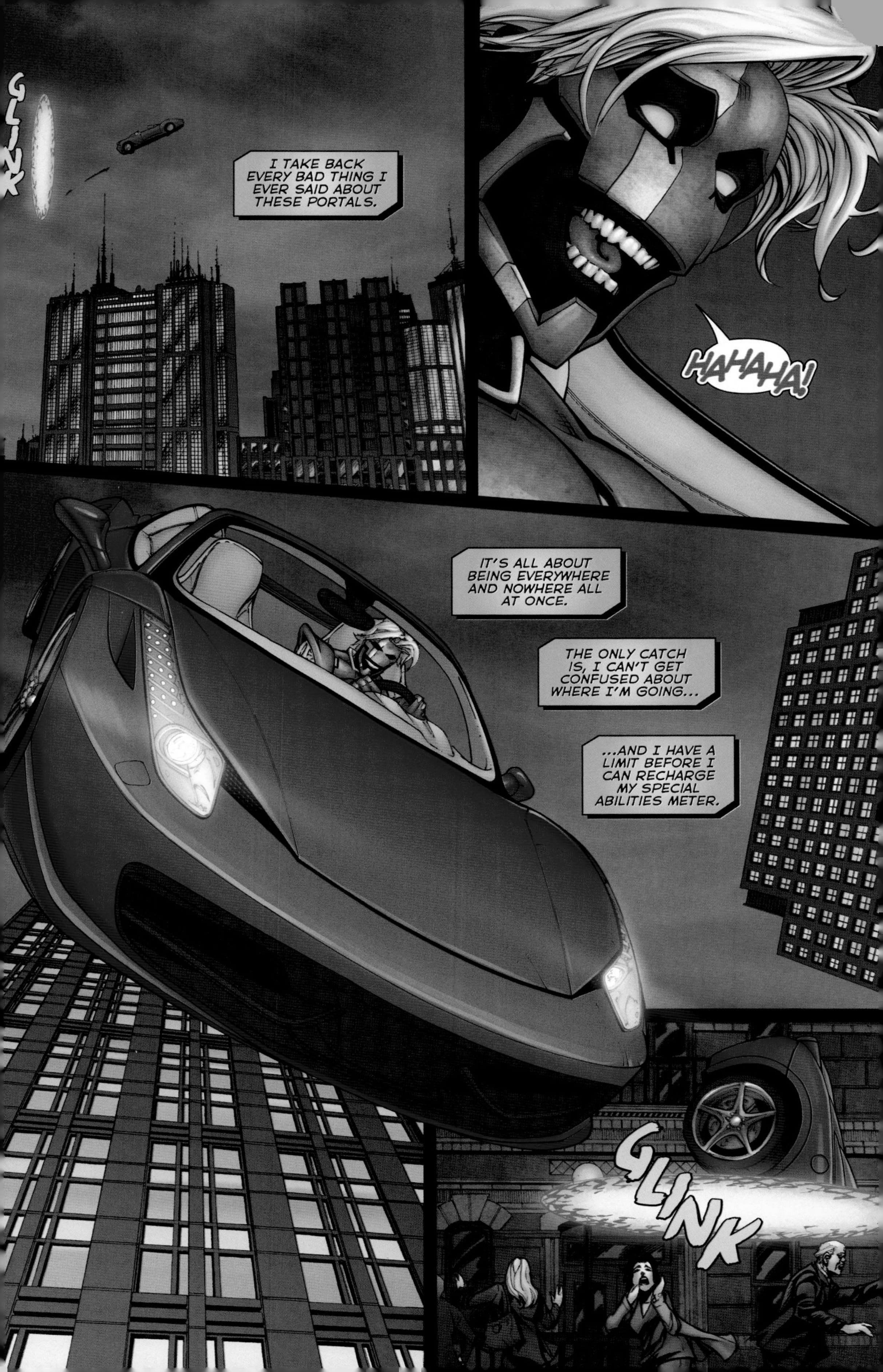
GLINK
I TAKE BACK EVERY BAD THING I EVER SAID ABOUT THESE PORTALS.
HAHAHA!
IT'S ALL ABOUT BEING EVERYWHERE AND NOWHERE ALL AT ONCE.
THE ONLY CATCH IS, I CAN'T GET CONFUSED ABOUT WHERE I'M GOING...
...AND I HAVE A LIMIT BEFORE I CAN RECHARGE MY SPECIAL ABILITIES METER.
GLINK

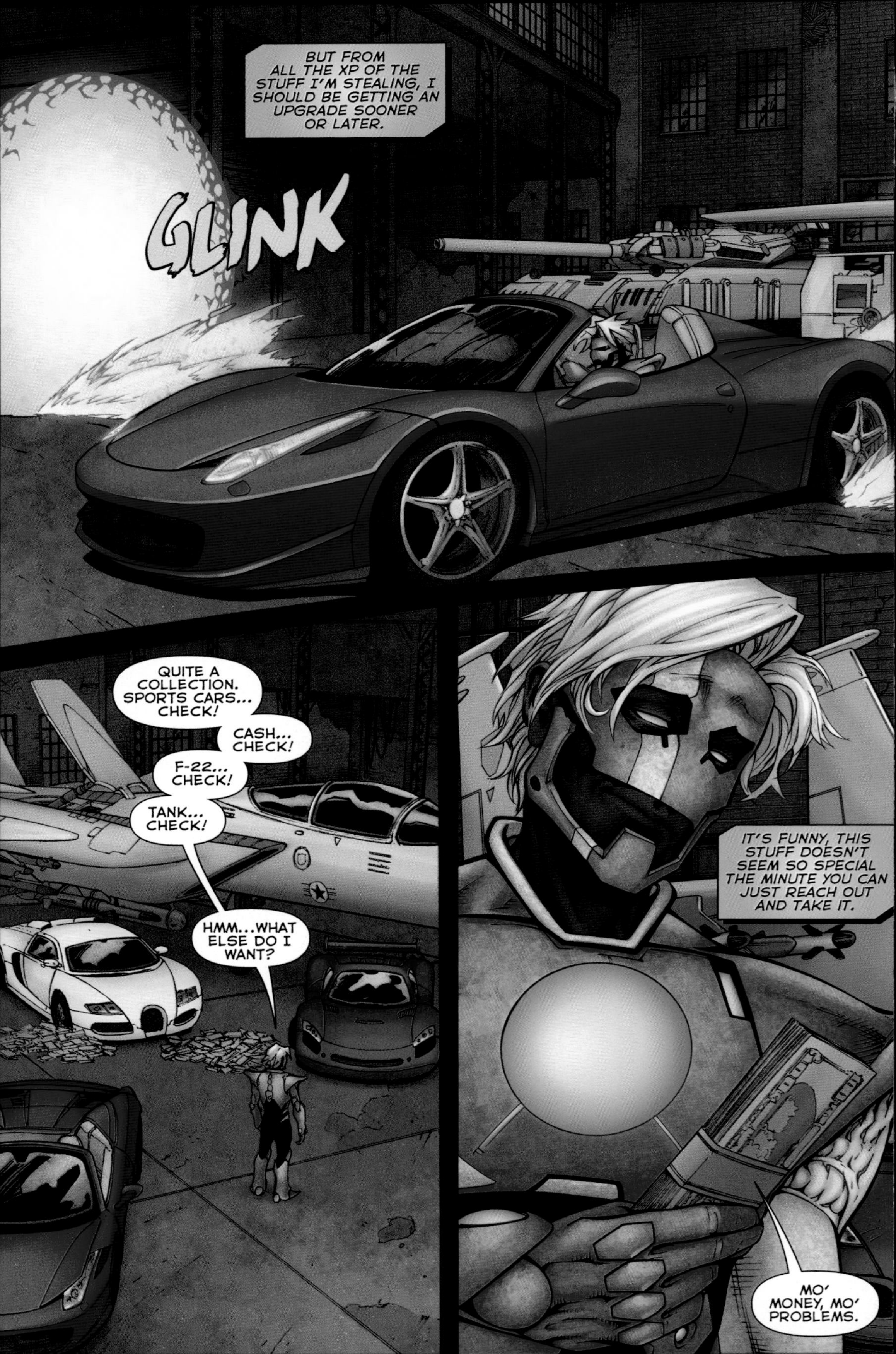
BUT FROM ALL THE XP OF THE STUFF I'M STEALING, I SHOULD BE GETTING AN UPGRADE SOONER OR LATER.
GLINK
QUITE A COLLECTION. SPORTS CARS... CHECK!
CASH... CHECK!
F-22... CHECK!
TANK... CHECK!
HMM...WHAT ELSE DO I WANT?
IT'S FUNNY, THIS STUFF DOESN'T SEEM SO SPECIAL THE MINUTE YOU CAN JUST REACH OUT AND TAKE IT.
MO' MONEY, MO' PROBLEMS.

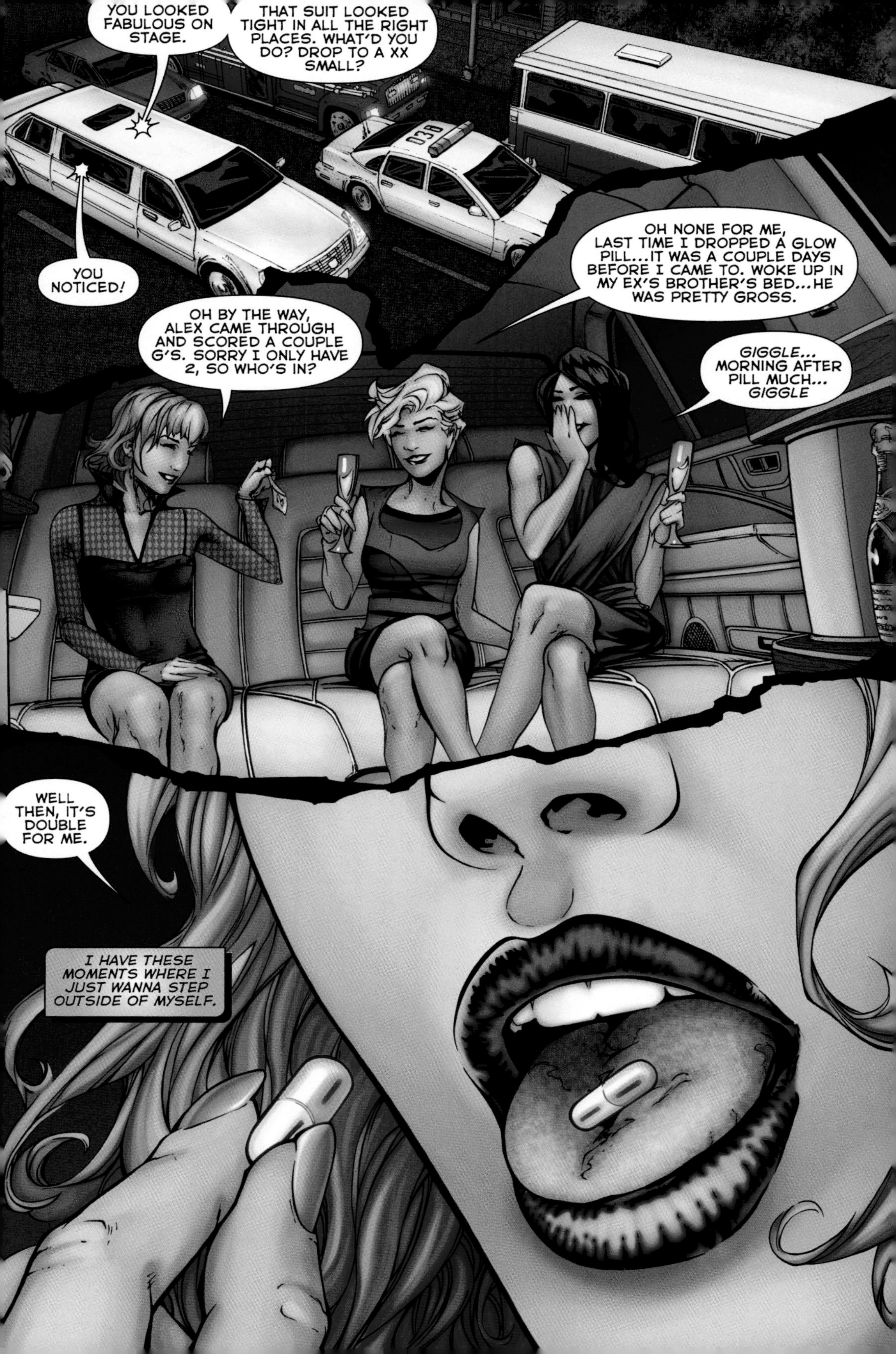
YOU LOOKED FABULOUS ON STAGE.
THAT SUIT LOOKED TIGHT IN ALL THE RIGHT PLACES. WHAT'D YOU DO? DROP TO A XX SMALL?
YOU NOTICED!
OH NONE FOR ME, LAST TIME I DROPPED A GLOW PILL...IT WAS A COUPLE DAYS BEFORE I CAME TO. WOKE UP IN MY EX'S BROTHER'S BED...HE WAS PRETTY GROSS.
OH BY THE WAY, ALEX CAME THROUGH AND SCORED A COUPLE G'S. SORRY I ONLY HAVE 2, SO WHO'S IN?
GIGGLE... MORNING AFTER PILL MUCH... GIGGLE
WELL THEN, IT'S DOUBLE FOR ME.
I HAVE THESE MOMENTS WHERE I JUST WANNA STEP OUTSIDE OF MYSELF.

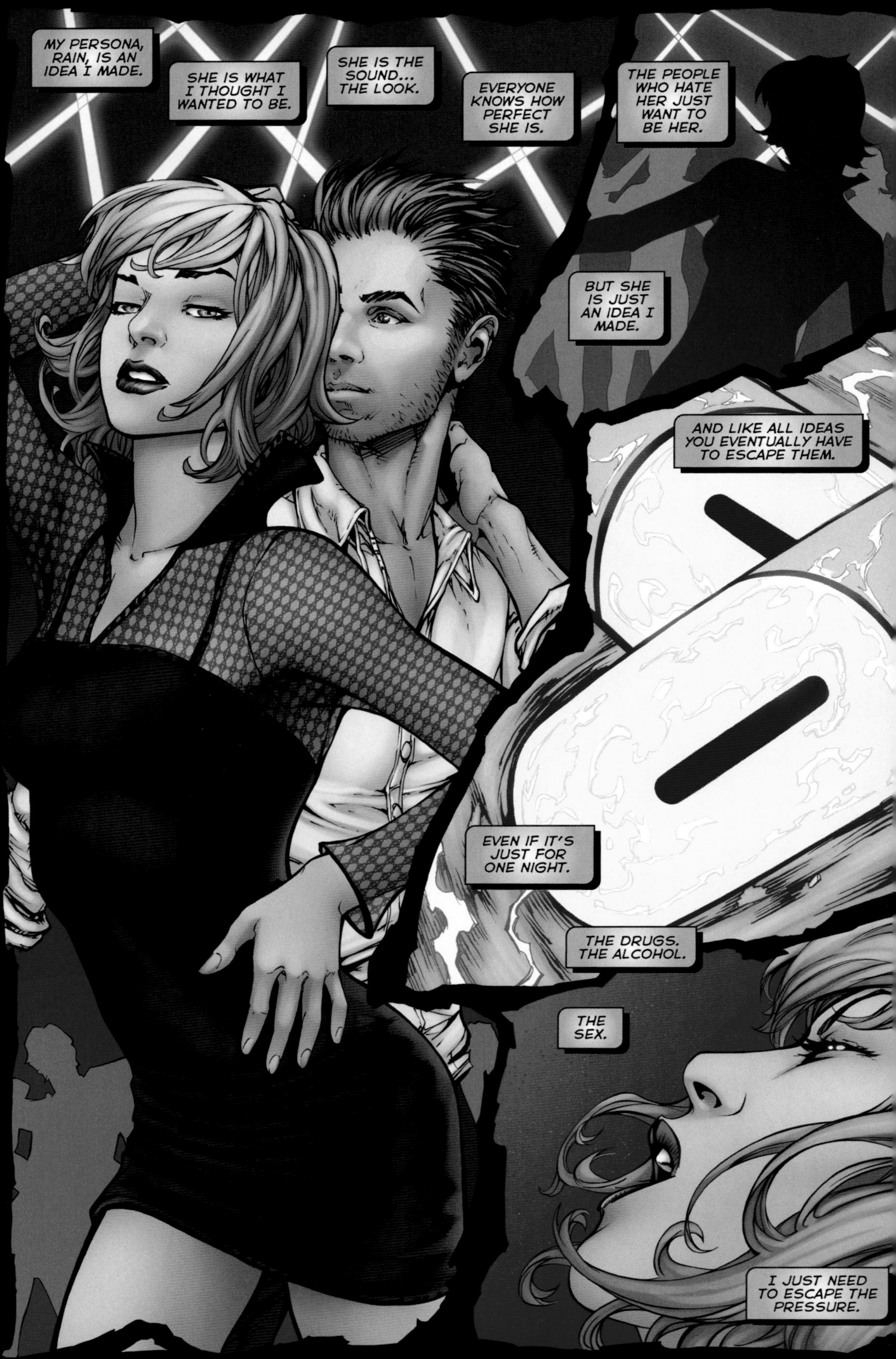
MY PERSONA, RAIN, IS AN IDEA I MADE.
SHE IS WHAT I THOUGHT I WANTED TO BE.
SHE IS THE SOUND... THE LOOK.
EVERYONE KNOWS HOW PERFECT SHE IS.
THE PEOPLE WHO HATE HER JUST WANT TO BE HER.
BUT SHE IS JUST AN IDEA I MADE.
AND LIKE ALL IDEAS YOU EVENTUALLY HAVE TO ESCAPE THEM.
EVEN IF IT'S JUST FOR ONE NIGHT.
THE DRUGS. THE ALCOHOL.
THE SEX.
I JUST NEED TO ESCAPE THE PRESSURE.

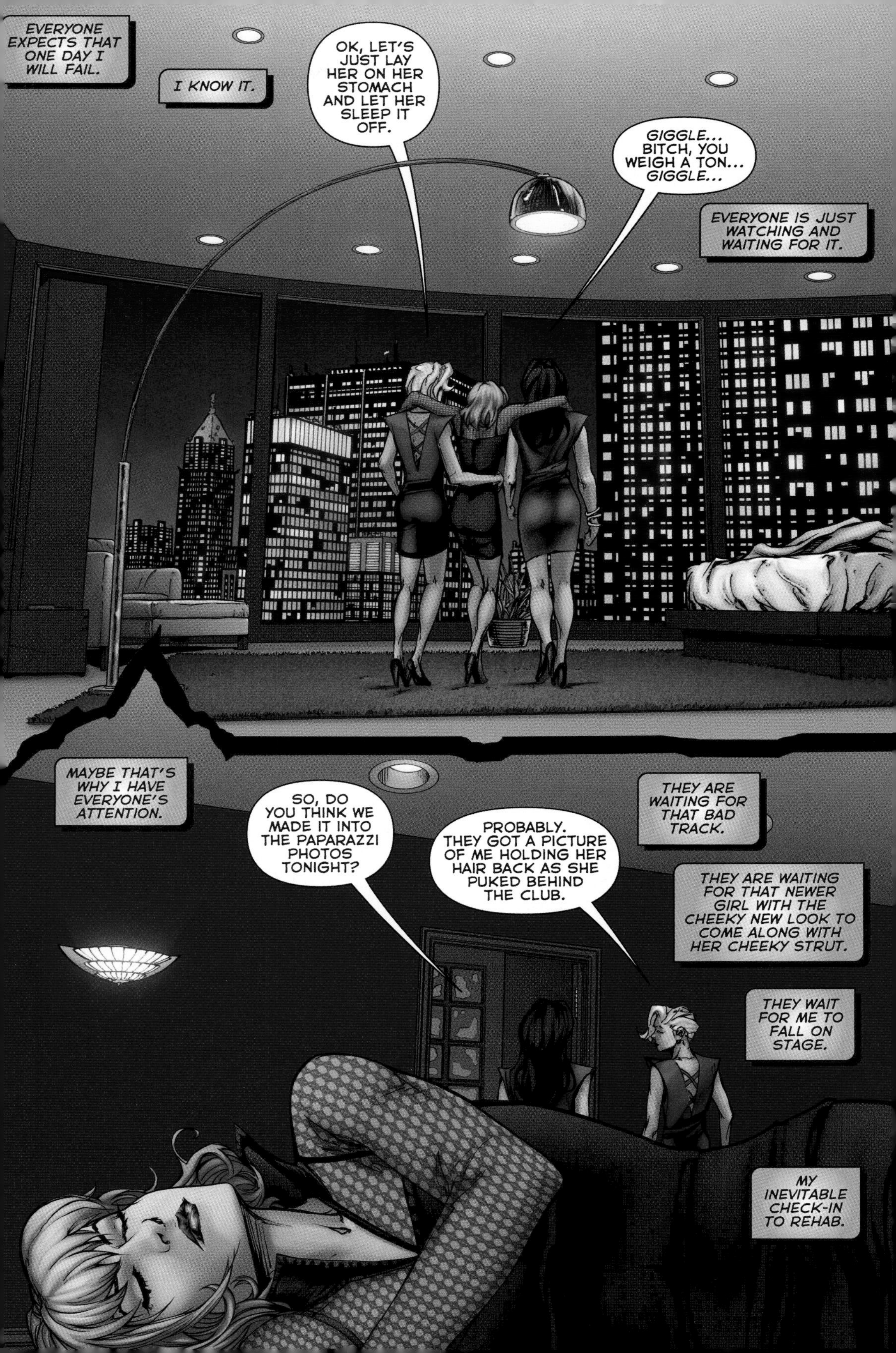
EVERYONE EXPECTS THAT ONE DAY I WILL FAIL.
I KNOW IT.
OK, LET'S JUST LAY HER ON HER STOMACH AND LET HER SLEEP IT OFF.
GIGGLE... BITCH, YOU WEIGH A TON... GIGGLE...
EVERYONE IS JUST WATCHING AND WAITING FOR IT.
MAYBE THAT'S WHY I HAVE EVERYONE'S ATTENTION.
SO, DO YOU THINK WE MADE IT INTO THE PAPARAZZI PHOTOS TONIGHT?
PROBABLY. THEY GOT A PICTURE OF ME HOLDING HER HAIR BACK AS SHE PUKED BEHIND THE CLUB.
THEY ARE WAITING FOR THAT BAD TRACK.
THEY ARE WAITING FOR THAT NEWER GIRL WITH THE CHEEKY NEW LOOK TO COME ALONG WITH HER CHEEKY STRUT.
THEY WAIT FOR ME TO FALL ON STAGE.
MY INEVITABLE CHECK-IN TO REHAB.

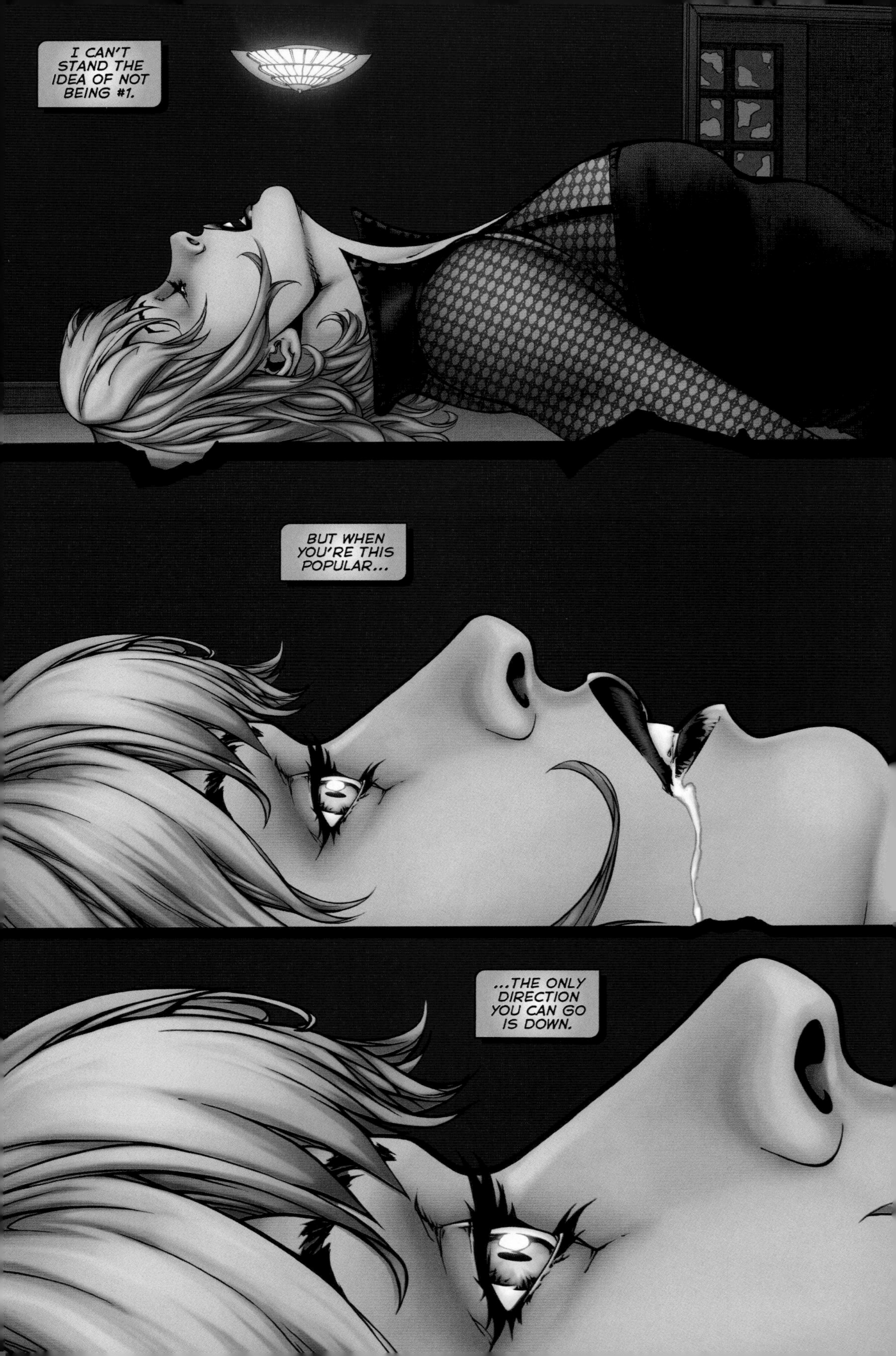
I CAN'T STAND THE IDEA OF NOT BEING #1.
BUT WHEN YOU'RE THIS POPULAR...
...THE ONLY DIRECTION YOU CAN GO IS DOWN.

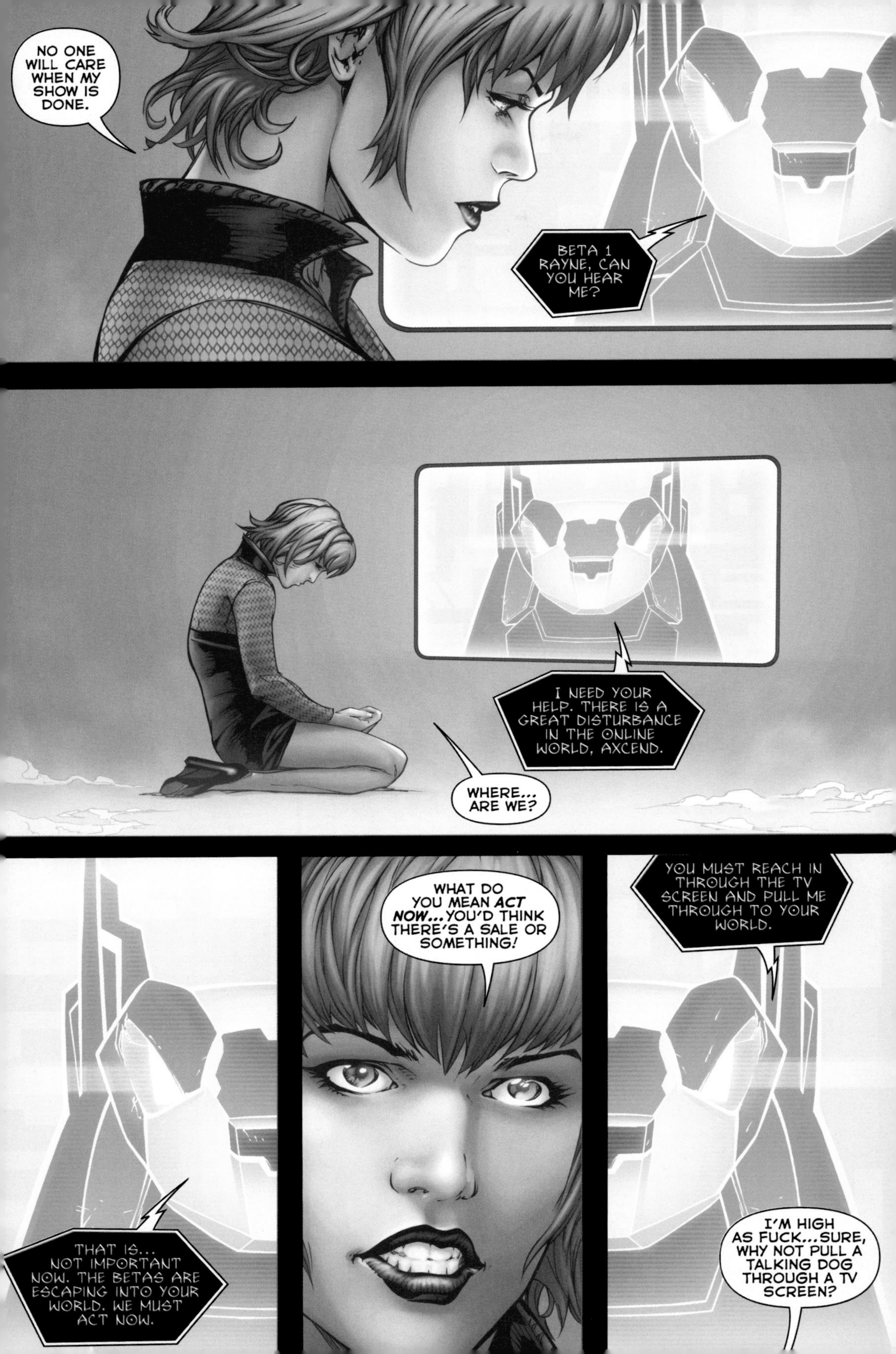
NO ONE WILL CARE WHEN MY SHOW IS DONE.
BETA 1 RAYNE, CAN YOU HEAR ME?
I NEED YOUR HELP. THERE IS A GREAT DISTURBANCE IN THE ONLINE WORLD, AXCEND.
WHERE... ARE WE?
THAT IS... NOT IMPORTANT NOW. THE BETAS ARE ESCAPING INTO YOUR WORLD. WE MUST ACT NOW.
WHAT DO YOU MEAN *ACT NOW*... YOU'D THINK THERE'S A SALE OR SOMETHING!
YOU MUST REACH IN THROUGH THE TV SCREEN AND PULL ME THROUGH TO YOUR WORLD.
I'M HIGH AS FUCK... SURE, WHY NOT PULL A TALKING DOG THROUGH A TV SCREEN?

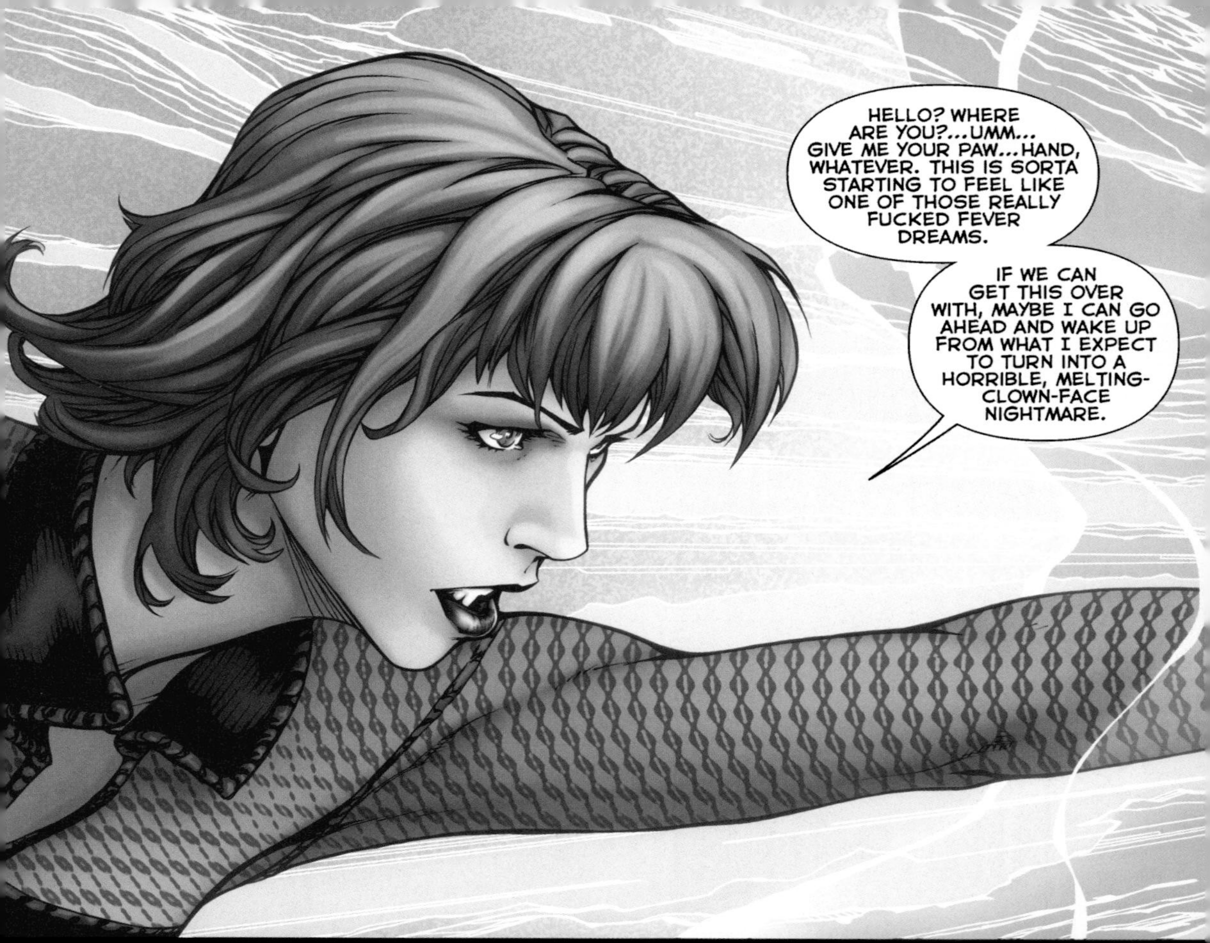
HELLO? WHERE ARE YOU?...UMM... GIVE ME YOUR PAW...HAND, WHATEVER. THIS IS SORTA STARTING TO FEEL LIKE ONE OF THOSE REALLY FUCKED FEVER DREAMS.
IF WE CAN GET THIS OVER WITH, MAYBE I CAN GO AHEAD AND WAKE UP FROM WHAT I EXPECT TO TURN INTO A HORRIBLE, MELTING-CLOWN-FACE NIGHTMARE.

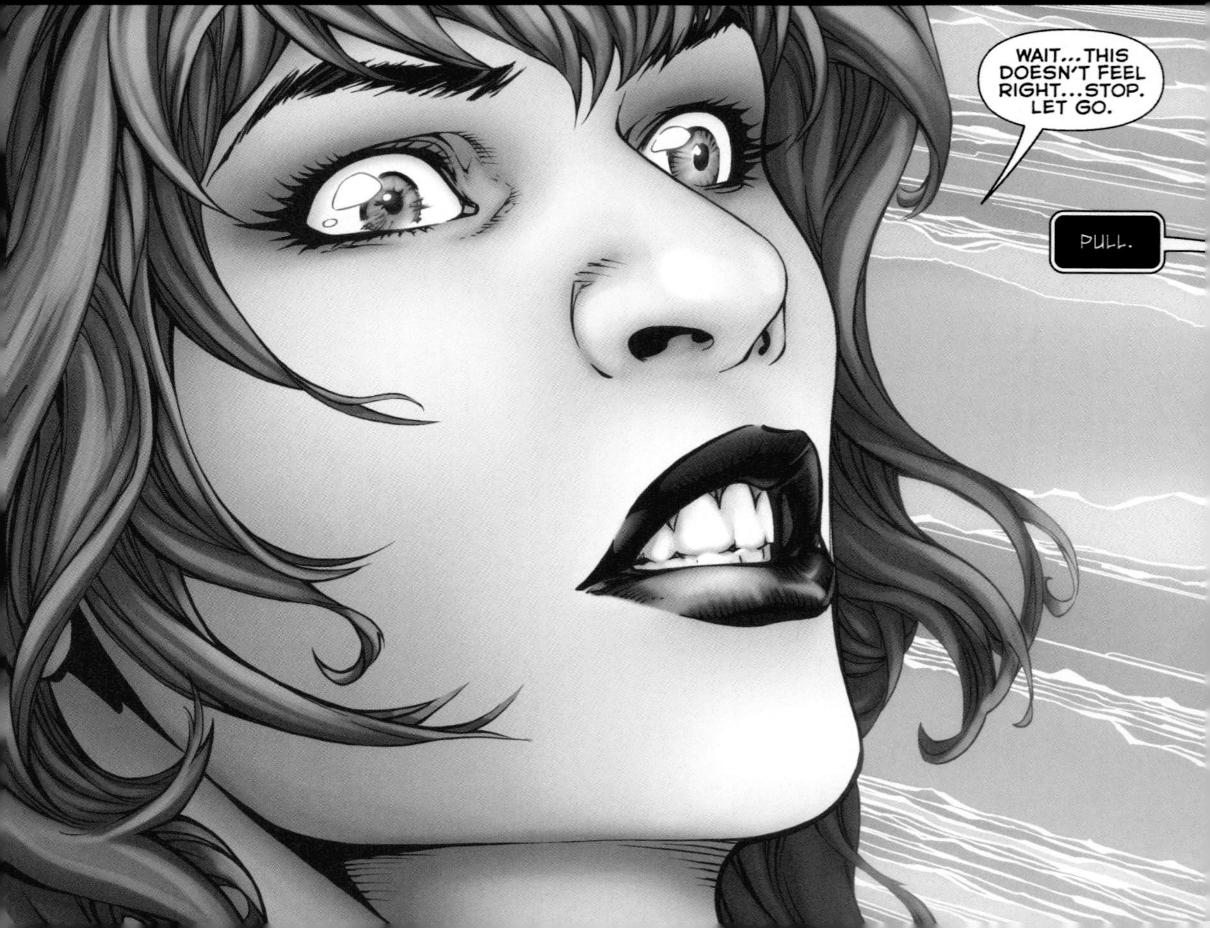
WAIT...THIS DOESN'T FEEL RIGHT...STOP. LET GO.
PULL.

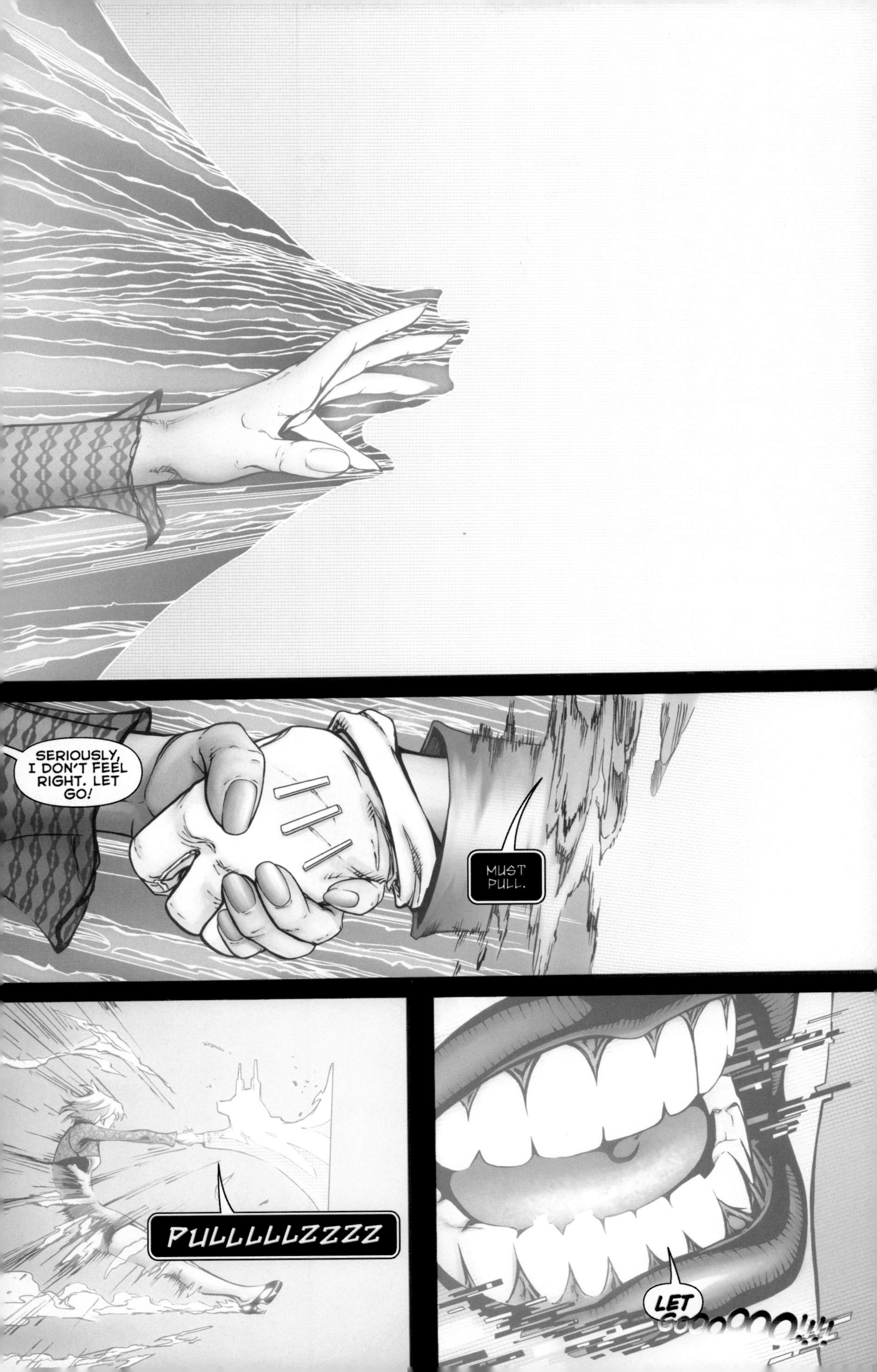
SERIOUSLY, I DON'T FEEL RIGHT. LET GO!
MUST PULL.
PULLLLLZZZZ
LET GOOOOOO!!!

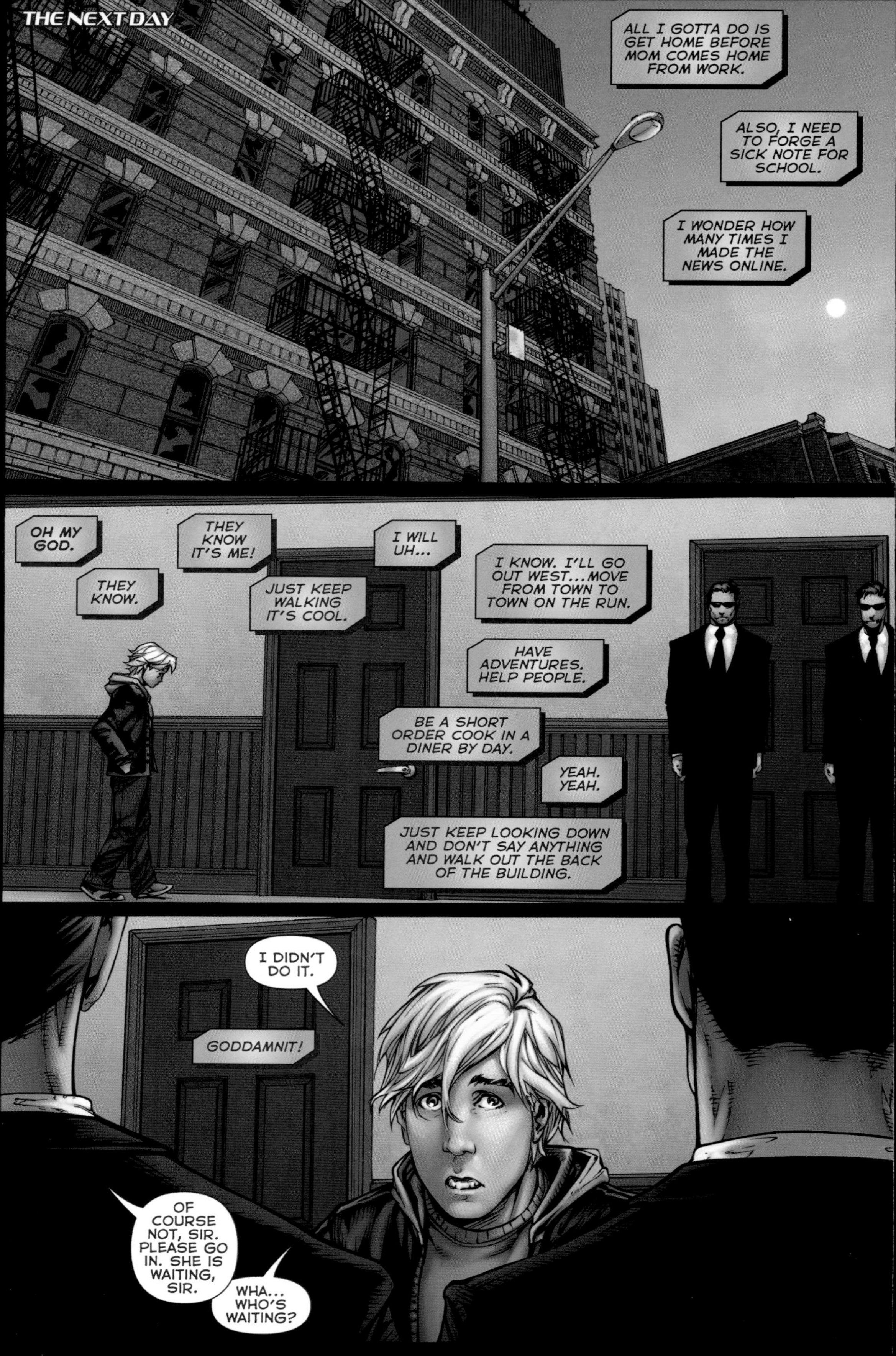
THE NEXT DAY
ALL I GOTTA DO IS GET HOME BEFORE MOM COMES HOME FROM WORK.
ALSO, I NEED TO FORGE A SICK NOTE FOR SCHOOL.
I WONDER HOW MANY TIMES I MADE THE NEWS ONLINE.
OH MY GOD.
THEY KNOW.
THEY KNOW IT'S ME!
JUST KEEP WALKING IT'S COOL.
I WILL UH...
I KNOW. I'LL GO OUT WEST...MOVE FROM TOWN TO TOWN ON THE RUN.
HAVE ADVENTURES. HELP PEOPLE.
BE A SHORT ORDER COOK IN A DINER BY DAY.
YEAH. YEAH.
JUST KEEP LOOKING DOWN AND DON'T SAY ANYTHING AND WALK OUT THE BACK OF THE BUILDING.
I DIDN'T DO IT.
GODDAMNIT!
OF COURSE NOT, SIR. PLEASE GO IN. SHE IS WAITING, SIR.
WHA... WHO'S WAITING?

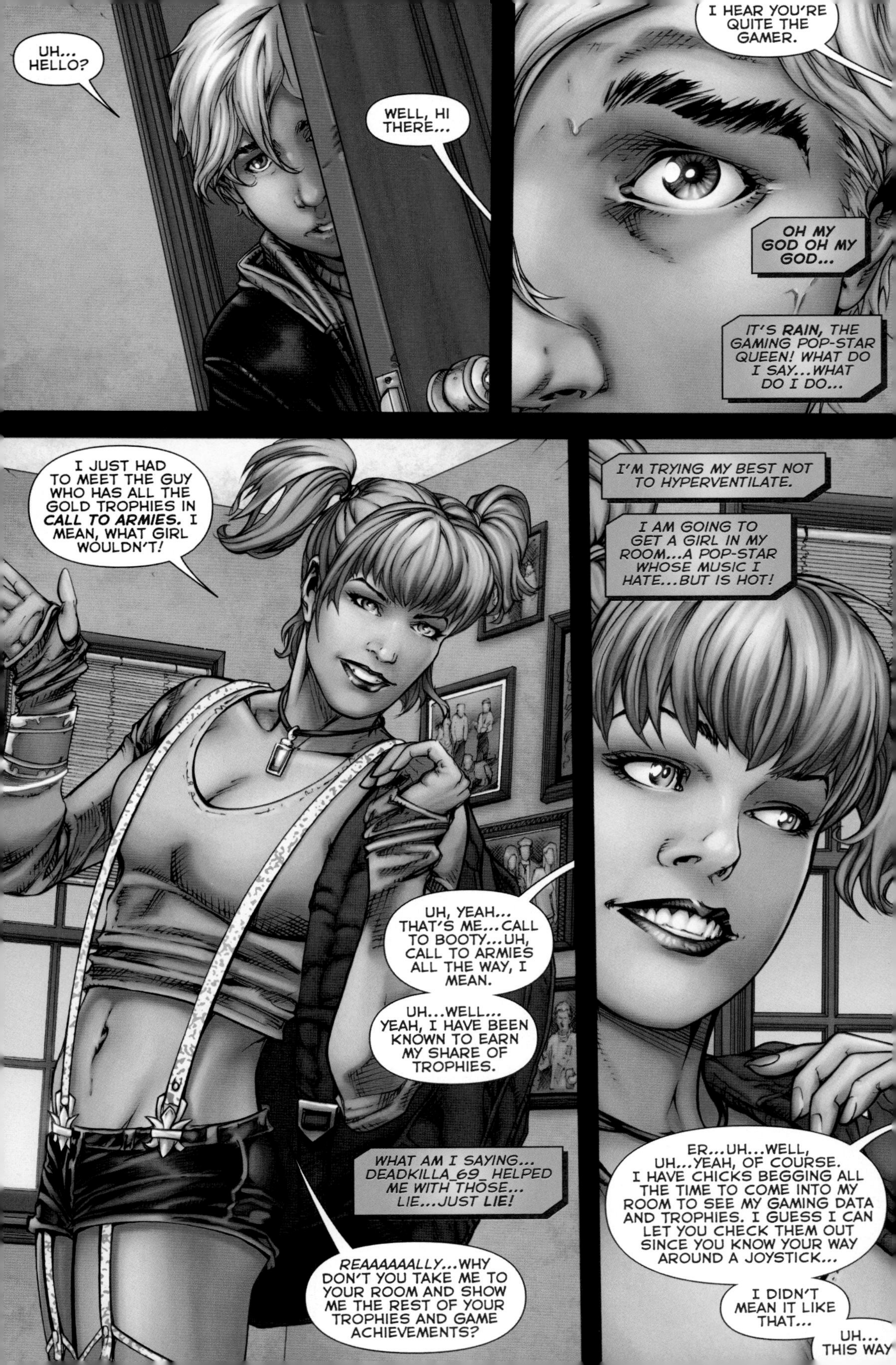
UH... HELLO?
WELL, HI THERE...
I HEAR YOU'RE QUITE THE GAMER.
OH MY GOD OH MY GOD...
IT'S RAIN, THE GAMING POP-STAR QUEEN! WHAT DO I SAY...WHAT DO I DO...
I JUST HAD TO MEET THE GUY WHO HAS ALL THE GOLD TROPHIES IN CALL TO ARMIES. I MEAN, WHAT GIRL WOULDN'T!
UH, YEAH... THAT'S ME...CALL TO BOOTY...UH, CALL TO ARMIES ALL THE WAY, I MEAN.
UH...WELL... YEAH, I HAVE BEEN KNOWN TO EARN MY SHARE OF TROPHIES.
WHAT AM I SAYING... DEADKILLA_69_ HELPED ME WITH THOSE... LIE...JUST LIE!
REAAAAAALLY...WHY DON'T YOU TAKE ME TO YOUR ROOM AND SHOW ME THE REST OF YOUR TROPHIES AND GAME ACHIEVEMENTS?
I'M TRYING MY BEST NOT TO HYPERVENTILATE.
I AM GOING TO GET A GIRL IN MY ROOM...A POP-STAR WHOSE MUSIC I HATE...BUT IS HOT!
ER...UH...WELL, UH...YEAH, OF COURSE. I HAVE CHICKS BEGGING ALL THE TIME TO COME INTO MY ROOM TO SEE MY GAMING DATA AND TROPHIES. I GUESS I CAN LET YOU CHECK THEM OUT SINCE YOU KNOW YOUR WAY AROUND A JOYSTICK...
I DIDN'T MEAN IT LIKE THAT...
UH... THIS WAY

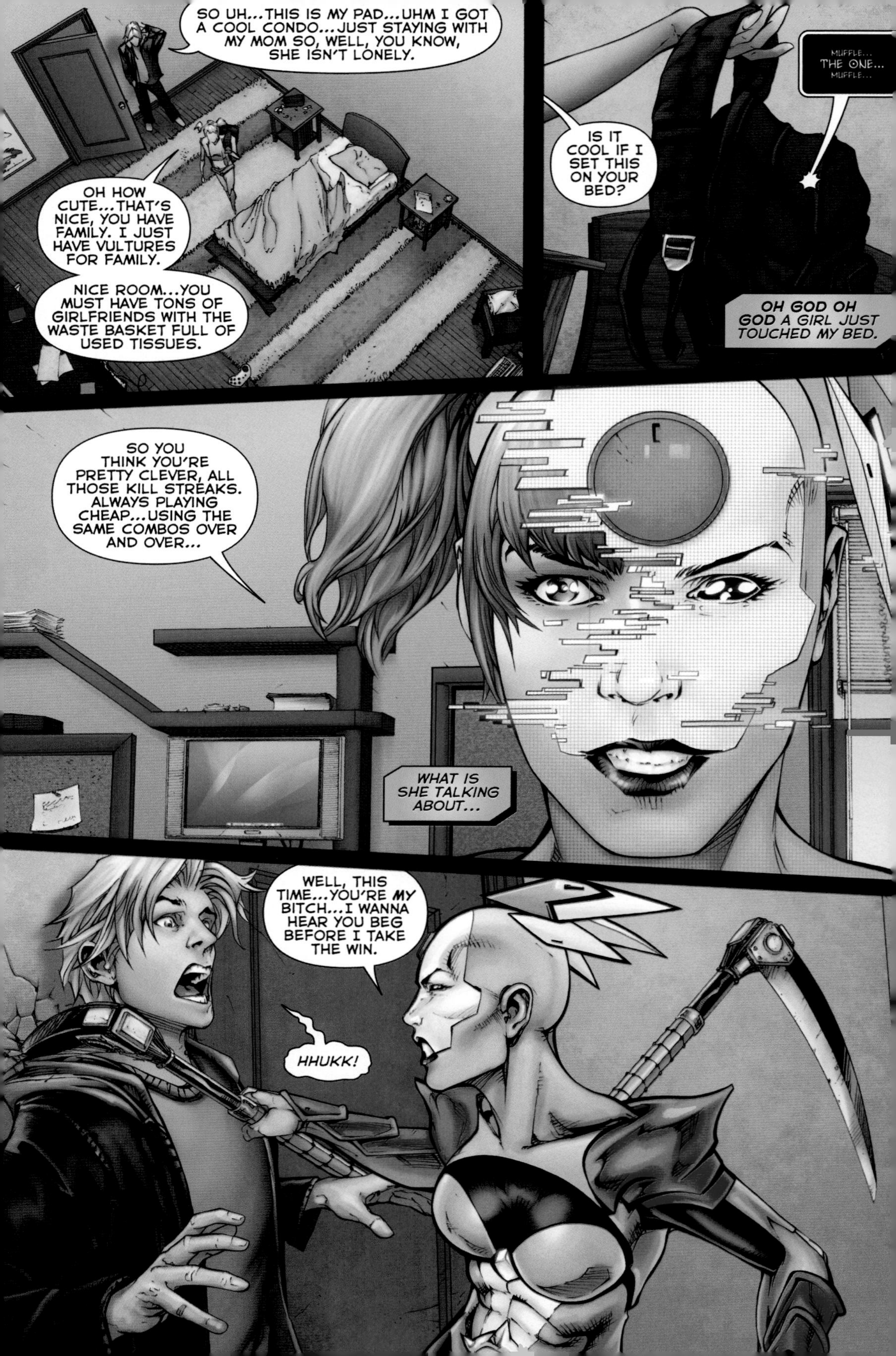
SO UH...THIS IS MY PAD...UHM I GOT A COOL CONDO...JUST STAYING WITH MY MOM SO, WELL, YOU KNOW, SHE ISN'T LONELY.
OH HOW CUTE...THAT'S NICE, YOU HAVE FAMILY. I JUST HAVE VULTURES FOR FAMILY.
NICE ROOM...YOU MUST HAVE TONS OF GIRLFRIENDS WITH THE WASTE BASKET FULL OF USED TISSUES.
IS IT COOL IF I SET THIS ON YOUR BED?
MUFFLE... THE ONE... MUFFLE...
OH GOD OH GOD A GIRL JUST TOUCHED MY BED.
SO YOU THINK YOU'RE PRETTY CLEVER, ALL THOSE KILL STREAKS. ALWAYS PLAYING CHEAP...USING THE SAME COMBOS OVER AND OVER...
WHAT IS SHE TALKING ABOUT...
WELL, THIS TIME...YOU'RE MY BITCH...I WANNA HEAR YOU BEG BEFORE I TAKE THE WIN.
HHUKK!

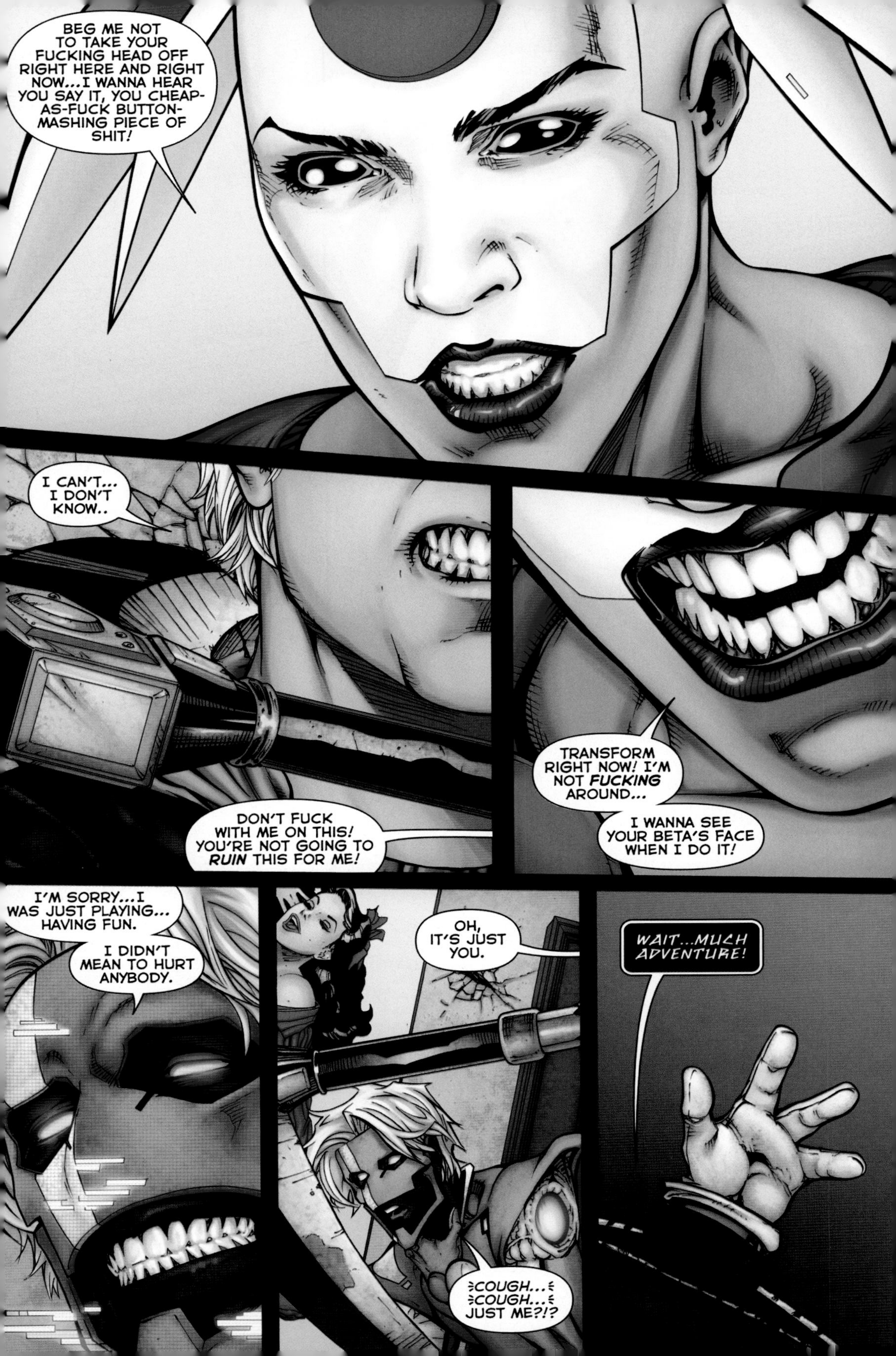
BEG ME NOT TO TAKE YOUR FUCKING HEAD OFF RIGHT HERE AND RIGHT NOW...I WANNA HEAR YOU SAY IT, YOU CHEAP-AS-FUCK BUTTON-MASHING PIECE OF SHIT!
I CAN'T... I DON'T KNOW..
DON'T FUCK WITH ME ON THIS! YOU'RE NOT GOING TO *RUIN* THIS FOR ME!
TRANSFORM RIGHT NOW! I'M NOT *FUCKING* AROUND...
I WANNA SEE YOUR BETA'S FACE WHEN I DO IT!
I'M SORRY...I WAS JUST PLAYING... HAVING FUN.
I DIDN'T MEAN TO HURT ANYBODY.
OH, IT'S JUST YOU.
COUGH... COUGH... JUST ME?!?
WAIT...MUCH ADVENTURE!

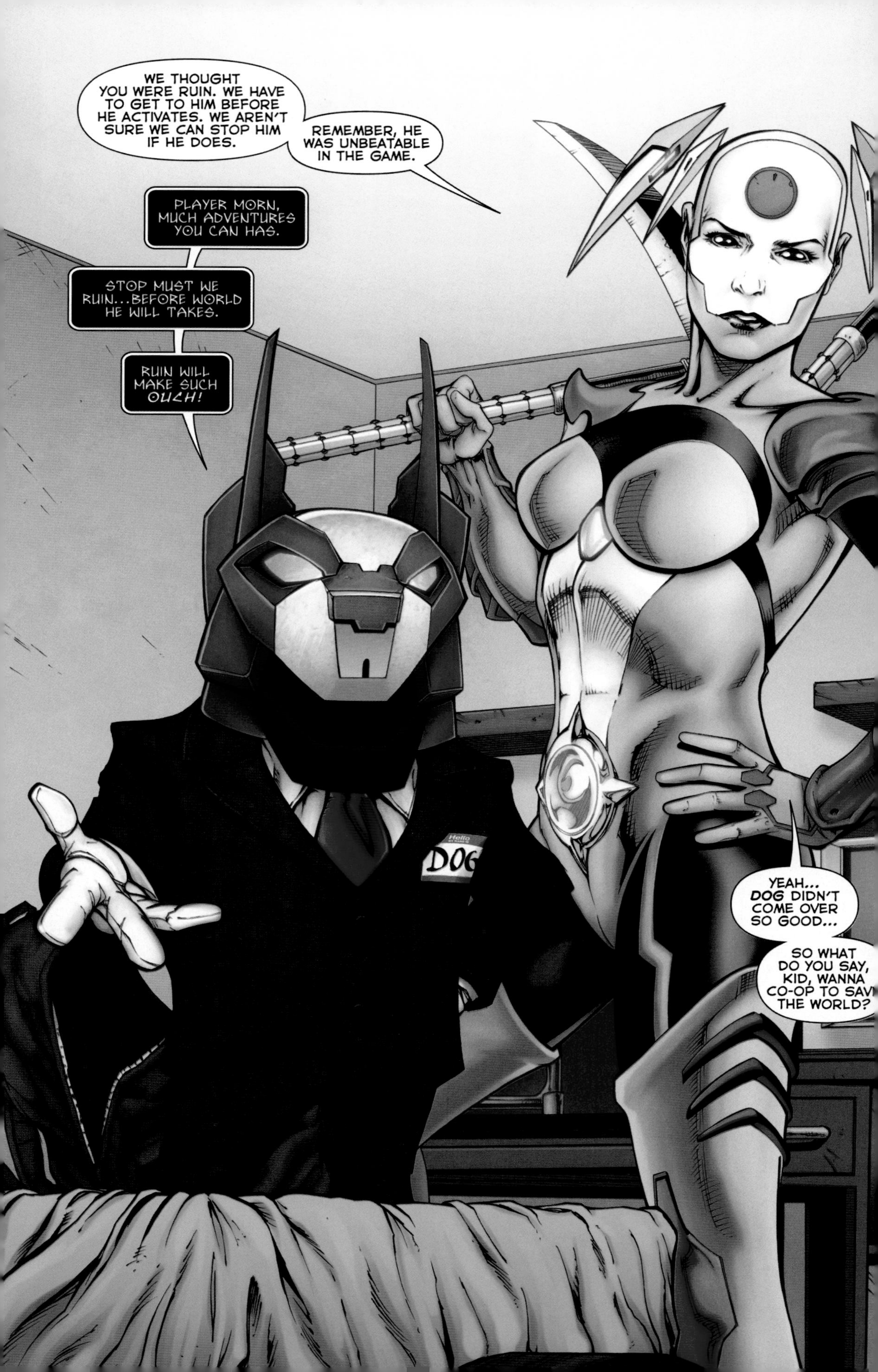
WE THOUGHT YOU WERE RUIN. WE HAVE TO GET TO HIM BEFORE HE ACTIVATES. WE AREN'T SURE WE CAN STOP HIM IF HE DOES.
REMEMBER, HE WAS UNBEATABLE IN THE GAME.
PLAYER MORN, MUCH ADVENTURES YOU CAN HAS.
STOP MUST WE RUIN...BEFORE WORLD HE WILL TAKES.
RUIN WILL MAKE SUCH OUCH!
DOG
YEAH... DOG DIDN'T COME OVER SO GOOD...
SO WHAT DO YOU SAY, KID, WANNA CO-OP TO SAV THE WORLD?

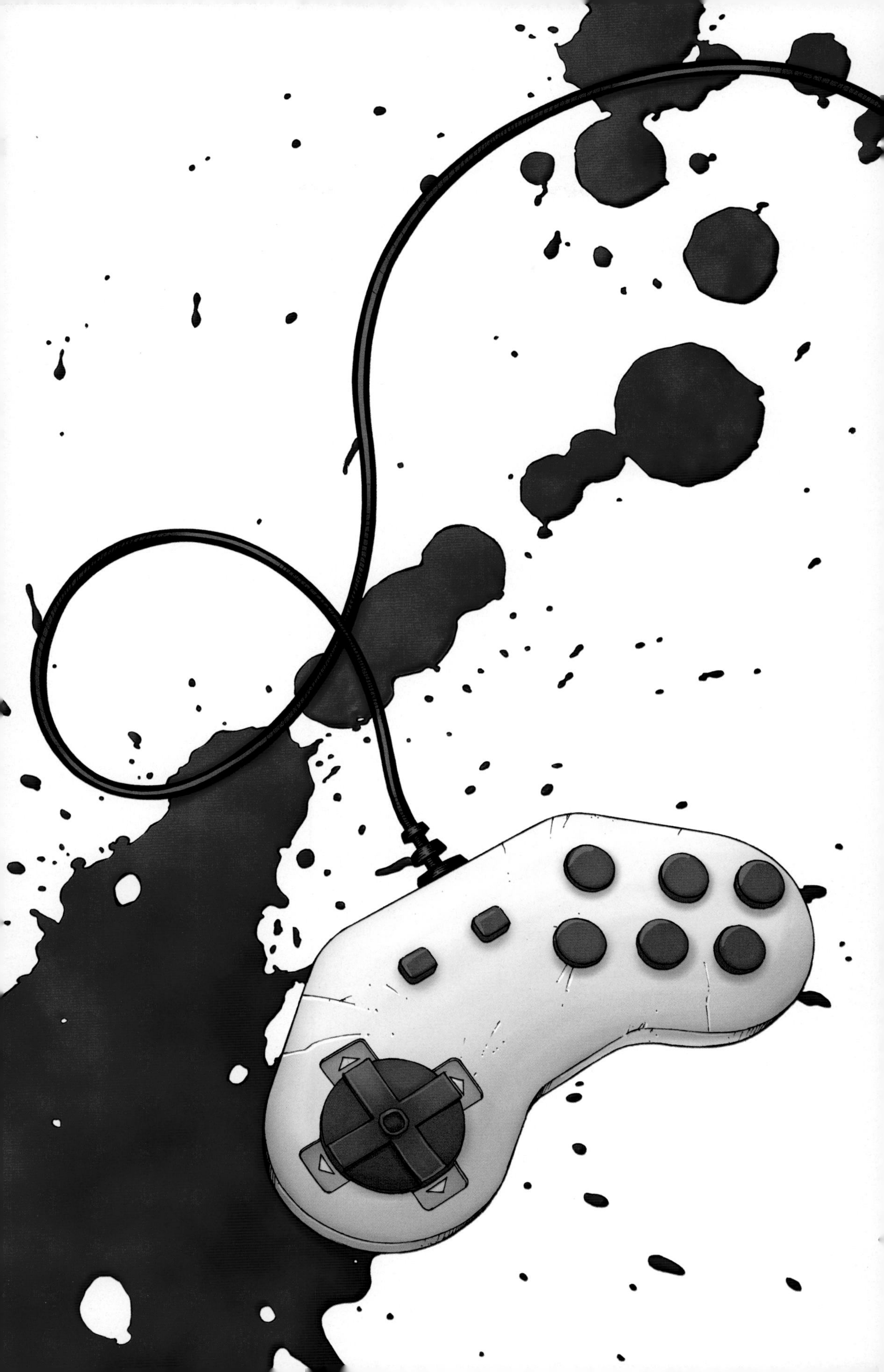

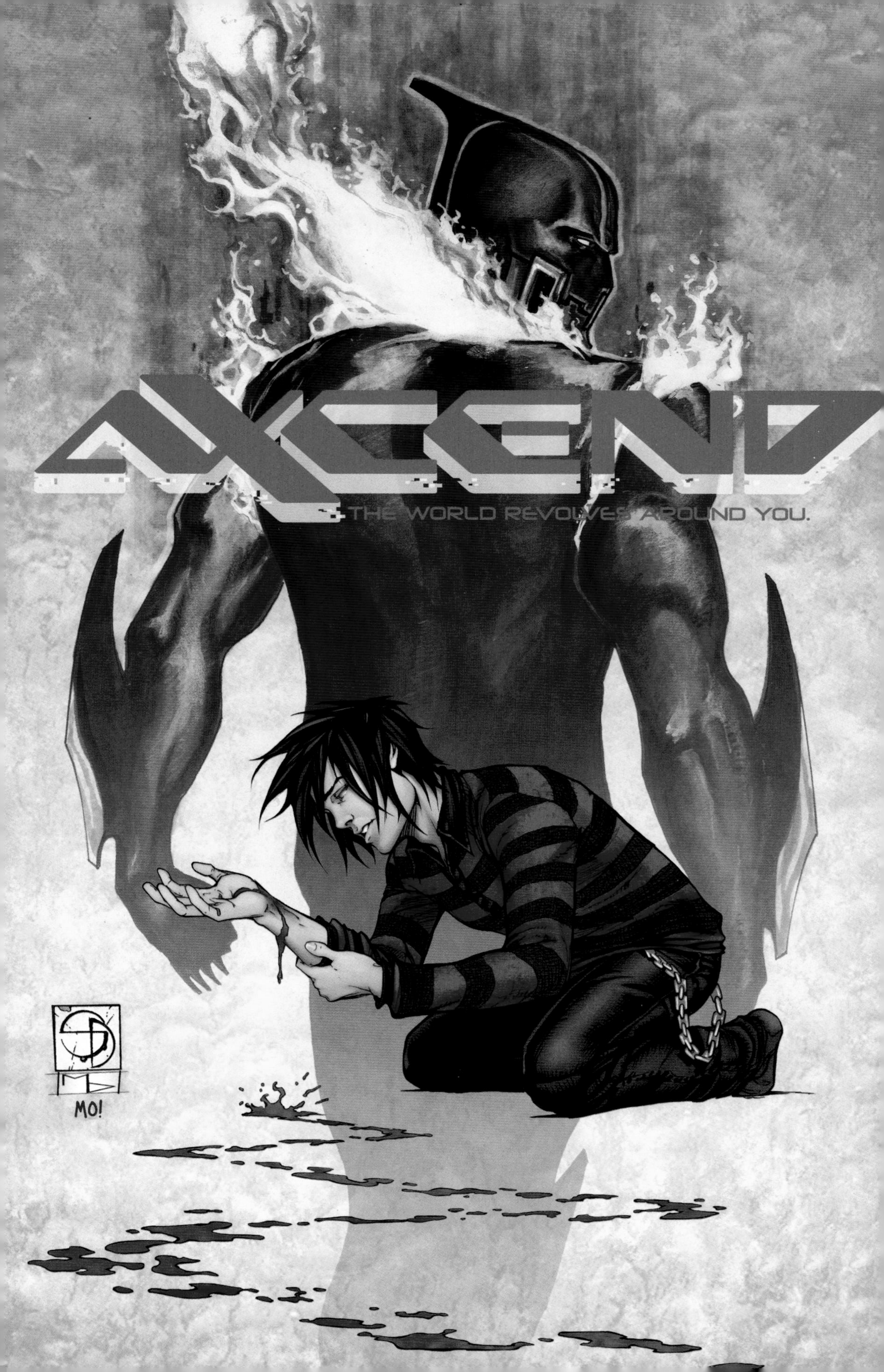
AXCEND
THE WORLD REVOLVES AROUND YOU.
MO!

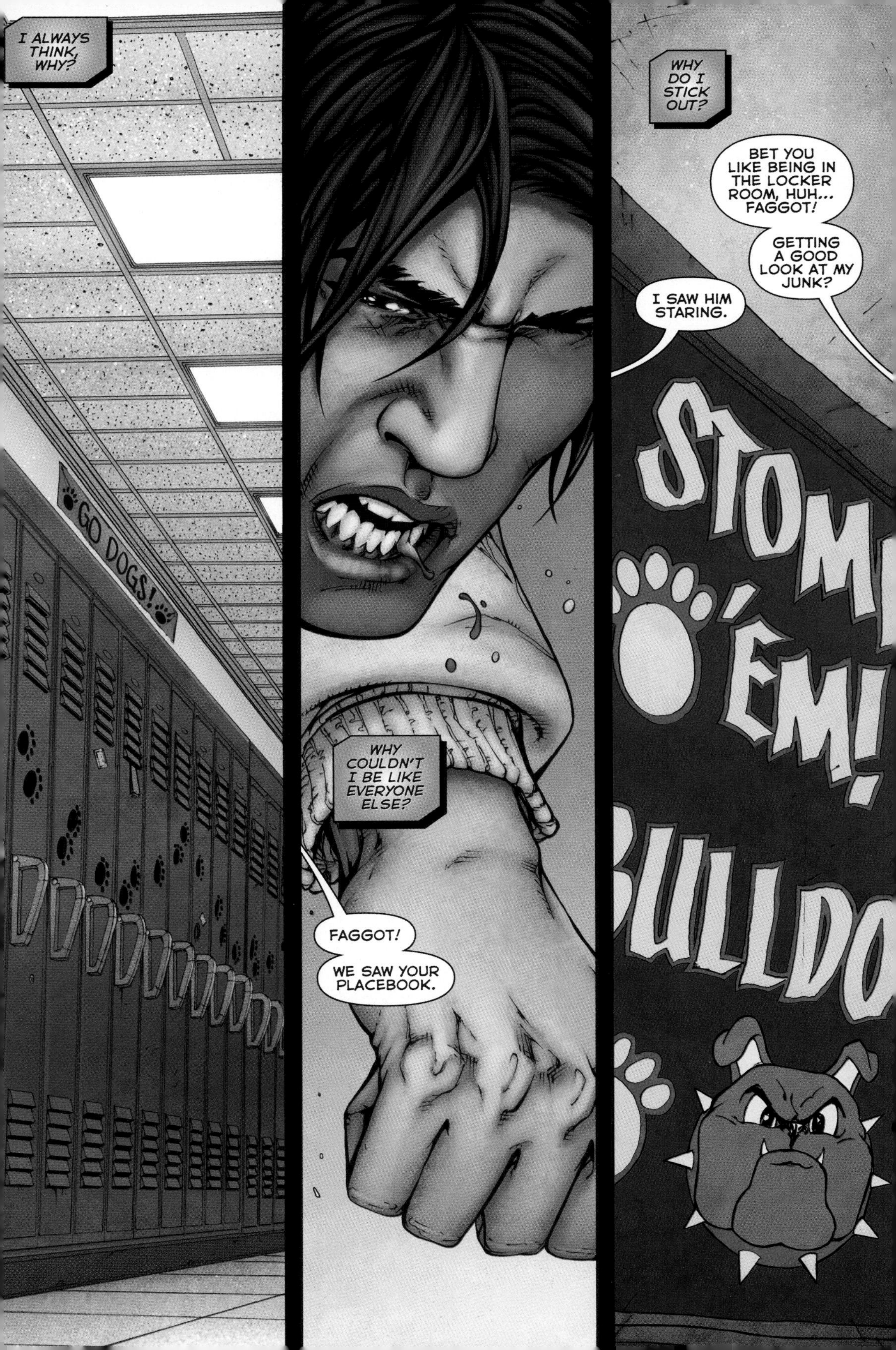
I ALWAYS THINK, WHY?
GO DOGS!
WHY COULDN'T I BE LIKE EVERYONE ELSE?
FAGGOT!
WE SAW YOUR PLACEBOOK.
WHY DO I STICK OUT?
BET YOU LIKE BEING IN THE LOCKER ROOM, HUH... FAGGOT!
GETTING A GOOD LOOK AT MY JUNK?
I SAW HIM STARING.

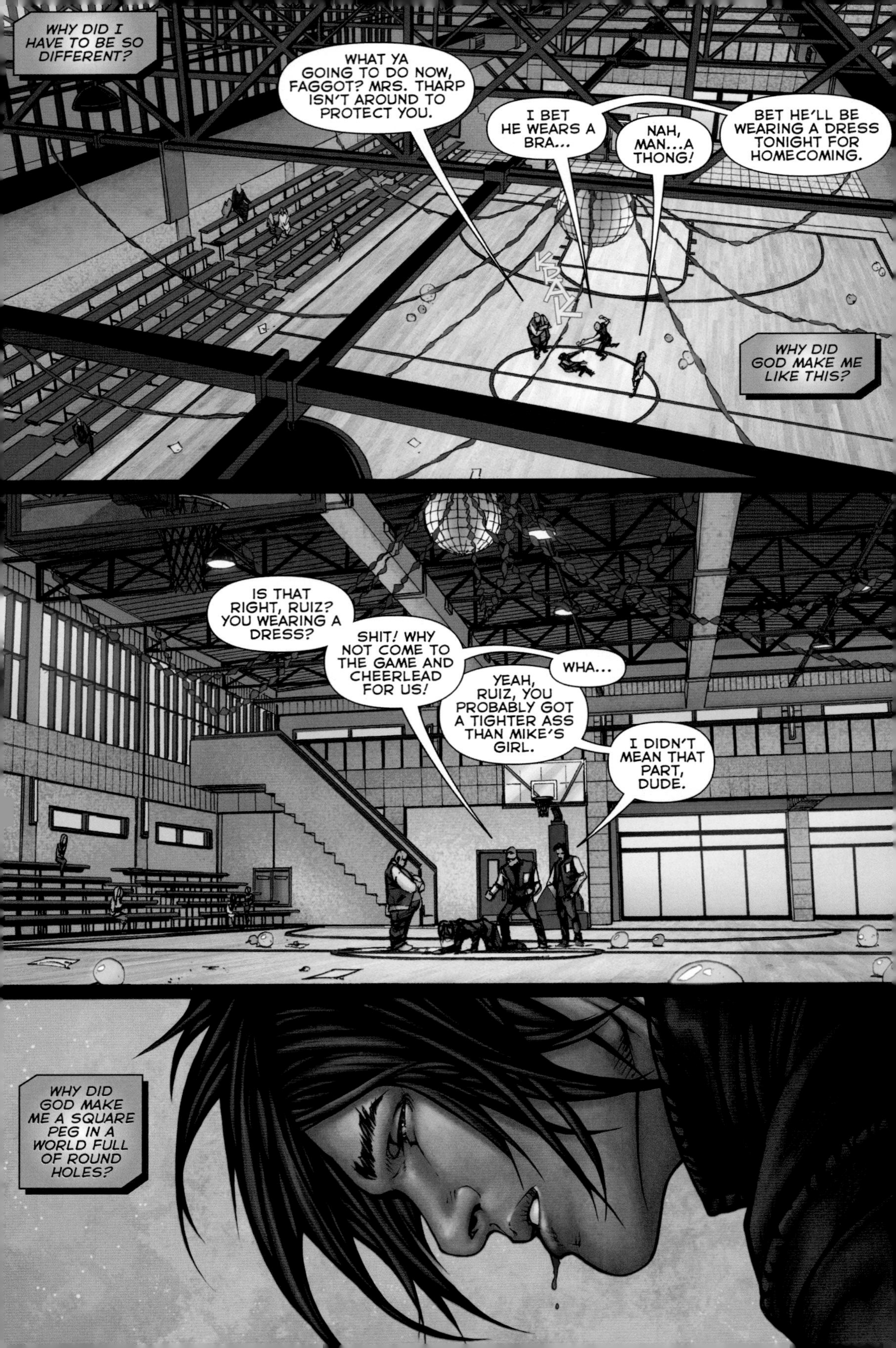
WHY DID I HAVE TO BE SO DIFFERENT?
WHAT YA GOING TO DO NOW, FAGGOT? MRS. THARP ISN'T AROUND TO PROTECT YOU.
I BET HE WEARS A BRA...
NAH, MAN...A THONG!
BET HE'LL BE WEARING A DRESS TONIGHT FOR HOMECOMING.
KRAK
WHY DID GOD MAKE ME LIKE THIS?
IS THAT RIGHT, RUIZ? YOU WEARING A DRESS?
SHIT! WHY NOT COME TO THE GAME AND CHEERLEAD FOR US!
WHA...
YEAH, RUIZ, YOU PROBABLY GOT A TIGHTER ASS THAN MIKE'S GIRL.
I DIDN'T MEAN THAT PART, DUDE.
WHY DID GOD MAKE ME A SQUARE PEG IN A WORLD FULL OF ROUND HOLES?

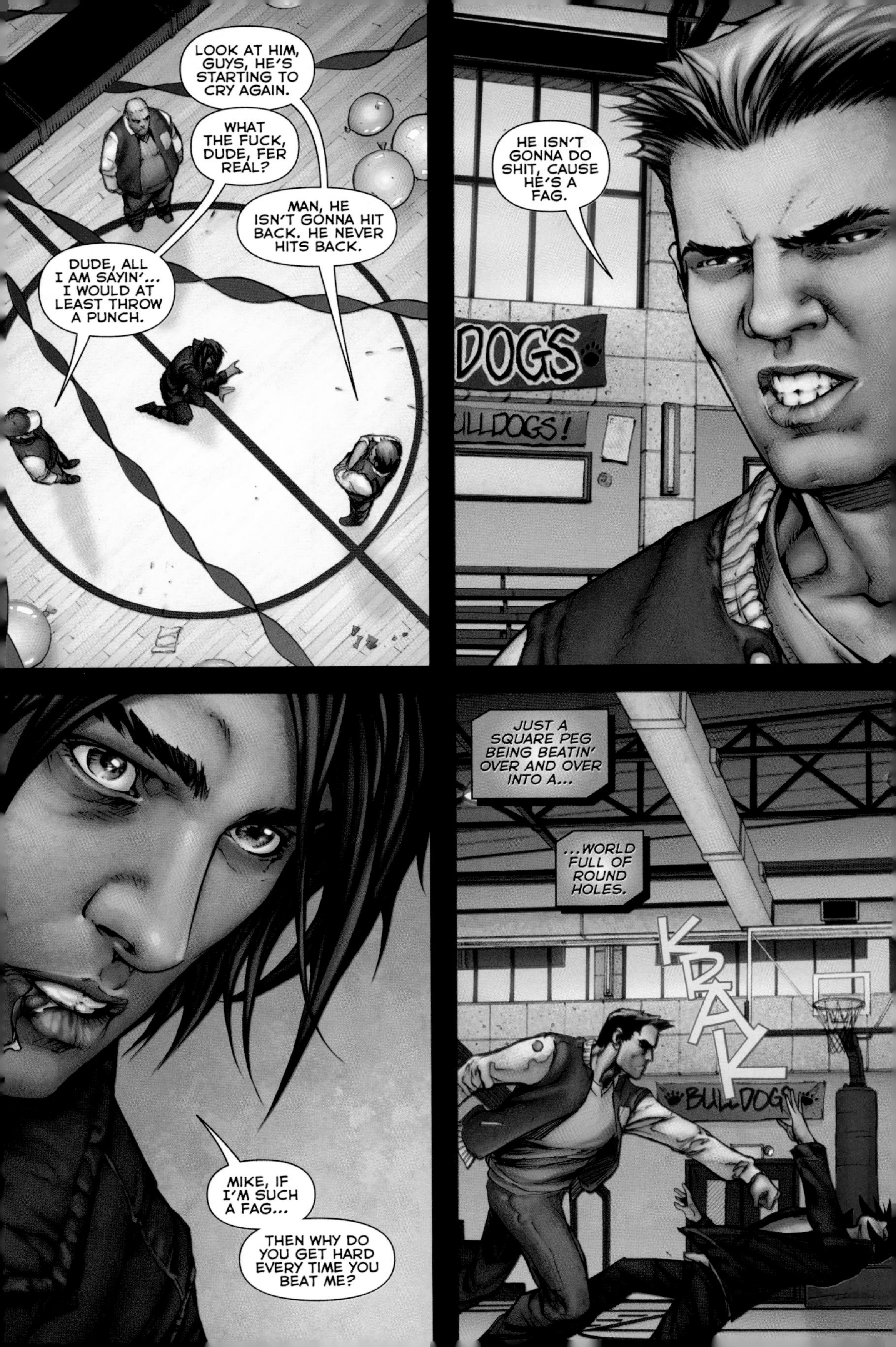
LOOK AT HIM, GUYS, HE'S STARTING TO CRY AGAIN.
WHAT THE FUCK, DUDE, FER REAL?
MAN, HE ISN'T GONNA HIT BACK. HE NEVER HITS BACK.
DUDE, ALL I AM SAYIN'... I WOULD AT LEAST THROW A PUNCH.
HE ISN'T GONNA DO SHIT, CAUSE HE'S A FAG.
DOGS
BULLDOGS!
MIKE, IF I'M SUCH A FAG...
THEN WHY DO YOU GET HARD EVERY TIME YOU BEAT ME?
JUST A SQUARE PEG BEING BEATIN' OVER AND OVER INTO A...
...WORLD FULL OF ROUND HOLES.
KRAK
BULLDOGS

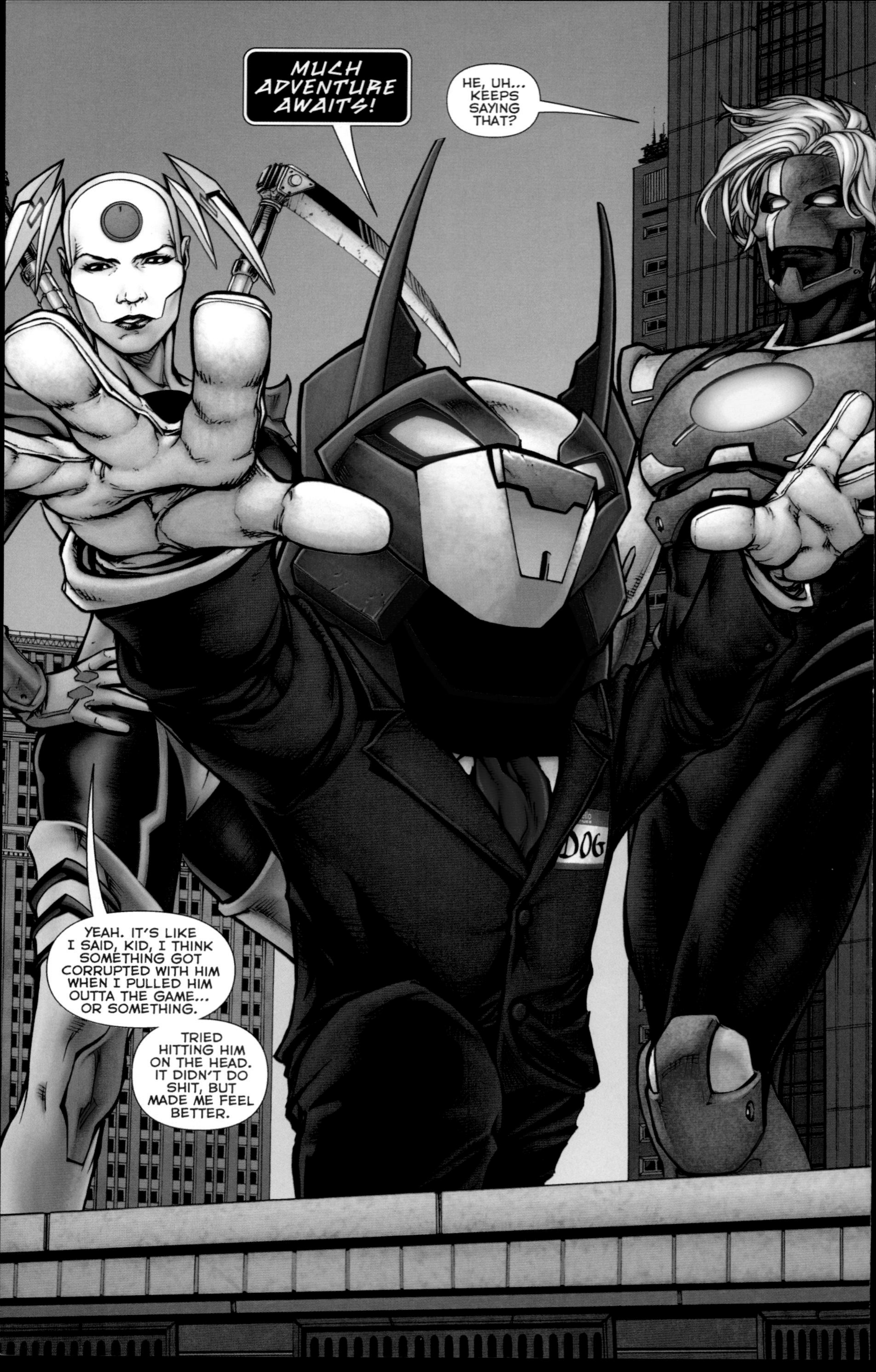
MUCH ADVENTURE AWAITS!
HE, UH... KEEPS SAYING THAT?
YEAH. IT'S LIKE I SAID, KID, I THINK SOMETHING GOT CORRUPTED WITH HIM WHEN I PULLED HIM OUTTA THE GAME... OR SOMETHING.
TRIED HITTING HIM ON THE HEAD. IT DIDN'T DO SHIT, BUT MADE ME FEEL BETTER.
DOG

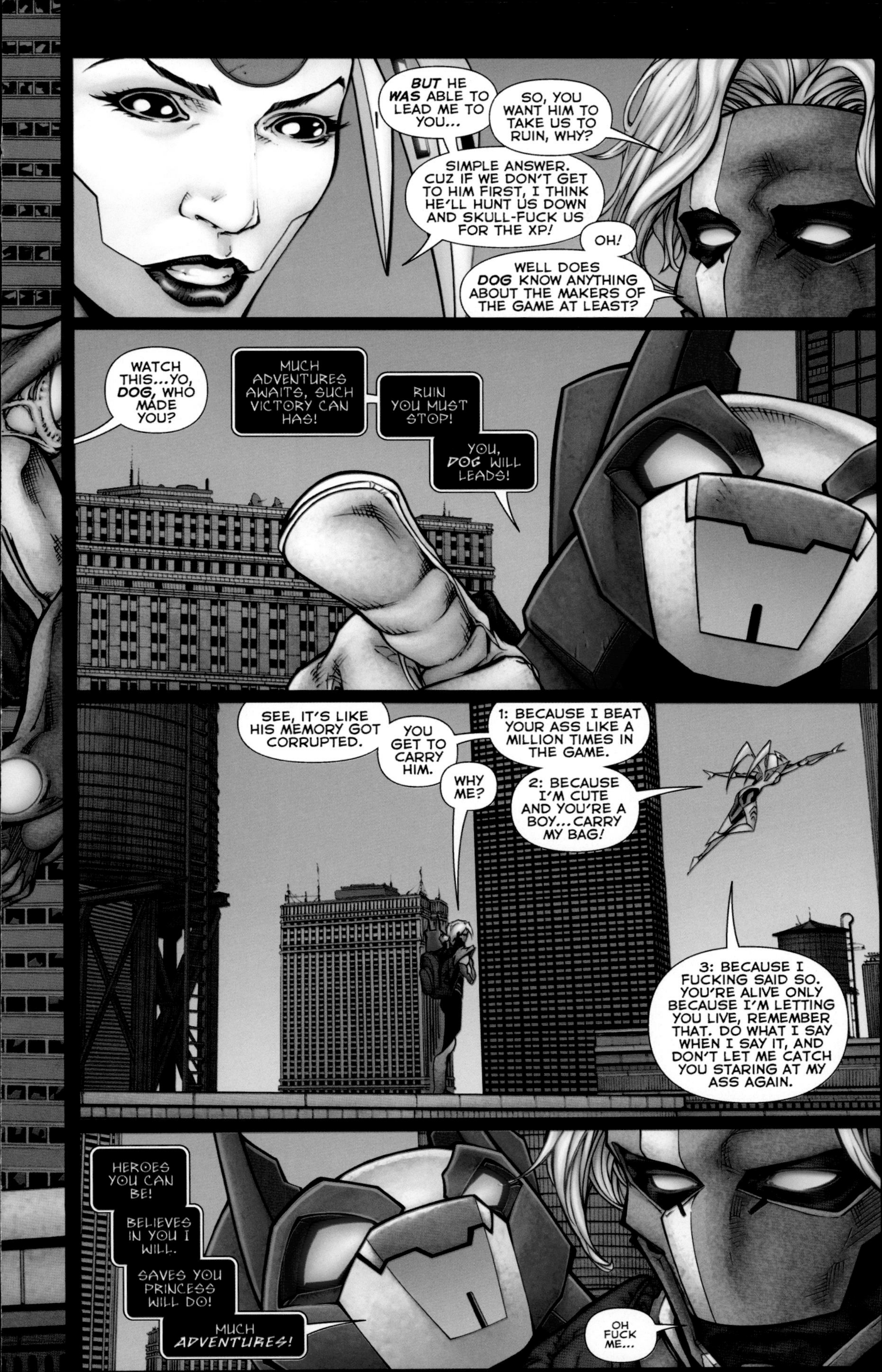
BUT HE WAS ABLE TO LEAD ME TO YOU...
SO, YOU WANT HIM TO TAKE US TO RUIN, WHY?
SIMPLE ANSWER. CUZ IF WE DON'T GET TO HIM FIRST, I THINK HE'LL HUNT US DOWN AND SKULL-FUCK US FOR THE XP!
OH!
WELL DOES DOG KNOW ANYTHING ABOUT THE MAKERS OF THE GAME AT LEAST?
WATCH THIS...YO, DOG, WHO MADE YOU?
MUCH ADVENTURES AWAITS, SUCH VICTORY CAN HAS!
RUIN YOU MUST STOP!
YOU, DOG WILL LEADS!
SEE, IT'S LIKE HIS MEMORY GOT CORRUPTED.
YOU GET TO CARRY HIM.
WHY ME?
1: BECAUSE I BEAT YOUR ASS LIKE A MILLION TIMES IN THE GAME.
2: BECAUSE I'M CUTE AND YOU'RE A BOY...CARRY MY BAG!
3: BECAUSE I FUCKING SAID SO. YOU'RE ALIVE ONLY BECAUSE I'M LETTING YOU LIVE, REMEMBER THAT. DO WHAT I SAY WHEN I SAY IT, AND DON'T LET ME CATCH YOU STARING AT MY ASS AGAIN.
HEROES YOU CAN BE!
BELIEVES IN YOU I WILL.
SAVES YOU PRINCESS WILL DO!
MUCH ADVENTURES!
OH FUCK ME...

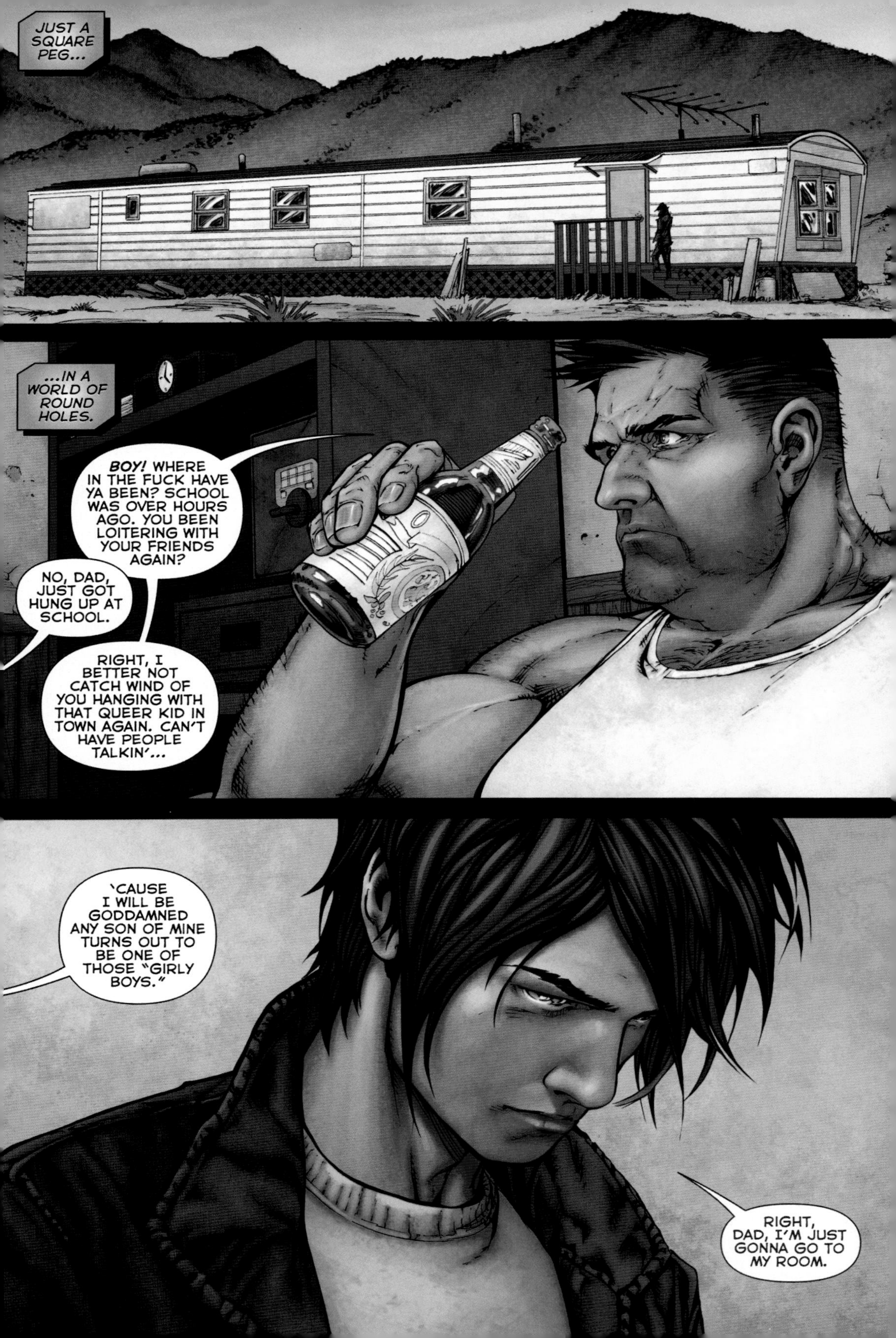
JUST A SQUARE PEG...
...IN A WORLD OF ROUND HOLES.
BOY! WHERE IN THE FUCK HAVE YA BEEN? SCHOOL WAS OVER HOURS AGO. YOU BEEN LOITERING WITH YOUR FRIENDS AGAIN?
NO, DAD, JUST GOT HUNG UP AT SCHOOL.
RIGHT, I BETTER NOT CATCH WIND OF YOU HANGING WITH THAT QUEER KID IN TOWN AGAIN. CAN'T HAVE PEOPLE TALKIN'...
'CAUSE I WILL BE GODDAMNED ANY SON OF MINE TURNS OUT TO BE ONE OF THOSE "GIRLY BOYS."
RIGHT, DAD, I'M JUST GONNA GO TO MY ROOM.

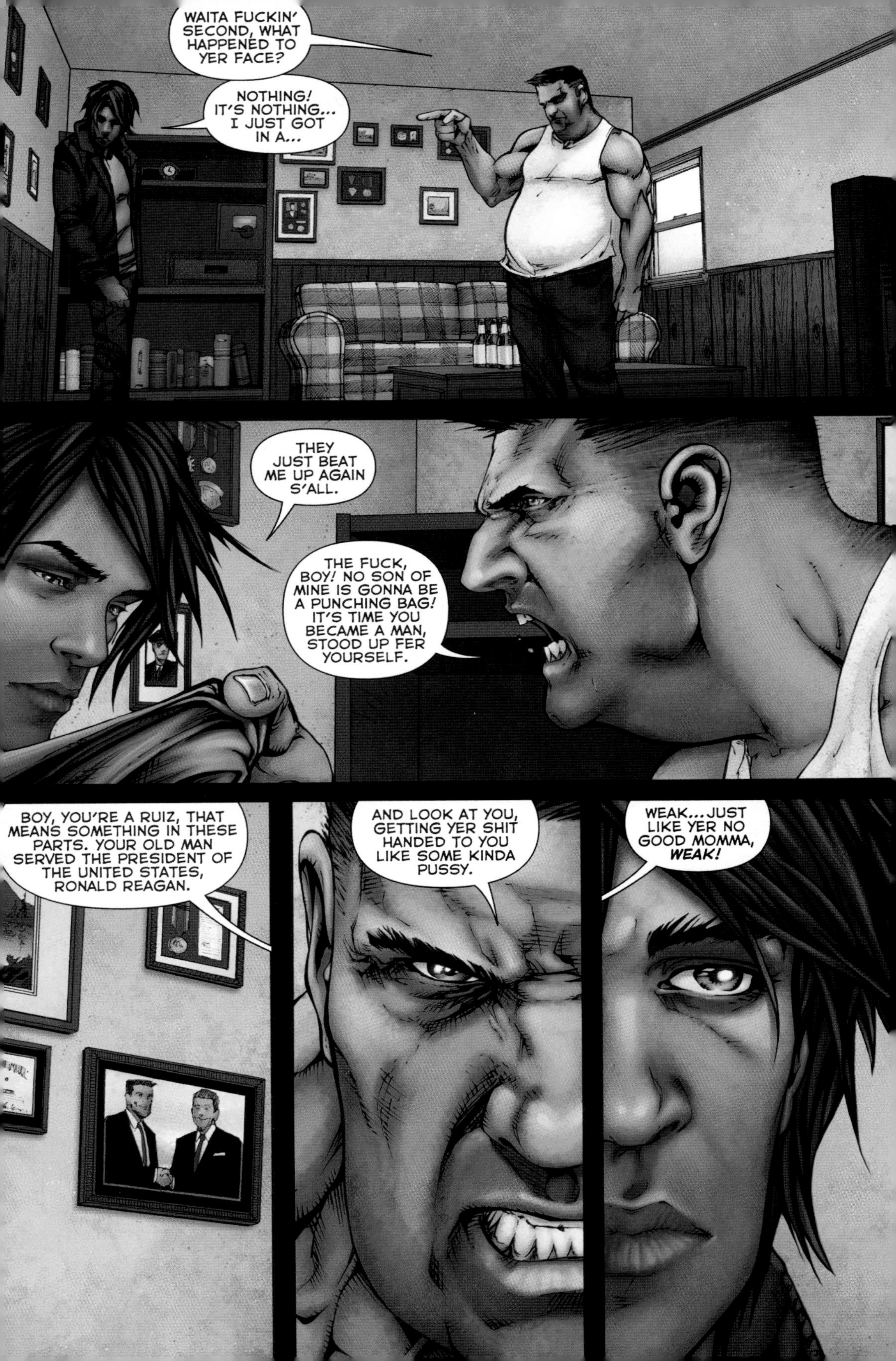
WAITA FUCKIN' SECOND, WHAT HAPPENED TO YER FACE?
NOTHING! IT'S NOTHING... I JUST GOT IN A...
THEY JUST BEAT ME UP AGAIN S'ALL.
THE FUCK, BOY! NO SON OF MINE IS GONNA BE A PUNCHING BAG! IT'S TIME YOU BECAME A MAN, STOOD UP FER YOURSELF.
BOY, YOU'RE A RUIZ, THAT MEANS SOMETHING IN THESE PARTS. YOUR OLD MAN SERVED THE PRESIDENT OF THE UNITED STATES, RONALD REAGAN.
AND LOOK AT YOU, GETTING YER SHIT HANDED TO YOU LIKE SOME KINDA PUSSY.
WEAK... JUST LIKE YER NO GOOD MOMMA, **WEAK!**

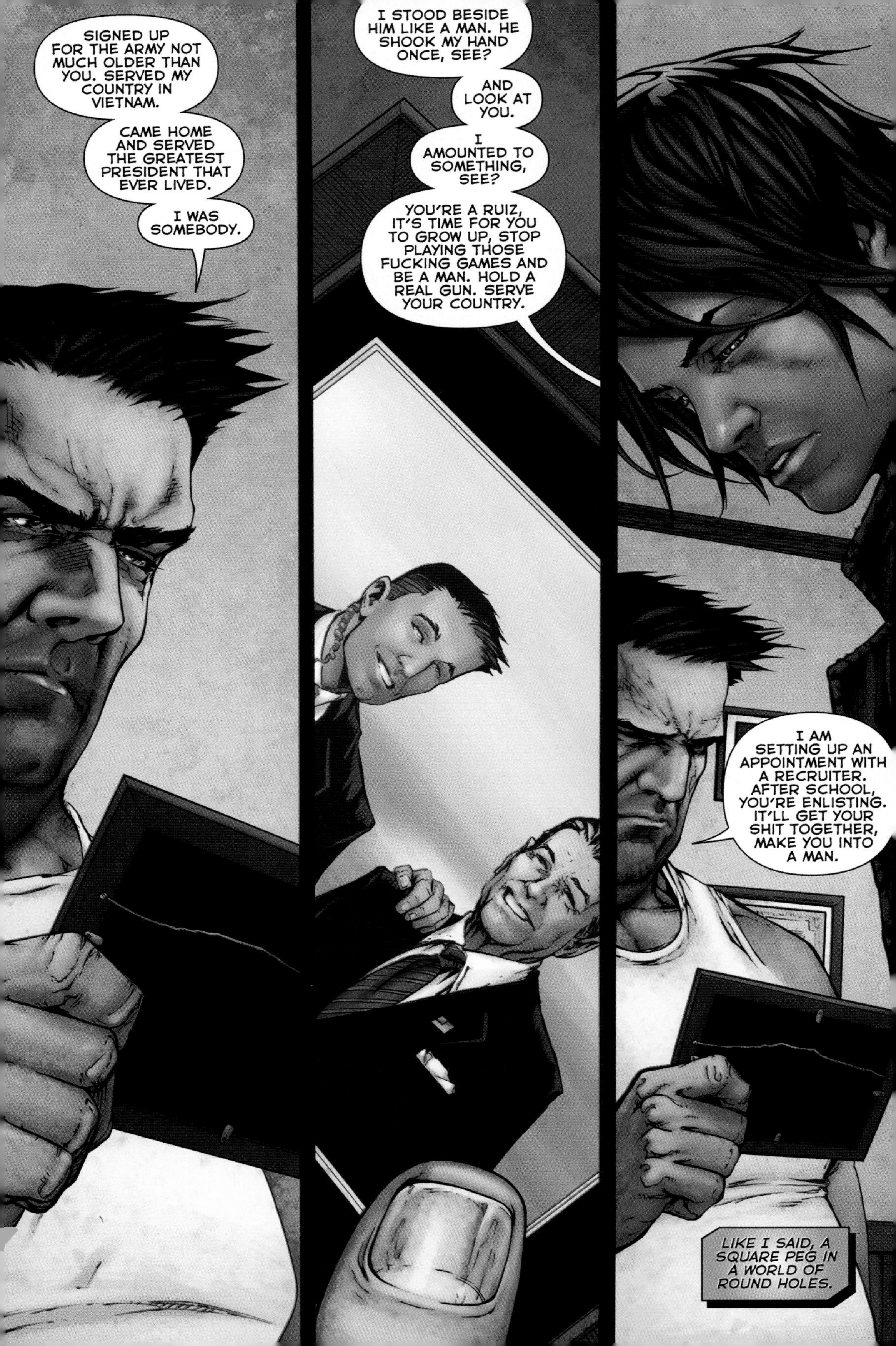
SIGNED UP FOR THE ARMY NOT MUCH OLDER THAN YOU. SERVED MY COUNTRY IN VIETNAM.
CAME HOME AND SERVED THE GREATEST PRESIDENT THAT EVER LIVED.
I WAS SOMEBODY.
I STOOD BESIDE HIM LIKE A MAN. HE SHOOK MY HAND ONCE, SEE?
AND LOOK AT YOU.
I AMOUNTED TO SOMETHING, SEE?
YOU'RE A RUIZ, IT'S TIME FOR YOU TO GROW UP, STOP PLAYING THOSE FUCKING GAMES AND BE A MAN. HOLD A REAL GUN. SERVE YOUR COUNTRY.
I AM SETTING UP AN APPOINTMENT WITH A RECRUITER. AFTER SCHOOL, YOU'RE ENLISTING. IT'LL GET YOUR SHIT TOGETHER, MAKE YOU INTO A MAN.
LIKE I SAID, A SQUARE PEG IN A WORLD OF ROUND HOLES.

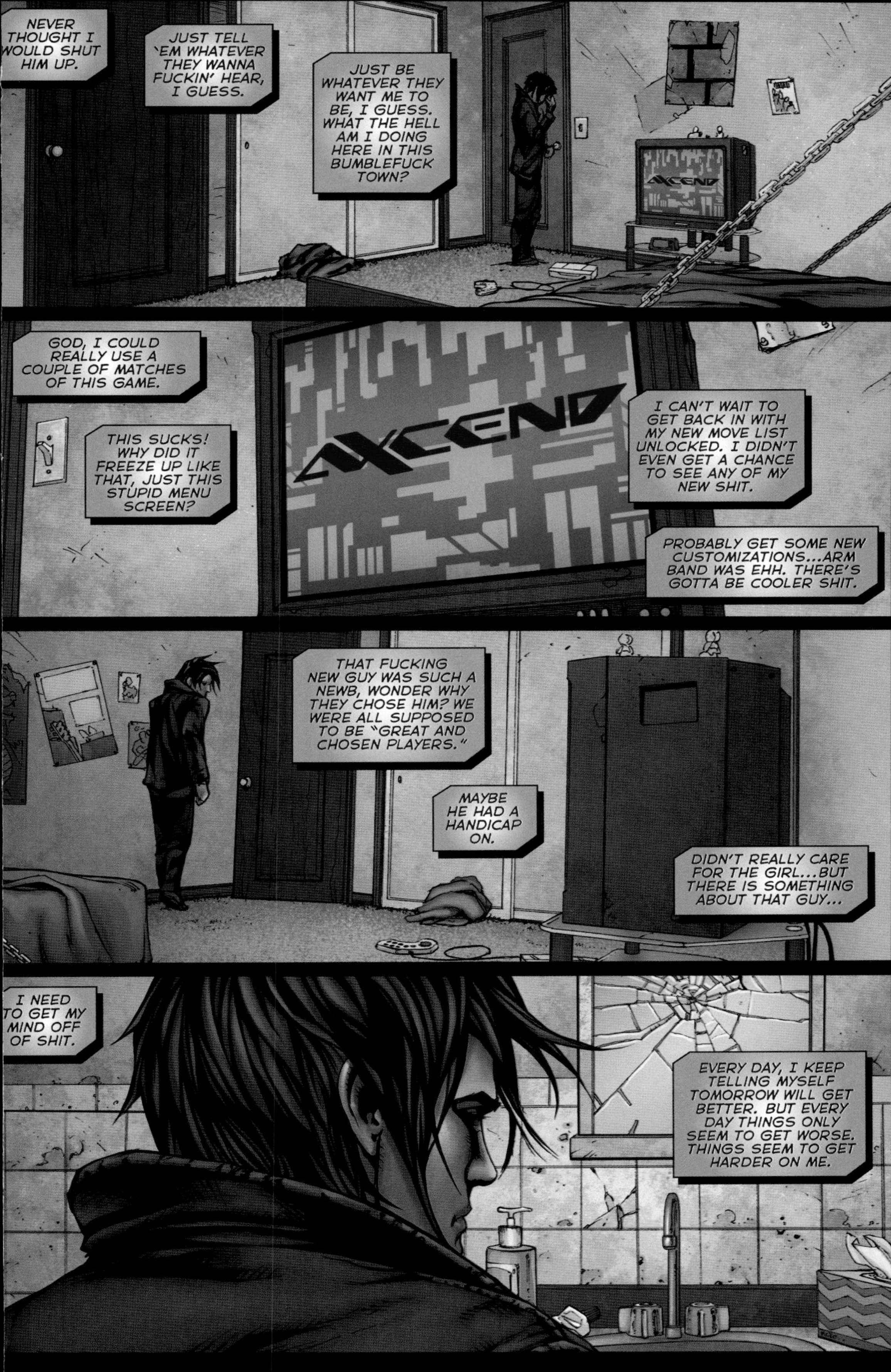
NEVER THOUGHT I WOULD SHUT HIM UP.
JUST TELL 'EM WHATEVER THEY WANNA FUCKIN' HEAR, I GUESS.
JUST BE WHATEVER THEY WANT ME TO BE, I GUESS. WHAT THE HELL AM I DOING HERE IN THIS BUMBLEFUCK TOWN?
AXCEND
GOD, I COULD REALLY USE A COUPLE OF MATCHES OF THIS GAME.
THIS SUCKS! WHY DID IT FREEZE UP LIKE THAT, JUST THIS STUPID MENU SCREEN?
AXCEND
I CAN'T WAIT TO GET BACK IN WITH MY NEW MOVE LIST UNLOCKED. I DIDN'T EVEN GET A CHANCE TO SEE ANY OF MY NEW SHIT.
PROBABLY GET SOME NEW CUSTOMIZATIONS...ARM BAND WAS EHH. THERE'S GOTTA BE COOLER SHIT.
THAT FUCKING NEW GUY WAS SUCH A NEWB, WONDER WHY THEY CHOSE HIM? WE WERE ALL SUPPOSED TO BE "GREAT AND CHOSEN PLAYERS."
MAYBE HE HAD A HANDICAP ON.
DIDN'T REALLY CARE FOR THE GIRL...BUT THERE IS SOMETHING ABOUT THAT GUY...
I NEED TO GET MY MIND OFF OF SHIT.
EVERY DAY, I KEEP TELLING MYSELF TOMORROW WILL GET BETTER. BUT EVERY DAY THINGS ONLY SEEM TO GET WORSE. THINGS SEEM TO GET HARDER ON ME.

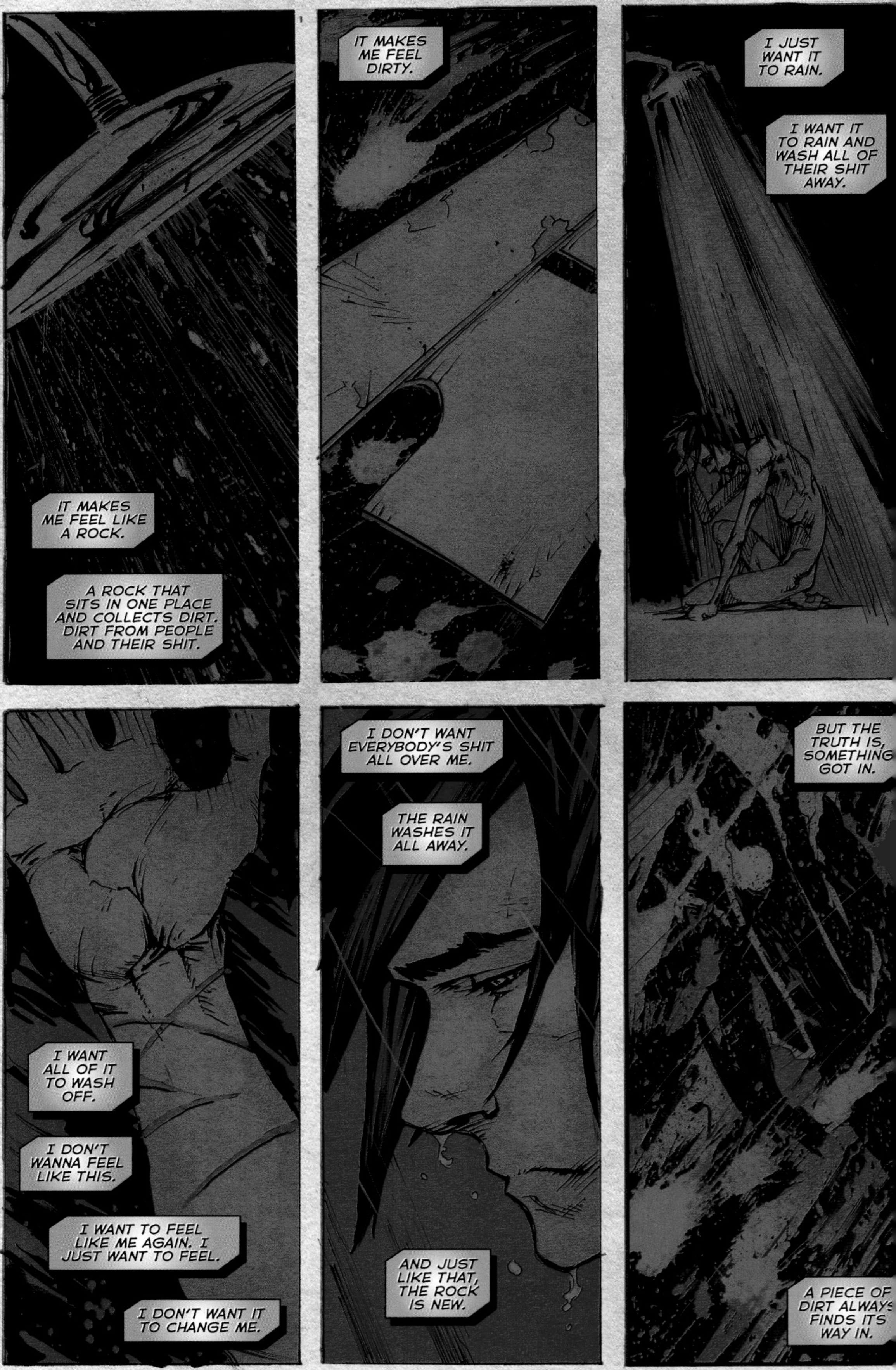
IT MAKES ME FEEL LIKE A ROCK.
A ROCK THAT SITS IN ONE PLACE AND COLLECTS DIRT. DIRT FROM PEOPLE AND THEIR SHIT.
IT MAKES ME FEEL DIRTY.
I JUST WANT IT TO RAIN.
I WANT IT TO RAIN AND WASH ALL OF THEIR SHIT AWAY.
I WANT ALL OF IT TO WASH OFF.
I DON'T WANNA FEEL LIKE THIS.
I WANT TO FEEL LIKE ME AGAIN. I JUST WANT TO FEEL.
I DON'T WANT IT TO CHANGE ME.
I DON'T WANT EVERYBODY'S SHIT ALL OVER ME.
THE RAIN WASHES IT ALL AWAY.
AND JUST LIKE THAT, THE ROCK IS NEW.
BUT THE TRUTH IS, SOMETHING GOT IN.
A PIECE OF DIRT ALWAYS FINDS ITS WAY IN.

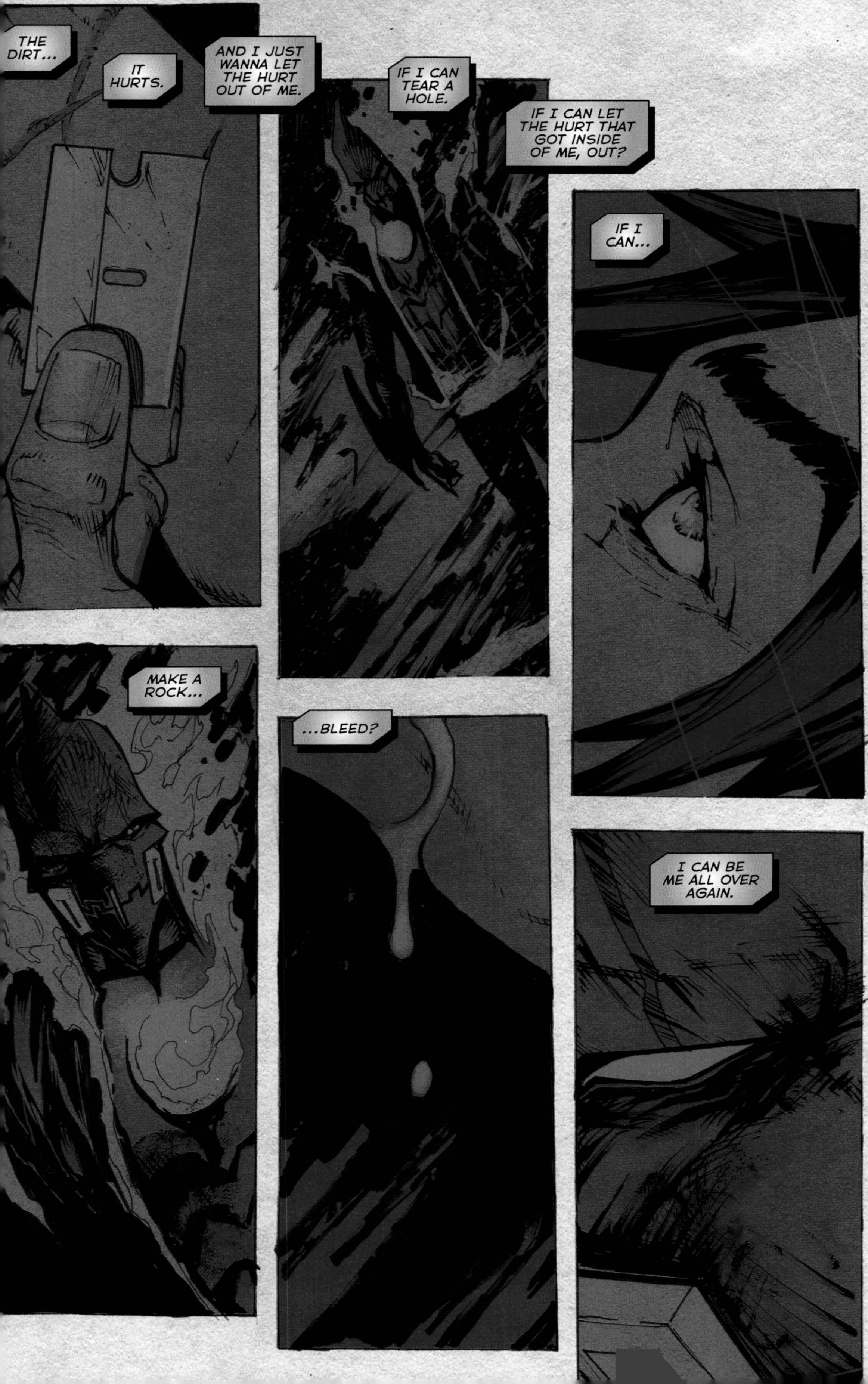
THE DIRT...
IT HURTS.
AND I JUST WANNA LET THE HURT OUT OF ME.
IF I CAN TEAR A HOLE.
IF I CAN LET THE HURT THAT GOT INSIDE OF ME, OUT?
IF I CAN...
MAKE A ROCK...
...BLEED?
I CAN BE ME ALL OVER AGAIN.

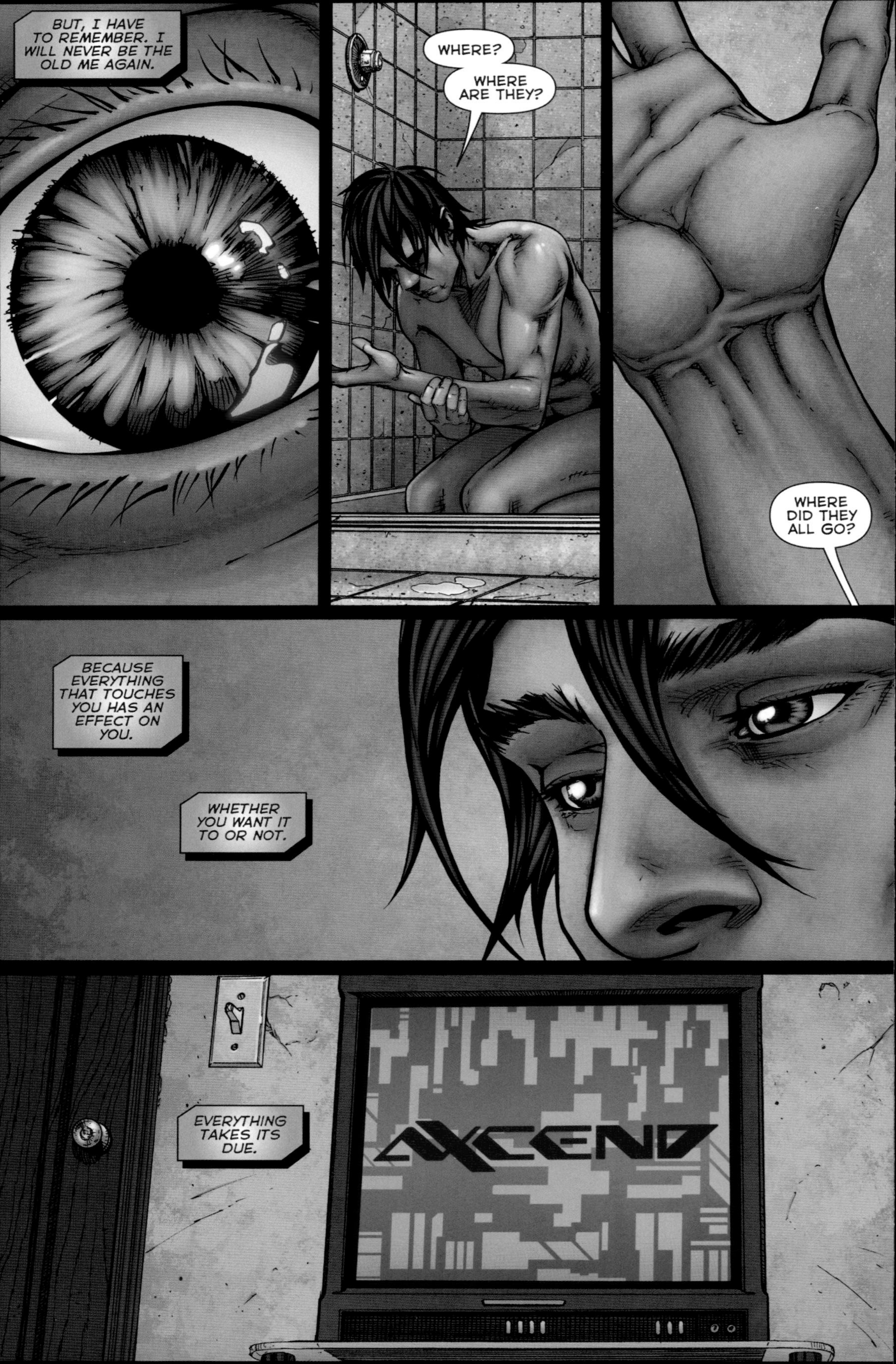
BUT, I HAVE TO REMEMBER. I WILL NEVER BE THE OLD ME AGAIN.
WHERE?
WHERE ARE THEY?
WHERE DID THEY ALL GO?
BECAUSE EVERYTHING THAT TOUCHES YOU HAS AN EFFECT ON YOU.
WHETHER YOU WANT IT TO OR NOT.
EVERYTHING TAKES ITS DUE.
AXCEND

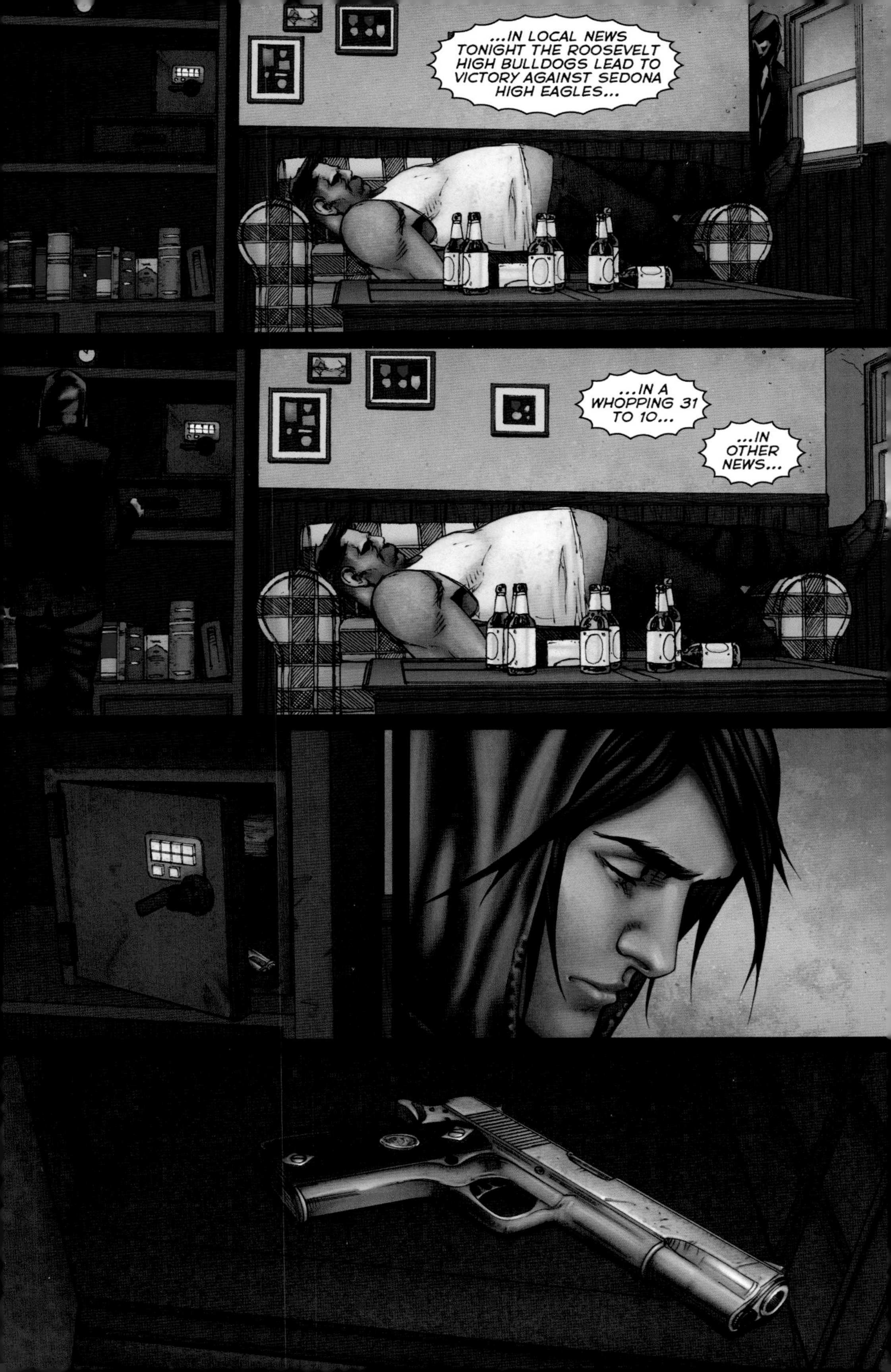
...IN LOCAL NEWS TONIGHT THE ROOSEVELT HIGH BULLDOGS LEAD TO VICTORY AGAINST SEDONA HIGH EAGLES...
...IN A WHOPPING 31 TO 10...
...IN OTHER NEWS...

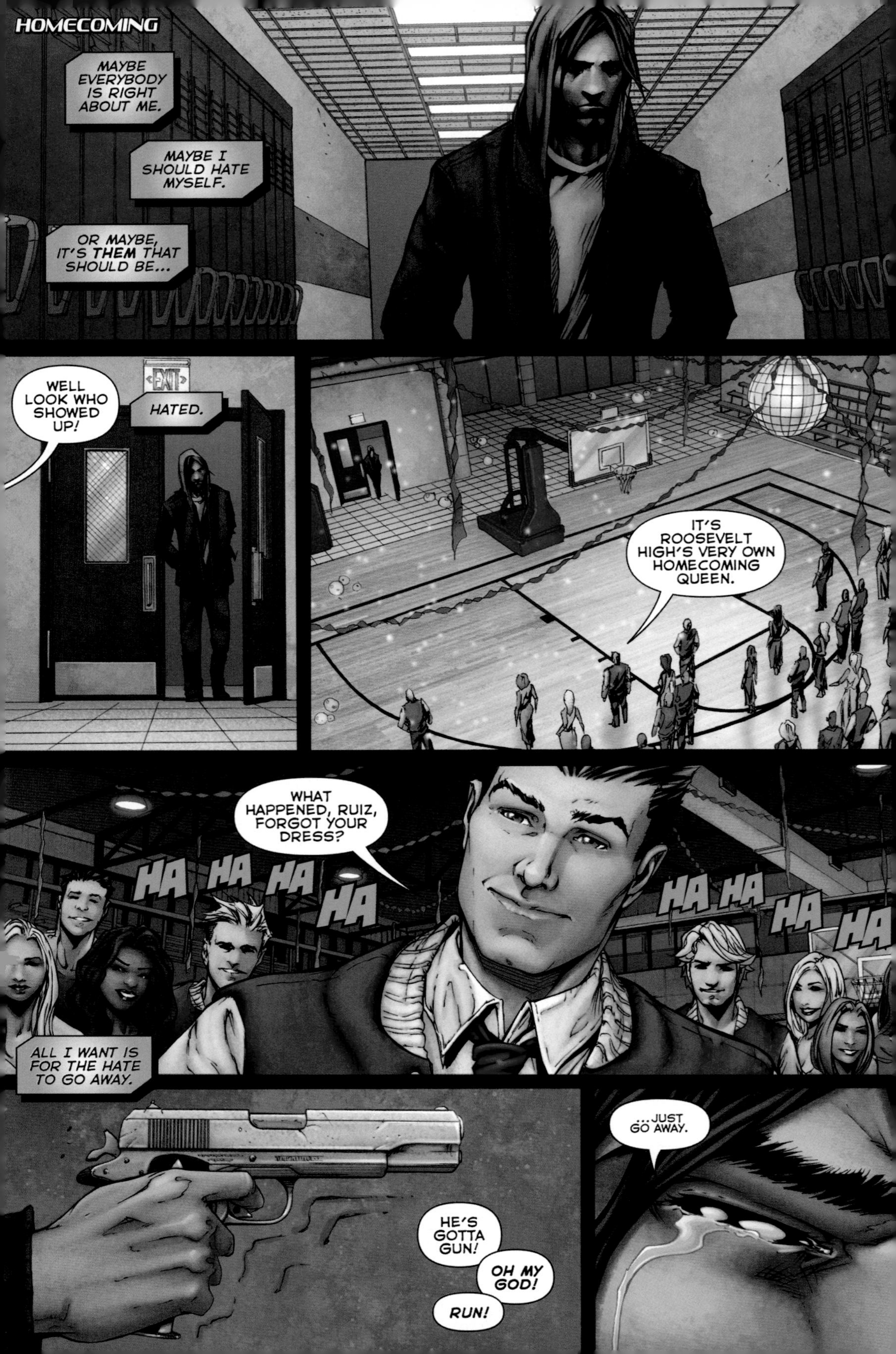
MAYBE EVERYBODY IS RIGHT ABOUT ME.
MAYBE I SHOULD HATE MYSELF.
OR MAYBE, IT'S **THEM** THAT SHOULD BE...
WELL LOOK WHO SHOWED UP!
HATED.
EXIT
IT'S ROOSEVELT HIGH'S VERY OWN HOMECOMING QUEEN.
WHAT HAPPENED, RUIZ, FORGOT YOUR DRESS?
HA HA HA HA
HA HA HA HA
ALL I WANT IS FOR THE HATE TO GO AWAY.
HE'S GOTTA GUN!
OH MY GOD!
RUN!
...JUST GO AWAY.

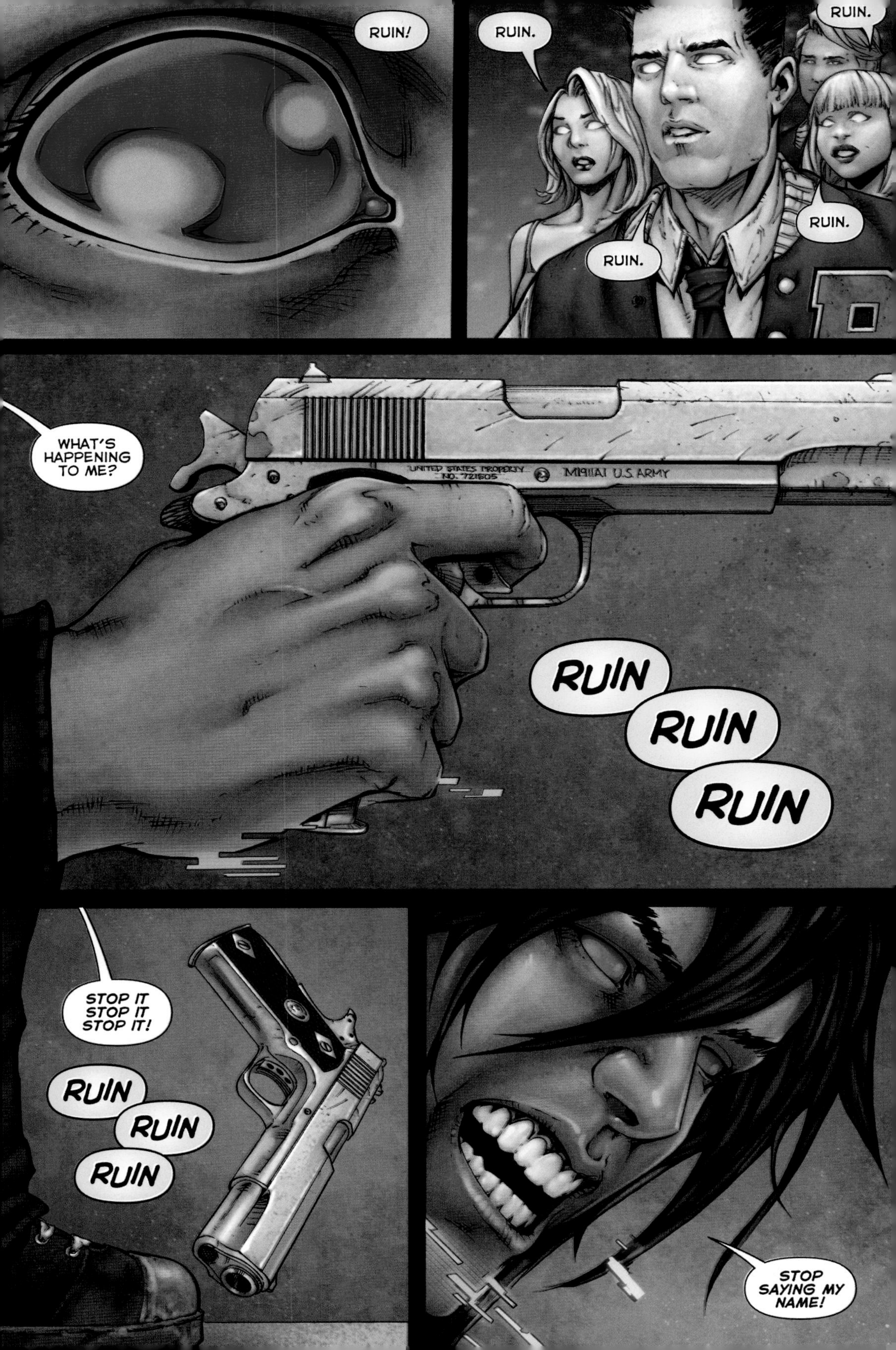
RUIN!
RUIN.
RUIN.
RUIN.
RUIN.
WHAT'S HAPPENING TO ME?
UNITED STATES PROPERTY NO. 721605
M1911A1 U.S. ARMY
RUIN
RUIN
RUIN
STOP IT STOP IT STOP IT!
RUIN
RUIN
RUIN
STOP SAYING MY NAME!

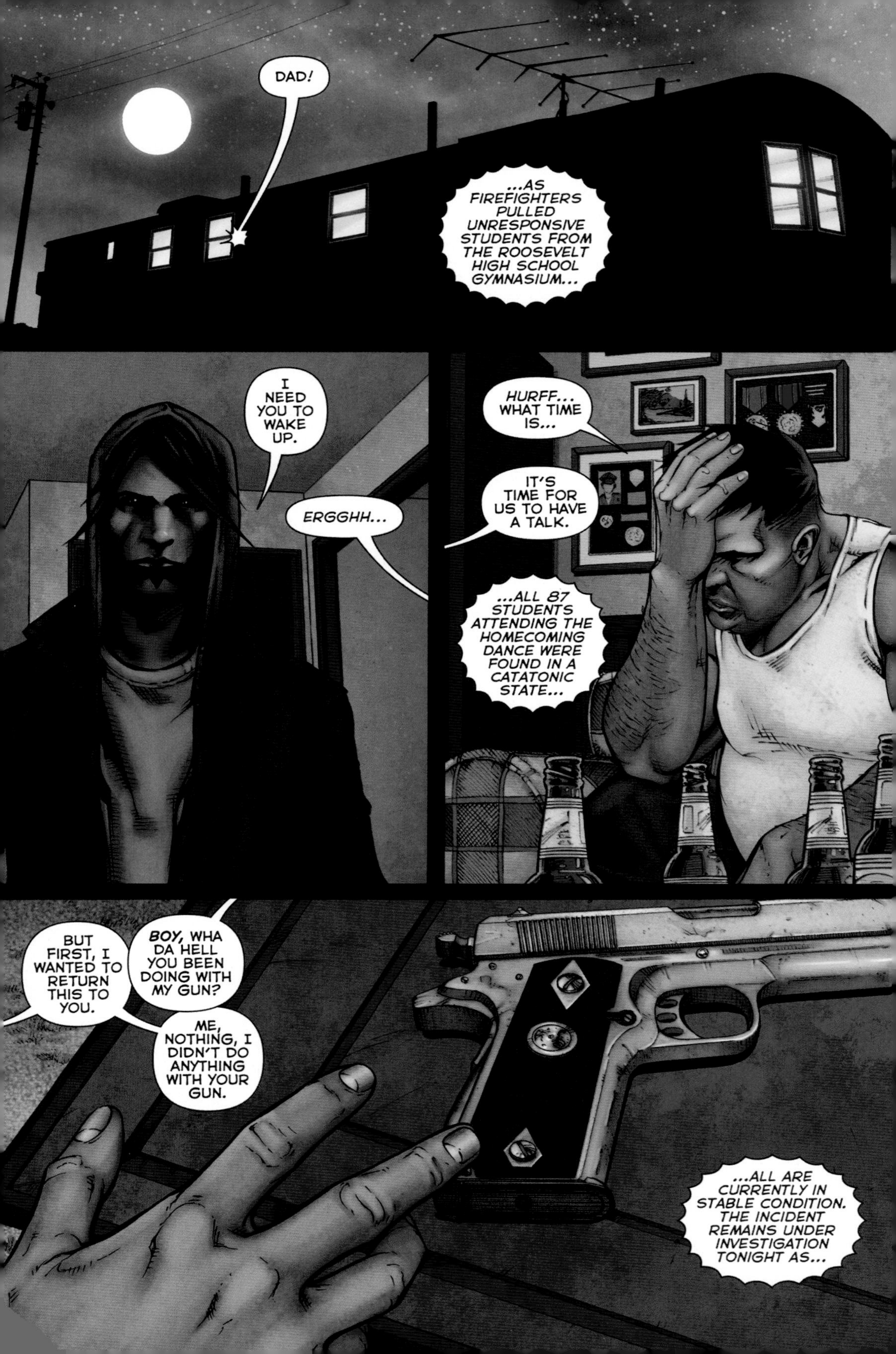
DAD!
...AS FIREFIGHTERS PULLED UNRESPONSIVE STUDENTS FROM THE ROOSEVELT HIGH SCHOOL GYMNASIUM...
I NEED YOU TO WAKE UP.
ERGGHH...
HURFF... WHAT TIME IS...
IT'S TIME FOR US TO HAVE A TALK.
...ALL 87 STUDENTS ATTENDING THE HOMECOMING DANCE WERE FOUND IN A CATATONIC STATE...
BUT FIRST, I WANTED TO RETURN THIS TO YOU.
BOY, WHA DA HELL YOU BEEN DOING WITH MY GUN?
ME, NOTHING, I DIDN'T DO ANYTHING WITH YOUR GUN.
...ALL ARE CURRENTLY IN STABLE CONDITION. THE INCIDENT REMAINS UNDER INVESTIGATION TONIGHT AS...

YOU GET THE HELL TA BED NOW.

NO.

NO? YOU DON'T SAY NO TO ME...

I SAID WE NEED TO TALK.

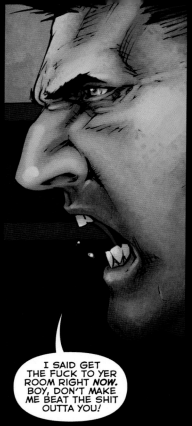

SEE THE THING IS, I REALLY WANT TO TALK.

HUKKKK!

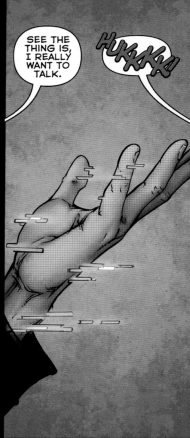

I SAID GET THE FUCK TO YER ROOM RIGHT *NOW*. BOY, DON'T MAKE ME BEAT THE SHIT OUTTA YOU!

I WANNA TELL YOU THAT I UNDERSTAND WHAT YOU HAVE BEEN TRYING TO TELL ME IN YOUR OWN WAY. THAT I HAVE BEEN WEAK.

THAT I HAVE TAKEN WEAK POSITION IN MY LIFE. THAT EVERYBODY TAKES ADVANTAGE OF THE WEAK. ALL YOU WANTED WAS FOR ME TO BE STRONG.

TO BE A *MAN*. WHAT IS IT YOU USED TO SAY TO DO IN A FIGHT?

GRAB SOMETHING THAT BENDS...

...AND BEND IT IN THE OPPOSITE DIRECTION.

EEEARGGGHHHAAA!!

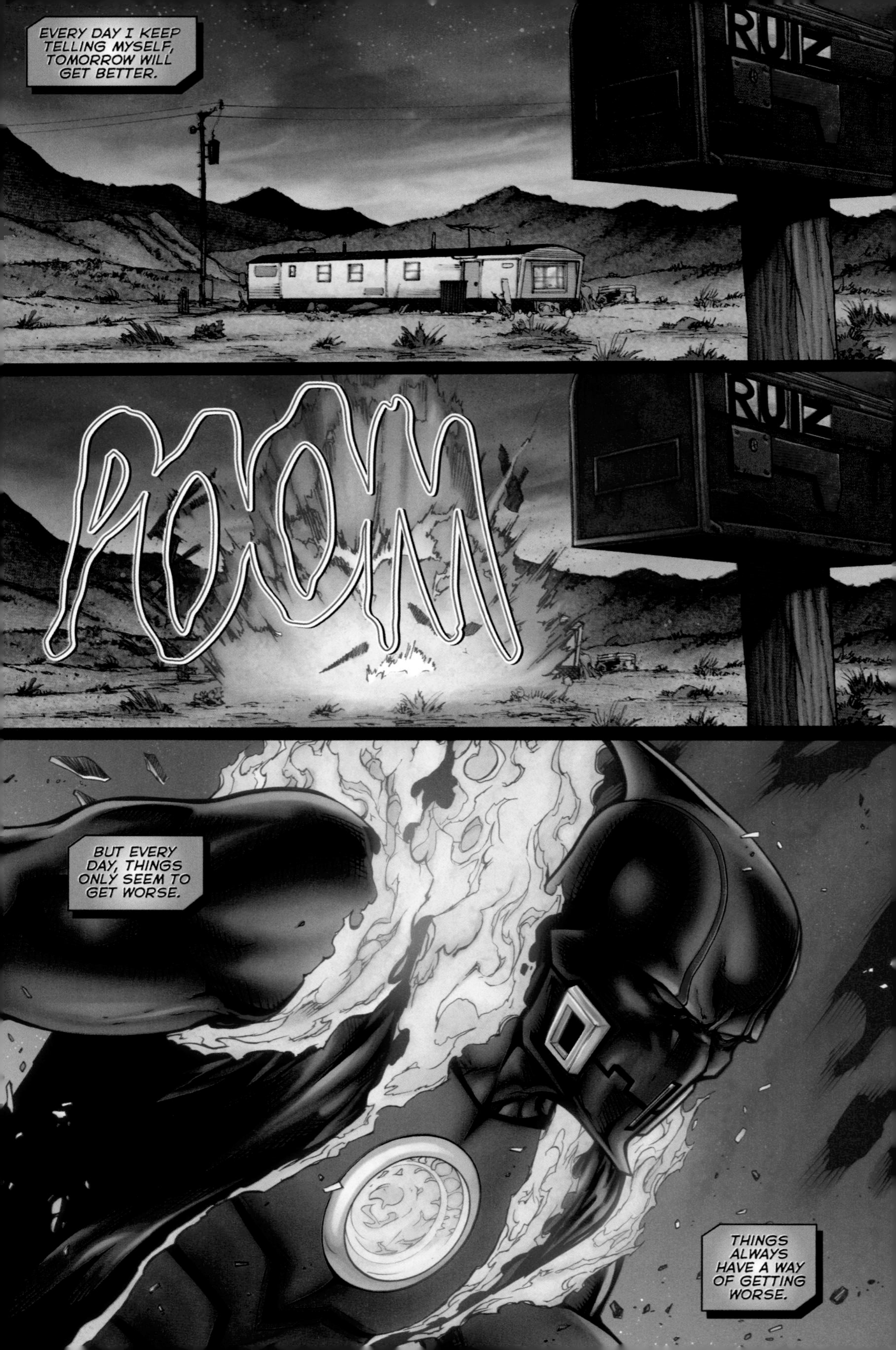
EVERY DAY I KEEP TELLING MYSELF, TOMORROW WILL GET BETTER.
RUIZ
BOOM
RUIZ
BUT EVERY DAY, THINGS ONLY SEEM TO GET WORSE.
THINGS ALWAYS HAVE A WAY OF GETTING WORSE.

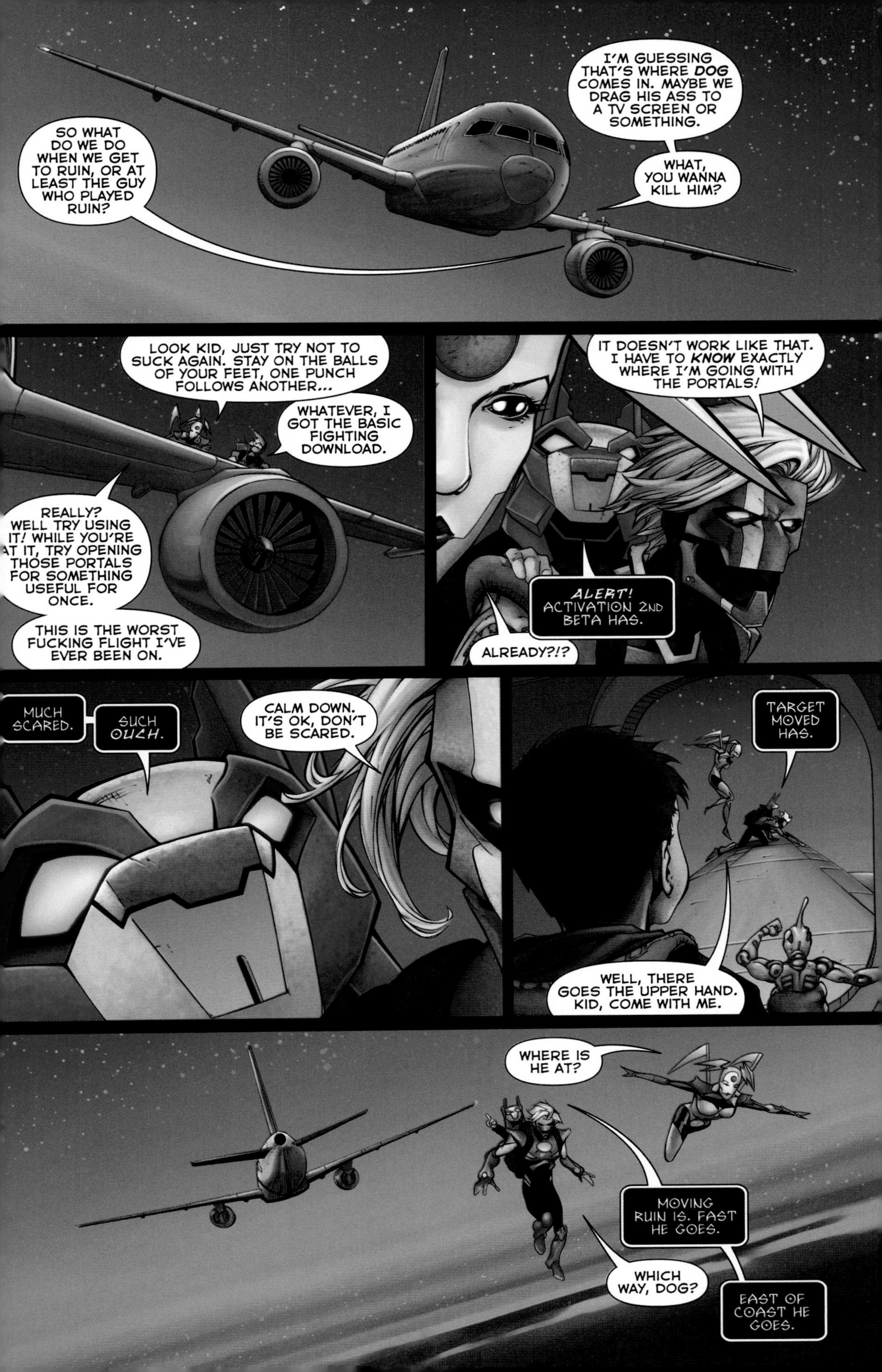
SO WHAT DO WE DO WHEN WE GET TO RUIN, OR AT LEAST THE GUY WHO PLAYED RUIN?
I'M GUESSING THAT'S WHERE DOG COMES IN. MAYBE WE DRAG HIS ASS TO A TV SCREEN OR SOMETHING.
WHAT, YOU WANNA KILL HIM?
LOOK KID, JUST TRY NOT TO SUCK AGAIN. STAY ON THE BALLS OF YOUR FEET, ONE PUNCH FOLLOWS ANOTHER...
WHATEVER, I GOT THE BASIC FIGHTING DOWNLOAD.
REALLY? WELL TRY USING IT! WHILE YOU'RE AT IT, TRY OPENING THOSE PORTALS FOR SOMETHING USEFUL FOR ONCE.
THIS IS THE WORST FUCKING FLIGHT I'VE EVER BEEN ON.
IT DOESN'T WORK LIKE THAT. I HAVE TO KNOW EXACTLY WHERE I'M GOING WITH THE PORTALS!
ALERT! ACTIVATION 2ND BETA HAS.
ALREADY?!?
MUCH SCARED.
SUCH OUCH.
CALM DOWN. IT'S OK, DON'T BE SCARED.
TARGET MOVED HAS.
WELL, THERE GOES THE UPPER HAND. KID, COME WITH ME.
WHERE IS HE AT?
MOVING RUIN IS. FAST HE GOES.
WHICH WAY, DOG?
EAST OF COAST HE GOES.

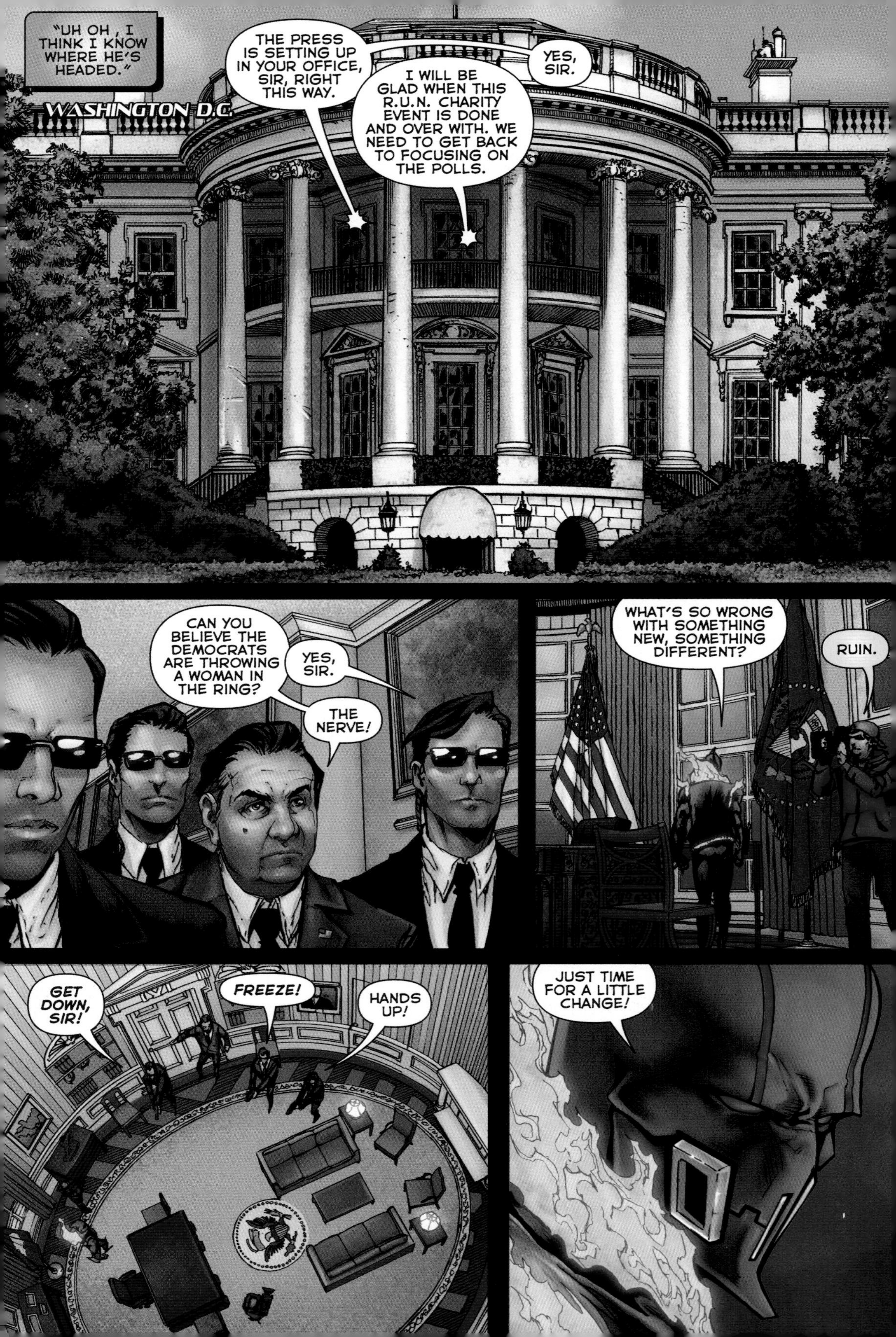
"UH OH, I THINK I KNOW WHERE HE'S HEADED."
WASHINGTON D.C.
THE PRESS IS SETTING UP IN YOUR OFFICE, SIR, RIGHT THIS WAY.
YES, SIR.
I WILL BE GLAD WHEN THIS R.U.N. CHARITY EVENT IS DONE AND OVER WITH. WE NEED TO GET BACK TO FOCUSING ON THE POLLS.
CAN YOU BELIEVE THE DEMOCRATS ARE THROWING A WOMAN IN THE RING?
YES, SIR.
THE NERVE!
WHAT'S SO WRONG WITH SOMETHING NEW, SOMETHING DIFFERENT?
RUIN.
GET DOWN, SIR!
FREEZE!
HANDS UP!
JUST TIME FOR A LITTLE CHANGE!

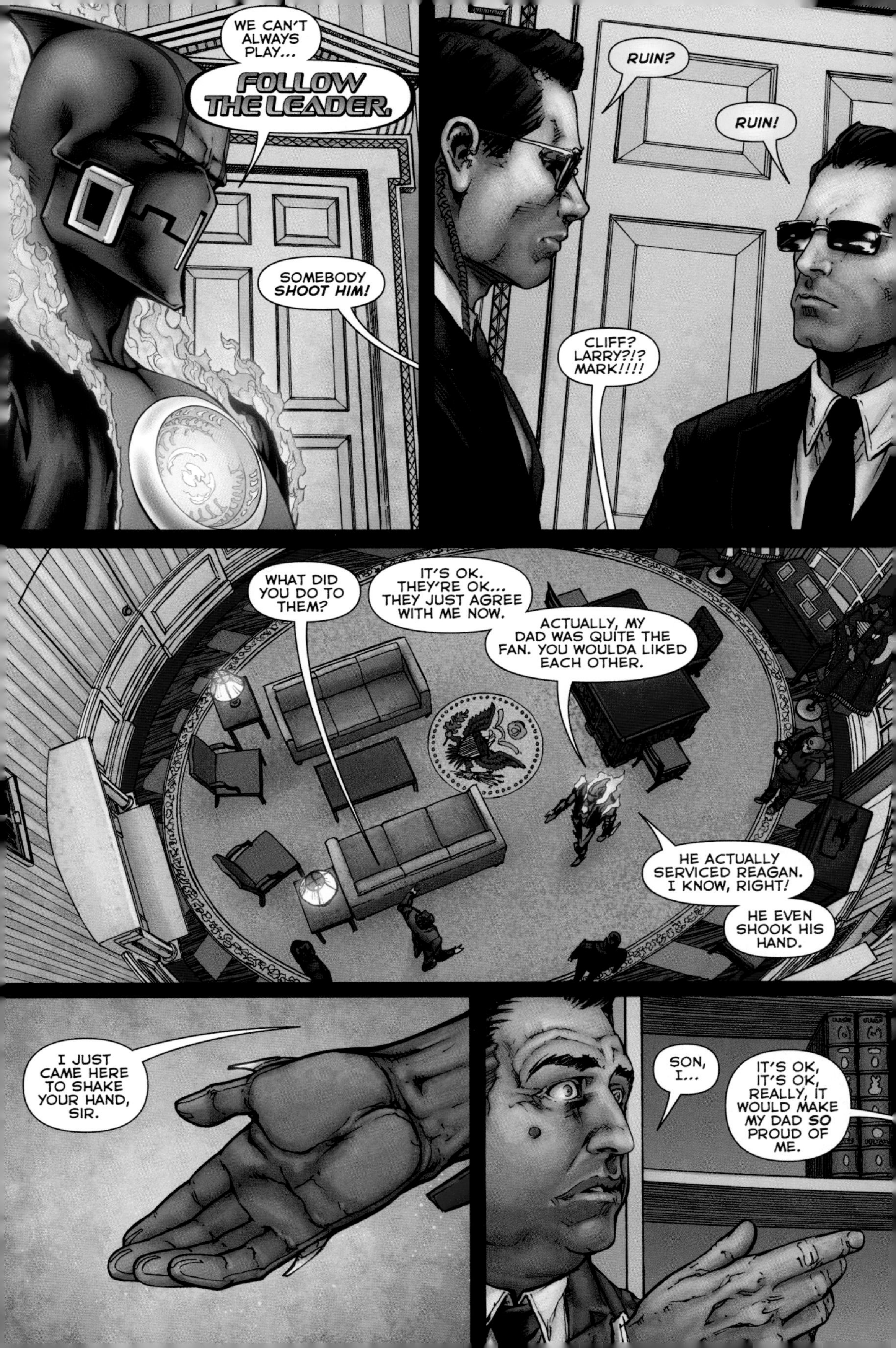
WE CAN'T ALWAYS PLAY...
FOLLOW THE LEADER.
SOMEBODY SHOOT HIM!
RUIN?
RUIN!
CLIFF? LARRY?!? MARK!!!!
WHAT DID YOU DO TO THEM?
IT'S OK. THEY'RE OK... THEY JUST AGREE WITH ME NOW.
ACTUALLY, MY DAD WAS QUITE THE FAN. YOU WOULDA LIKED EACH OTHER.
HE ACTUALLY SERVICED REAGAN. I KNOW, RIGHT!
HE EVEN SHOOK HIS HAND.
I JUST CAME HERE TO SHAKE YOUR HAND, SIR.
SON, I...
IT'S OK, IT'S OK, REALLY, IT WOULD MAKE MY DAD SO PROUD OF ME.

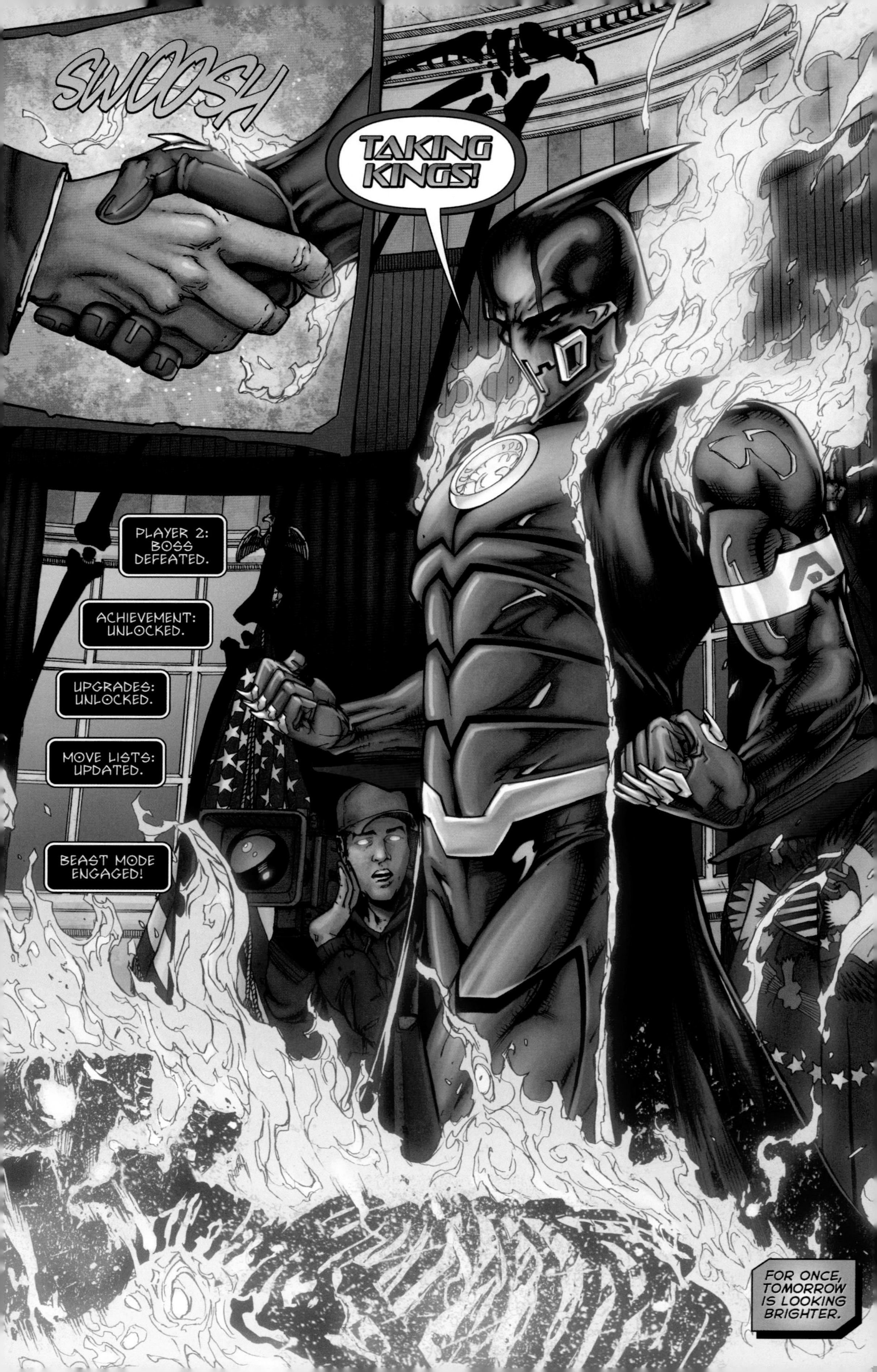
SWOOSH
TAKING KINGS!
PLAYER 2: BOSS DEFEATED.
ACHIEVEMENT: UNLOCKED.
UPGRADES: UNLOCKED.
MOVE LISTS: UPDATED.
BEAST MODE ENGAGED!
FOR ONCE, TOMORROW IS LOOKING BRIGHTER.

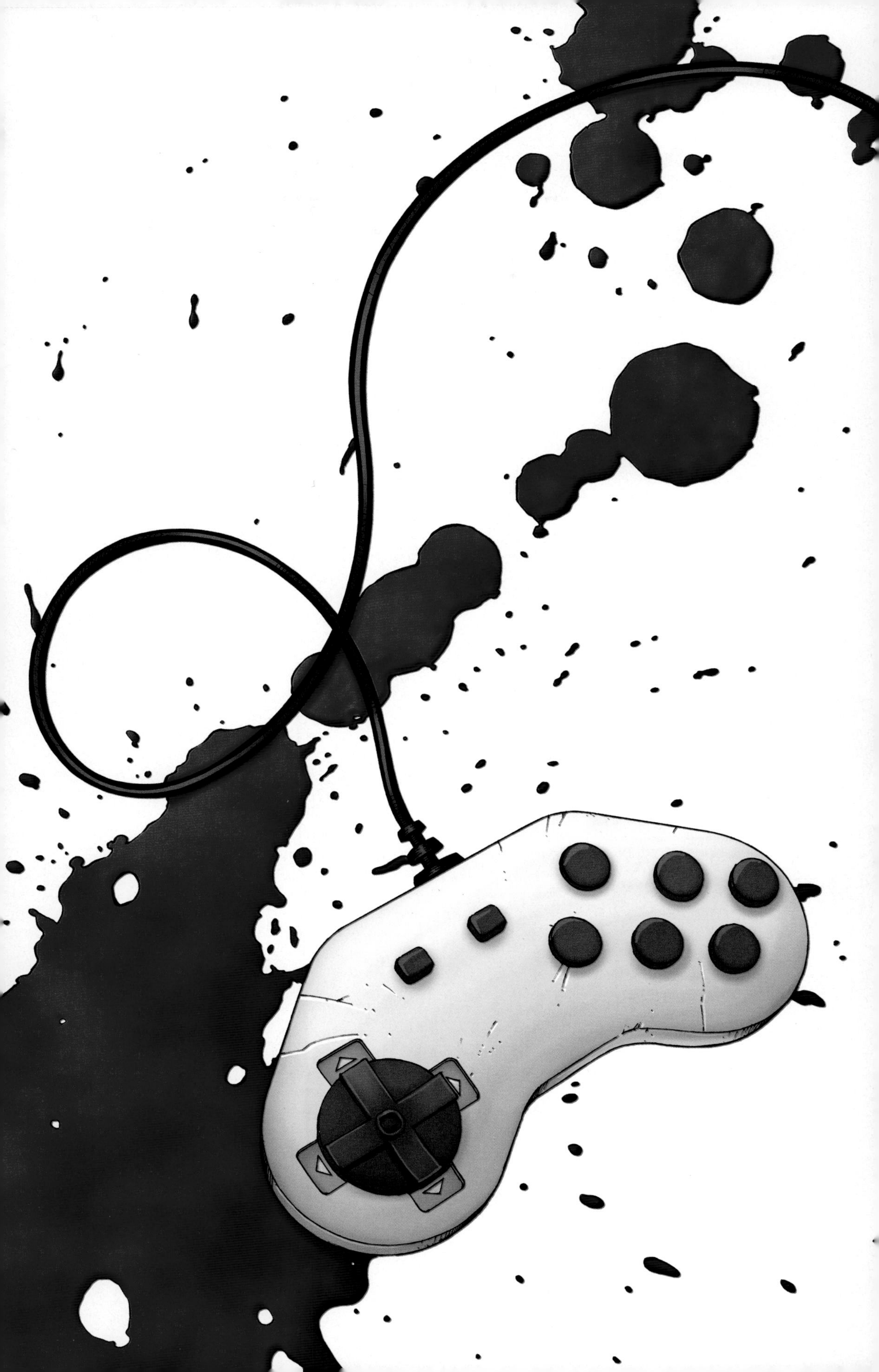

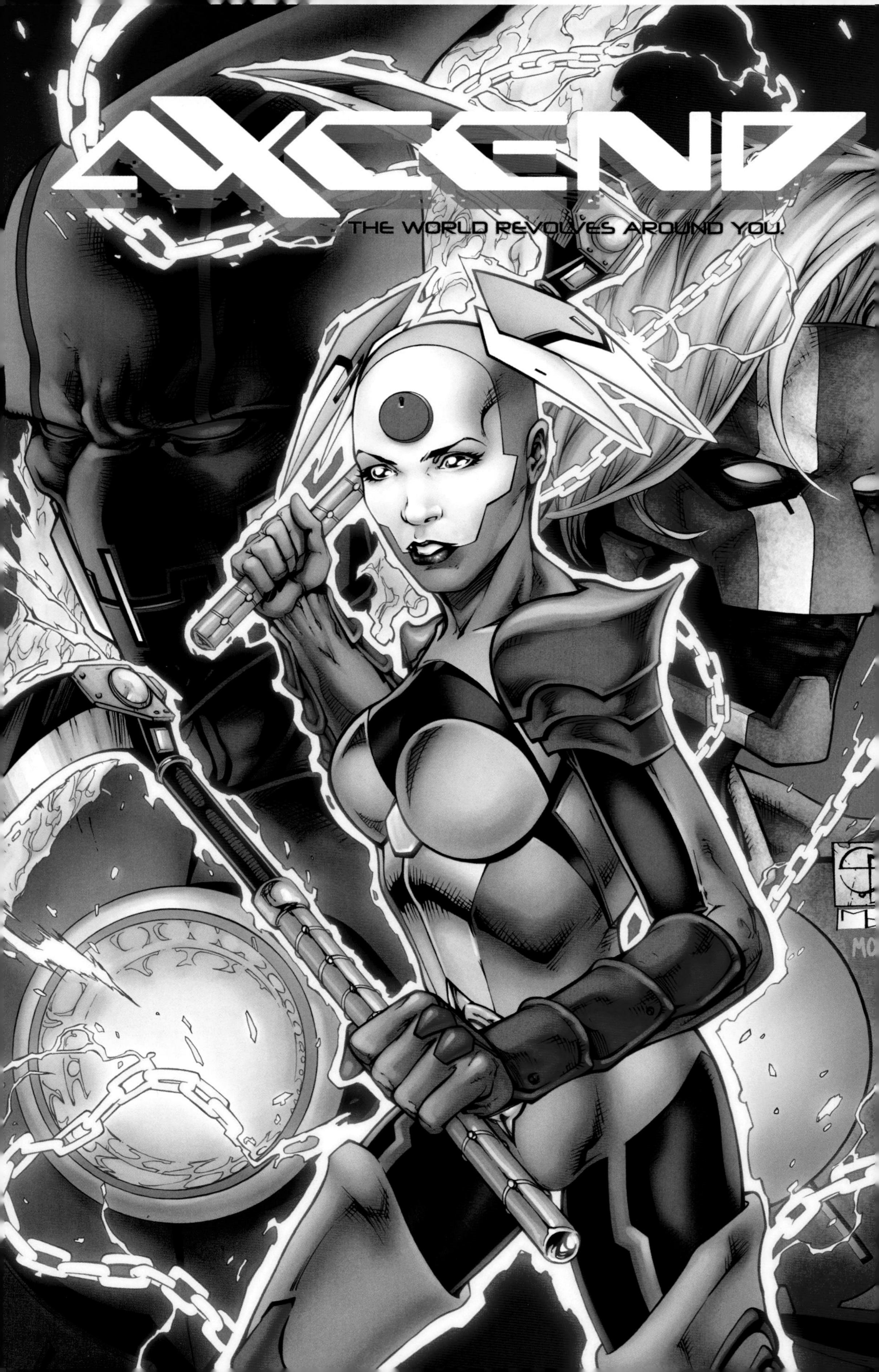
AXCEND
THE WORLD REVOLVES AROUND YOU.

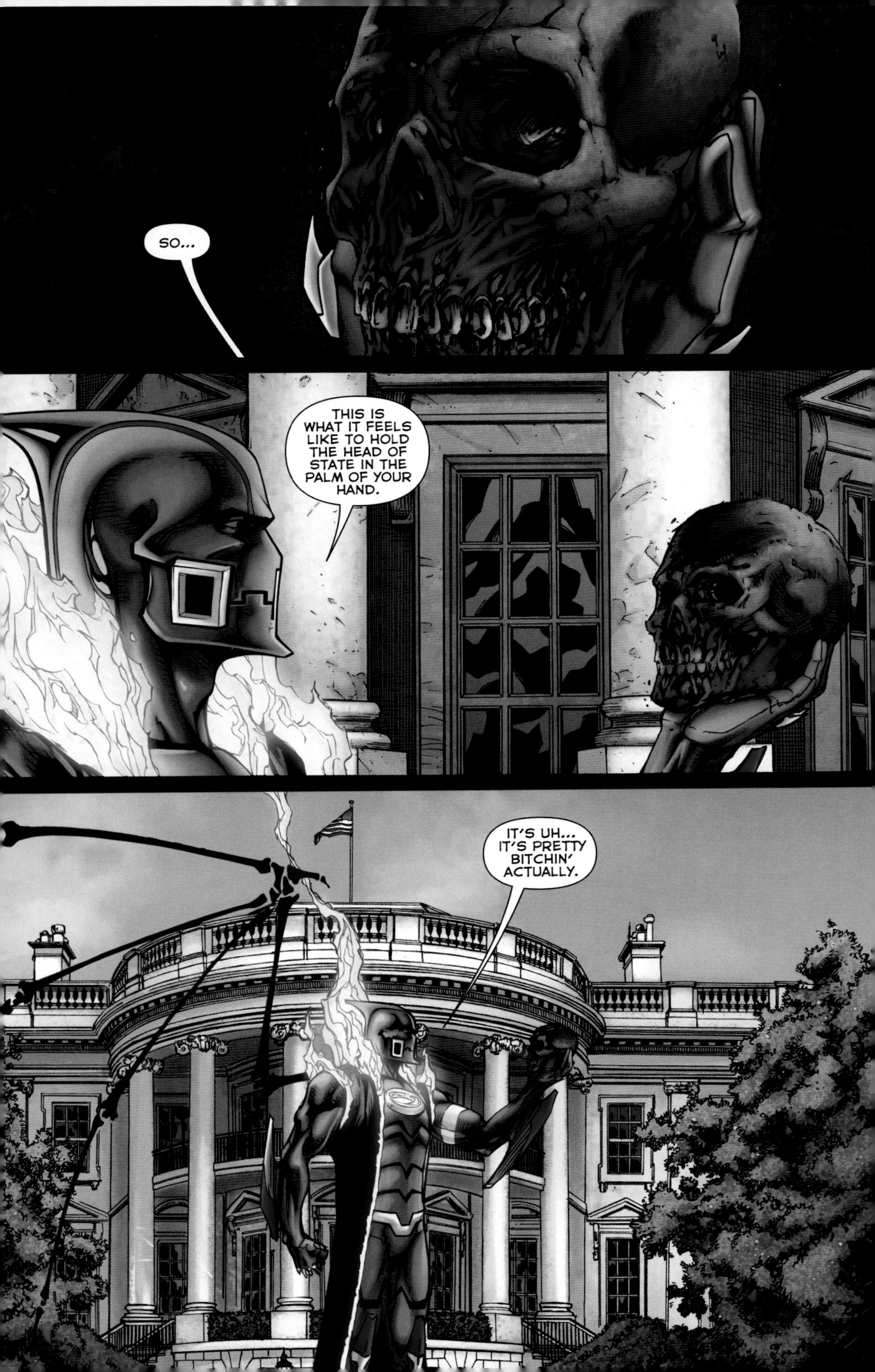
SO...
THIS IS WHAT IT FEELS LIKE TO HOLD THE HEAD OF STATE IN THE PALM OF YOUR HAND.
IT'S UH... IT'S PRETTY BITCHIN' ACTUALLY.

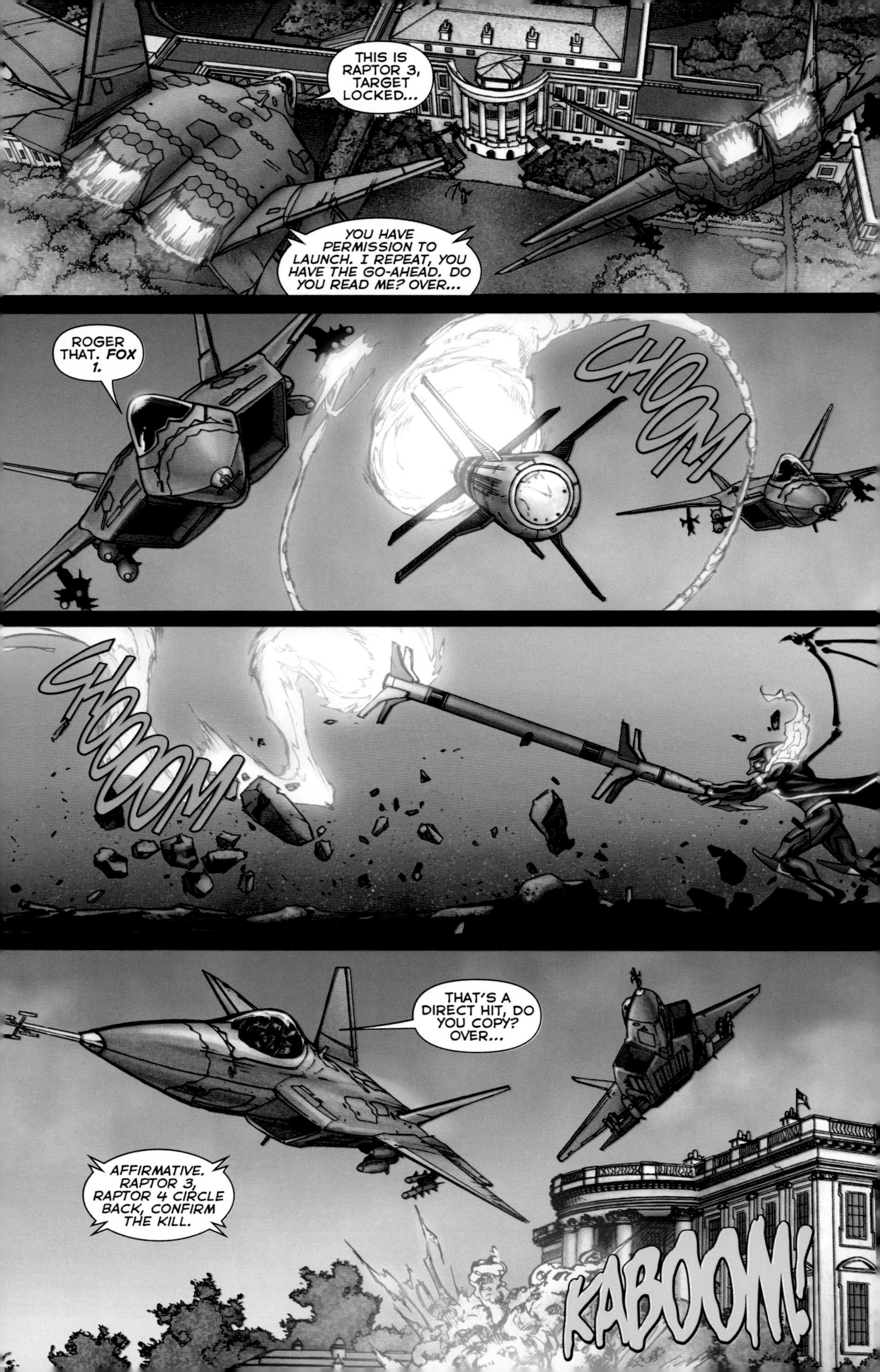
THIS IS RAPTOR 3, TARGET LOCKED...
YOU HAVE PERMISSION TO LAUNCH. I REPEAT, YOU HAVE THE GO-AHEAD. DO YOU READ ME? OVER...
ROGER THAT. *FOX 1.*
CHOOM
CHOOOOM
THAT'S A DIRECT HIT, DO YOU COPY? OVER...
AFFIRMATIVE. RAPTOR 3, RAPTOR 4 CIRCLE BACK, CONFIRM THE KILL.
KABOOM!

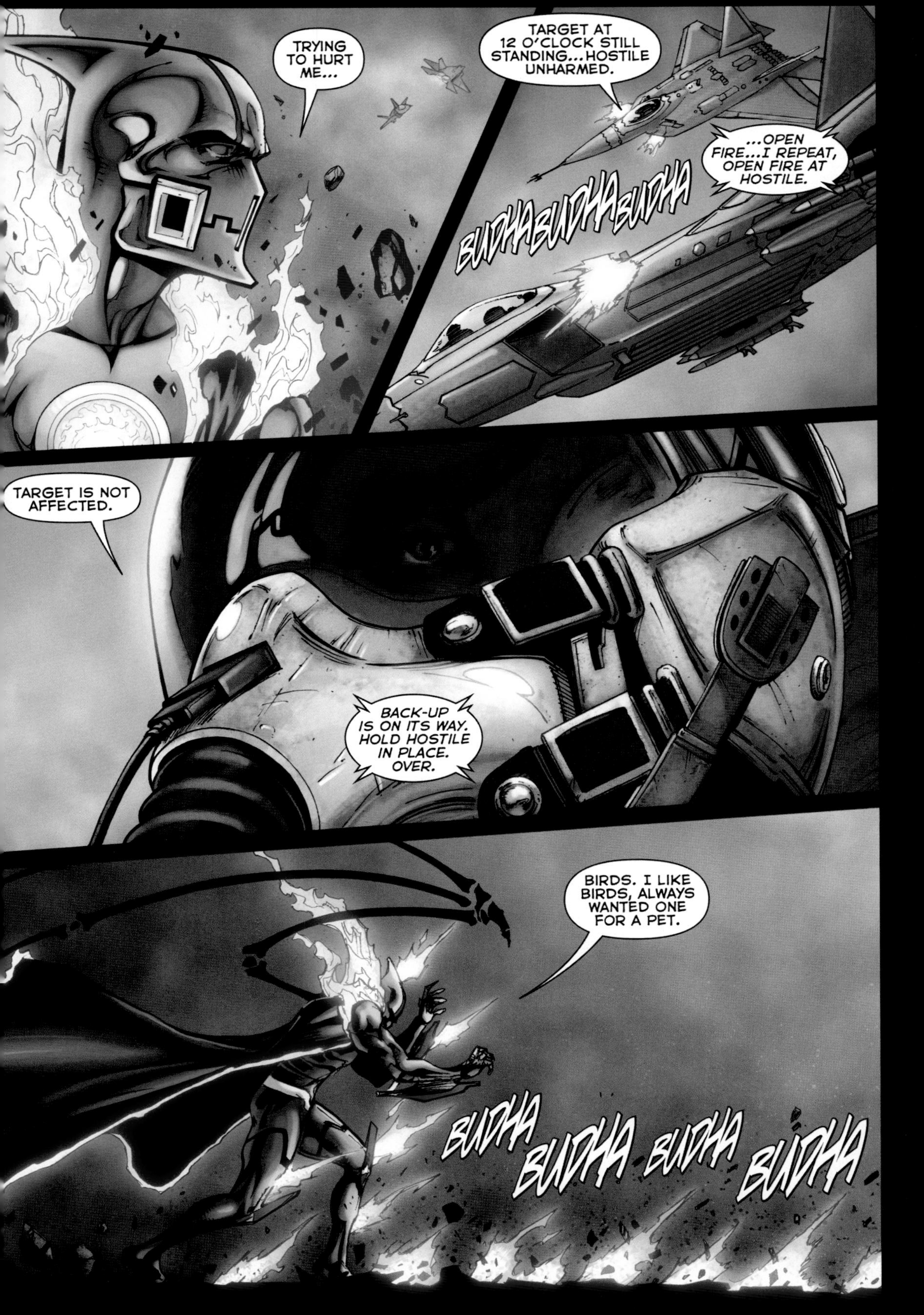
TRYING TO HURT ME...
TARGET AT 12 O'CLOCK STILL STANDING...HOSTILE UNHARMED.
...OPEN FIRE...I REPEAT, OPEN FIRE AT HOSTILE.
BUDHABUDHABUDHA
TARGET IS NOT AFFECTED.
BACK-UP IS ON ITS WAY. HOLD HOSTILE IN PLACE. OVER.
BIRDS. I LIKE BIRDS, ALWAYS WANTED ONE FOR A PET.
BUDHA BUDHA BUDHA BUDHA

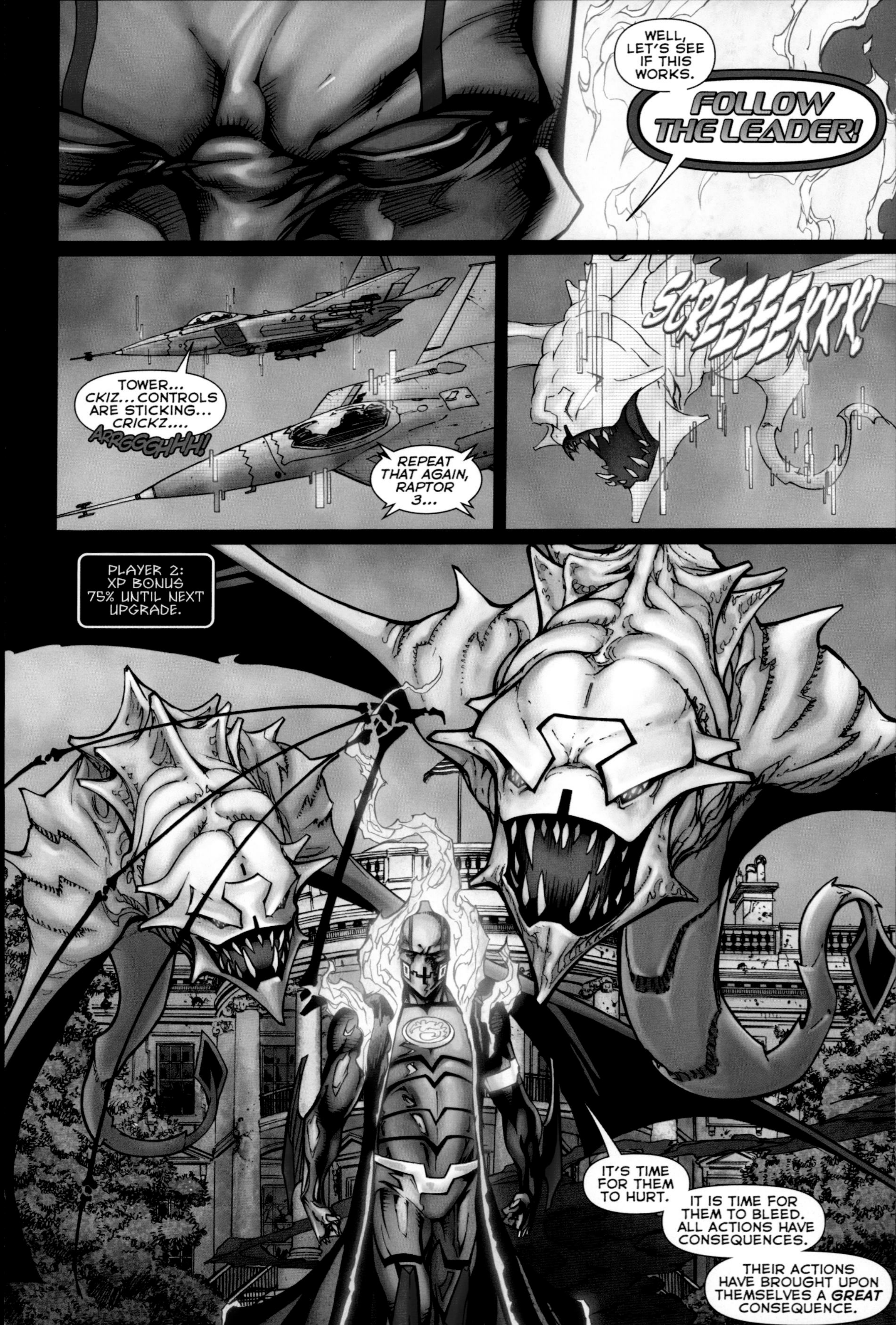
WELL, LET'S SEE IF THIS WORKS.
FOLLOW THE LEADER!
TOWER... CKIZ...CONTROLS ARE STICKING... CRICKZ.... ARRGGGHHH!
REPEAT THAT AGAIN, RAPTOR 3...
SCREEEEEKKK!
PLAYER 2: XP BONUS 75% UNTIL NEXT UPGRADE.
IT'S TIME FOR THEM TO HURT.
IT IS TIME FOR THEM TO BLEED. ALL ACTIONS HAVE CONSEQUENCES.
THEIR ACTIONS HAVE BROUGHT UPON THEMSELVES A GREAT CONSEQUENCE.

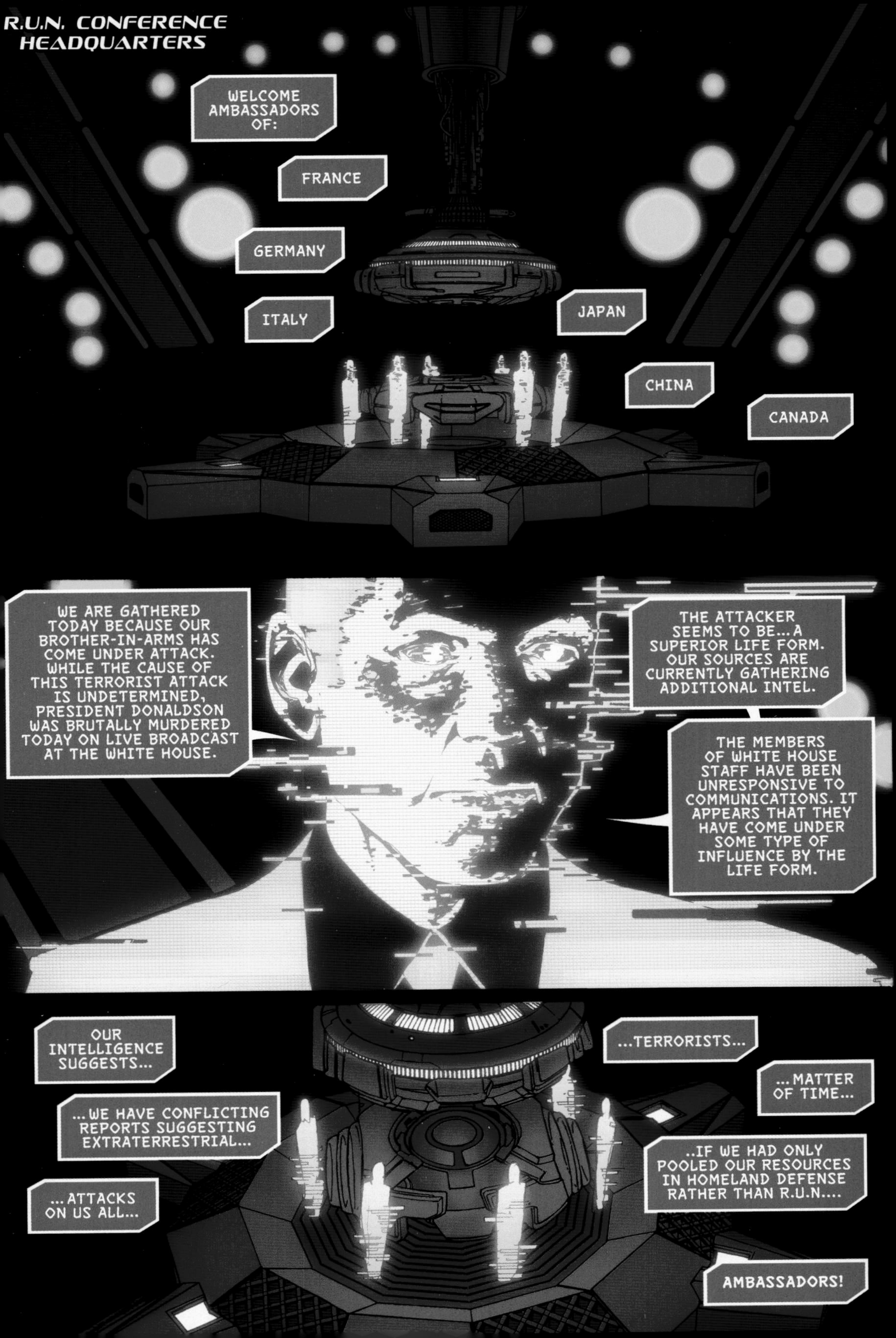
R.U.N. CONFERENCE HEADQUARTERS
WELCOME AMBASSADORS OF:
FRANCE
GERMANY
ITALY
JAPAN
CHINA
CANADA
WE ARE GATHERED TODAY BECAUSE OUR BROTHER-IN-ARMS HAS COME UNDER ATTACK. WHILE THE CAUSE OF THIS TERRORIST ATTACK IS UNDETERMINED, PRESIDENT DONALDSON WAS BRUTALLY MURDERED TODAY ON LIVE BROADCAST AT THE WHITE HOUSE.
THE ATTACKER SEEMS TO BE... A SUPERIOR LIFE FORM. OUR SOURCES ARE CURRENTLY GATHERING ADDITIONAL INTEL.
THE MEMBERS OF WHITE HOUSE STAFF HAVE BEEN UNRESPONSIVE TO COMMUNICATIONS. IT APPEARS THAT THEY HAVE COME UNDER SOME TYPE OF INFLUENCE BY THE LIFE FORM.
OUR INTELLIGENCE SUGGESTS...
...WE HAVE CONFLICTING REPORTS SUGGESTING EXTRATERRESTRIAL...
...ATTACKS ON US ALL...
...TERRORISTS...
...MATTER OF TIME...
..IF WE HAD ONLY POOLED OUR RESOURCES IN HOMELAND DEFENSE RATHER THAN R.U.N....
AMBASSADORS!

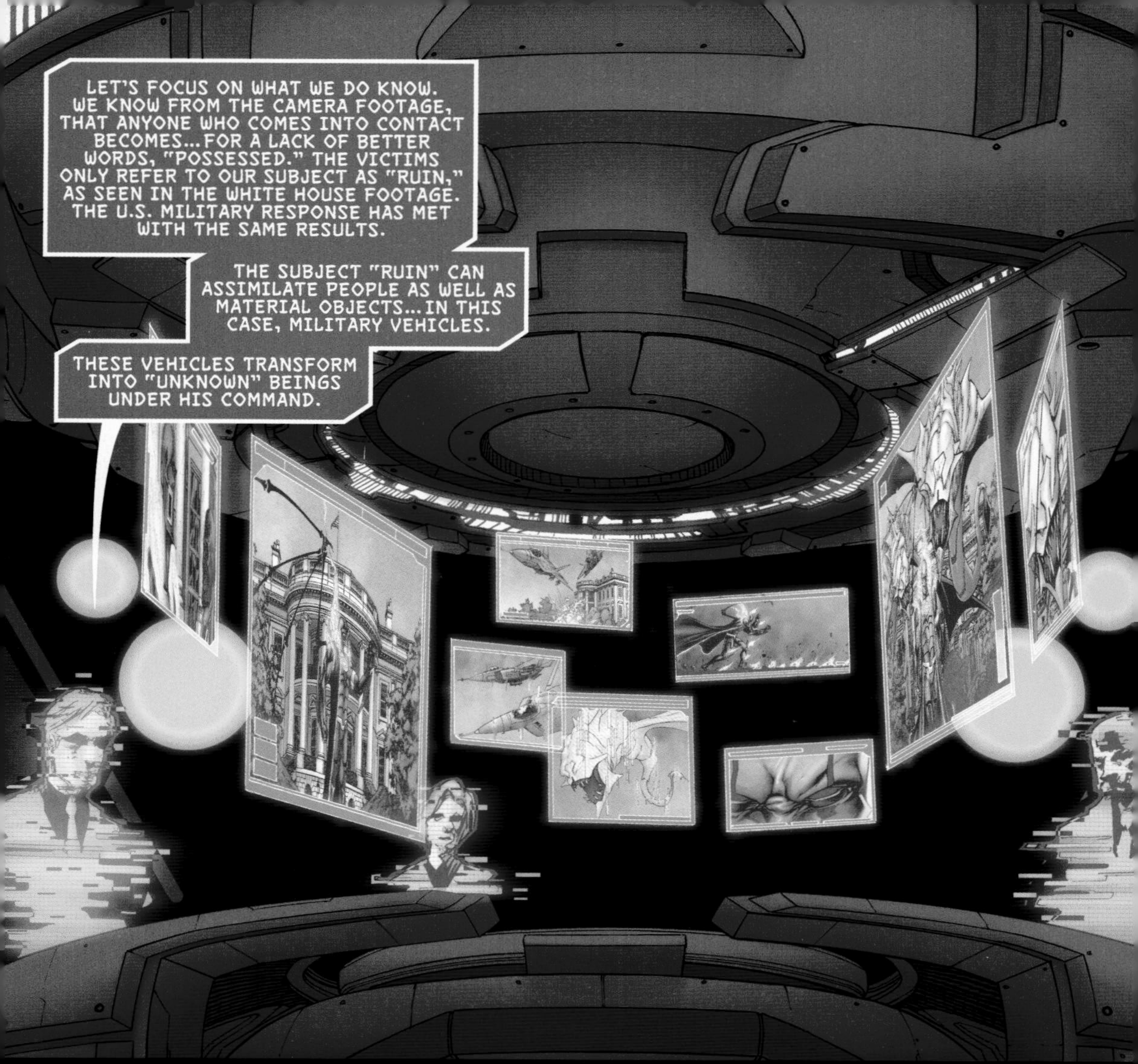
LET'S FOCUS ON WHAT WE DO KNOW. WE KNOW FROM THE CAMERA FOOTAGE, THAT ANYONE WHO COMES INTO CONTACT BECOMES...FOR A LACK OF BETTER WORDS, "POSSESSED." THE VICTIMS ONLY REFER TO OUR SUBJECT AS "RUIN," AS SEEN IN THE WHITE HOUSE FOOTAGE. THE U.S. MILITARY RESPONSE HAS MET WITH THE SAME RESULTS.
THE SUBJECT "RUIN" CAN ASSIMILATE PEOPLE AS WELL AS MATERIAL OBJECTS...IN THIS CASE, MILITARY VEHICLES.
THESE VEHICLES TRANSFORM INTO "UNKNOWN" BEINGS UNDER HIS COMMAND.

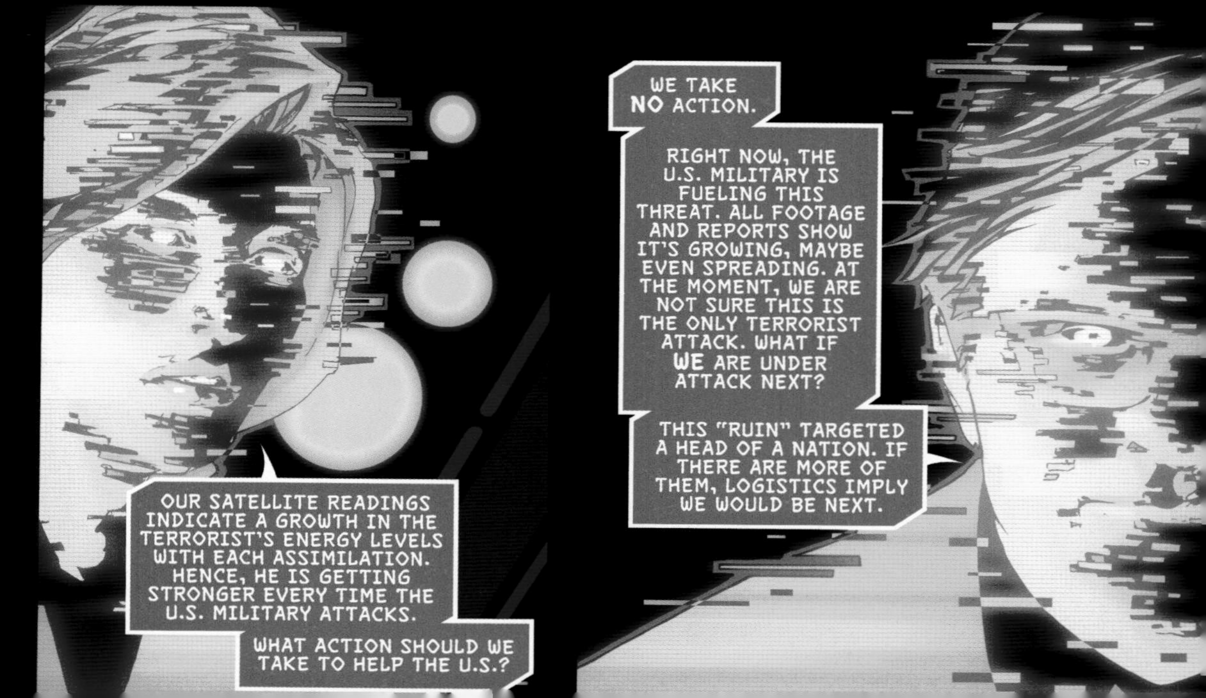
OUR SATELLITE READINGS INDICATE A GROWTH IN THE TERRORIST'S ENERGY LEVELS WITH EACH ASSIMILATION. HENCE, HE IS GETTING STRONGER EVERY TIME THE U.S. MILITARY ATTACKS.
WHAT ACTION SHOULD WE TAKE TO HELP THE U.S.?
WE TAKE **NO** ACTION.
RIGHT NOW, THE U.S. MILITARY IS FUELING THIS THREAT. ALL FOOTAGE AND REPORTS SHOW IT'S GROWING, MAYBE EVEN SPREADING. AT THE MOMENT, WE ARE NOT SURE THIS IS THE ONLY TERRORIST ATTACK. WHAT IF **WE** ARE UNDER ATTACK NEXT?
THIS "RUIN" TARGETED A HEAD OF A NATION. IF THERE ARE MORE OF THEM, LOGISTICS IMPLY WE WOULD BE NEXT.

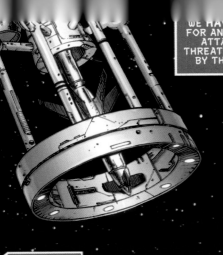

WE **HAVE** TO PLAN FOR AN IMPENDING ATTACK. THIS THREAT IS GROWING BY THE MINUTE.

WHAT ARE YOU SUGGESTING WE DO?

R.U.N. WAS FORMED BY 7 NATIONS TO POLICE GLOBAL THREATS. IT'S LIKELY WE MAY BE LOOKING AT ONE RIGHT NOW. IT MAY BE TIME TO TAKE A VOTE.

LUDICROUS!

...ARE YOU INSANE? YOU'RE GOING TO ANNIHILATE 150 MILLION AMERICANS! YOU'LL WIPE THE U.S. OFF THE MAP!

...**YOU**... YOU NEVER AGREED WITH AMERICA. ARE WE SUPPOSED TO AGREE WITH **YOU** NOW?...

WAIT, WE CAN TRY HITTING IT AT ALL ANGLES WITH GROUND SUPPORT!

THAT'S MAKING THE THREAT STRONGER. HAVEN'T YOU PEOPLE BEEN LISTENING?

...WHAT DO YOU MEAN "**YOU** PEOPLE?!"

EXACTLY...

THE THREAT IS GROWING. I'M NOT STANDING BY, SO MY COUNTRY CAN FALL.

...YOU'RE SAYING THIS BECAUSE THE VOTE ON THE OIL TRADE DIDN'T GO YOUR WAY..

I ALSO SUGGEST...

WHAT? THAT WE TAKE A VOTE?

THE VOTE.

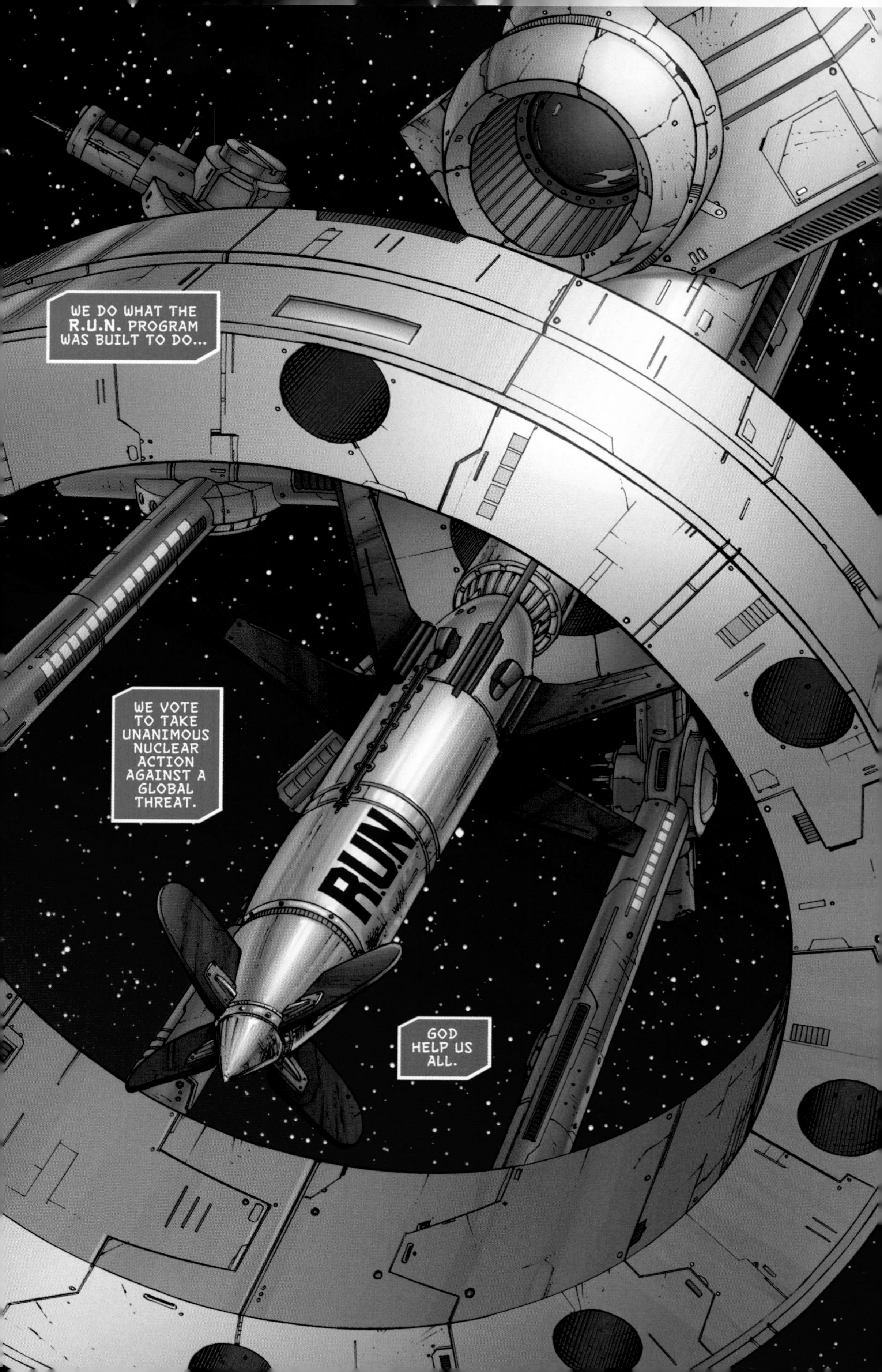
WE DO WHAT THE R.U.N. PROGRAM WAS BUILT TO DO...
WE VOTE TO TAKE UNANIMOUS NUCLEAR ACTION AGAINST A GLOBAL THREAT.
R.U.N.
GOD HELP US ALL.

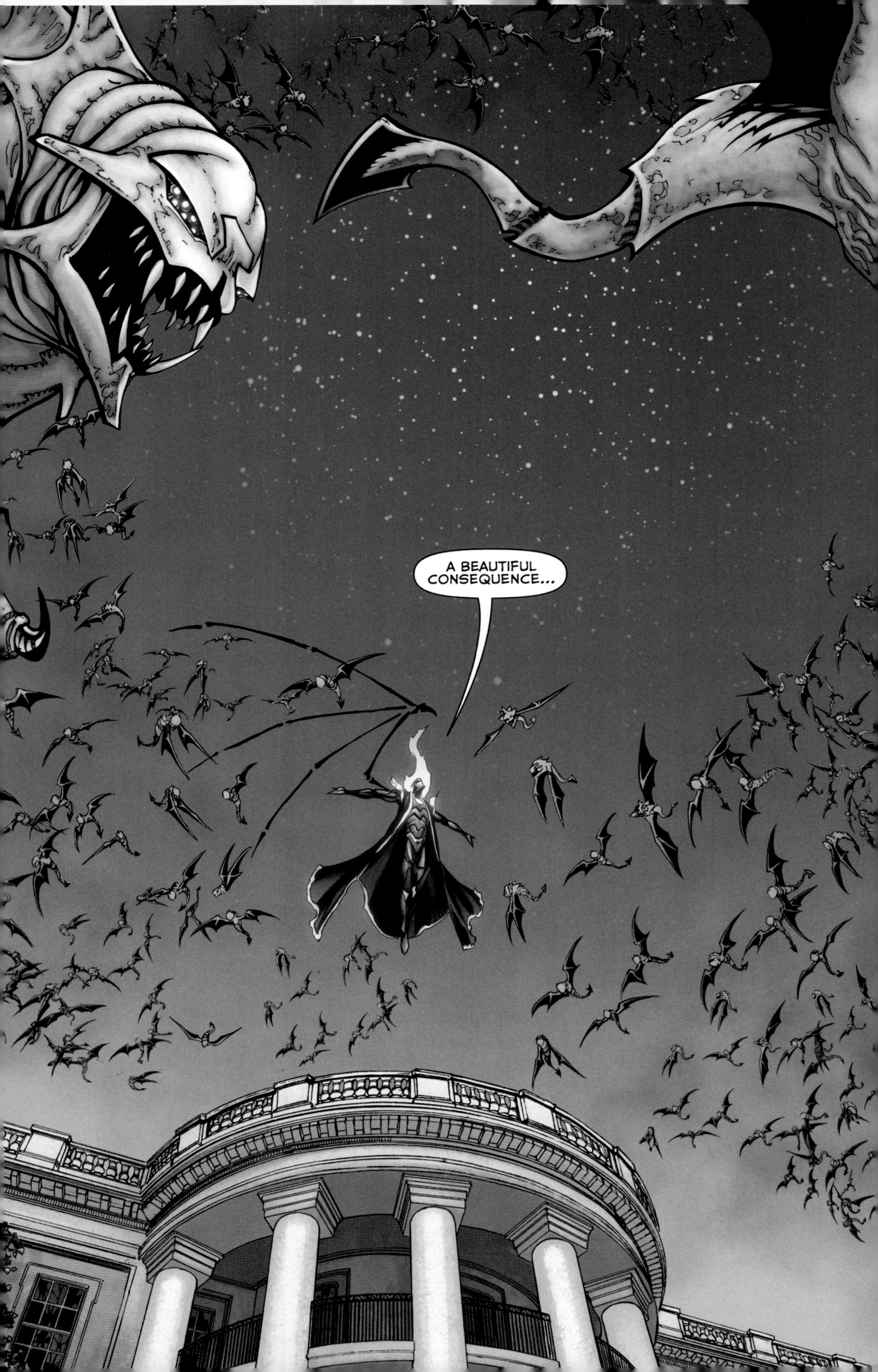
A BEAUTIFUL CONSEQUENCE...

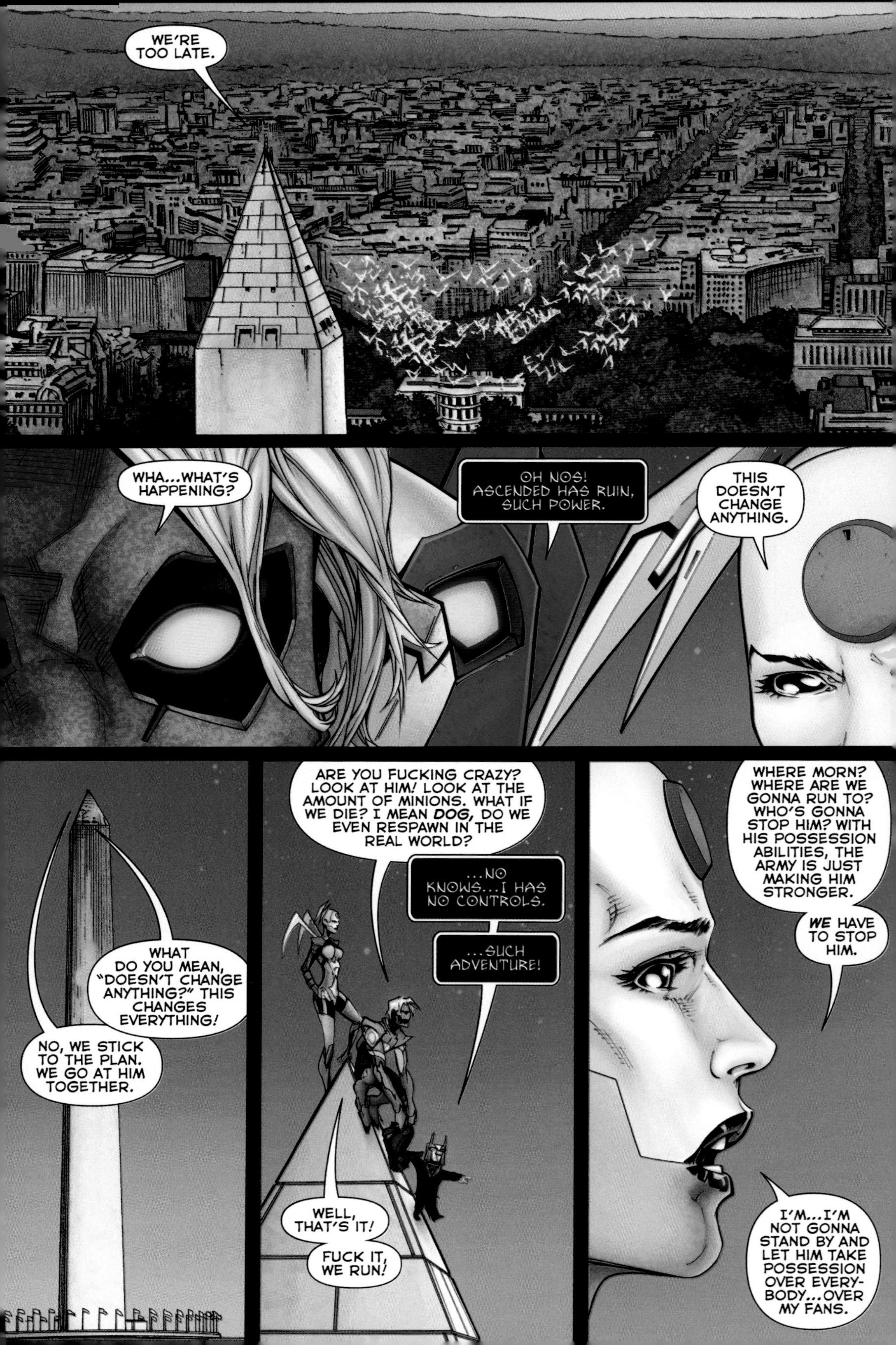
WE'RE TOO LATE.
WHA...WHAT'S HAPPENING?
OH NOS! ASCENDED HAS RUIN, SUCH POWER.
THIS DOESN'T CHANGE ANYTHING.
WHAT DO YOU MEAN, "DOESN'T CHANGE ANYTHING?" THIS CHANGES EVERYTHING!
NO, WE STICK TO THE PLAN. WE GO AT HIM TOGETHER.
ARE YOU FUCKING CRAZY? LOOK AT HIM! LOOK AT THE AMOUNT OF MINIONS. WHAT IF WE DIE? I MEAN DOG, DO WE EVEN RESPAWN IN THE REAL WORLD?
...NO KNOWS...I HAS NO CONTROLS.
...SUCH ADVENTURE!
WELL, THAT'S IT!
FUCK IT, WE RUN!
WHERE MORN? WHERE ARE WE GONNA RUN TO? WHO'S GONNA STOP HIM? WITH HIS POSSESSION ABILITIES, THE ARMY IS JUST MAKING HIM STRONGER.
WE HAVE TO STOP HIM.
I'M...I'M NOT GONNA STAND BY AND LET HIM TAKE POSSESSION OVER EVERY-BODY...OVER MY FANS.

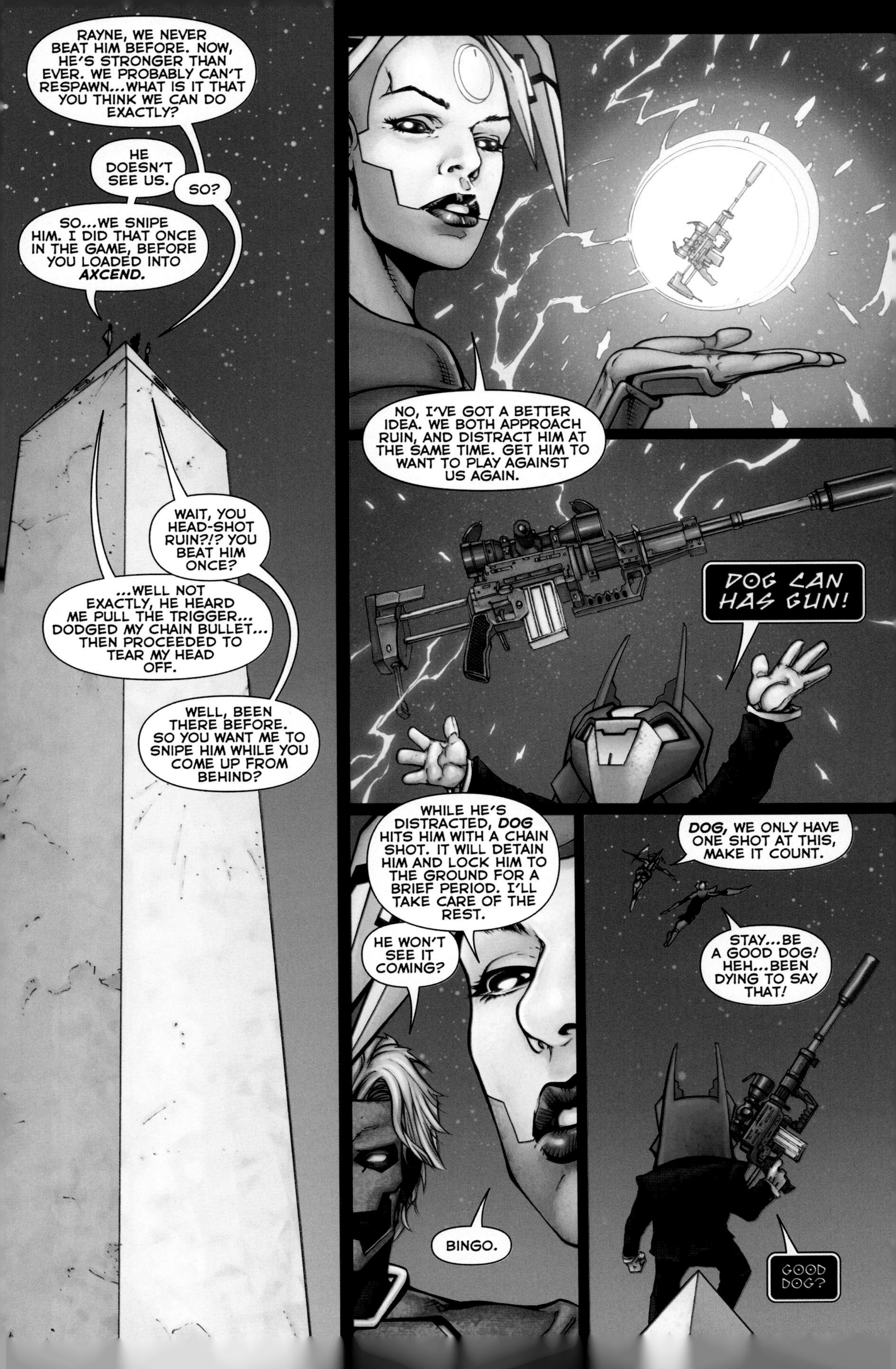
RAYNE, WE NEVER BEAT HIM BEFORE. NOW, HE'S STRONGER THAN EVER. WE PROBABLY CAN'T RESPAWN...WHAT IS IT THAT YOU THINK WE CAN DO EXACTLY?
HE DOESN'T SEE US.
SO?
SO...WE SNIPE HIM. I DID THAT ONCE IN THE GAME, BEFORE YOU LOADED INTO ***AXCEND.***
WAIT, YOU HEAD-SHOT RUIN?!? YOU BEAT HIM ONCE?
...WELL NOT EXACTLY, HE HEARD ME PULL THE TRIGGER... DODGED MY CHAIN BULLET... THEN PROCEEDED TO TEAR MY HEAD OFF.
WELL, BEEN THERE BEFORE. SO YOU WANT ME TO SNIPE HIM WHILE YOU COME UP FROM BEHIND?
NO, I'VE GOT A BETTER IDEA. WE BOTH APPROACH RUIN, AND DISTRACT HIM AT THE SAME TIME. GET HIM TO WANT TO PLAY AGAINST US AGAIN.
DOG CAN HAS GUN!
WHILE HE'S DISTRACTED, ***DOG*** HITS HIM WITH A CHAIN SHOT. IT WILL DETAIN HIM AND LOCK HIM TO THE GROUND FOR A BRIEF PERIOD. I'LL TAKE CARE OF THE REST.
HE WON'T SEE IT COMING?
BINGO.
DOG, WE ONLY HAVE ONE SHOT AT THIS, MAKE IT COUNT.
STAY...BE A GOOD DOG! HEH...BEEN DYING TO SAY THAT!
GOOD DOG?

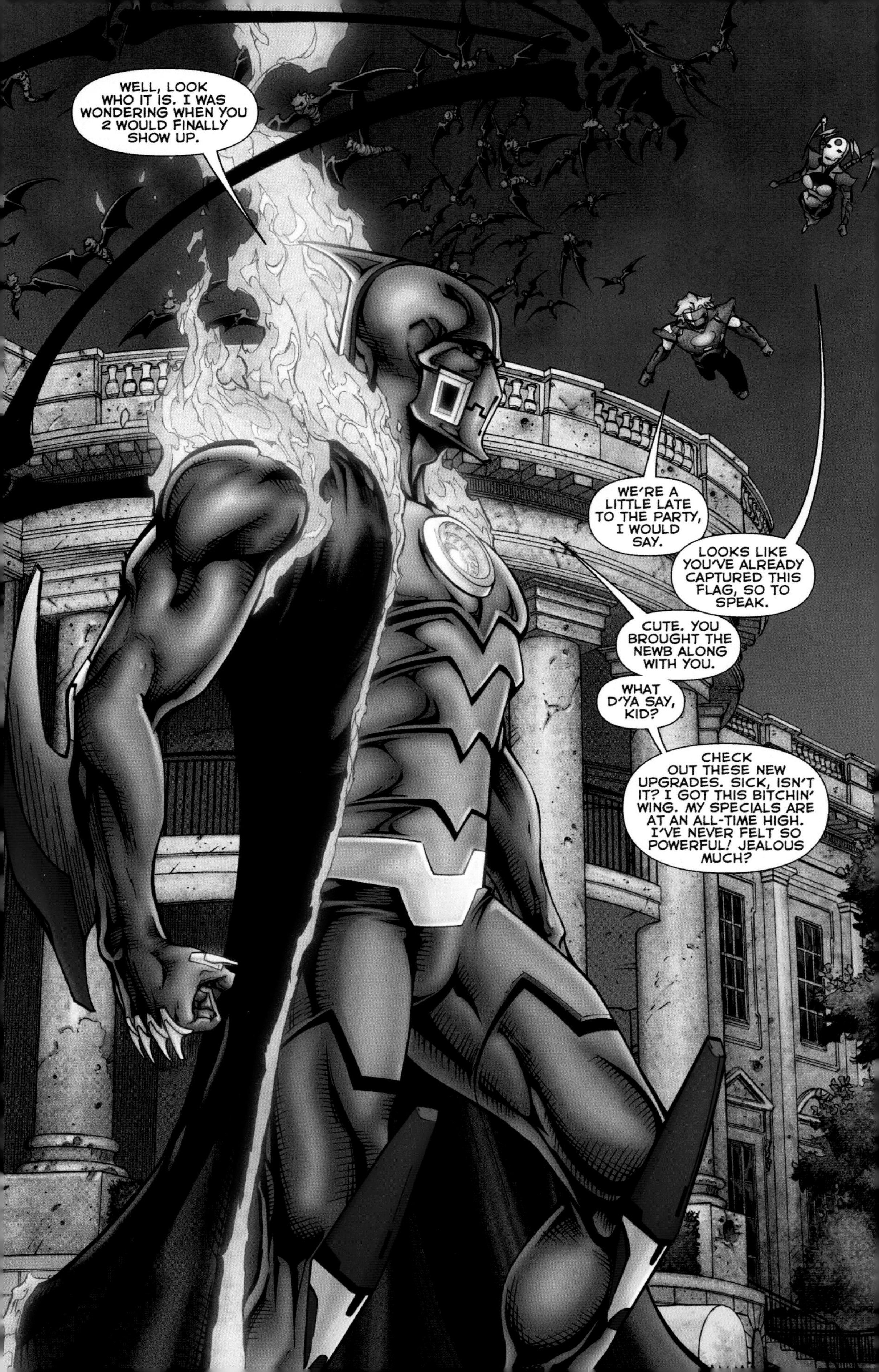
WELL, LOOK WHO IT IS. I WAS WONDERING WHEN YOU 2 WOULD FINALLY SHOW UP.
WE'RE A LITTLE LATE TO THE PARTY, I WOULD SAY.
LOOKS LIKE YOU'VE ALREADY CAPTURED THIS FLAG, SO TO SPEAK.
CUTE. YOU BROUGHT THE NEWB ALONG WITH YOU.
WHAT D'YA SAY, KID?
CHECK OUT THESE NEW UPGRADES. SICK, ISN'T IT? I GOT THIS BITCHIN' WING. MY SPECIALS ARE AT AN ALL-TIME HIGH. I'VE NEVER FELT SO POWERFUL! JEALOUS MUCH?

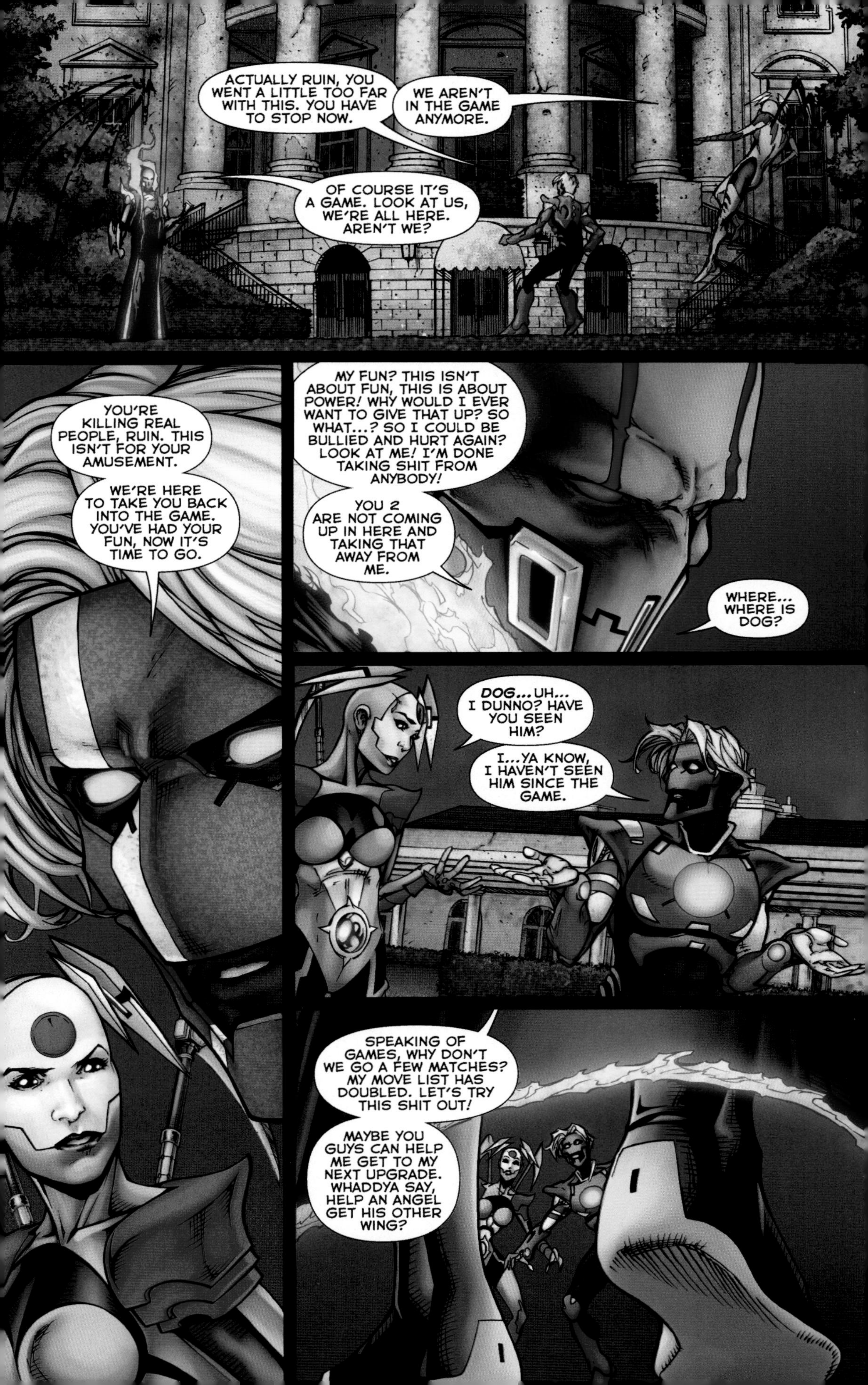
ACTUALLY RUIN, YOU WENT A LITTLE TOO FAR WITH THIS. YOU HAVE TO STOP NOW.
WE AREN'T IN THE GAME ANYMORE.
OF COURSE IT'S A GAME. LOOK AT US, WE'RE ALL HERE. AREN'T WE?
YOU'RE KILLING REAL PEOPLE, RUIN. THIS ISN'T FOR YOUR AMUSEMENT.
WE'RE HERE TO TAKE YOU BACK INTO THE GAME. YOU'VE HAD YOUR FUN, NOW IT'S TIME TO GO.
MY FUN? THIS ISN'T ABOUT FUN, THIS IS ABOUT POWER! WHY WOULD I EVER WANT TO GIVE THAT UP? SO WHAT...? SO I COULD BE BULLIED AND HURT AGAIN? LOOK AT ME! I'M DONE TAKING SHIT FROM ANYBODY!
YOU 2 ARE NOT COMING UP IN HERE AND TAKING THAT AWAY FROM ME.
WHERE... WHERE IS DOG?
DOG... UH... I DUNNO? HAVE YOU SEEN HIM?
I... YA KNOW, I HAVEN'T SEEN HIM SINCE THE GAME.
SPEAKING OF GAMES, WHY DON'T WE GO A FEW MATCHES? MY MOVE LIST HAS DOUBLED. LET'S TRY THIS SHIT OUT!
MAYBE YOU GUYS CAN HELP ME GET TO MY NEXT UPGRADE. WHADDYA SAY, HELP AN ANGEL GET HIS OTHER WING?

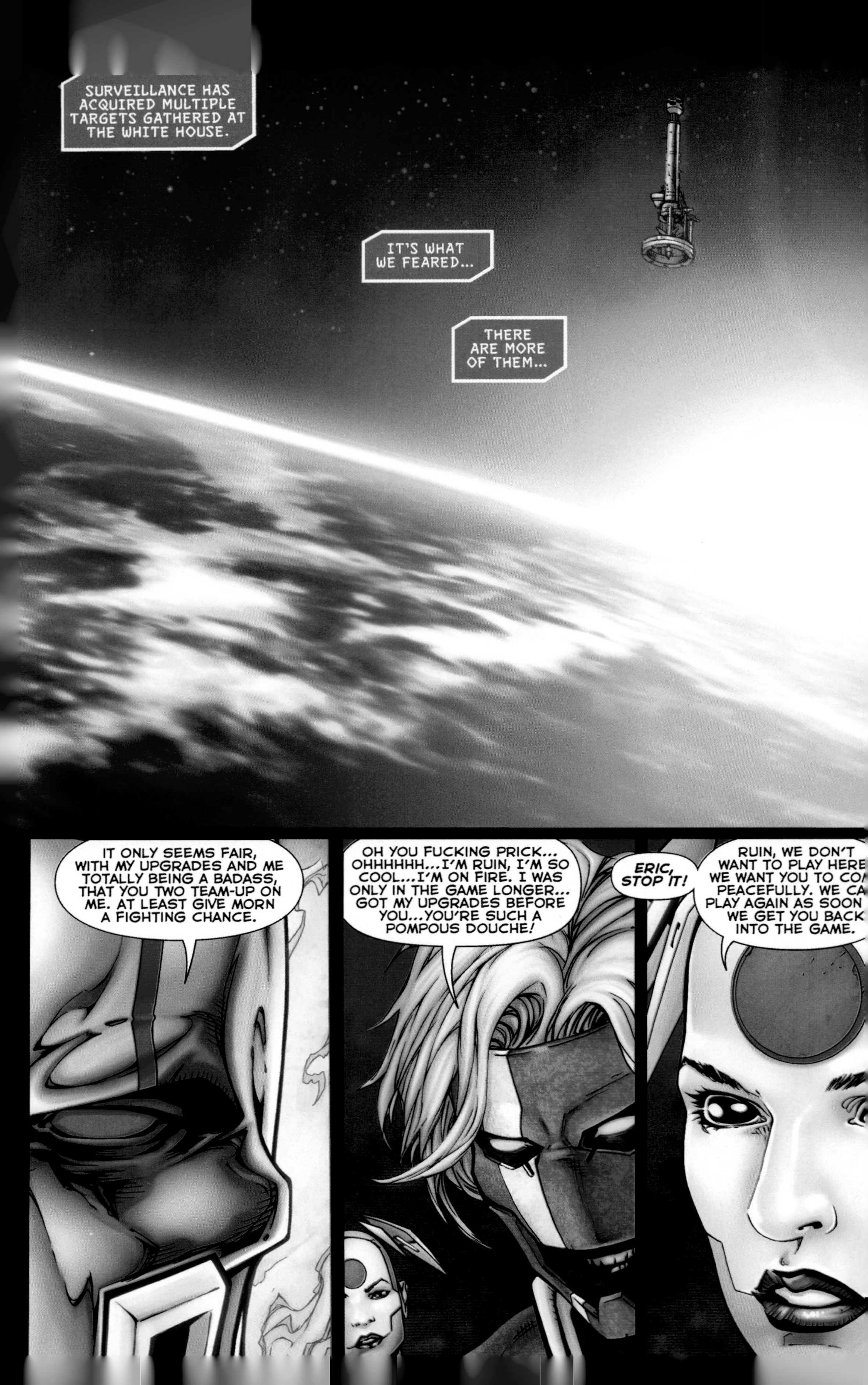
SURVEILLANCE HAS ACQUIRED MULTIPLE TARGETS GATHERED AT THE WHITE HOUSE.
IT'S WHAT WE FEARED...
THERE ARE MORE OF THEM...
IT ONLY SEEMS FAIR, WITH MY UPGRADES AND ME TOTALLY BEING A BADASS, THAT YOU TWO TEAM-UP ON ME. AT LEAST GIVE MORN A FIGHTING CHANCE.
OH YOU FUCKING PRICK... OHHHHHH...I'M RUIN, I'M SO COOL...I'M ON FIRE. I WAS ONLY IN THE GAME LONGER... GOT MY UPGRADES BEFORE YOU...YOU'RE SUCH A POMPOUS DOUCHE!
ERIC, STOP IT!
RUIN, WE DON'T WANT TO PLAY HERE WE WANT YOU TO CO PEACEFULLY. WE CA PLAY AGAIN AS SOON WE GET YOU BACK INTO THE GAME.

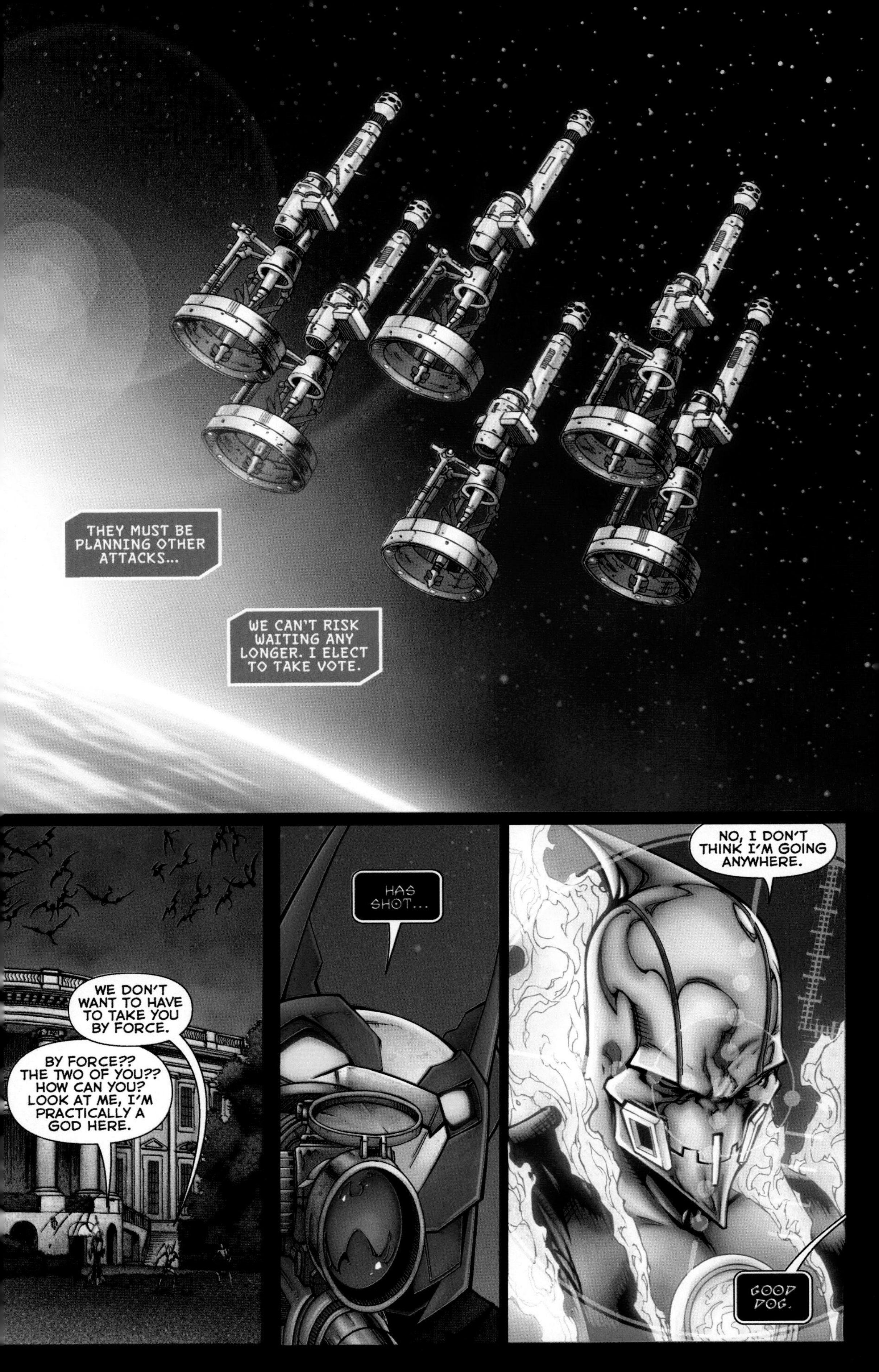
THEY MUST BE PLANNING OTHER ATTACKS...
WE CAN'T RISK WAITING ANY LONGER. I ELECT TO TAKE VOTE.
WE DON'T WANT TO HAVE TO TAKE YOU BY FORCE.
BY FORCE?? THE TWO OF YOU?? HOW CAN YOU? LOOK AT ME, I'M PRACTICALLY A GOD HERE.
HAS SHOT...
NO, I DON'T THINK I'M GOING ANYWHERE.
GOOD DOG.

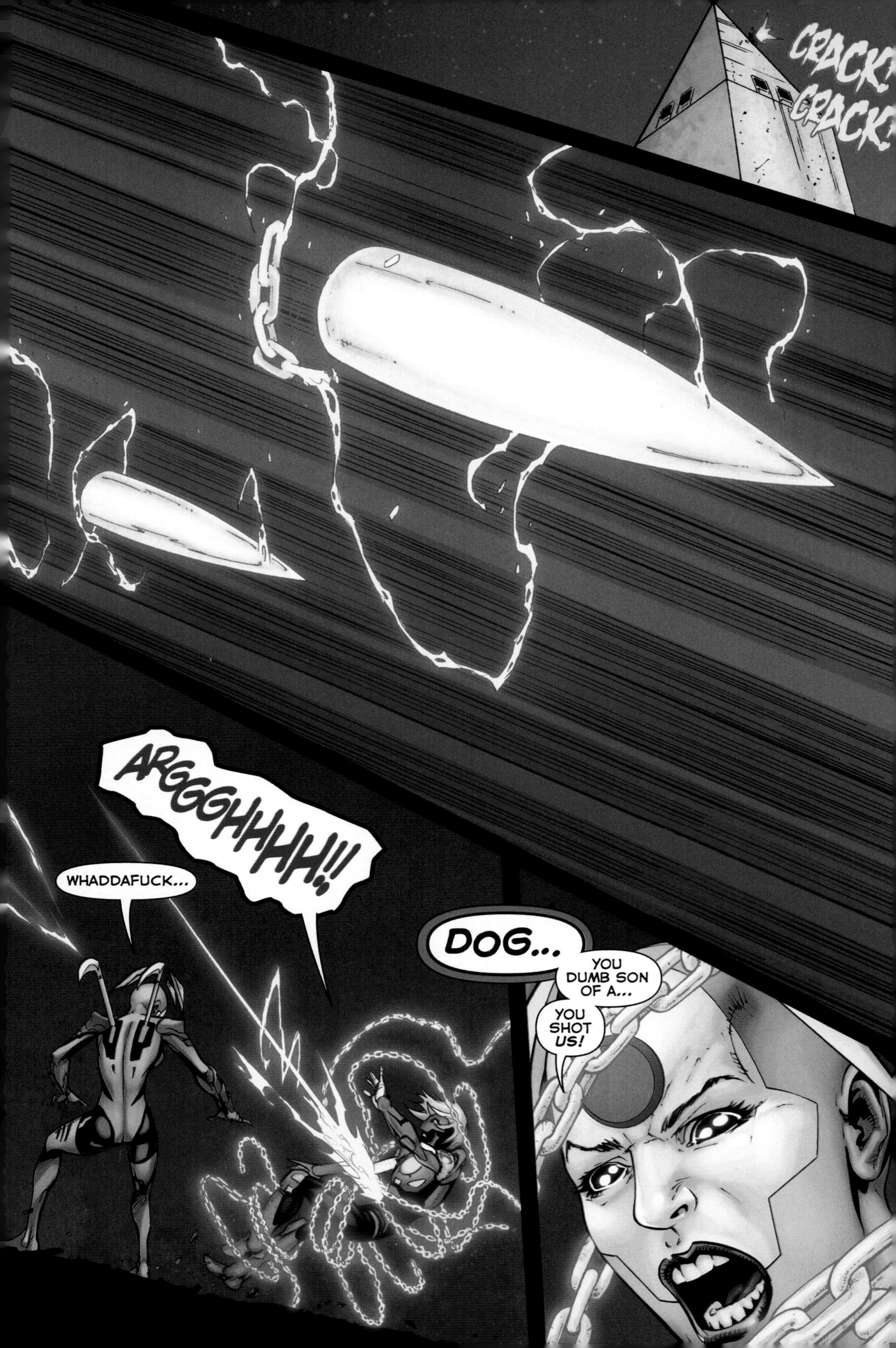
CRACK!
CRACK!
ARGGGHHHHH!!
WHADDAFUCK...
DOG...
YOU DUMB SON OF A...
YOU SHOT US!

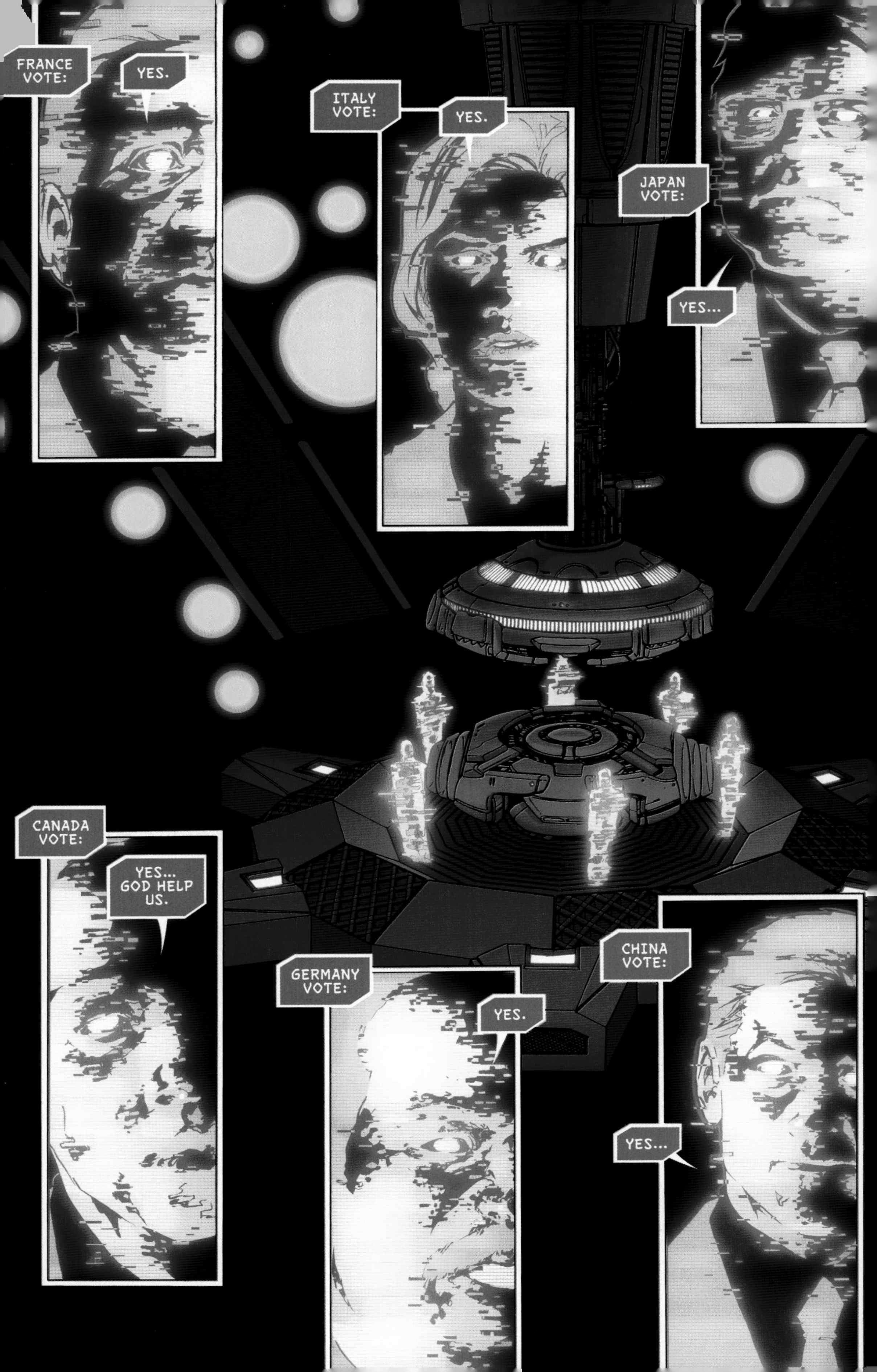
FRANCE VOTE:
YES.
ITALY VOTE:
YES.
JAPAN VOTE:
YES...
CANADA VOTE:
YES... GOD HELP US.
GERMANY VOTE:
YES.
CHINA VOTE:
YES...

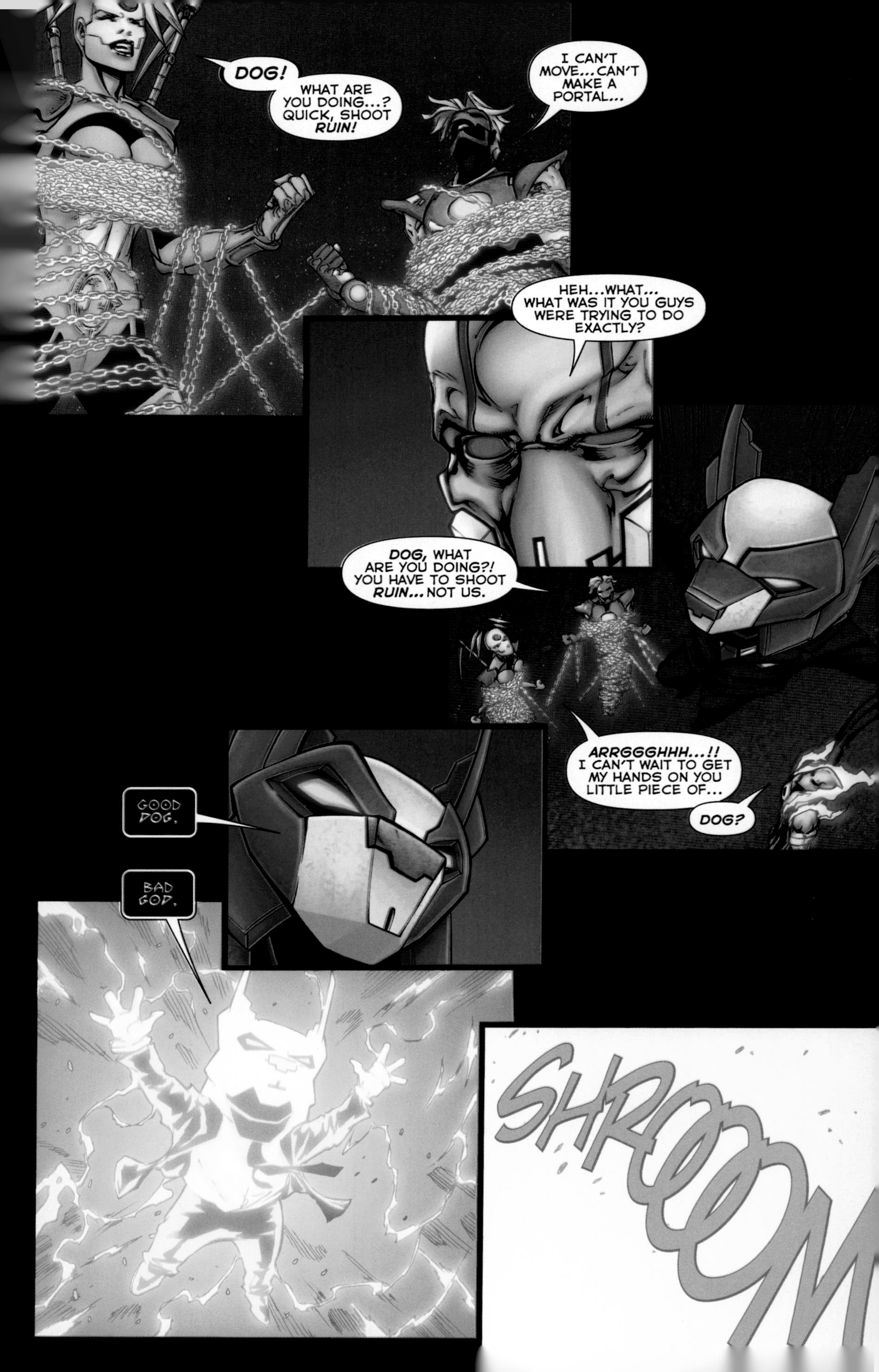
DOG!
WHAT ARE YOU DOING...? QUICK, SHOOT RUIN!
I CAN'T MOVE...CAN'T MAKE A PORTAL...
HEH...WHAT... WHAT WAS IT YOU GUYS WERE TRYING TO DO EXACTLY?
DOG, WHAT ARE YOU DOING?! YOU HAVE TO SHOOT RUIN...NOT US.
ARRGGGHHH...!! I CAN'T WAIT TO GET MY HANDS ON YOU LITTLE PIECE OF...
DOG?
GOOD DOG.
BAD GOD.
SHROOOOM

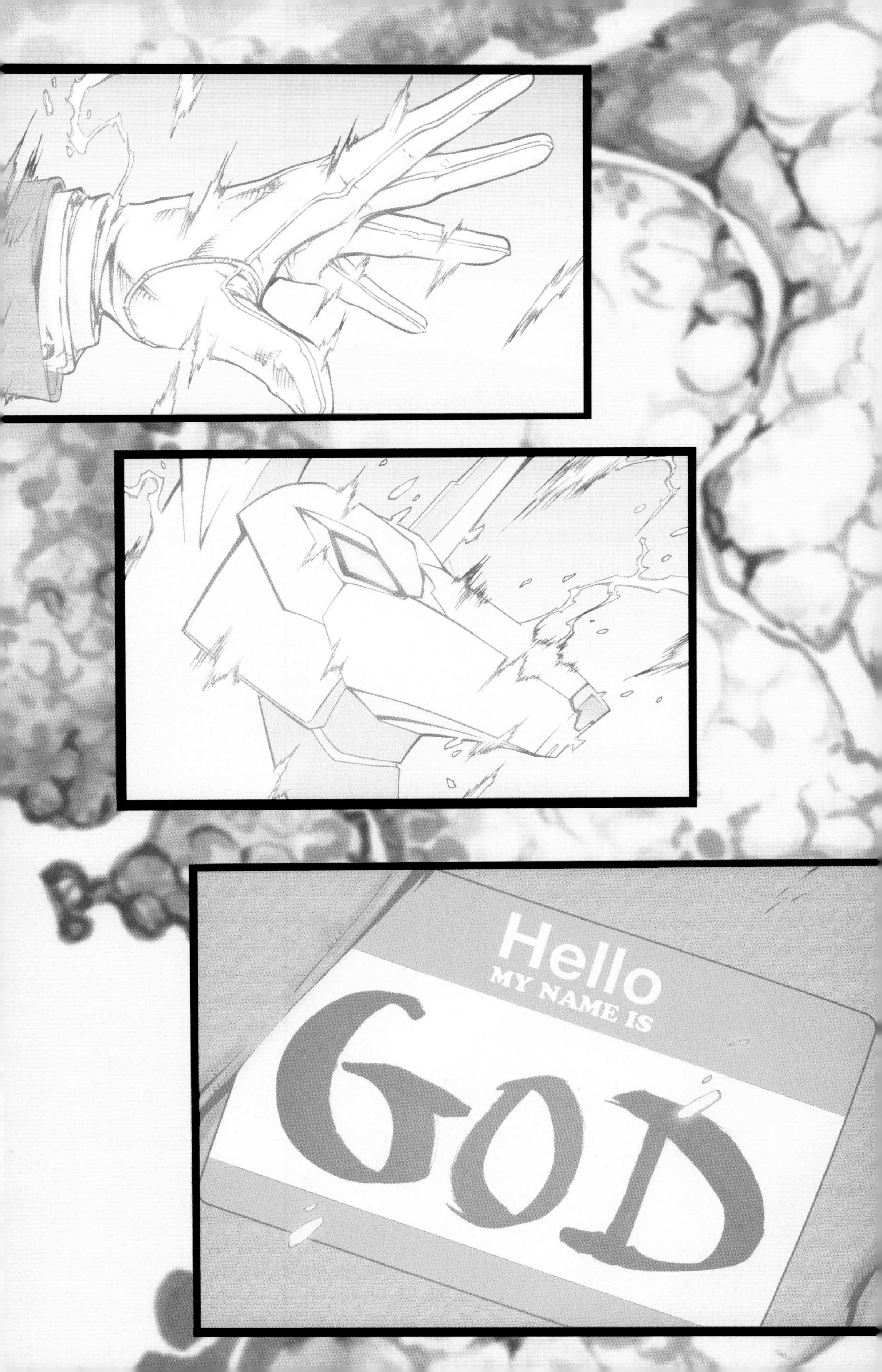
Hello
MY NAME IS
GOD

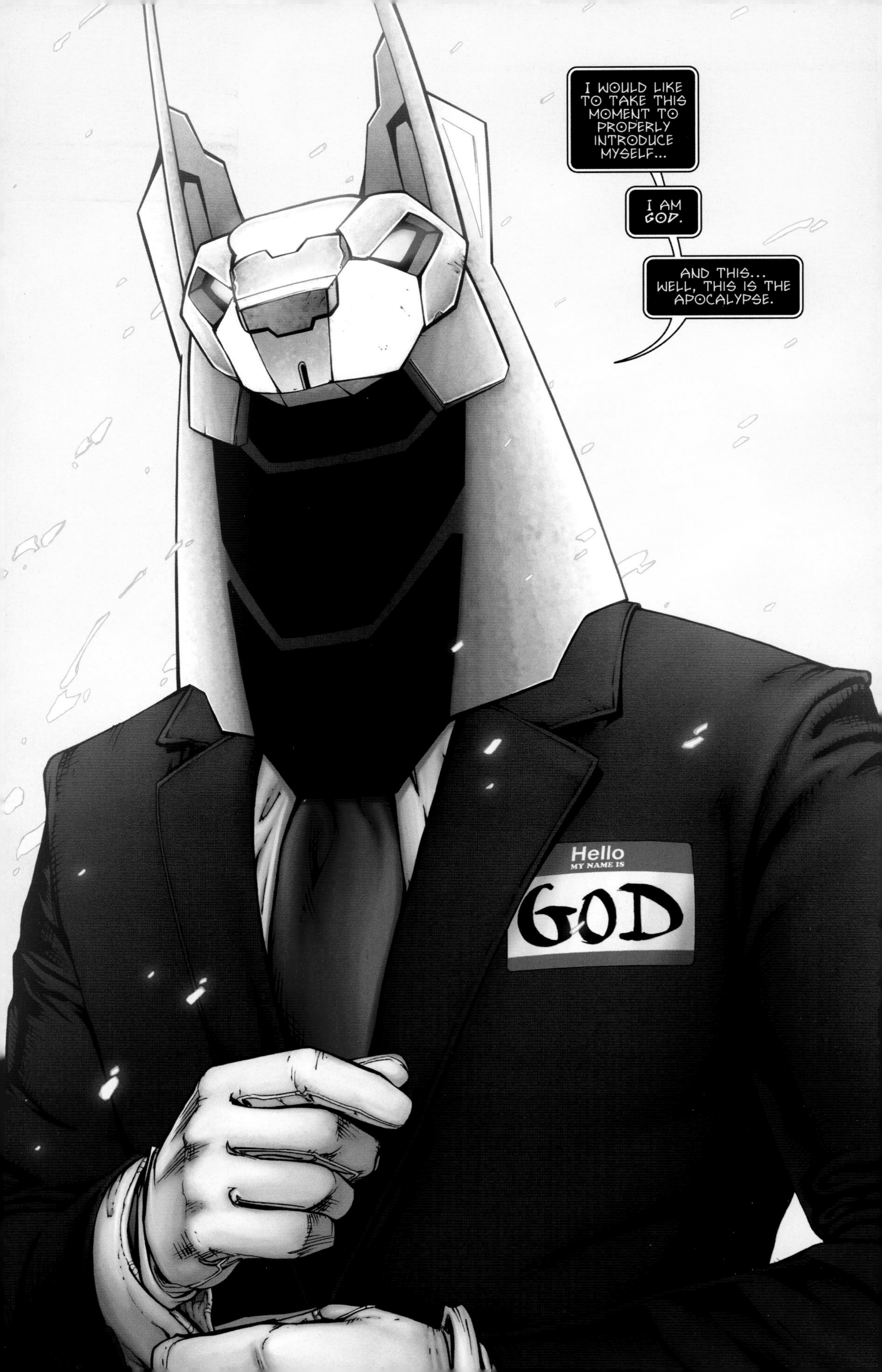
I WOULD LIKE TO TAKE THIS MOMENT TO PROPERLY INTRODUCE MYSELF...
I AM GOD.
AND THIS... WELL, THIS IS THE APOCALYPSE.
Hello
MY NAME IS
GOD

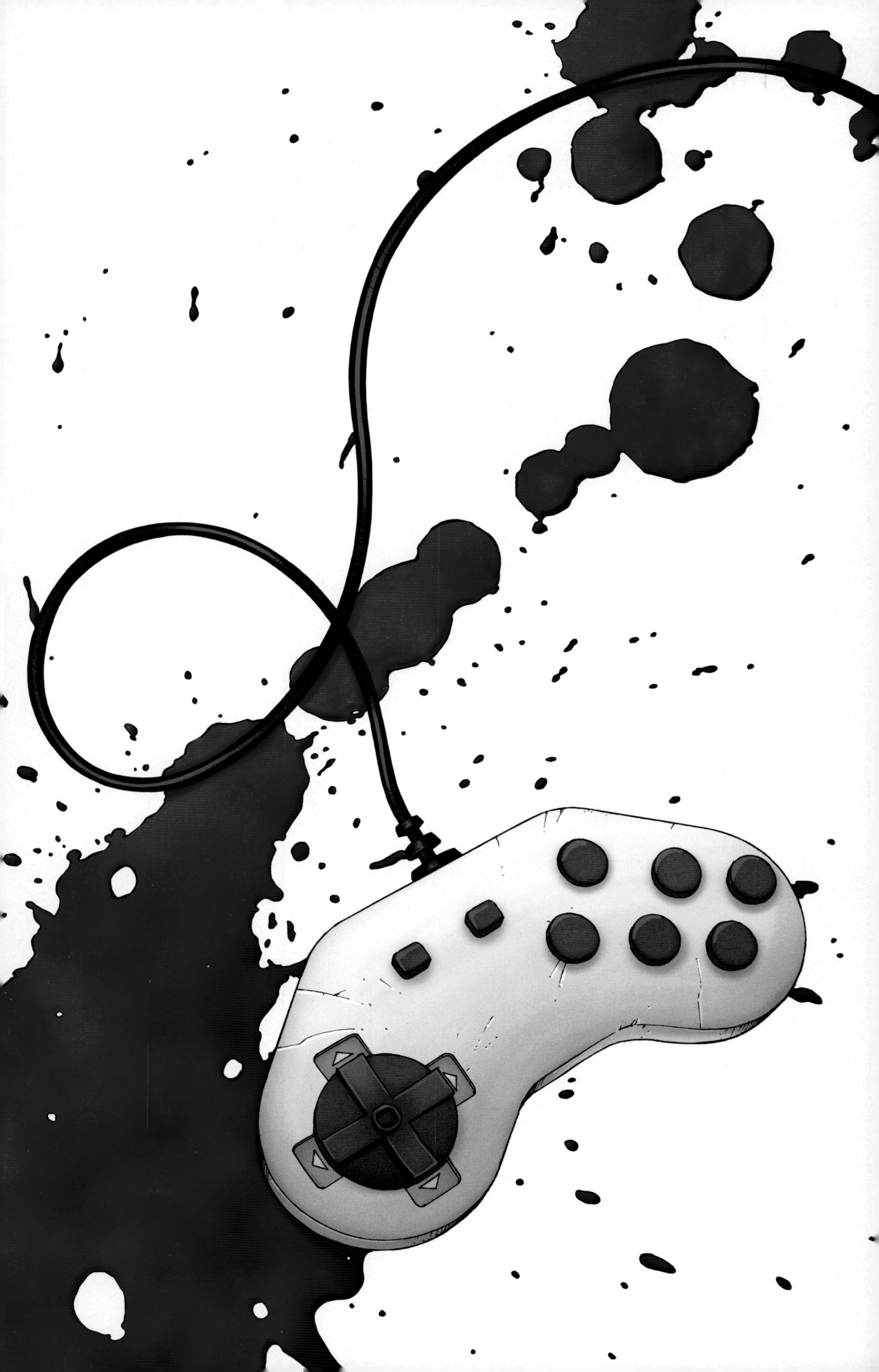

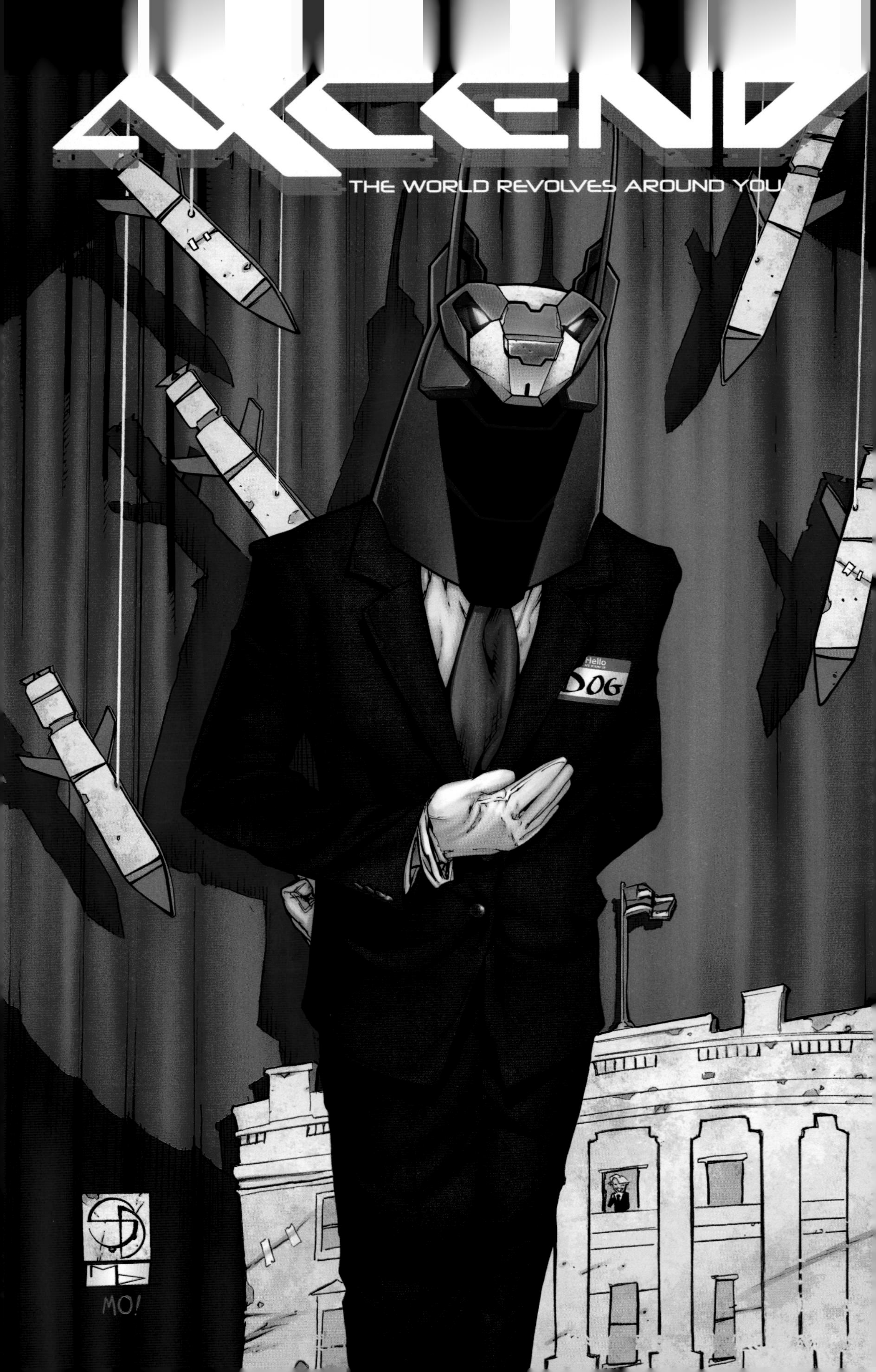
THE WORLD REVOLVES AROUND YOU.
Hello
DOG
MO!

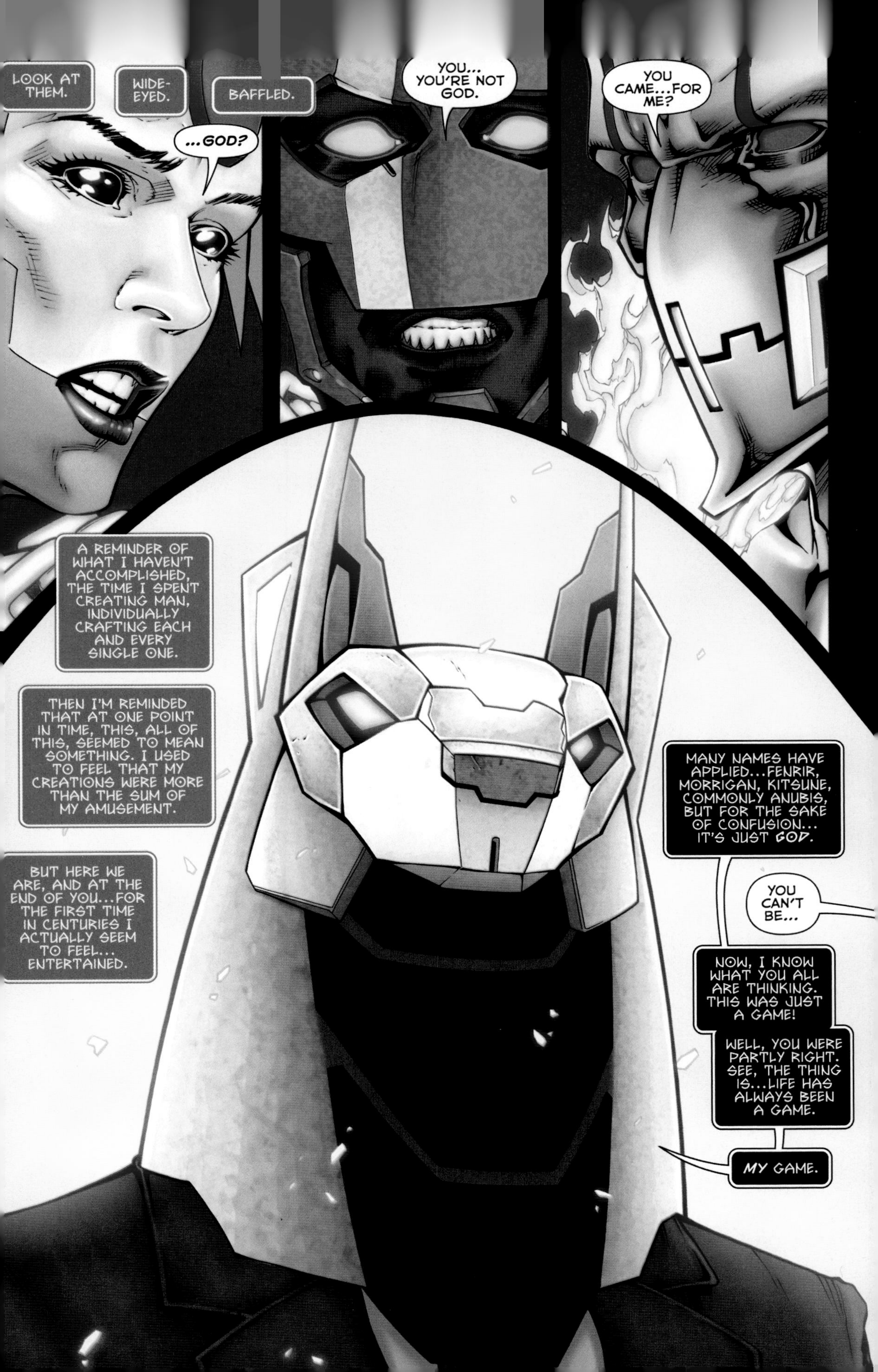
LOOK AT THEM.
WIDE-EYED.
BAFFLED.
...GOD?
YOU... YOU'RE NOT GOD.
YOU CAME...FOR ME?
A REMINDER OF WHAT I HAVEN'T ACCOMPLISHED, THE TIME I SPENT CREATING MAN, INDIVIDUALLY CRAFTING EACH AND EVERY SINGLE ONE.
THEN I'M REMINDED THAT AT ONE POINT IN TIME, THIS, ALL OF THIS, SEEMED TO MEAN SOMETHING. I USED TO FEEL THAT MY CREATIONS WERE MORE THAN THE SUM OF MY AMUSEMENT.
BUT HERE WE ARE, AND AT THE END OF YOU...FOR THE FIRST TIME IN CENTURIES I ACTUALLY SEEM TO FEEL... ENTERTAINED.
MANY NAMES HAVE APPLIED...FENRIR, MORRIGAN, KITSUNE, COMMONLY ANUBIS, BUT FOR THE SAKE OF CONFUSION... IT'S JUST GOD.
YOU CAN'T BE...
NOW, I KNOW WHAT YOU ALL ARE THINKING. THIS WAS JUST A GAME!
WELL, YOU WERE PARTLY RIGHT. SEE, THE THING IS...LIFE HAS ALWAYS BEEN A GAME.
MY GAME.

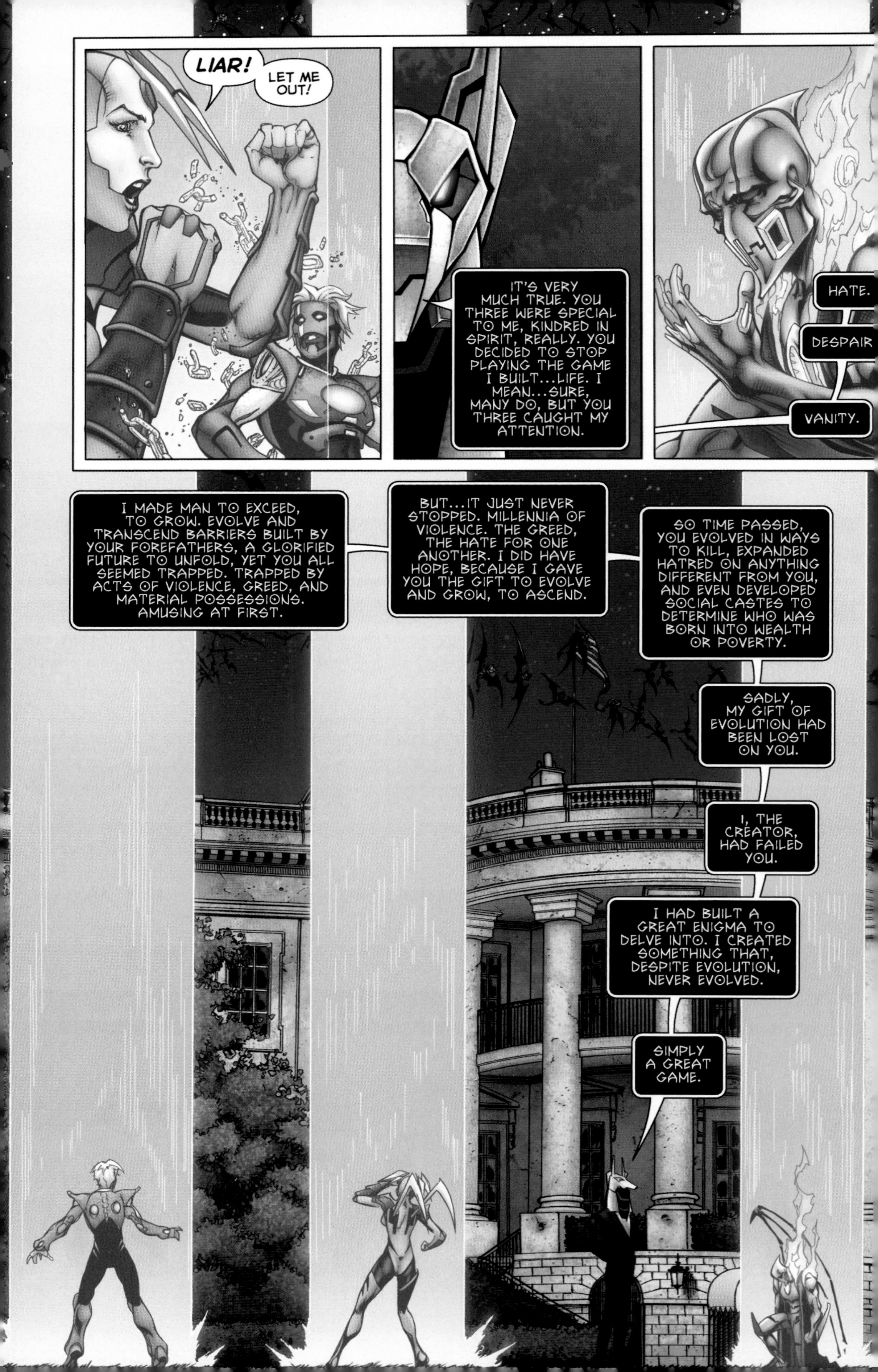
LIAR!
LET ME OUT!
IT'S VERY MUCH TRUE. YOU THREE WERE SPECIAL TO ME, KINDRED IN SPIRIT, REALLY. YOU DECIDED TO STOP PLAYING THE GAME I BUILT...LIFE. I MEAN...SURE, MANY DO, BUT YOU THREE CAUGHT MY ATTENTION.
HATE.
DESPAIR
VANITY.
I MADE MAN TO EXCEED, TO GROW. EVOLVE AND TRANSCEND BARRIERS BUILT BY YOUR FOREFATHERS, A GLORIFIED FUTURE TO UNFOLD, YET YOU ALL SEEMED TRAPPED. TRAPPED BY ACTS OF VIOLENCE, GREED, AND MATERIAL POSSESSIONS. AMUSING AT FIRST.
BUT...IT JUST NEVER STOPPED. MILLENNIA OF VIOLENCE. THE GREED, THE HATE FOR ONE ANOTHER. I DID HAVE HOPE, BECAUSE I GAVE YOU THE GIFT TO EVOLVE AND GROW, TO ASCEND.
SO TIME PASSED, YOU EVOLVED IN WAYS TO KILL, EXPANDED HATRED ON ANYTHING DIFFERENT FROM YOU, AND EVEN DEVELOPED SOCIAL CASTES TO DETERMINE WHO WAS BORN INTO WEALTH OR POVERTY.
SADLY, MY GIFT OF EVOLUTION HAD BEEN LOST ON YOU.
I, THE CREATOR, HAD FAILED YOU.
I HAD BUILT A GREAT ENIGMA TO DELVE INTO. I CREATED SOMETHING THAT, DESPITE EVOLUTION, NEVER EVOLVED.
SIMPLY A GREAT GAME.

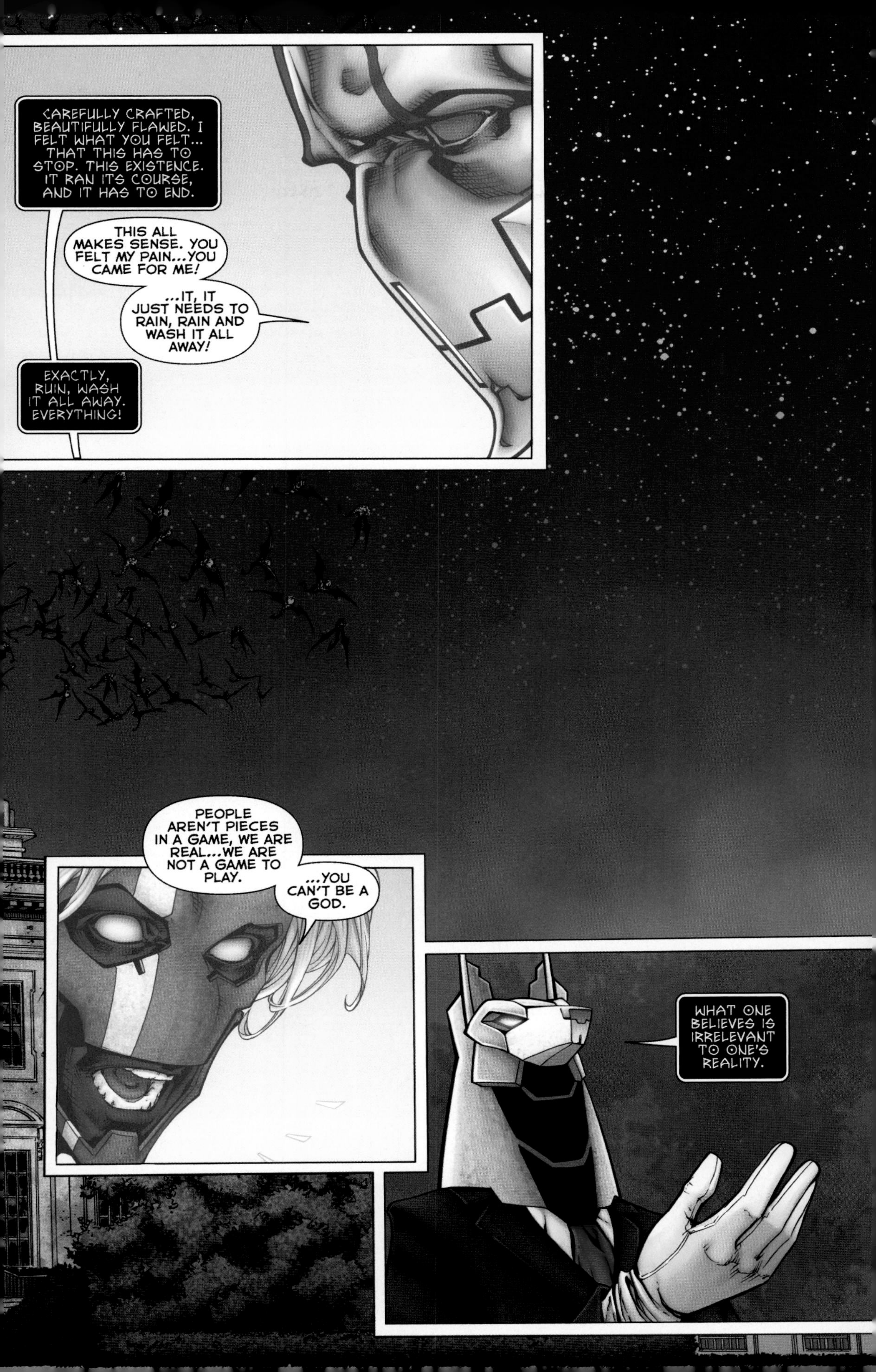
CAREFULLY CRAFTED, BEAUTIFULLY FLAWED. I FELT WHAT YOU FELT... THAT THIS HAS TO STOP. THIS EXISTENCE. IT RAN ITS COURSE, AND IT HAS TO END.
THIS ALL MAKES SENSE. YOU FELT MY PAIN...YOU CAME FOR ME!
...IT, IT JUST NEEDS TO RAIN, RAIN AND WASH IT ALL AWAY!
EXACTLY, RUIN, WASH IT ALL AWAY. EVERYTHING!
PEOPLE AREN'T PIECES IN A GAME, WE ARE REAL...WE ARE NOT A GAME TO PLAY.
...YOU CAN'T BE A GOD.
WHAT ONE BELIEVES IS IRRELEVANT TO ONE'S REALITY.

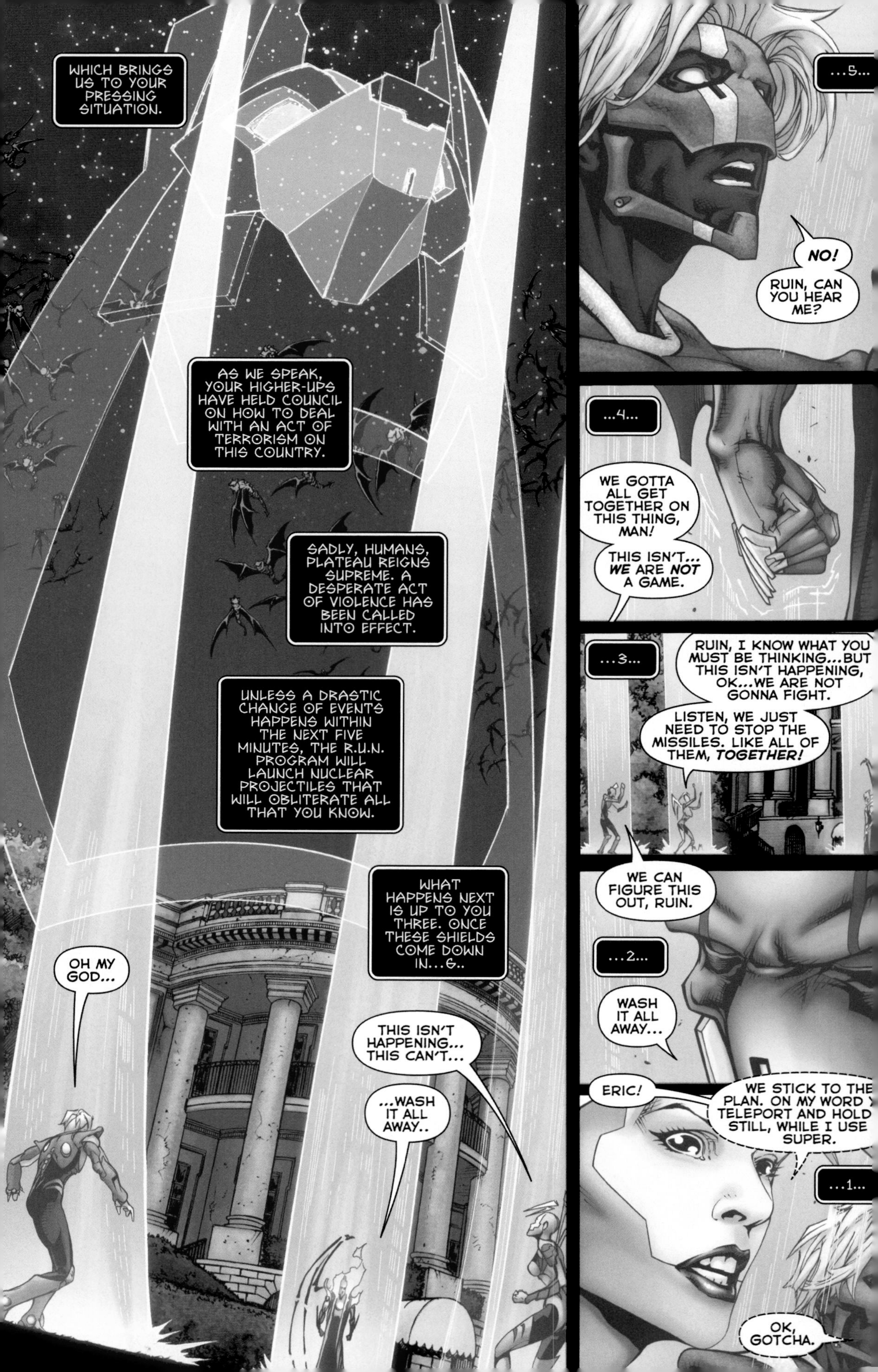

WHICH BRINGS US TO YOUR PRESSING SITUATION.
AS WE SPEAK, YOUR HIGHER-UPS HAVE HELD COUNCIL ON HOW TO DEAL WITH AN ACT OF TERRORISM ON THIS COUNTRY.
SADLY, HUMANS, PLATEAU REIGNS SUPREME. A DESPERATE ACT OF VIOLENCE HAS BEEN CALLED INTO EFFECT.
UNLESS A DRASTIC CHANGE OF EVENTS HAPPENS WITHIN THE NEXT FIVE MINUTES, THE R.U.N. PROGRAM WILL LAUNCH NUCLEAR PROJECTILES THAT WILL OBLITERATE ALL THAT YOU KNOW.
WHAT HAPPENS NEXT IS UP TO YOU THREE. ONCE THESE SHIELDS COME DOWN IN...6..
OH MY GOD...
THIS ISN'T HAPPENING... THIS CAN'T...
...WASH IT ALL AWAY..
...5...
NO!
RUIN, CAN YOU HEAR ME?
...4...
WE GOTTA ALL GET TOGETHER ON THIS THING, MAN!
THIS ISN'T... WE ARE NOT A GAME.
...3...
RUIN, I KNOW WHAT YOU MUST BE THINKING...BUT THIS ISN'T HAPPENING, OK...WE ARE NOT GONNA FIGHT.
LISTEN, WE JUST NEED TO STOP THE MISSILES. LIKE ALL OF THEM, TOGETHER!
WE CAN FIGURE THIS OUT, RUIN.
...2...
WASH IT ALL AWAY...
ERIC!
WE STICK TO THE PLAN. ON MY WORD Y TELEPORT AND HOLD STILL, WHILE I USE SUPER.
...1...
OK, GOTCHA.

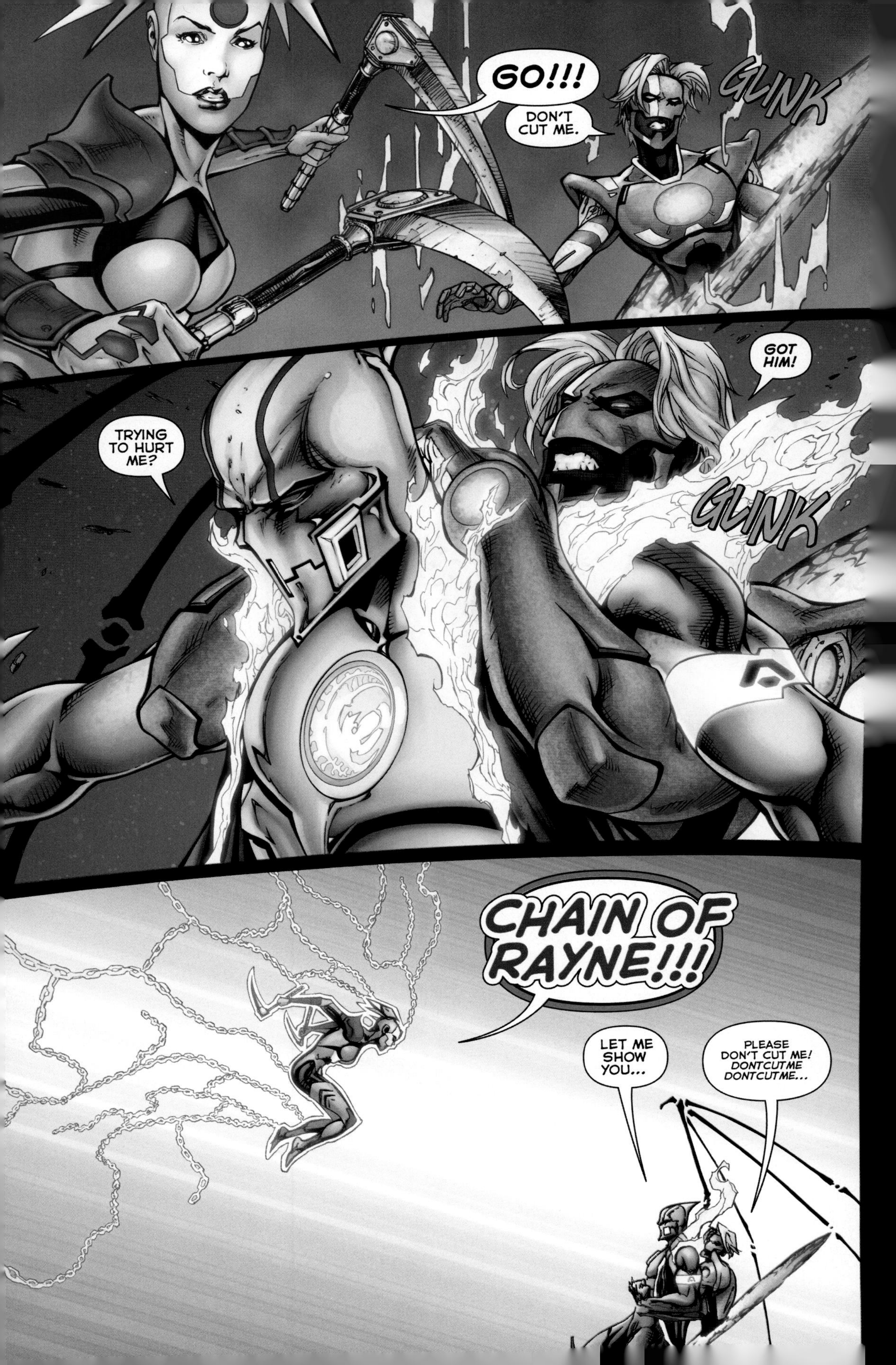
GO!!!
DON'T CUT ME.
GLINK
GOT HIM!
TRYING TO HURT ME?
GLINK
CHAIN OF RAYNE!!!
LET ME SHOW YOU...
PLEASE DON'T CUT ME! DONTCUTME DONTCUTME...

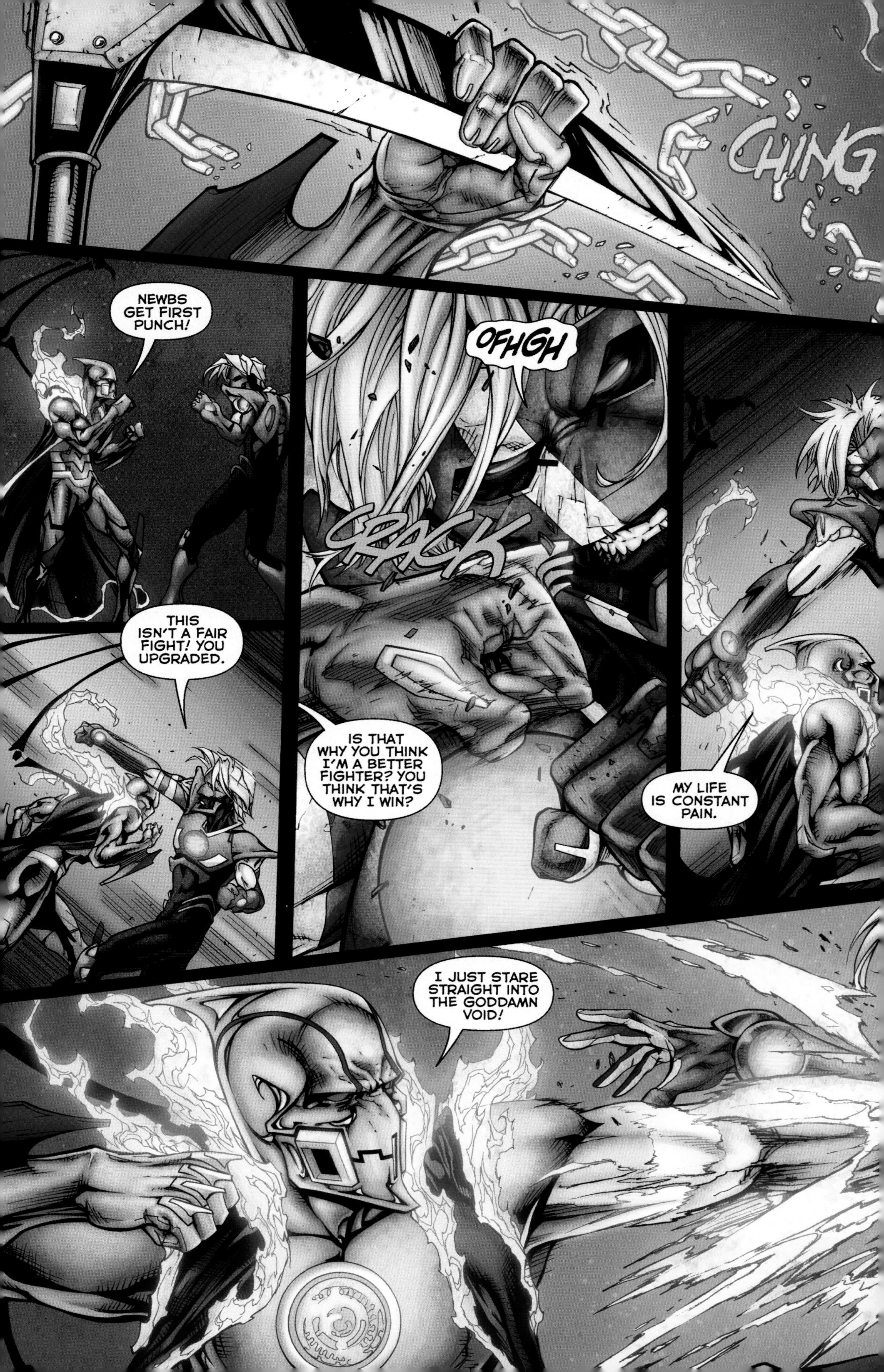
CHING
NEWBS GET FIRST PUNCH!
OFHGH
CRACK
THIS ISN'T A FAIR FIGHT! YOU UPGRADED.
IS THAT WHY YOU THINK I'M A BETTER FIGHTER? YOU THINK THAT'S WHY I WIN?
MY LIFE IS CONSTANT PAIN.
I JUST STARE STRAIGHT INTO THE GODDAMN VOID!

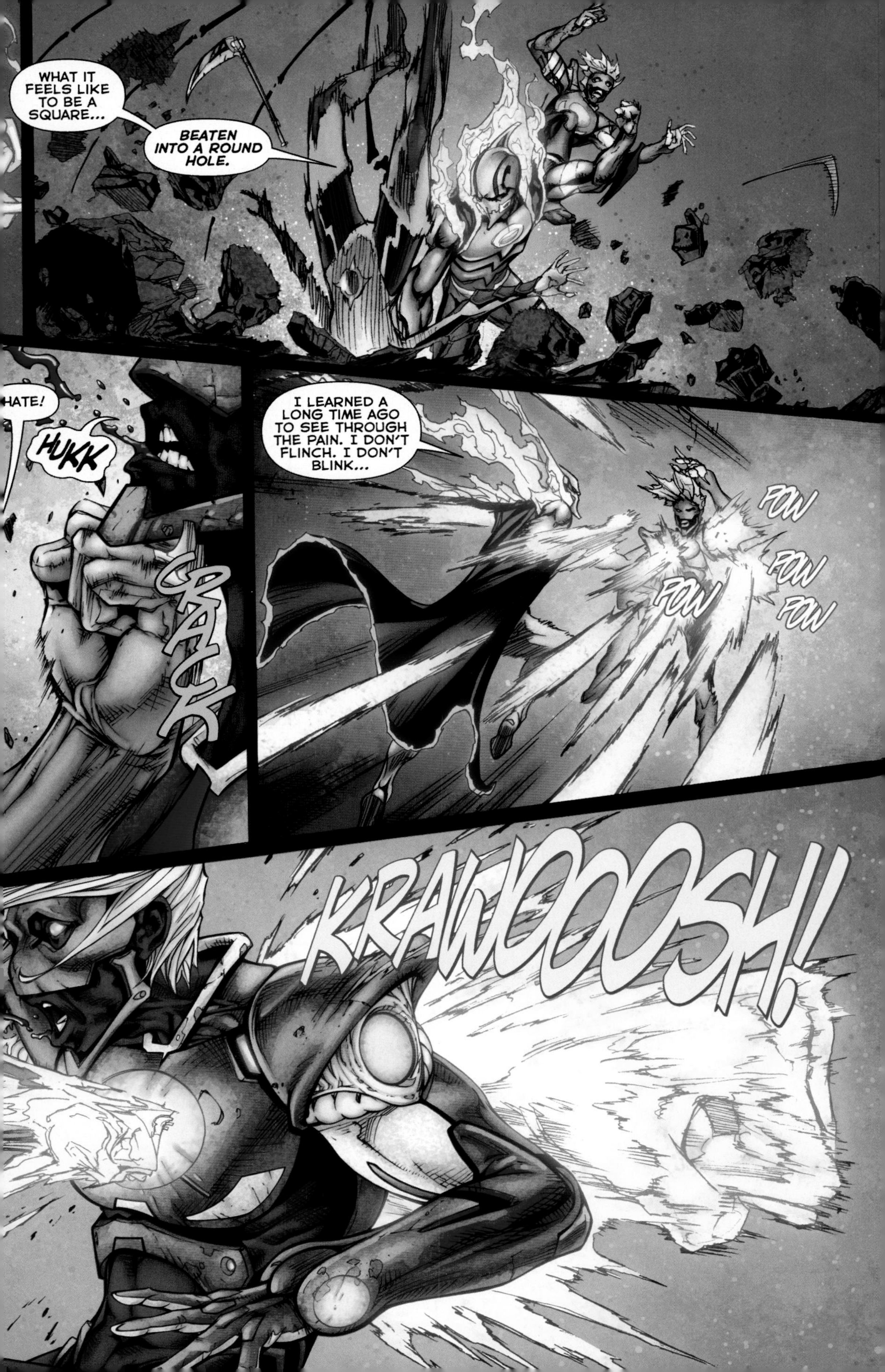
WHAT IT FEELS LIKE TO BE A SQUARE...
BEATEN INTO A ROUND HOLE.
HATE!
HUKK
CRACK
I LEARNED A LONG TIME AGO TO SEE THROUGH THE PAIN. I DON'T FLINCH. I DON'T BLINK...
POW
POW
POW
POW
KRAWOOOSH!

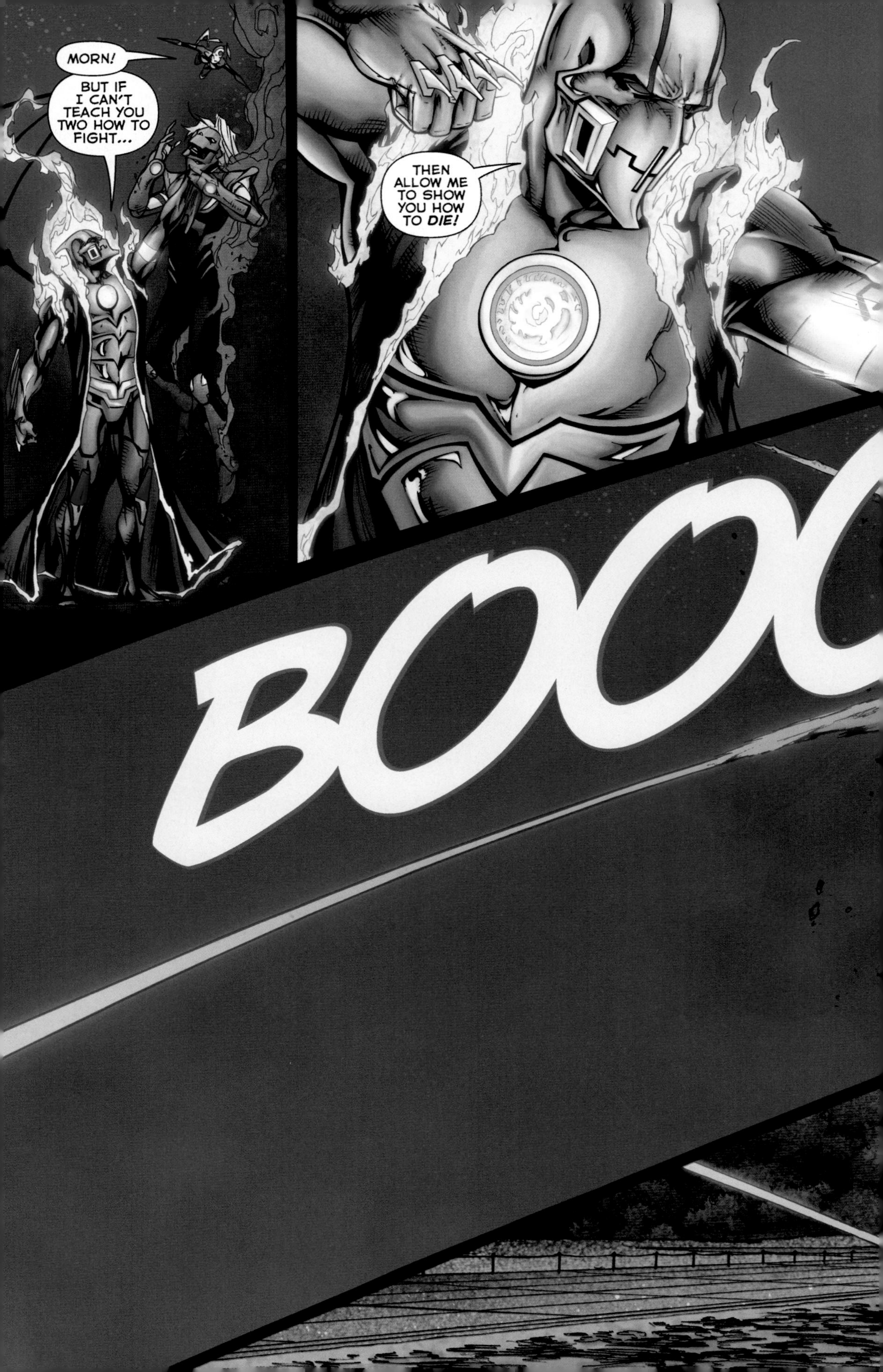
MORN!
BUT IF I CAN'T TEACH YOU TWO HOW TO FIGHT...
THEN ALLOW ME TO SHOW YOU HOW TO *DIE!*
BOOO

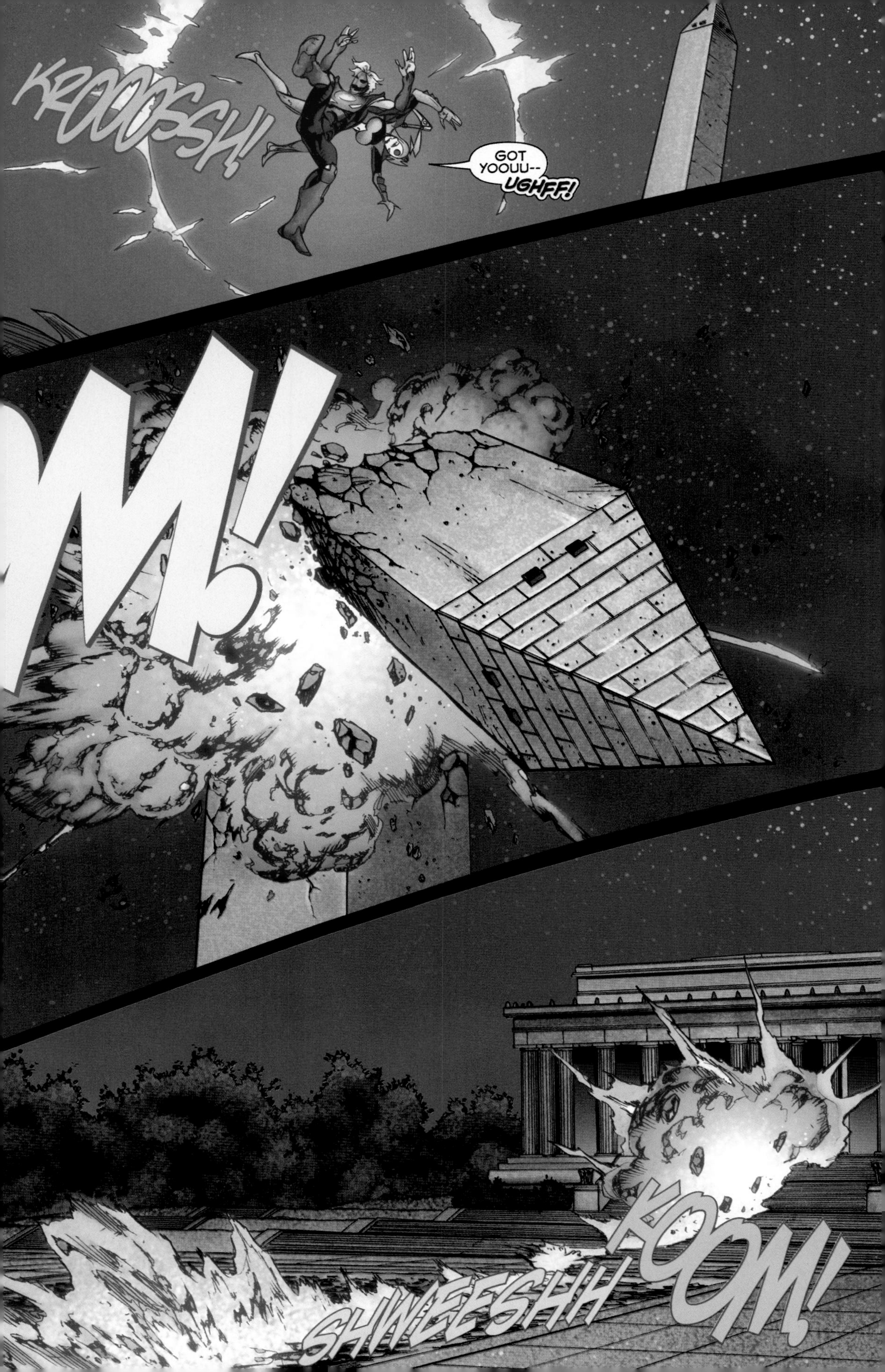
KROOOSSH!
GOT YOOUU-- UGHFF!
M!
SHWEESHH
KOOM!

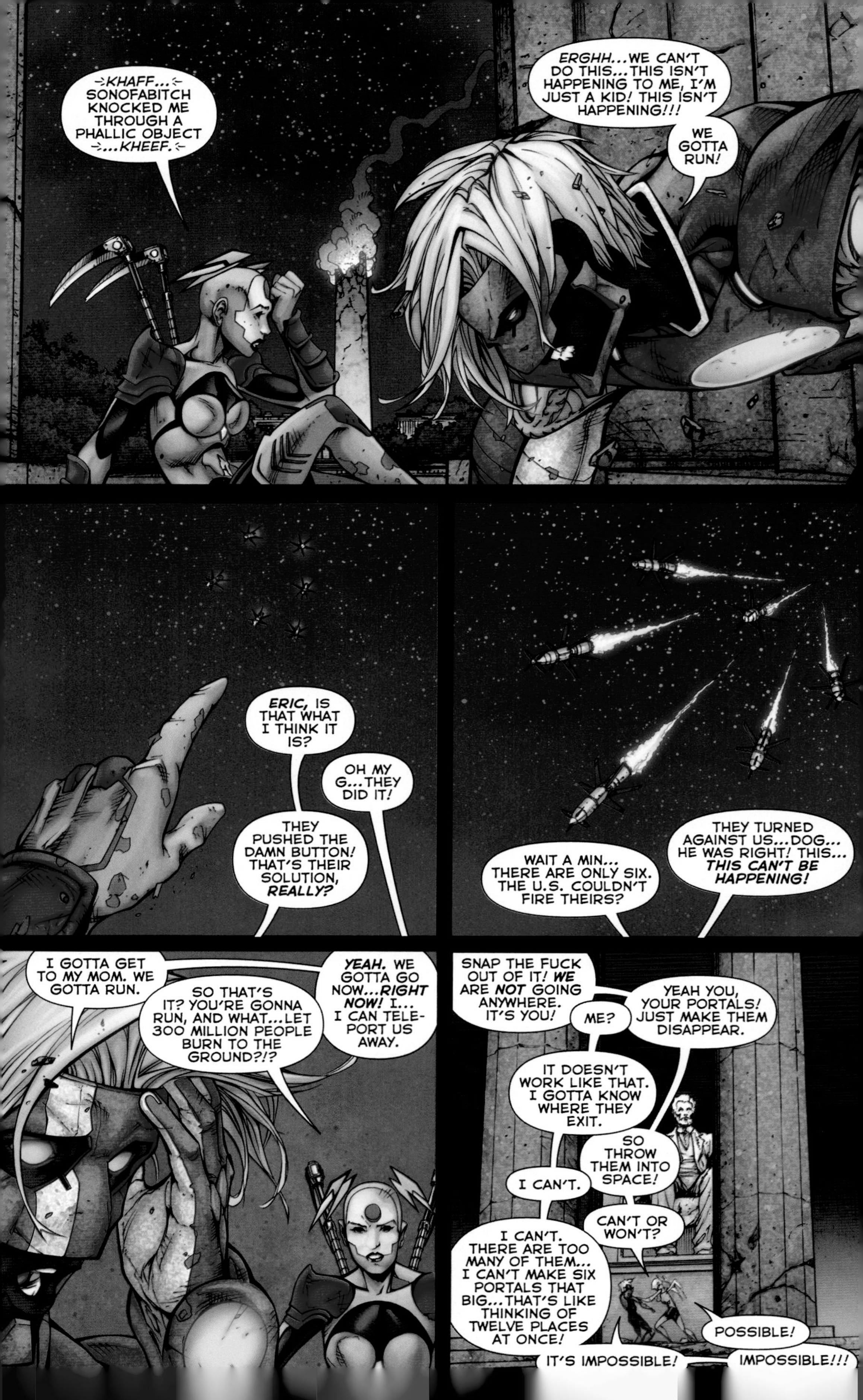

KHAFF... SONOFABITCH KNOCKED ME THROUGH A PHALLIC OBJECT ...KHEEF.
ERGHH...WE CAN'T DO THIS...THIS ISN'T HAPPENING TO ME, I'M JUST A KID! THIS ISN'T HAPPENING!!!
WE GOTTA RUN!
ERIC, IS THAT WHAT I THINK IT IS?
OH MY G...THEY DID IT!
THEY PUSHED THE DAMN BUTTON! THAT'S THEIR SOLUTION, REALLY?
WAIT A MIN... THERE ARE ONLY SIX. THE U.S. COULDN'T FIRE THEIRS?
THEY TURNED AGAINST US...DOG... HE WAS RIGHT! THIS... THIS CAN'T BE HAPPENING!
I GOTTA GET TO MY MOM. WE GOTTA RUN.
SO THAT'S IT? YOU'RE GONNA RUN, AND WHAT...LET 300 MILLION PEOPLE BURN TO THE GROUND?!?
YEAH. WE GOTTA GO NOW...RIGHT NOW! I... I CAN TELE-PORT US AWAY.
SNAP THE FUCK OUT OF IT! WE ARE NOT GOING ANYWHERE. IT'S YOU!
ME?
YEAH YOU, YOUR PORTALS! JUST MAKE THEM DISAPPEAR.
IT DOESN'T WORK LIKE THAT. I GOTTA KNOW WHERE THEY EXIT.
SO THROW THEM INTO SPACE!
I CAN'T.
CAN'T OR WON'T?
I CAN'T. THERE ARE TOO MANY OF THEM... I CAN'T MAKE SIX PORTALS THAT BIG...THAT'S LIKE THINKING OF TWELVE PLACES AT ONCE!
POSSIBLE!
IT'S IMPOSSIBLE!
IMPOSSIBLE!!!

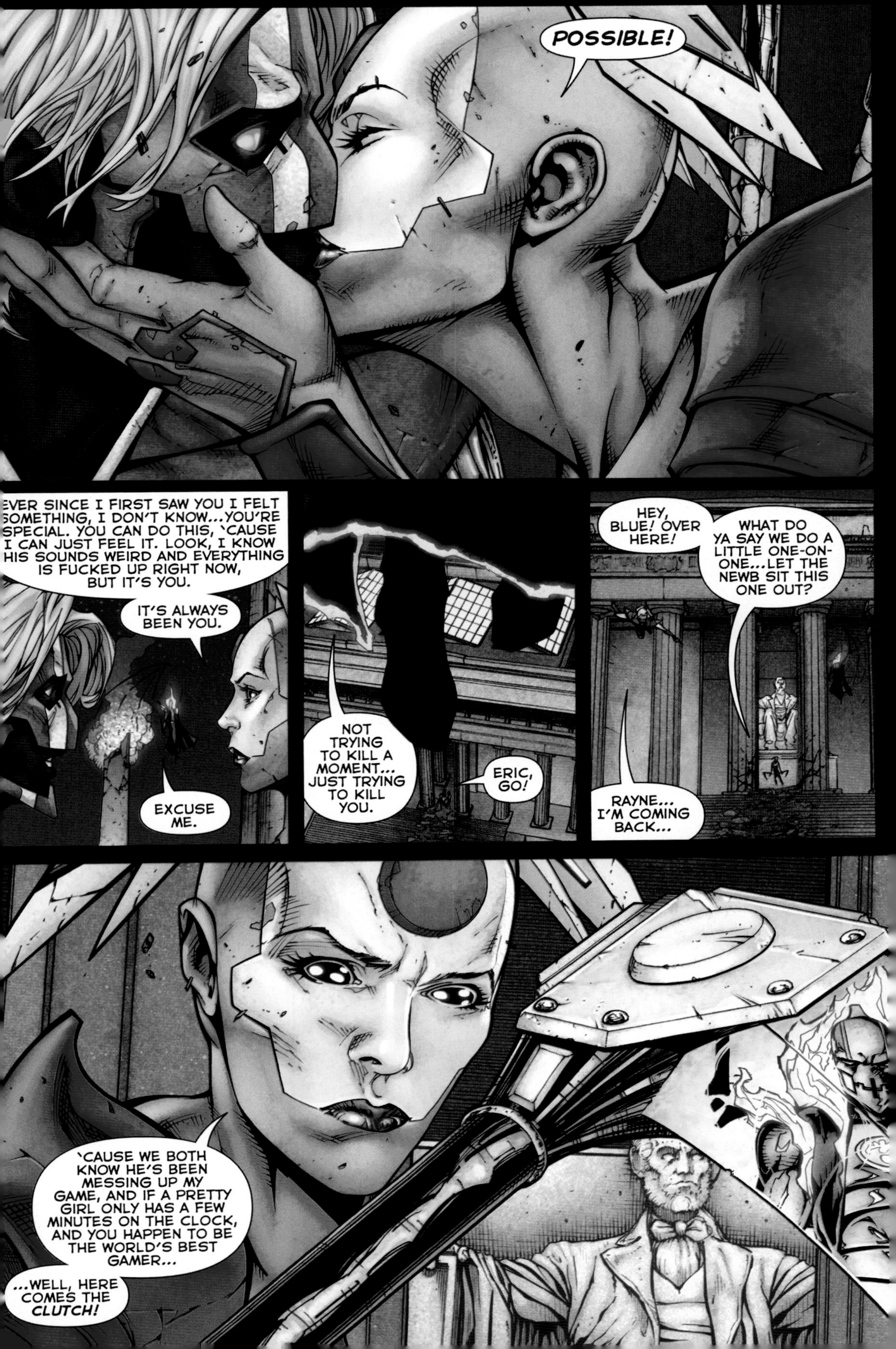
POSSIBLE!
EVER SINCE I FIRST SAW YOU I FELT SOMETHING, I DON'T KNOW...YOU'RE SPECIAL. YOU CAN DO THIS, 'CAUSE I CAN JUST FEEL IT. LOOK, I KNOW HIS SOUNDS WEIRD AND EVERYTHING IS FUCKED UP RIGHT NOW, BUT IT'S YOU.
IT'S ALWAYS BEEN YOU.
EXCUSE ME.
NOT TRYING TO KILL A MOMENT... JUST TRYING TO KILL YOU.
ERIC, GO!
HEY, BLUE! OVER HERE!
WHAT DO YA SAY WE DO A LITTLE ONE-ON-ONE...LET THE NEWB SIT THIS ONE OUT?
RAYNE... I'M COMING BACK...
'CAUSE WE BOTH KNOW HE'S BEEN MESSING UP MY GAME, AND IF A PRETTY GIRL ONLY HAS A FEW MINUTES ON THE CLOCK, AND YOU HAPPEN TO BE THE WORLD'S BEST GAMER...
...WELL, HERE COMES THE CLUTCH!

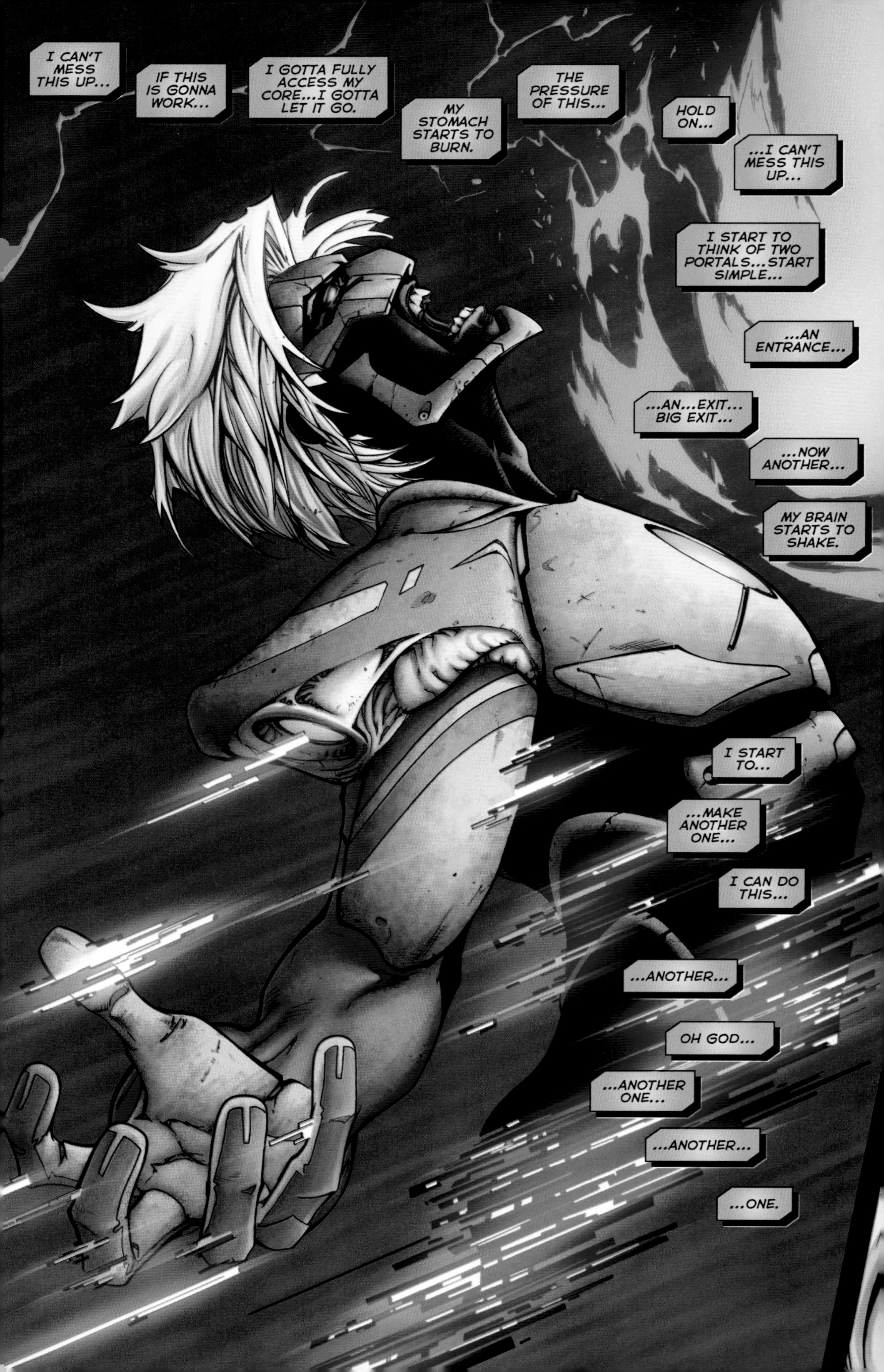
I CAN'T MESS THIS UP...
IF THIS IS GONNA WORK...
I GOTTA FULLY ACCESS MY CORE...I GOTTA LET IT GO.
MY STOMACH STARTS TO BURN.
THE PRESSURE OF THIS...
HOLD ON...
...I CAN'T MESS THIS UP...
I START TO THINK OF TWO PORTALS...START SIMPLE...
...AN ENTRANCE...
...AN...EXIT... BIG EXIT...
...NOW ANOTHER...
MY BRAIN STARTS TO SHAKE.
I START TO...
...MAKE ANOTHER ONE...
I CAN DO THIS...
...ANOTHER...
OH GOD...
...ANOTHER ONE...
...ANOTHER...
...ONE.

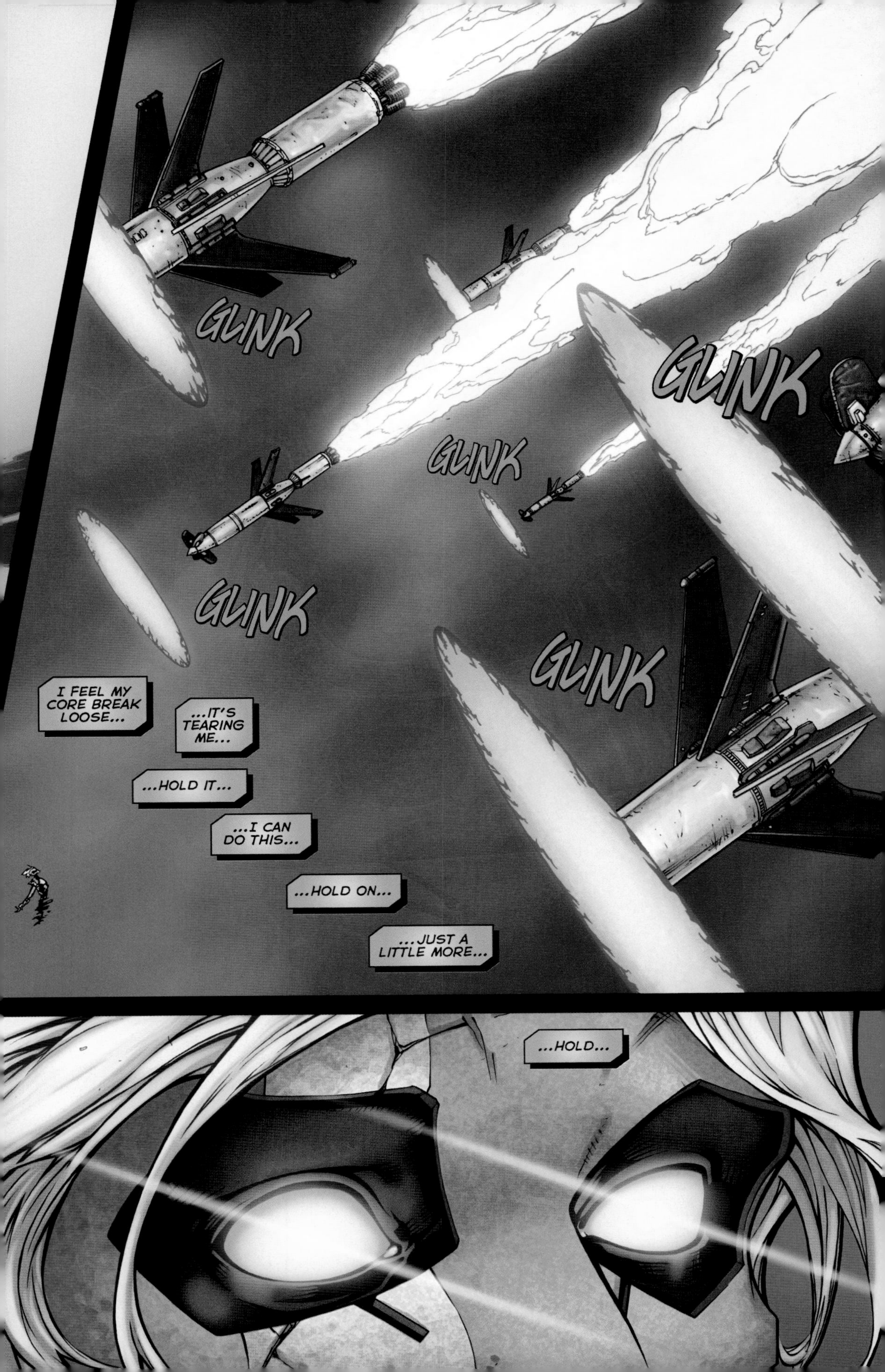
GLINK
GLINK
GLINK
GLINK
GLINK
I FEEL MY CORE BREAK LOOSE...
...IT'S TEARING ME...
...HOLD IT...
...I CAN DO THIS...
...HOLD ON...
...JUST A LITTLE MORE...
...HOLD...

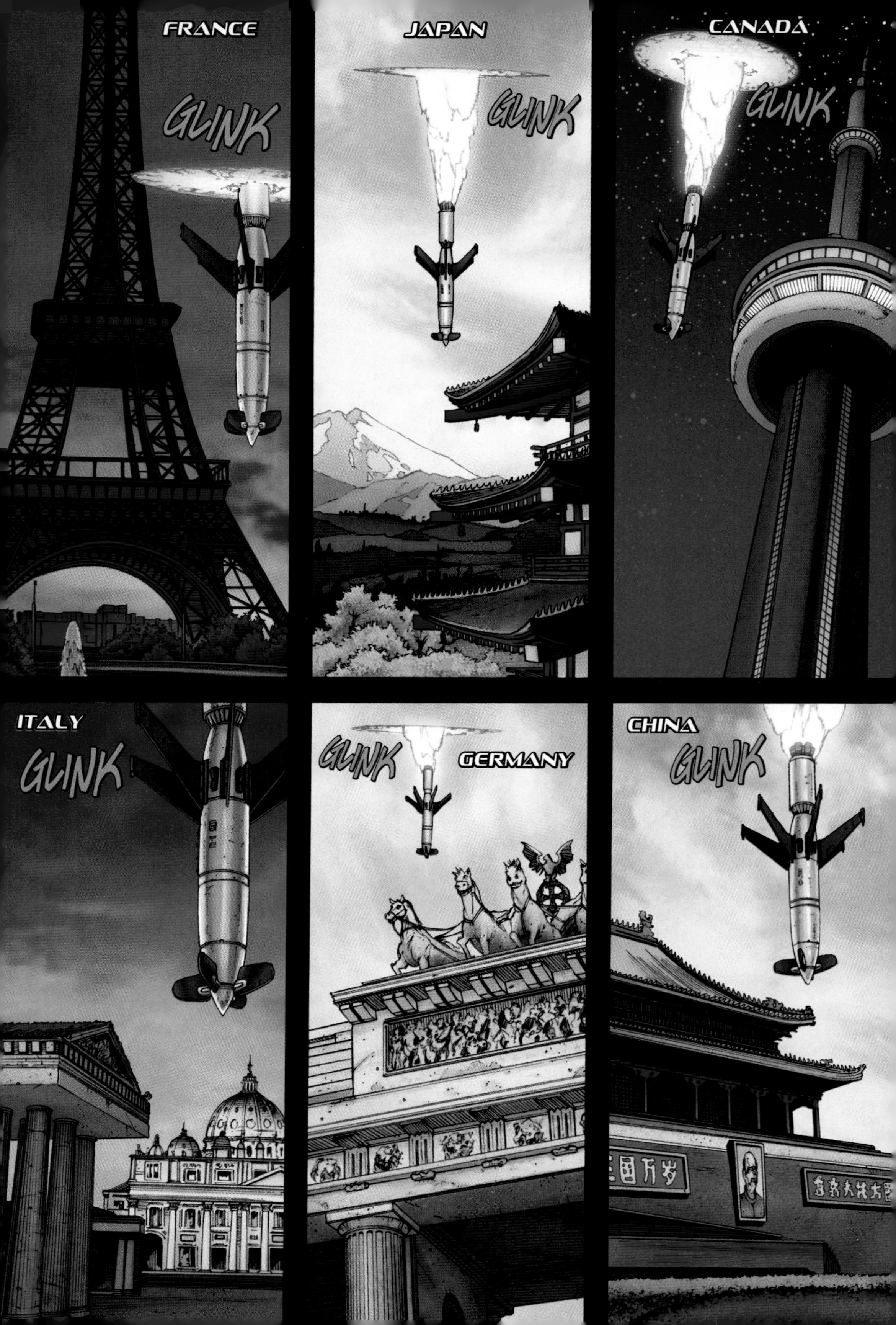
FRANCE
GLINK
JAPAN
GLINK
CANADA
GLINK
ITALY
GLINK
GLINK
GERMANY
CHINA
GLINK

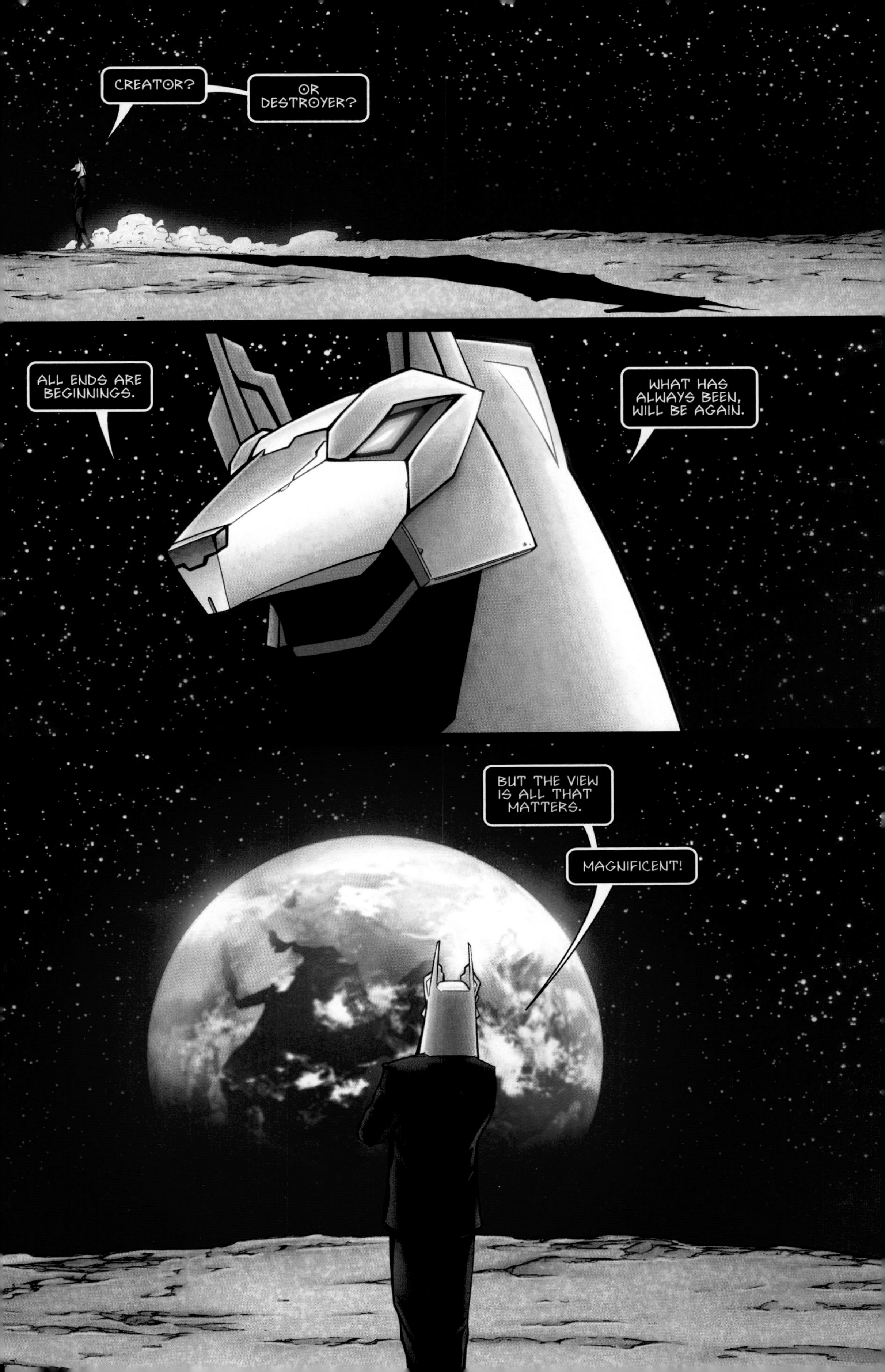
CREATOR?
OR DESTROYER?
ALL ENDS ARE BEGINNINGS.
WHAT HAS ALWAYS BEEN, WILL BE AGAIN.
BUT THE VIEW IS ALL THAT MATTERS.
MAGNIFICENT!

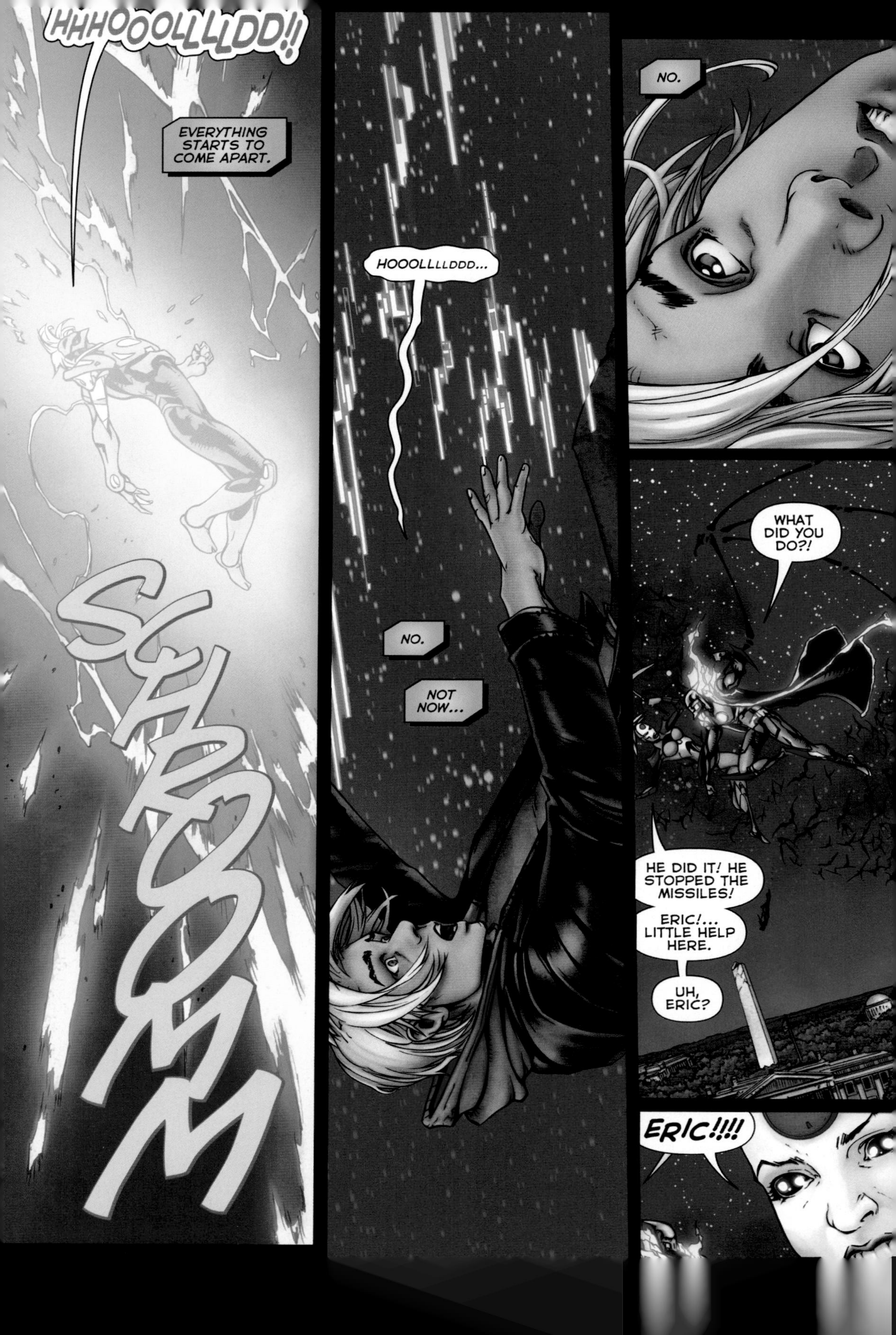
HHHOOOLLLLDD!!
EVERYTHING STARTS TO COME APART.
SHHROOOMM
HOOOLLLLLDDD...
NO.
NOT NOW...
NO.
WHAT DID YOU DO?!
HE DID IT! HE STOPPED THE MISSILES!
ERIC!... LITTLE HELP HERE.
UH, ERIC?
ERIC!!!!

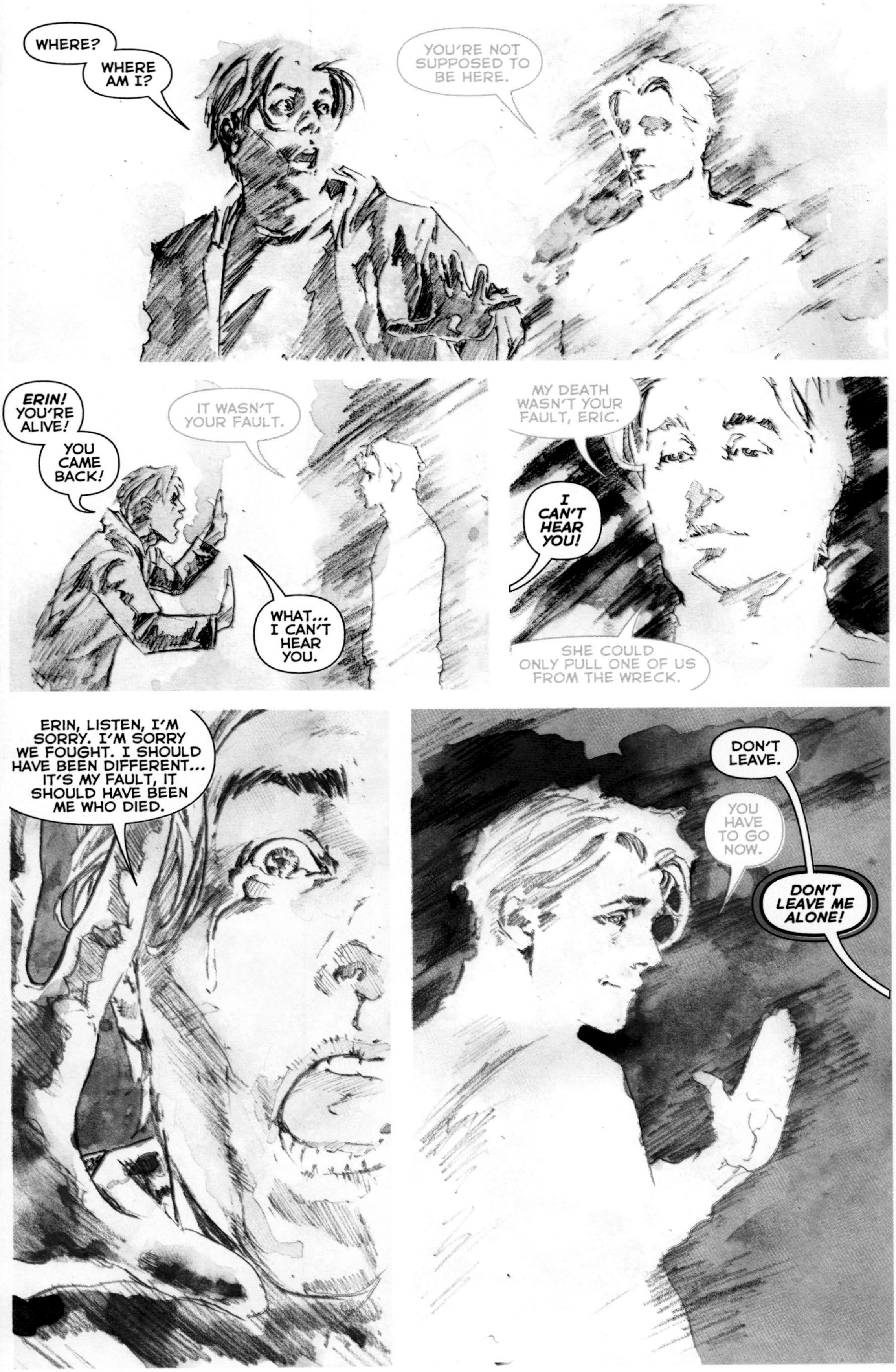
WHERE?
WHERE AM I?
YOU'RE NOT SUPPOSED TO BE HERE.
ERIN! YOU'RE ALIVE!
YOU CAME BACK!
IT WASN'T YOUR FAULT.
WHAT... I CAN'T HEAR YOU.
MY DEATH WASN'T YOUR FAULT, ERIC.
I CAN'T HEAR YOU!
SHE COULD ONLY PULL ONE OF US FROM THE WRECK.
ERIN, LISTEN, I'M SORRY. I'M SORRY WE FOUGHT. I SHOULD HAVE BEEN DIFFERENT... IT'S MY FAULT, IT SHOULD HAVE BEEN ME WHO DIED.
DON'T LEAVE.
YOU HAVE TO GO NOW.
DON'T LEAVE ME ALONE!

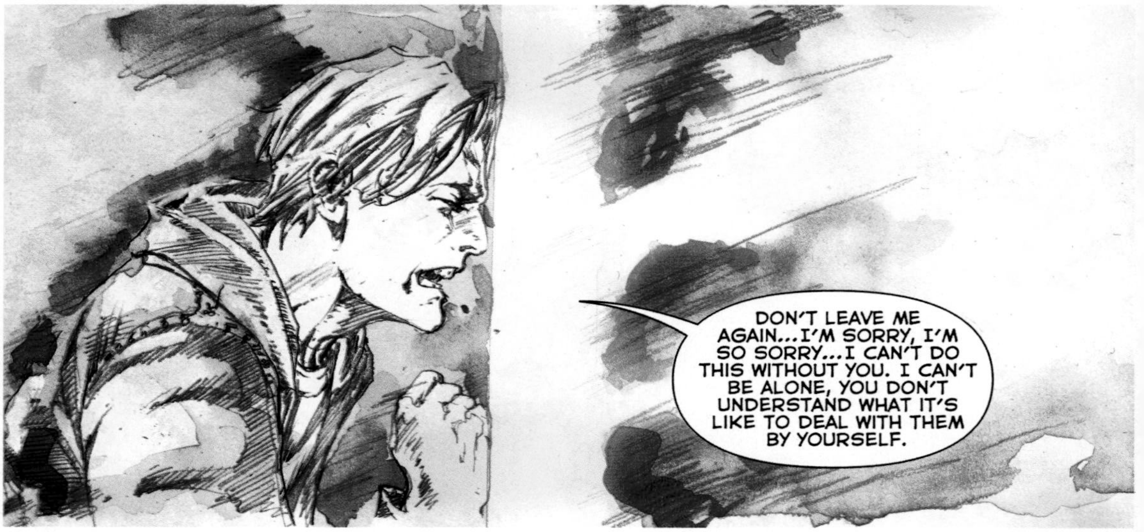
DON'T LEAVE ME AGAIN...I'M SORRY, I'M SO SORRY...I CAN'T DO THIS WITHOUT YOU. I CAN'T BE ALONE, YOU DON'T UNDERSTAND WHAT IT'S LIKE TO DEAL WITH THEM BY YOURSELF.

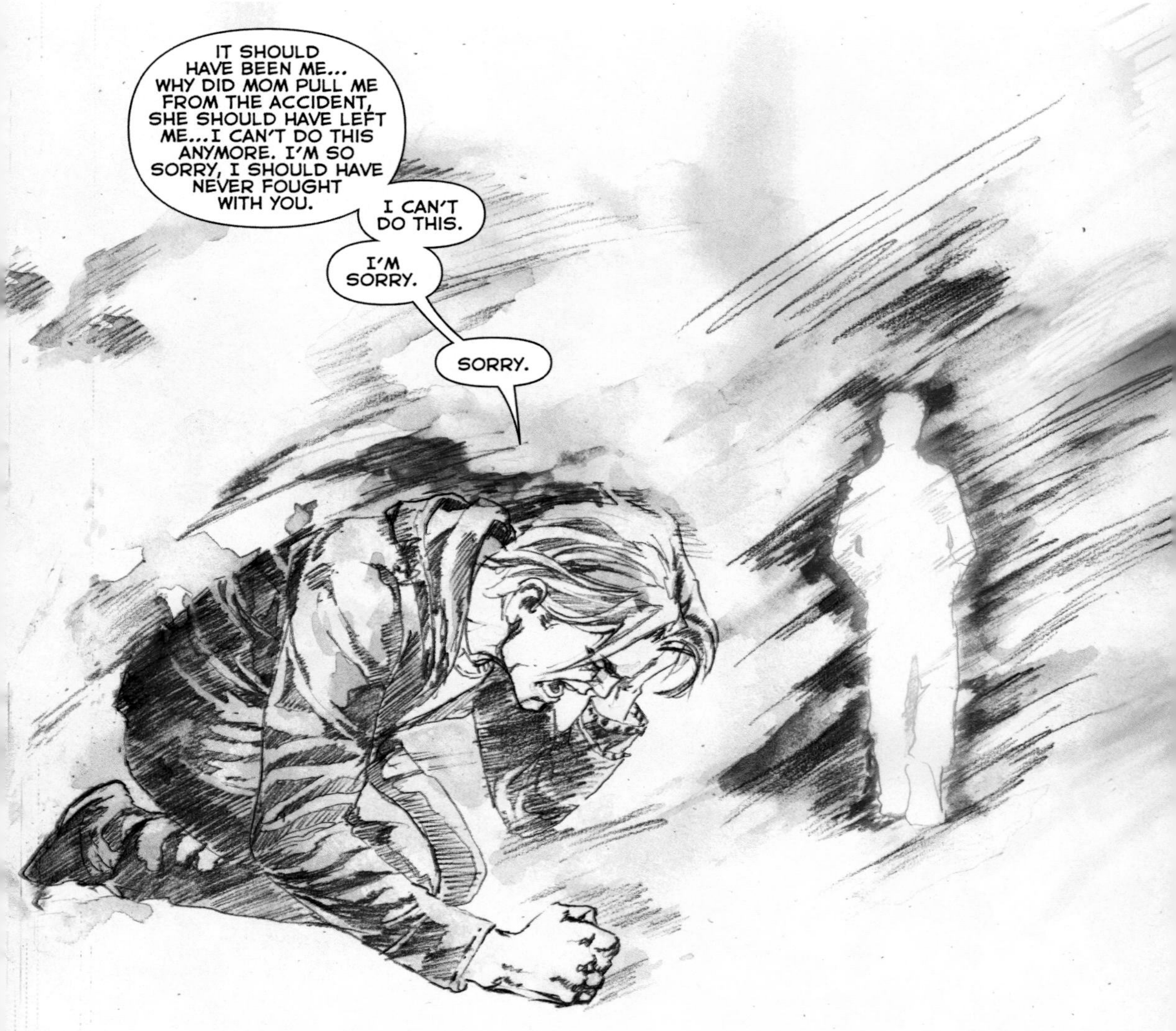
IT SHOULD HAVE BEEN ME... WHY DID MOM PULL ME FROM THE ACCIDENT, SHE SHOULD HAVE LEFT ME...I CAN'T DO THIS ANYMORE. I'M SO SORRY, I SHOULD HAVE NEVER FOUGHT WITH YOU.
I CAN'T DO THIS.
I'M SORRY.
SORRY.

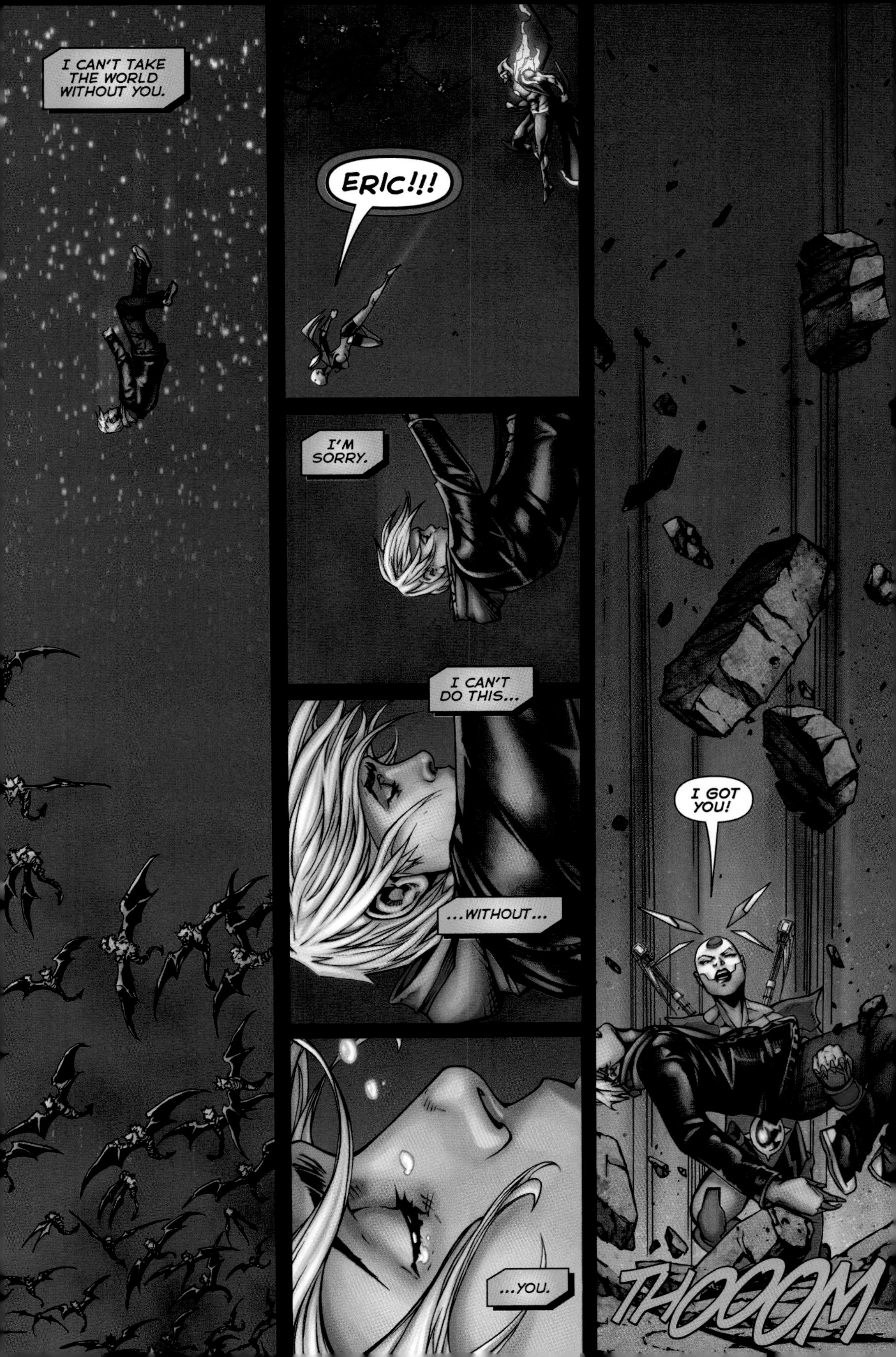
I CAN'T TAKE THE WORLD WITHOUT YOU.
ERIC!!!
I'M SORRY.
I CAN'T DO THIS...
...WITHOUT...
...YOU.
I GOT YOU!
THOOOM

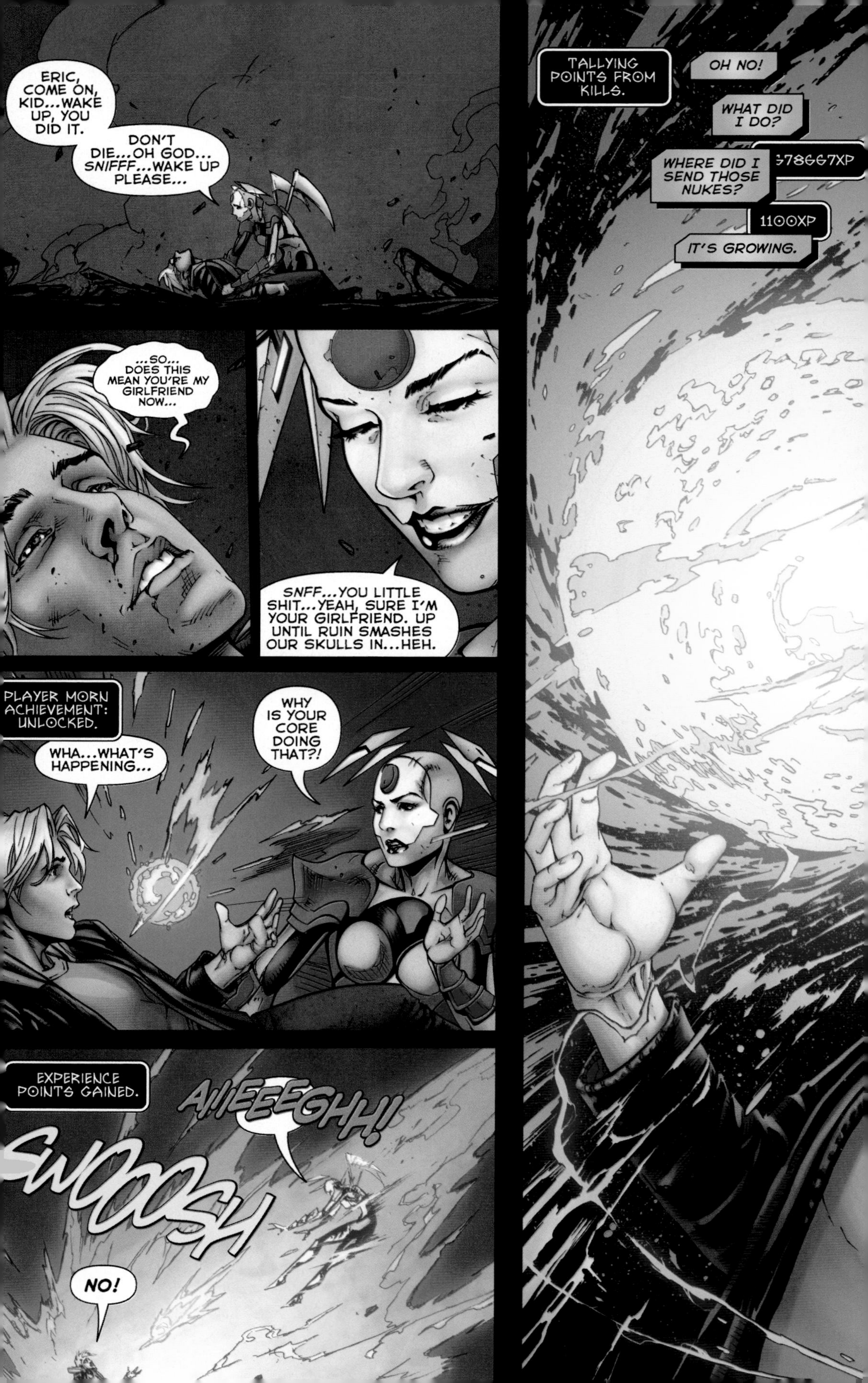
ERIC, COME ON, KID...WAKE UP, YOU DID IT.
DON'T DIE...OH GOD... SNIFFF...WAKE UP PLEASE...
...SO... DOES THIS MEAN YOU'RE MY GIRLFRIEND NOW...
SNFF...YOU LITTLE SHIT...YEAH, SURE I'M YOUR GIRLFRIEND. UP UNTIL RUIN SMASHES OUR SKULLS IN...HEH.
PLAYER MORN ACHIEVEMENT: UNLOCKED.
WHA...WHAT'S HAPPENING...
WHY IS YOUR CORE DOING THAT?!
EXPERIENCE POINTS GAINED.
AIIEEEGHH!
SWOOSH
NO!
TALLYING POINTS FROM KILLS.
OH NO!
WHAT DID I DO?
78667XP
WHERE DID I SEND THOSE NUKES?
1100XP
IT'S GROWING.

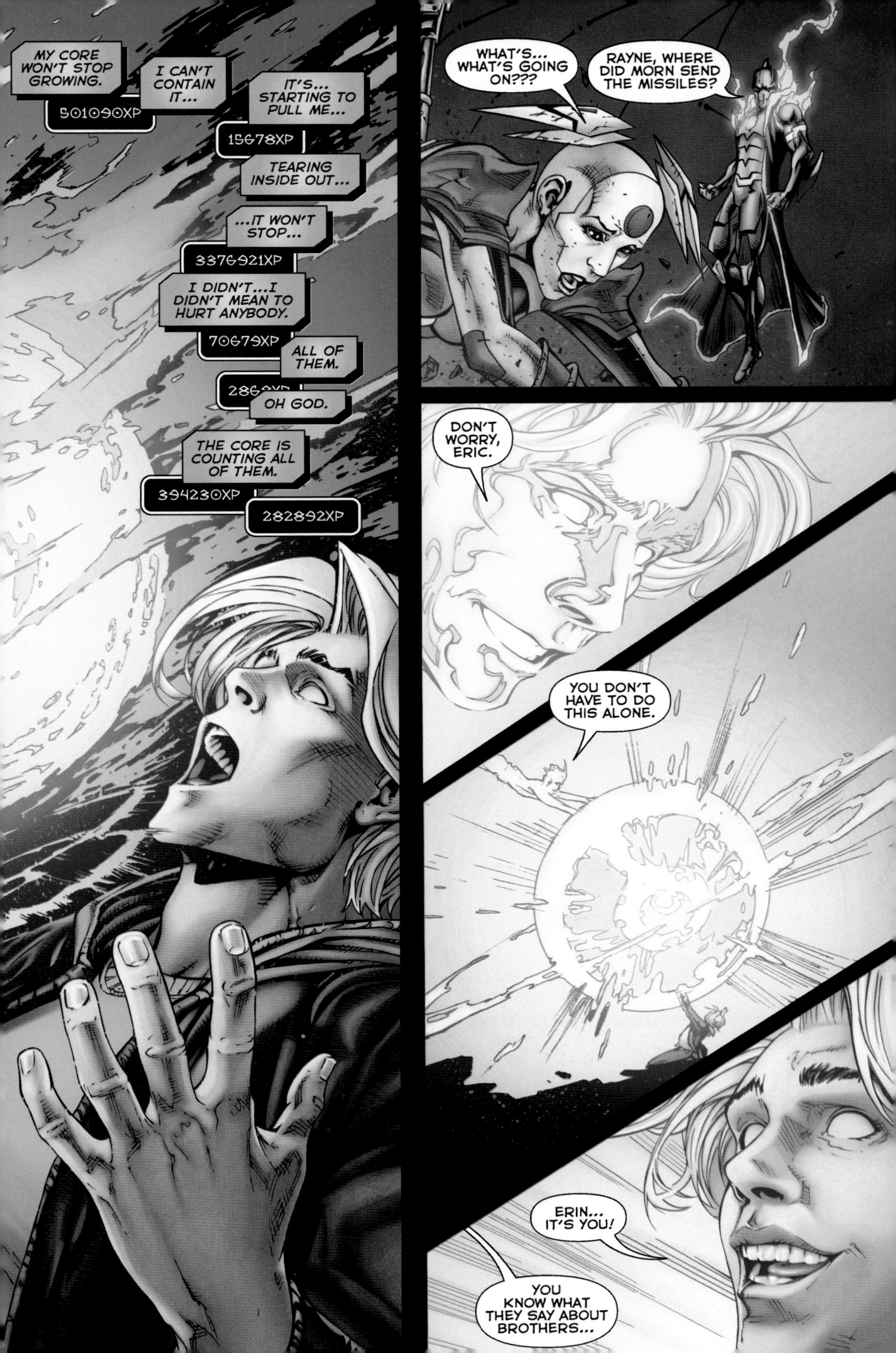
MY CORE WON'T STOP GROWING.
501090XP
I CAN'T CONTAIN IT...
IT'S... STARTING TO PULL ME...
15678XP
TEARING INSIDE OUT...
...IT WON'T STOP...
3376921XP
I DIDN'T...I DIDN'T MEAN TO HURT ANYBODY.
70679XP
ALL OF THEM.
OH GOD.
THE CORE IS COUNTING ALL OF THEM.
394230XP
282892XP
WHAT'S... WHAT'S GOING ON???
RAYNE, WHERE DID MORN SEND THE MISSILES?
DON'T WORRY, ERIC.
YOU DON'T HAVE TO DO THIS ALONE.
ERIN... IT'S YOU!
YOU KNOW WHAT THEY SAY ABOUT BROTHERS...

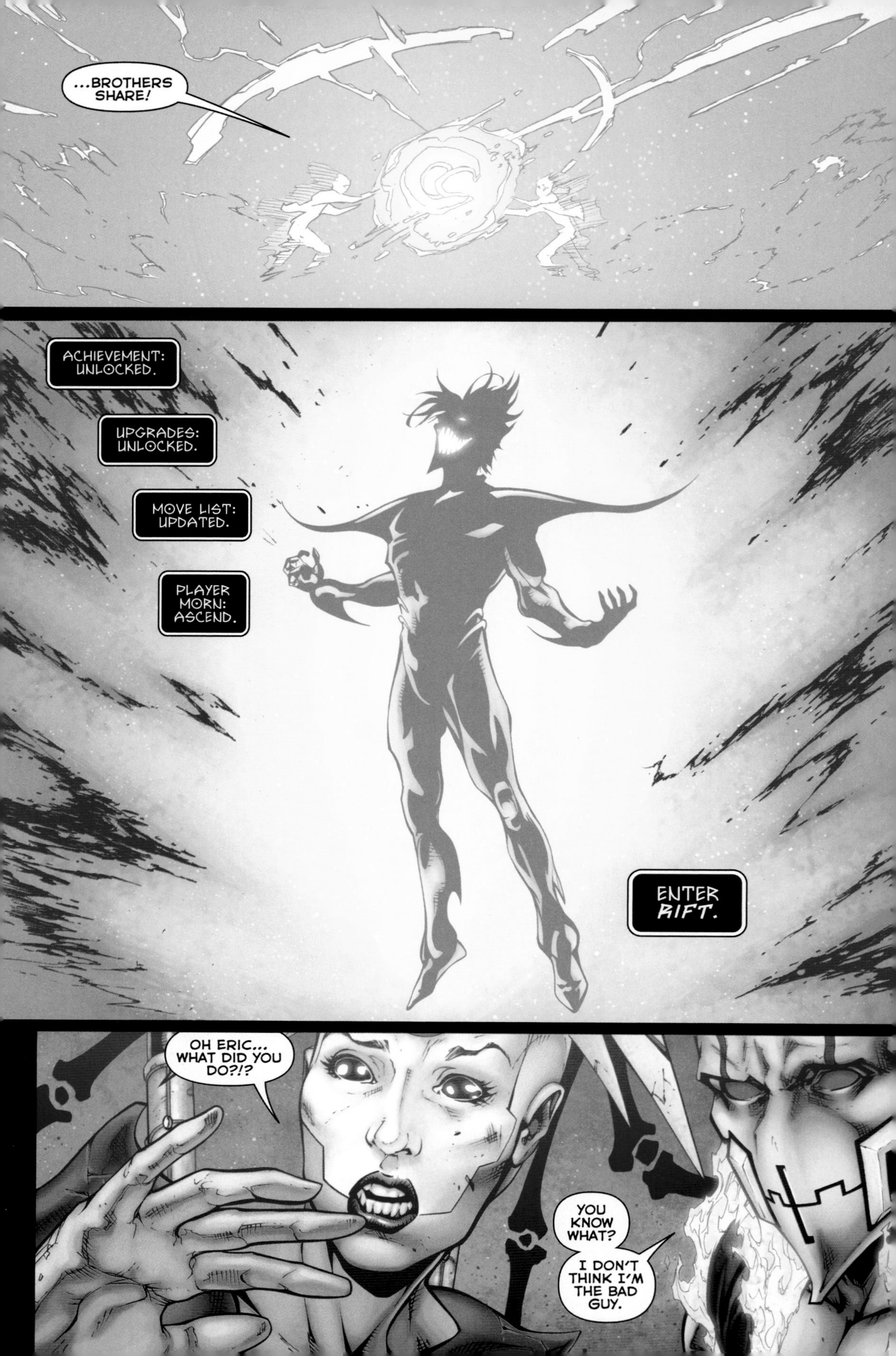
...BROTHERS SHARE!
ACHIEVEMENT: UNLOCKED.
UPGRADES: UNLOCKED.
MOVE LIST: UPDATED.
PLAYER MORN: ASCEND.
ENTER RIFT.
OH ERIC... WHAT DID YOU DO?!?
YOU KNOW WHAT?
I DON'T THINK I'M THE BAD GUY.

SHANE DAVIS

Most people know Shane Davis as the co-creator of the majority of the Red Lantern Corps and the wildly popular *New York Times* bestsellers, *Superman: Earth One*, volumes one and two. He has worked in comics for over a decade and entertained a world-wide legion of fans with his visionary creativity and lifelike illustrations. He wrote *Legends of the Dark Knight* for DC Comics. *Axcend* is Shane's first creator-owned project at Image. He is the most interesting man in the world.

MICHELLE DELECKI

Michelle Delecki, graduate of TCNJ, has built a robust career in inks within the comic industry, working for such giants as Marvel, DC, Image, and Valiant. Her work encompasses a broad range of media. She spends much of her time listening to shred metal and learning the ancient ways of hand to hand combat from her resident sifu, Mr. Kitten.

MORRY HOLLOWELL

Kubert School trained. Industry sharpened. Professional colorist Morry Hollowell has worked for Marvel, Image, Legendary & Crossgen Comics. Widely known for his work on Marvel's *Civil War* and *Wolverine: Old Man Logan.*

PATRICK BROSSEAU

Trained somewhere in the Burmese mountains by Gaspar Saladino worshiping Tibetan monks in the lost art of comic book lettering many moons ago. Patrick quickly rose to the top of the lettering game, only to fall back to the bottom after becoming addicted to sniffing felt-tip markers. He now letters many fine comic books while daydreaming of lettering the perfect sound effect.

GABE BRIDWELL

Gabe is a cartoonist, illustrator & designer from central Illinois and a 2002 alumnus of The Kubert School, where he would later go on to teach and become program development coordinator.

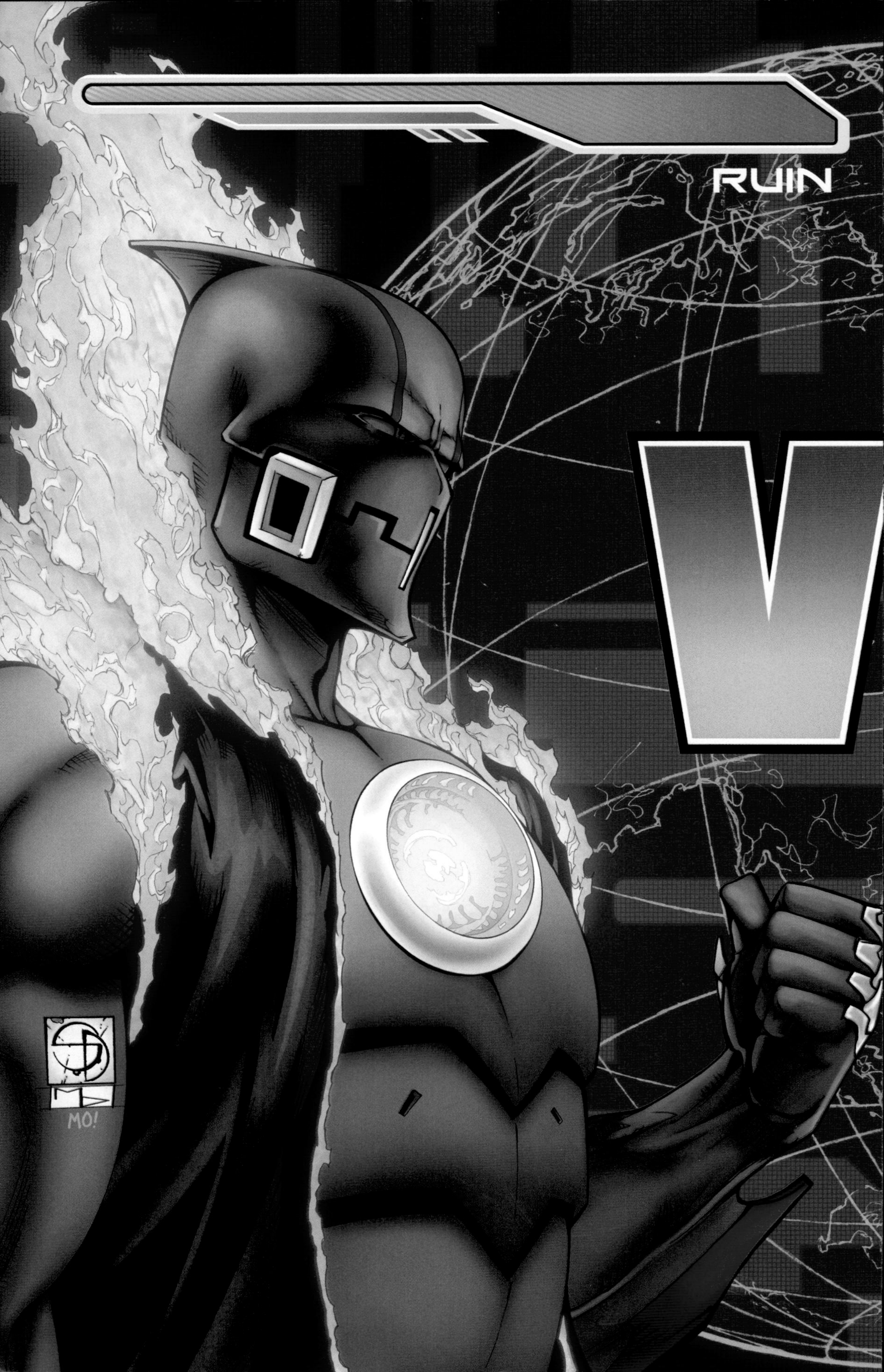
RUIN
V
MO!

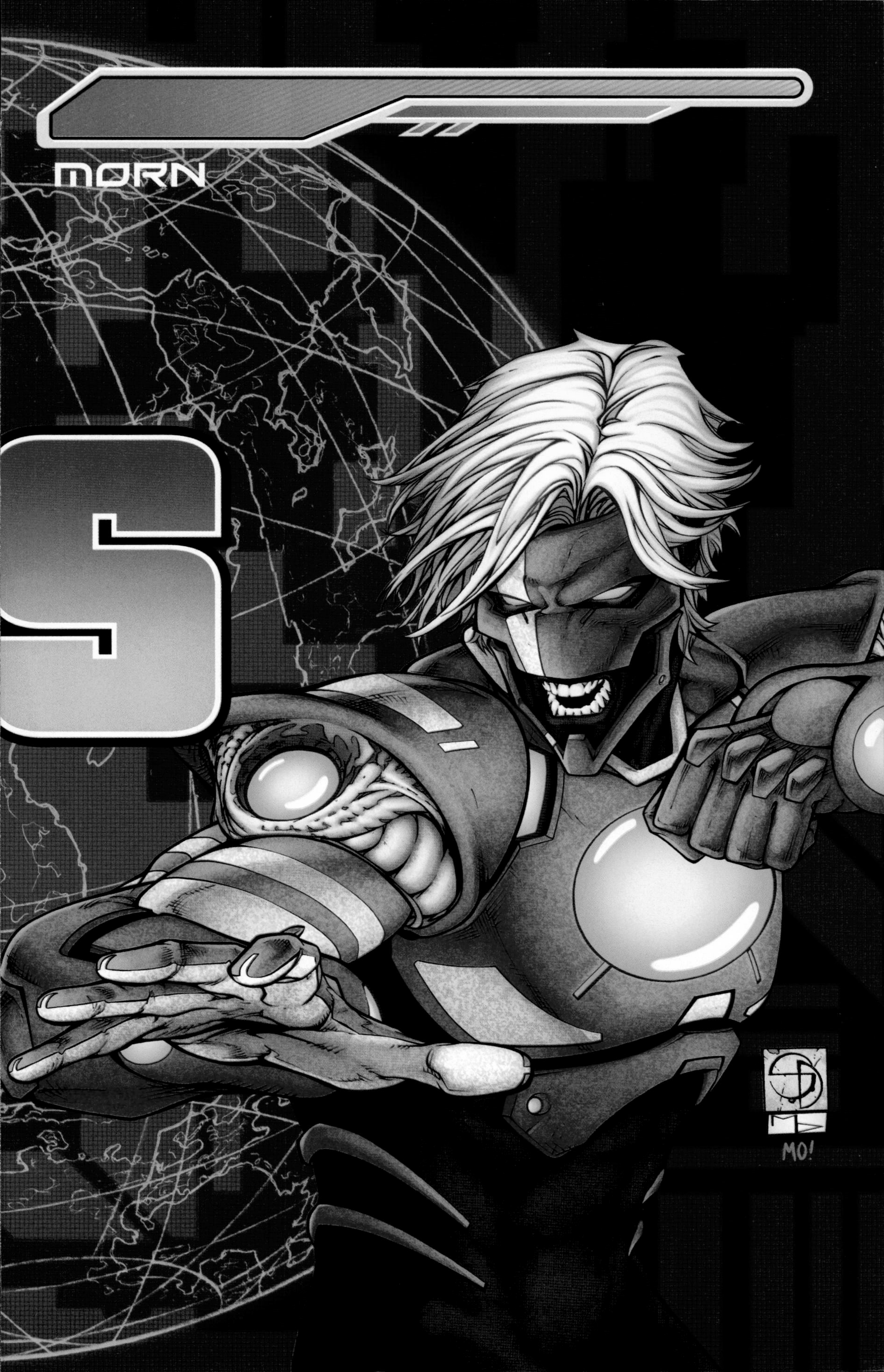
MORN
MO!

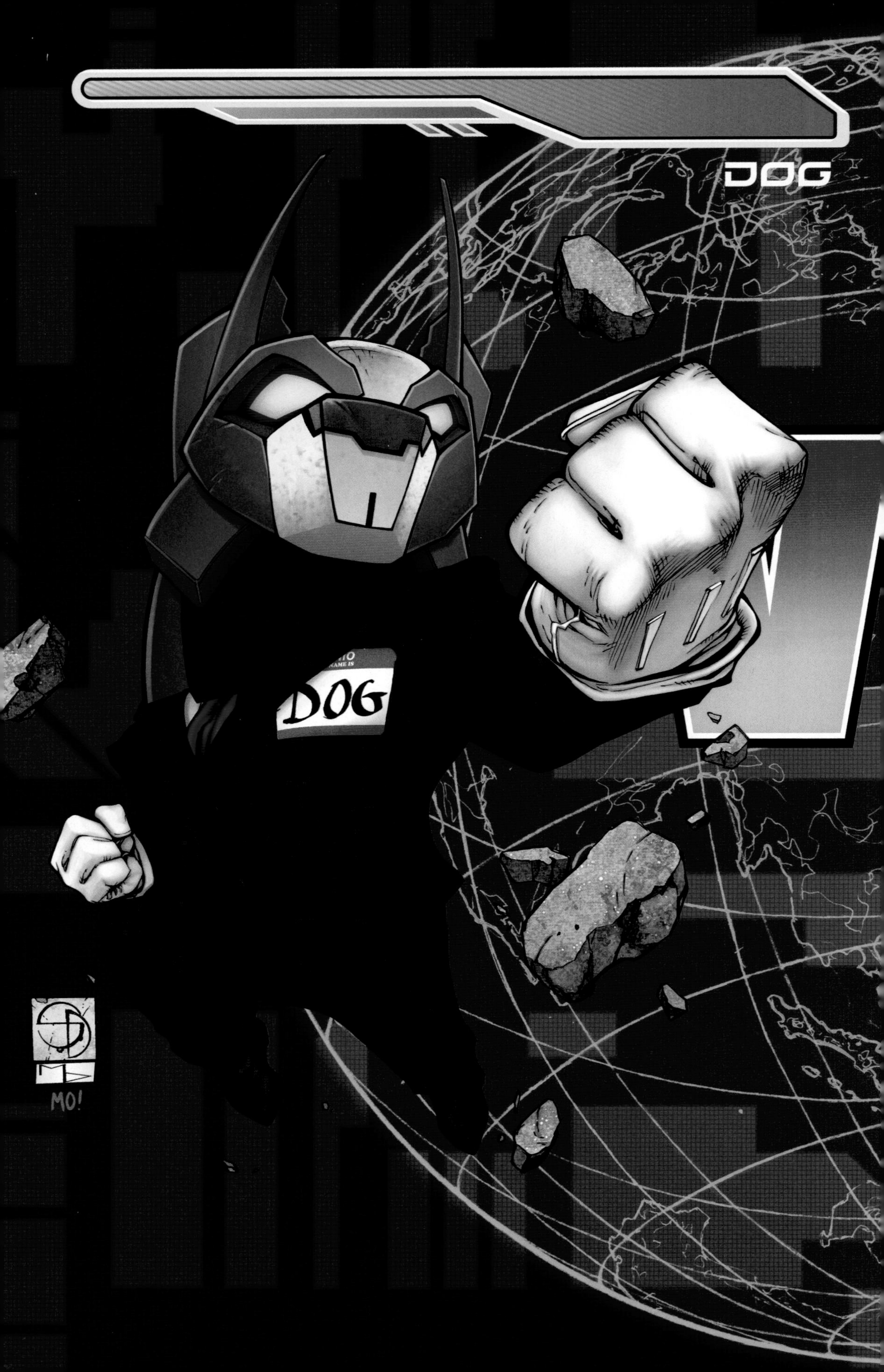
DOG
HELLO MY NAME IS
DOG
MO!

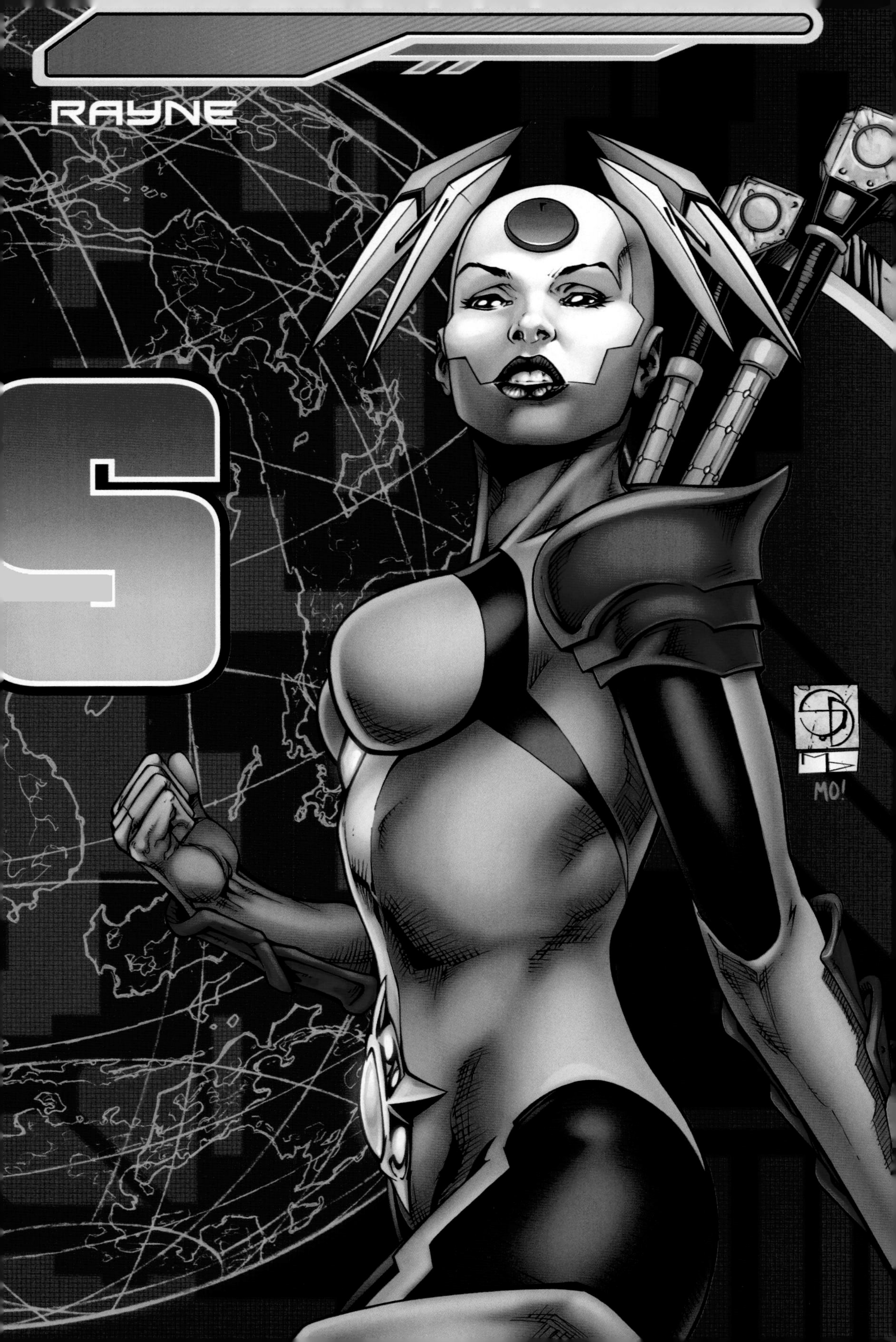
RAYNE
MO!

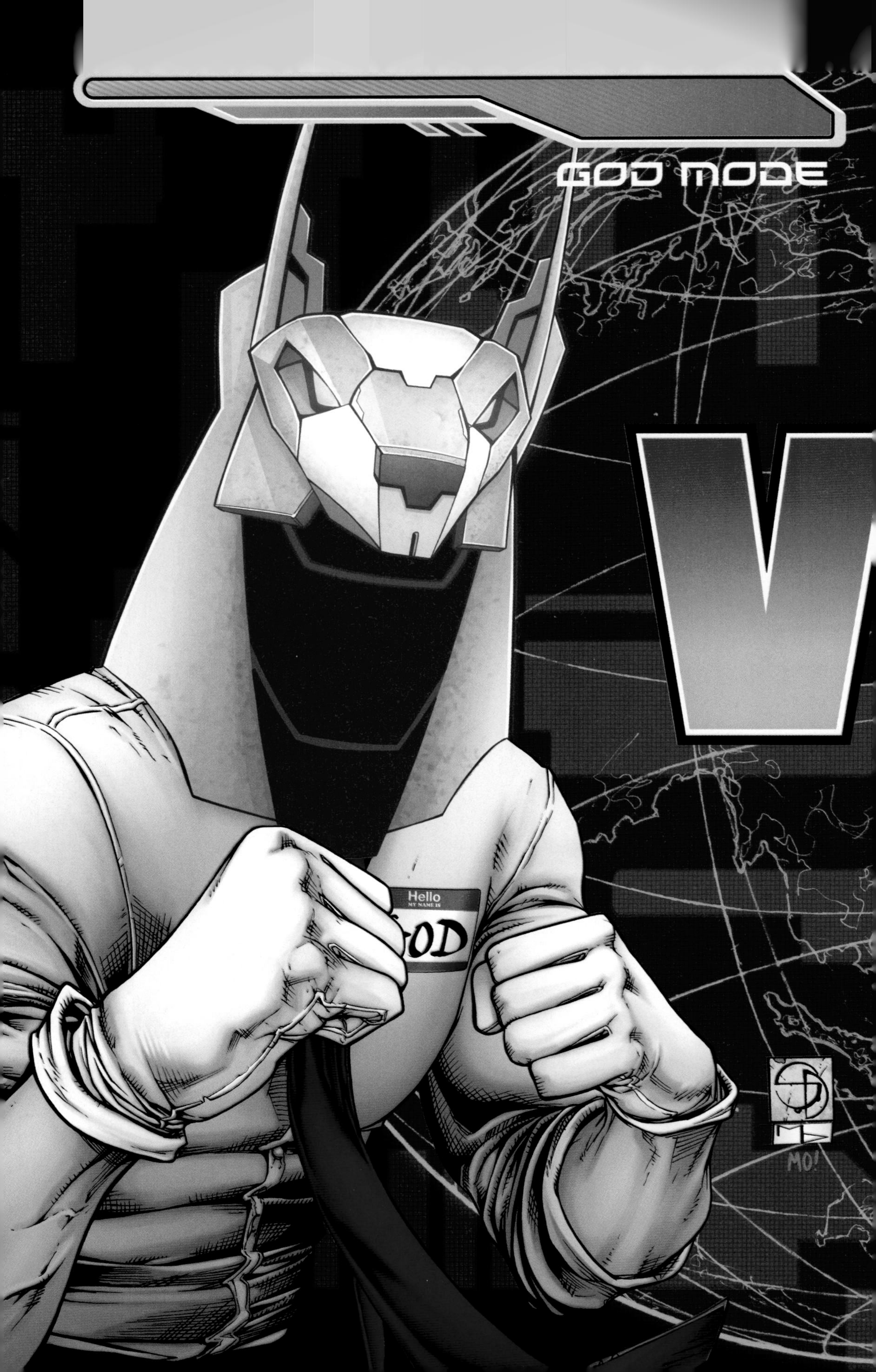
GOD MODE
V
Hello
MY NAME IS
GOD
MO!

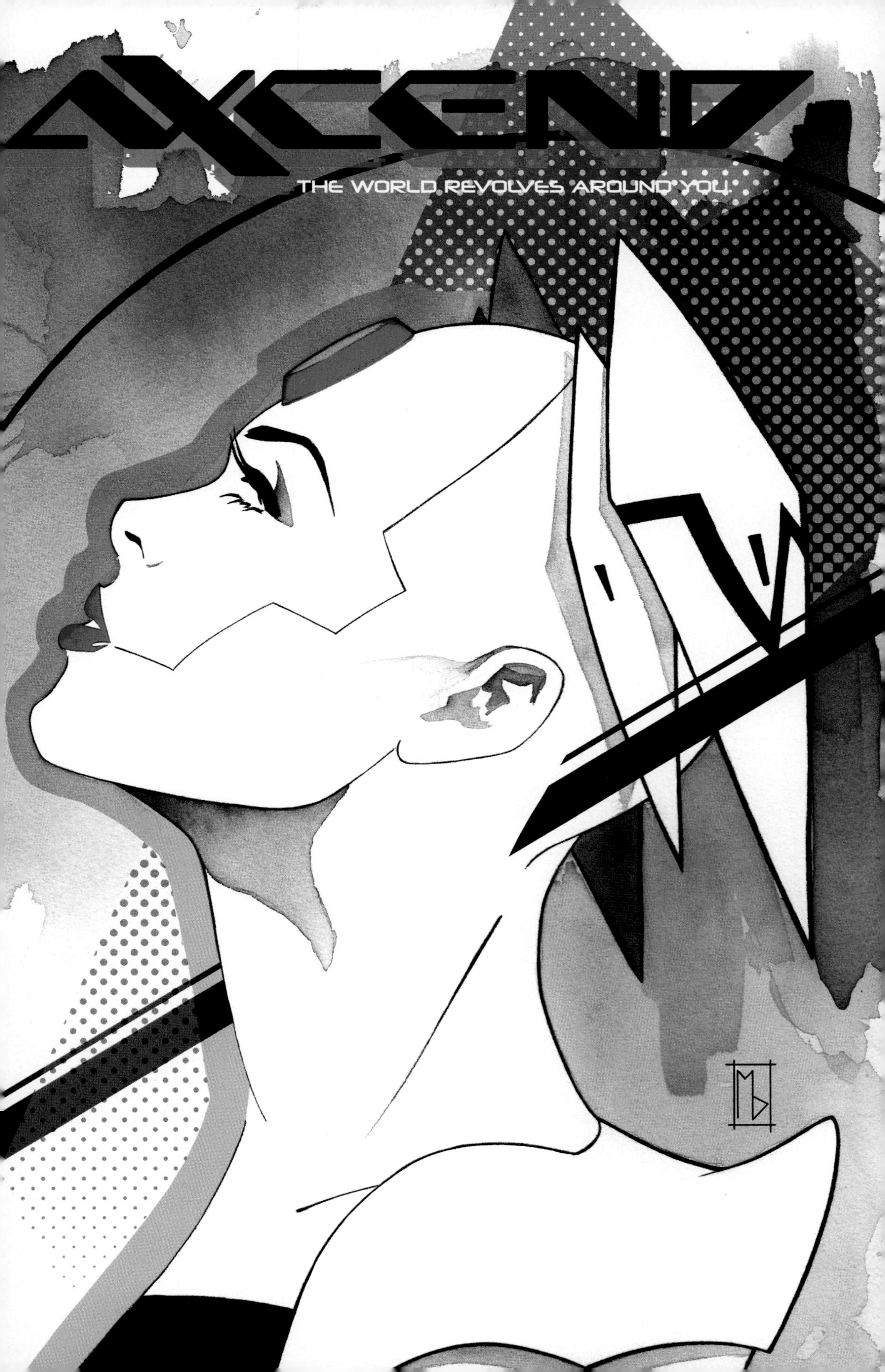
AXCEND
THE WORLD REVOLVES AROUND YOU

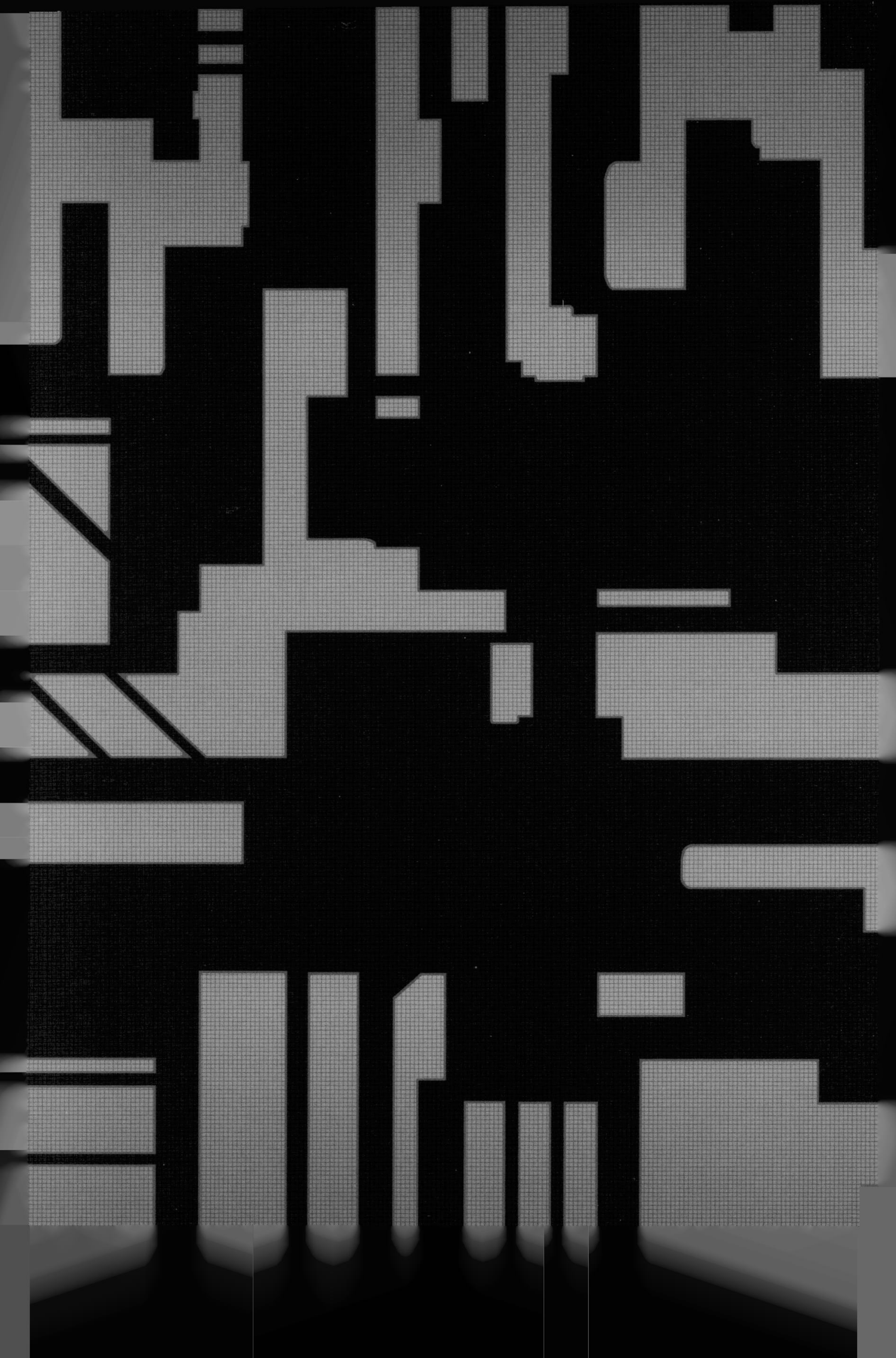